THE VENGEFUL DEAD

A DUNHAM RAYNOR NOVEL

BY

C.R. RICHARDS

CHAPTER ONE

Missouri - 1865

I don't recall how the painted snake had come to embed itself within my skin or why it insisted upon eating its tail. In the years I'd possessed the mark, my inky friend hadn't revealed any clues about its origins.

Small teeth sunk into the flesh covering my chest with sudden ferocity. Though conjured with paint and needle upon my skin, the enchanted snake tattoo came alive when the Dead drew near. I pressed a hand to my chest, hoping to quiet the agitated serpent. The Ouroboros, as the Greeks and Egyptians referred to it, was never wrong.

The unearthly intruder had found me. Or rather, my curiosity had landed me in the soup again.

A tall man dressed in Sunday black stood in the alley off Prairie Town's business district. Two revolvers dangled from a worn leather gun belt around his waist. The weapons were perfectly balanced and within easy reach.

An eerie light struck the silver star pinned to his chest. Its shimmer drew the eye to Prairie Town's former sheriff like a beacon of righteous fury. However, the faded red stains on his shirt were the most disturbing features of his imposing visage. Turning my attention from the cluster of bloodied bullet holes surrounding his badge, I swallowed hard.

"Evening, Sheriff. My name's Dunham Raynor, but you can call me Dun. Everyone does." I cleared my throat uncomfortably when the ghost made no reply. "Some of the town folk would like you to consider moving on to your final reward."

"I don't like the looks of you, stranger." The ghostly sheriff's voice struck my mind like the sudden boom of thunder on a moonless night.

Small pockets of dirt exploded on the alley floor as he spoke. Bits of glass and wood slammed against the sides of the buildings about us. Poltergeist. Nothing said 'time to leave' like a ghost who could throw things.

"You think you can ambush me?" The ghost pulled his revolvers. "Get out of my town, Bushwacker!"

Then the ghostly sheriff fired. Otherworldly energy propelled a loose board straight for my head. Yowling an unmanly yelp, I turned tail and ran as fast as I could for the streets of Prairie Town.

Arms gripped my shoulders, guiding me to a nearby trough. I plunged my face into the water and blew out rapid bubbles. Two men stood wringing their hands as they waited for me to stand. Nels Anderson and Bart Jessup were the unlucky owners of the buildings lining the alley.

"Well? Is he gone?" Jessup asked. "You promised you could get rid of him for us."

"I promised I would politely ask him to leave," I said. "That sheriff is one nasty poltergeist. Be thankful he's bound to the alley and can't roam around town."

"That's it?" Anderson poked a sausage finger at my chest. "We paid you fifty dollars to get rid of him."

Funny thing about Poltergeists. Rage and angst gave the haunters abilities other ghosts didn't possess. The ghostly sheriff, for instance, had spent his afterlife haunting the alley where he'd died. I suspected he chose to haunt the spot rather than being forced to stay. Nothing said he couldn't change his mind. The thought motivated me to try my luck in another town.

"This is a challenging case. Yes. Indeed. I must confer with my associates," I said, taking quick steps toward our camp. "I'll be in touch soon."

"But you'll be back?" Jessop called.

It wouldn't be easy convincing my friends to pack up. The little troupe had made themselves comfortable in Prairie Town. I'd have to rely on my charm to persuade them rather than admitting I'd bungled things again.

Chapter Two

A tattered canvas banner bucked and snapped over the makeshift stage of Madame Angelina's Traveling Medicine Show. It was the lone fanfare sounding a lukewarm welcome for our performance on the gusty Missouri night.

Faded red letters upon the canvas announced, "Fortunes Told. The Mystical Madame Angelina knows all."

Stuck in the ground beneath it was my less notable sign painted on a discarded board. "Featuring Professor Edgar Eden, Psychic Medium and Messenger of the Dearly Departed."

It was utter nonsense. I don't consider myself a psychic, or a man of letters. I'm a professional confidence man. One of the best. Of course, I can't claim success from my cleverness alone. I know things about the marks I meet in my travels. Intimate tidbits no one outside their skin could know.

The Dead see everything and know what's inside a man's soul. Many newly Dead, burdened by the knowledge and their own desperate need to move off this plane onto the next, search for someone who can help them. I am their favorite attentive ear.

Tin stars and moons danced upon bits of tattered rope strung from the wagon's roof. The frayed strands sagged toward poles positioned in the center of the dirt field. These trinkets plunged our audience into a state of wonder. The spectacle was everything, according to my business partner, Angelina.

A group of boys dressed in moderately clean overalls waited for me beside the fire as they'd done for the last three nights. The camp was otherwise empty. Checking my impatience, I shrugged and sat on a log by our campfire.

Twisting my wrists, I deftly tucked the jack of spades inside my sleeve. The group of boys gasped with delight as I wiggled my empty fingers before them. Then I made the card appear again with a pouf of magician's flash paper. My small audience clapped in enthusiastic appreciation.

"You young'uns ought to be getting home. It's gotta be past your suppertime. Don't make your fathers come looking for you." Trip, our stagehand, entered the camp with his tin bucket rattling. The noise, if not Trip's surly expression, sent the youths scattering toward town.

"Put those damn cards away," Trip told me. "Save your tricks for the paying customers. If we have any at tonight's show, that is."

"You sound like Angelina," I told him. "Don't you remember what it was like to be a bored little boy?"

"Hell, I don't remember last week!"

Trip's weathered face was etched with wrinkles earned under a harsh sun. Thinning gray hair showed slight signs of the light auburn that crowned his head in youth. A hard life spent on the road had taken his looks and right arm. I had no intention of sharing his fate in my elder years. Performing in this medicine show was temporary. I had grander plans.

"My incomparable skill at cards will get me noticed by the right people in San Francisco," I said, tucking the deck into my jacket. "Goodbye dirt water towns like this one. Hello, fancy suits and expensive cigars. You'll see, Trip. I'll own the best gambling house on the California coast one day."

"Yeah. So, you've said many times. We aren't out of Missouri yet. I chopped up those dried rabbit bones for Angelina." Trip dropped the bucket of tiny bones next to the log. "It says something about the world we live in when she runs out of hex bags before love potions."

"Angelina's colored pond water isn't selling, eh?" I straightened my hat with a grin. "Maybe it's a sign we should move on?"

"Don't be stupid. This town is still plump. Angelina isn't about to leave before we've emptied a few more purses. Why are you acting so squirrelly?" Trip gave me a frown. "You haven't found trouble, have you?"

"I wasn't looking," I said with an angelic smile.

"See that you don't." Trip pointed over my shoulder. "Silent Dan has a job for you."

Built like a bull and just about as intelligent, Silent Dan had found the medicine show a few years ago in a dirt water part of Kansas. The boy followed our wagons like a stray pup. Trip fed him and gave him a place to sleep and a job. Dan had been with us ever since. In all that time, I'd never heard him utter a word.

Silent Dan presented a carefully folded newspaper as if the rag was an original scroll written by the Apostles.

Shaking my head, I gave him a sour frown. Silent Dan rubbed a massive hand atop his short sandy hair as his pale blue eyes watered with irritation. He tapped my chest and thrust the paper at me.

"Again? I've read it to you a hundred times," I said. "We need to find you a new paper. This is months old. Look. It says April 9th, 1865. We're full-on into summer now."

Trip sat his lantern down beside me and turned up the flame. "Don't strain your eyes."

"Come on, Trip," I said, casting a troubled glance into the darkness. "You've both heard me read this last night."

The boy pushed my chest harder, nearly sending me backward off the log. I'd tried to spare myself the agony of being Silent Dan's sole source of entertainment, but neither he nor Trip had put much effort into learning how to read.

"Fine! Give it." I snatched the paper and opened it to the first page, where a bold headline announced, "Lee Surrenders. The War Is Over!"

"Lee and Grant met at Appomattox today," I began. "Why do you suppose these newspapermen always list Lee first? He was the loser, after all. Shouldn't it be Grant and Lee?"

"Stop your teasing and read the damn thing," Trip growled. "Silent Dan is about to explode."

"Fine," I said with an affronted sniff. "The two men came to terms. Lee signed a treaty, allowing the men from both sides to lay down their guns. The soldiers can at long last return home to their families." I lowered the paper and looked at the boy. "Don't make me read this next flowery part about faded glory."

Silent Dan shrugged and flipped the pages to the cartoon depicting Lee and Grant with absurdly large heads. His laugh exploded in great honks of air. I don't think the boy favored either the Union or Confederacy, but rather he enjoyed comedy where he could find it.

Our little troupe shared a neutral attitude toward the North and the South. Gold was gold, as far as we were concerned, whether it came from Union or Confederate pockets. Neutrality, however, was a dangerous balancing act even after the war ended. We kept our eyes and ears sharp for any signs of a town's loyalty. Expressing the wrong opinions to the right folks was a sure way to get chased out of town.

"The boss is coming," Trip said. "She's in an awful hurry too."

Our painted queen of the gypsies ran down Prairie Town's main street with her skirts lifted to the knees. Her purple socks flashed vibrant shimmers of silk at stunned male passersby. Though Angelina had celebrated her fortieth birthday at least twice since I'd known her, she'd remained nimble.

"What did you do this time, Dun!" Angelina jutted her arm back toward town. "All the lamp posts on Main Street have exploded. Barrels are rolling down the street like tumbleweeds."

The Ouroboros sunk its teeth into my chest. I sprang off the log with a yelp as the ghostly sheriff stormed toward camp with guns drawn. His first shot sent our lantern flying toward the dangling tin stars. Silent Dan threw his big body under the wagon. He peeked through the wheel spokes, watching as the lantern danced wildly through the air.

"It's not my fault," I told Angelina.

The poltergeist's second shot hit Trip's bucket of animal bones spilling the contents into the fire. I pulled a cursing Angelina under the wagon. Trip pushed her flaying legs between the wheels and joined us. He rested a hand on Silent Dan's shoulder, offering soothing words.

"We have a poltergeist," I said. "It's Prairie Town's Dead sheriff."

"What the hell does he want?" Trip asked.

"He's inviting us to leave his town," I said with what I hoped was a contrite grin. "We may have had a brief conversation earlier about him crossing over. He declined."

"Ya don't say?" Trip cursed and slapped me on the shoulder. "How many times have you been told to avoid poltergeists? They're a pain in the backside and always bring us trouble."

Angelina fixed her gaze upon the show's banner as it sailed toward the fire. She scurried out from under the wagon on all fours and caught the fabric before it touched the flames. Smoothing her skirts as she stood, Angelina began to fold the banner lovingly.

"Y'all start packing the wagons," Angelina said. "We leave tonight."

"What? In the dark?" Trip shook his head. "What if one of the team breaks a leg?"

"Would you like that ghost to go for the mules next?" Angelina's accusing eyes were on me. "Tell the ghost we're leaving and beg him to stop attacking us. Damn it, Dun! I'm not going to ask what happened because I don't care," she said, throwing open the wagon's door with an angry flourish. "But if you did try to conjure that ghost, be better at it next time. Get packing, and don't take your own sweet time about it either."

"It's not my fault," I said. "You know I don't mean for these things to happen."

"Don't. You'll only make it worse. Come on," Trip said. "We'd better start packing before the real sheriff of Prairie Town decides to help us leave."

CHAPTER THREE

Trip's wagon rolled lazily on the trail ahead of me. Its hypnotic side-to-side shuffle lulled my eyelids shut despite the garish red paint plastered on the surface. I took another sip of water, trying to stay awake. We were in Nowhere, Missouri, between Saint Louis and Independence. Points of interest were scarce. Desperate to relieve my excruciating boredom, I began whistling a cheery little tune I'd heard in a saloon outside of Saint Louis.

"You sound like an idiot."

Patchouli perfume engulfed me as our prickly gypsy queen poked her head through the curtain behind me. She'd sulked inside the wagon since we'd departed Prairie Town. I can't say I missed her waspish temper.

"You're speaking to me again," I murmured. "Hooray."

"It would serve you right if I never spoke to you again," she said. "It isn't like you're pulling your weight."

"I'm driving the wagon, aren't I?"

"Silent Dan can do as much," Angelina said. "You're supposed to be this miraculous medium who can charm secrets from the Dead. But, instead, you cause us problems. We lost weeks of profit because you had to play with that poltergeist."

"I was only trying to help," I said, shrinking from her disapproving sneer. "A little goodwill from the town makes our stay easier. Right?"

I pulled out the heavy coin purse and shook it when she didn't answer. "Lady Luck kissed me in Prairie Town. Fifty dollars buys a few good steak dinners. I suppose I can throw in some tobacco for Trip and a new shirt for Silent Dan." I let my lips form a slight grin. "We may even find more thread for your hex bags in the next town."

"Poker?" She asked, fingering the coin purse.

"You know me." I winked, handing her the fifty dollars Anderson and Jessop had paid me to consult on their ghost problem.

Nothing put the color back in Angelina's cheeks like money. She climbed through the wagon's opening. Spreading her skirts like a silk fan, Angelina began to lower her body onto the bench. Fate picked that precise moment for our wagon to hit a bump in the road. Her backside bounced on the seat beside me. I judiciously swallowed my laughter.

Clutching the coin purse tighter, she stared into the vast landscape. "My daddy was a gambler."

I cast a look at her expressive face. In her features, I saw something rare. Honesty. Though I'd been in the troupe since I was a youngster, many things about Angelina, especially her real past, remained a mystery.

"I remember Daddy's hot streaks. He'd buy Mama fine clothes, and we children had plenty to eat." Her voice grew softer as her memory took her back in time. "But Daddy wasn't lucky often. More times than not, he'd come home drunk and broke. He'd take out his frustrations on Mama until she couldn't take the beatings anymore."

Then the grifter's well-formed mask returned to her face. She sighed and gave me the charming smile I'd seen her favor on dozens of gullible marks.

"Stay in the confidence game, Dun. We control the marks, not the other way around." Angelina tucked the coin purse back into my jacket pocket. "Your time is better spent practicing summoning your ghost friends. They can make us some real money."

"I've told you before I don't call them. The spirits come to me."

Trip waved his arm to the wagon's side with a shrill whistle. I edged our team a few feet to the right, affording Angelina and me a better view. A town grew out of the horizon on the road ahead.

"I thought we were a few days away from civilization," Angelina said.

I shrugged. "Don't ask me. Trip is the one steering this ship."

In truth, I hadn't been paying much attention to my surroundings for the past several hours. My fickle attention, suddenly awakened, registered fence posts standing stoically in the prairie grass alongside the dirt trail. Farmhouses and barns made shadows in the Missouri morning. Their presence gave my mood a considerable boost at the promise of real civilization.

"I see a mercantile and a saloon," Angelina said, leaning precariously to the side for a better view. "This town has money, Dun. I feel it!"

Buildings sprouted from the ground to line each side of the town's one street. Angelina's hawk eyes were correct. Mercantile and saloon signs, under the dour shadow of a dilapidated old church, made cheery welcomes as we rode closer. We'd found the heart of this farming community.

"Welcome to Lester. Population 252," Angelina recited from the town's welcome sign. "What a delightful surprise! I hadn't expected a sizeable town this far away from Independence."

Serpent's fangs bit into my chest. The Ouroboros was awake again. Its warnings were coming too frequently for my liking. I released a resigned sigh as a translucent shape began to form beside the town's welcome sign. It was the ghostly form of an old woman. Mangled and bloody, she'd met a violent end. Judging by the scowl on her face, the old bag was still angry about how she departed this life. Thrusting both hands before her, she began to glide toward our wagon.

"Let's keep moving," I said. "There's bound to be better towns up ahead."

"You see something, don't you?" Angelina slapped my arm. "What is it? Don't hold out on me."

"It's an old woman. She was murdered."

Deep cuts caked with blood made canyons in the old woman's severe face. Her stern jawline clenched tightly under a sour frown. Hard eyes kept me in their sights as the full force of her stubborn determination pinned my body against the driver's seat.

"We don't want to be rude. Let's go meet her." The predator smile stretched across Angelina's face. "Never keep a lady waiting, especially when she may have interesting secrets."

"No need. She's here."

The old woman's ghostly form passed unhindered through our mules. She levitated above the animals until her ghastly face was inches from mine. The ghost screeched in unbound fury as she pressed her hands against my arms to hold me in place. I tried to pull away from her, but my body was trapped. What was happening? The Dead couldn't restrain the Living. This was impossible! Twisting in panicked jerks, I was desperate to escape. The ghostly woman bared her teeth until I stilled.

"Listen to me, magician! First, a murderess stole my property, and then she stole my life!" The ghostly face leaned in closer until I thought she'd try to pass through my body. "I'm not leaving Lester until things have been set right!"

"I'm not the law. So what do you want from me?"

"Revenge!" She screamed as her stick fingers bore into my chest. "Swear you'll make it right, or I will haunt you the rest of your days."

Then she spoke of murder. Minutes passed like hours as she recounted her death and the desecration of her body afterward. I took in the sensations. The physical trauma of her death to the impotent rage she'd felt toward the heinous murderer who'd taken her life. Finally, she let me go. I put my aching head in my hands. Had Heaven or Hell claimed her soul? I didn't care. I was just glad the old hag was gone.

"What happened?" Angelina rested a hand on my arm. "You were gone for a long time."

I leaned forward, trying to ease the sick feeling in my soul. Since receiving my ability to speak with the Dead, I'd seen plenty of gruesome things. It wasn't the gory images the old woman had seared into my brain. Instead, the ghost's power over my body had unsettled me to the core. I'd never experienced such a feeling of helplessness and loss of control.

"We have to leave," I said. "Something's not right about that ghost or this town."

"Take a drink." Angelina handed me her flask of brandy. "Now, tell me what she said. I want every detail you can remember. Come on, Dun. This isn't our first blackmail job."

"We're talking about murder this time." I thrust the flask back into her hand. "That old woman's ghost wasn't right. I've warned you before my ghostly visitors are coming more often. Now this old woman was able to bind my body. The Dead should not be able to touch the Living. I don't like it."

"What's not to like? These ghosts of yours want to tell you things." Angelina gripped my arm with a playful squeeze. "They're practically begging you to take the money they've left behind. Let them help us get to San Francisco."

"I suppose," I acquiesced. "If it keeps the old hag in her grave, I'm in."

"That's the spirit!" Angelina rubbed her hands together with a grin.

I recognized the terrier look on her face. Angelina smelled money, and nothing would keep her from it. Not even me.

Chapter Four

Trip had a gift for finding the perfect location to pitch our camp. He'd chosen a large dirt field near the center of Lester. Our troupe circled our wagons in full view of every curious lookie-loo who passed by. Not satisfied with the level of interest, Angelina set out to prowl Lester for customers.

I'd spent the afternoon sitting in the shade cast by our wagon. Our quick departure from Prairie Town had damaged a small gear wheel on the collapsible stage. I'd been able to fix its bent tooth and was lovingly greasing it when Angelina returned from her tour of Lester.

"Am I the only one in this troupe who works?"

Angelina's Tennessee twang dripped like sweet syrup over the camp. She may have sounded as if she were joking to the unpracticed ear. Unfortunately for Trip, Silent Dan, and me, Angelina suffered a common malady among most put upon women. She hated seeing a man spend his spare time relaxing rather than engaging in practical labor.

The gold Egyptian cloak she'd picked up in a secondhand store in New Orleans rustled around her ankles. Painted lips quivered in a poorly suppressed smile as she majestically crossed the dirt toward us.

"You look happier than a fox in a chicken coop," Trip said. "Did you find our new best friend?"

Performing her best imitation of Cleopatra, Angelina alighted upon the portable stool beside our campfire. Trip and Silent Dan, their gaze riveted upon her, waited as she brushed the dust off her hem. I fiddled with the greasy gear, completely ignoring her posturing.

Finally, when she could stand my indifference no more, Angelina clasped her hands together. "I made it a point to 'accidentally' cross paths with her. Our mark is the spiritual type." Angelina turned her sparkling eyes upon me. "She is giddy to meet you, professor."

"I'll bet." I rested the gear on a cloth beside me. "What farfetched tail did you spin?"

"It hardly matters. Do your job tonight, and we can leave Lester with a healthy stake." Angelina clasped her hands together as if in prayer. "Maybe if we hustle enough money on this scam, we can travel to San Francisco in style. No filthy wagon trains for our troupe! Wouldn't Lucky Sal be impressed if we stepped off a fancy steamship dressed in silks?"

Lucky Salvatore Moretti had arrived in the Americas with ten dollars in his pocket and a head full of ambition. He built a kingdom of gambling halls from Chicago to Saint Louis. Now in his seventies, Sal was ready to expand to San Francisco. For our part, the letter he'd sent Angelina offering her the chance to manage his new gambling hall venture was a fond dream come true.

"Go on, Angelina. Read Sal's letter again," Trip said.

She reverently pulled the folded letter from her chemise as if it were a holy relic. Trip and Silent Dan's eager eyes followed her teasing fingers as she unfolded the parchment. Then grinning with pleasure, Angelina held it before her with the blank side facing us.

"I'm not sure I should. The firelight strains my eyes."

"Allow me," I said, reaching for the letter. "I'm the one who taught you how to read, don't forget."

She yanked it away from my fingers as if I were a thief trying to snatch her most prized possession. "Don't you trust me, Dun? After all the years and miles we've spent together? I practically raised you."

"Then I took you back after you ran off. I made you a partner in our medicine show out of the goodness of my heart, mind you. Now you behave as if I'm trying to cheat you." Angelina sniffed back dramatic tears. "We're family."

"Why won't you let me see the letter?" I frowned and let my hand fall. "I can't talk to you when you're playing Cleopatra. We'll discuss Sal's letter after the show."

"Forget the letter. Keep your focus where it should be. I mean it, Dun!" Angelina warned. "No mistakes tonight. Any trouble, and I won't take you with us to San Francisco."

We both knew it was an empty threat, but it still rankled me. Our painted gypsy queen was hiding something. It had been foolish of me to try openly confronting her about it. Angelina, above all else, was a master of manipulation. I had yet to see an opponent with wit enough to outmaneuver her in a battle of words. It was time to try another means of getting that letter. Sometimes a lighter touch was best.

Our audience - a handful of farmers and one or two curious boys - stood under the temporary cathedral of spiritual wonders. A tiny ping from a pebble sent the line of tin stars swaying. The boys broke into fits of laughter. Rascals. One stern look from a disgruntled father quieted their youthful exuberance. I muttered a little prayer hoping theirs would be the only laughter I'd hear tonight.

The God-fearing women of Lester were suspiciously absent. They'd made the usual fuss when we erected the stage-circling about the wagons with their bibles waving. Dragging the sheriff to our camp, insisting he chase out the gypsies. I'd had the same greeting in every town we'd visited since leaving New Orleans. However, one glance at Angelina's love charms had drawn the romantically inclined back to our camp after the sun went down.

A tambourine rattled at the mouth of the fortune teller's tent where a caricature from every Romany Gypsy tale demanded attention. Madame Angelina danced under the tin stars, sweeping across the dirt in flowing scarlet skirts until every eye was upon her. The women of Lester trailed behind their new goddess of fortune, mesmerized. Having transformed into 'the Madame,' Angelina was a twisted pied piper. Wild and beautiful, her dark hair fell over bare shoulders. Gold-plated coins, dripping from her skirts, jingled as she moved. Intoxicating and exotic, she was one of the most ruthless grifters I'd ever met. Nevertheless, most men found her beautiful enough to make the risk worthwhile. Having seen beneath the heavily painted façade, I had made a game of predicting how soon she'd relieve her amorous admirers of their fortunes.

"The spirits are among us tonight. They yearn to speak with those left behind." Angelina's rich velvet voice embraced the crowd. "World-renowned psychic medium Professor Edgar Eden was drawn to Lester by the spirit world. He's here to deliver messages from the departed. Professor, if you please."

My cue received, I assumed the professor's character and pulled the red velvet curtains open. The rewarding gasps from the crowd were a shot of elixir to my waning confidence. Showtime. I'd seen a magician perform in Chicago once. He'd been a great source of inspiration for the persona I adopted now. I stepped purposefully on stage. The platform, attached by rusted hinges to the wagon, squeaked as I put my weight upon it. Eyeing the crowd with the right amount of solemn authority, I flung the cloak off my shoulders. The hidden wire tugged sluggishly as my garment flew to a waiting hook attached to the wagon's side. Pulleys squeaked under the Missouri grit, making the illusion fall flat. I made a mental note to lubricate them with axle grease or horse dung.

"So many spirits wish to speak. It is difficult to hear."

I touched thinning white gloves to my temples as if I were straining to hear whispered words from the great beyond. My hands suddenly dropped as I took in a ragged breath. The ladies gasped. Calico and lace fluttered wildly as the women of Lester clung to one another. Standing behind them, Angelina gave me a cat-like grin. Our jittery mice were ready for the tempting cheese.

Chanting in nonsensical gibberish, I paced slowly across the boards. Their curious eyes followed my body, jumping backward when I jutted a pointed finger into their numbers. I began moving the appendage as if a supernatural force guided it. The curious crowd stood rigid beneath the tin stars. Gasps of awe escape stubborn lips. Their full attention remained riveted upon my slow-moving finger.

"I have a message from the great beyond for someone here tonight!" I rolled my eyes and shuddered like a wet dog in winter. "Madame Angelina, the spirits are ready to speak. Feel my psychic vibrations."

The odor of nervous bodies pressed together filled my nostrils, prompting an unmanly digestive queasiness. Excited murmurs circled the audience. Their dull chatter echoed like a hammer on an anvil against my temples. My sudden fit of nerves was more than simple stage fright. Something unearthly was coming to Lester, and it had unfortunate theatrical timing.

"Please remain quiet," Angelina said, brushing her skirts behind her. "Professor Eden must have absolute silence to commune with the other side."

The crowd immediately fell silent. The sudden stillness made the pounding in my ears a thunderous howl. Angelina's lips set into a hard line of displeasure. She nodded at me with an impatient flash of her carnivorous eyes. I placed the shaking fingers of my other hand against my forehead—hair tonic mixed with the sweat beading on my skin. The unearthly thing was coming closer. I could sense its wrongness at the edge of town.

"Keep your head, Dun. Don't lose focus," I counseled myself in a low murmur.

Gliding like the silk skirts she wore, Angelina moved into the crowd. She lifted a discreet hand over a young woman at the back, our signal for a potential mark. Then Angelina danced through the crowd tapping her finger twice, indicating two rows up. She stopped behind a woman in pink whose youth had begun to drain under the yoke of farm life. Eyes sparkling with pleasure, our pink pigeon gasped when I moved a finger in her direction.

"You, my dear lady, have drawn the spirits to Lester." I bowed with a flourish and smiled as she gushed. "Yes. Their presence is blinding."

"What's your game, mister?" One of the sharp-eyed men challenged. "You watch yourself, Martha. This snake oil salesman is after your money."

"Hush, Frank," she said. "The spirits are here for me, not you."

Miss Martha tossed fading blond ringlets over her shoulder. Our new mark wiggled excitedly under the tin stars. Her generous bosom heaved in short gasps of breathless anticipation as the fortune teller twirled before her. The spark of greed inflamed Angelina's eyes as she wedged between the naysayer and her new prize. My partner, hungrily licking full lips, took the woman's arm in a protective embrace. She wasn't about to let our pink pigeon fly away.

"Pray, tell us what message the spirits would deliver to this fortunate lady, Professor."

I wouldn't precisely regard her as fortunate. One spirit, a particularly nasty one, wanted her message given plainly to Miss Martha in pink. I shivered at the memory of the old woman who'd spotted me as I'd driven our wagon past the field where she'd died. It was a simple message, but one bound to shake the Living.

"Your grandmother has come among us," I said, carefully regarding her blank expression. "She's here to give you a message."

Grandma wasn't really with us now, thank the generous Lord. After forcing me to listen to her message, the old witch had departed for good. Then she'd gone. Hell, I was sure, had taken her. By the look on Martha's face, she'd hoped the old woman was basking in flames as well.

"She says she doesn't like where she's buried," I said, holding her gaze. "Such disrespect for the dead."

"That old woman was buried in her hometown a hundred miles from here. What is Martha supposed to do? Dig her up?" The farmer shook his head. "This is all a fake."

Martha believed. Pale cheeks and wide guilty eyes betrayed her. Our pigeon knew exactly where Grandma was buried, having done the digging under a gloomy midnight moon. Pieces of the old woman's body were scattered in the fields exactly where Martha had planted them. Murder was an ugly business. There was always a reckoning in this life or the next.

"I think a private reading would be best in such a delicate situation, don't you?" Angelina asked sweetly and then turned to me. "Shall we say first thing in the morning, Professor?"

The anticipation in her voice emphasized every word. She smelled good blackmail. Once Angelina had her teeth into a mark, hell itself couldn't deter her. I harbored no sympathy for Martha. Murder was murder.

"It's a trick. That man is after your money." The farmer folded his arms obstinately. He was a problem. Other skeptics were beginning to take up his accusations of fraud. I took a tentative step back, losing eye contact with Martha. She suddenly pulled away from Angelina as if waking from a dream state. Angry rumblings circled the crowd.

Suddenly, heat exploded along the skin of my chest as anxious writhing pressed against the inside of my shirt. A sharp bite sent me stumbling forward. The Ouroboros had awakened.

Bloodied and gruesomely maimed, the Confederate soldier dragged his ruined leg behind as he moved. A hole, large enough to pass a fist through, opened in the middle of his gut. Light from the torches winked within the gruesome frame. Dead eyes found me upon the stage. I watched helplessly as his transparent body passed unhindered through the crowd of the Living.

"They shot me! My own men shot me. They called me a traitor when I tried to warn the farmers."

He lifted his ghostly face to the tin stars and sent an unearthly wail into the endless void. Hopefully, it would be his last outburst on this side of the veil. I zealously attempted to avoid those violently murdered. They were desperate for acts of justice I was not willing to pursue. Unfortunately, this time I had a personal stake in his message.

"Are they coming here?" I asked. "Tell me."

"This town will be the battlefield. Yankees or Confederates. Neither care about the fate of these people. Those men want to feed their hate. Run! Leave before midnight tonight, or you'll join these farmers in death." His duty done, the soldier closed his eyes with a deep sigh of relief.

Then a light, too pure for any creature of flesh to gaze upon, burst onto the dirt field. Its brilliant glare washed away all visible signs of the Living shuffling about in the dirt. I closed my eyes and turned away.

A sensation of comfort and the soft tinkling of crystal bells heralded the agents of the Light. God's angels had come to collect another soul. How those fortunate individuals ascended to the Pearly Gates, I couldn't say. I never looked. Madness waited for the mortal who peered into the Eternal Flame before their time.

I held tight fists before my eyes and waited on anxious feet for the Eternal Flame to fade. If the soldier's warning came to pass, reapers from Heaven and Hell would be coming to Lester soon. I had no intention of risking my sanity, waiting for their arrival.

CHAPTER FIVE

"What's ailing him? It looks like he's having a fit."

Fueled by the relentless prairie wind, the summer heat intensified Lester's nauseating odors of sweat and cheap soap. Someone ignited a cigar. My stomach lurched, and I threw my body in a prone position at the edge of the stage. I'd lingered upon the dead soldier's face a moment too long. The Eternal Flame had snatched away my sight and scrambled the nerves in my body. Regrettably, the best I could muster with arms and legs twitching was a blathering gurgle of panicked warning. Somewhere in the great beyond, I was sure Heaven's agents heaved the sigh of long-suffering martyrdom. Hell, most certainly, was in hysterics.

Angelina's overpowering perfume surrounded me as coins clinked close to the stage. The sick bubbled in my throat, threatening to explode. These Missouri farmers were about to see the unpleasant side of Professor Edgar Eden.

"Get up," she hissed. "You're taking things too far."

Then the platform creaked as quick feet raced toward me. Firm fingers tugged at my arm, pulling me to my feet with surprising strength. Angelina's coins clinked wildly as she insistently dragged me away from the audience. Blinking, I rubbed my eyes. Shapes began to form, but their details remained blurred.

"He's in a trance. Professor Eden needs a quiet place for meditation. Come back tomorrow night. He'll commune with the spirits again. My dear Miss Martha, perhaps you should visit us for that private reading in the morning?"

"Union and Confederate soldiers are headed this way. Lester is about to be demolished!" Those were my intended words, but unfortunately, what spewed incoherently from my lips were utterances blundered by a swollen tongue.

Air wheezed in and out of Angelina's mouth in angry gulps. Mentioning the war in any way was reckless. For the past four and some odd years, Missouri had been a tantalizing bone for two armies anxious to gain ground over the other. Caught up in a violent civil war amongst their fellow countrymen, the Union and Confederate Armies wanted to grip this land in their hungry jaws.

"Come along, Professor." Angelina's fingers dug into tender flesh as she pulled me backward.

My fingers smoothed at the almost imperceptible rectangle bump hiding beneath her belt - Sal's letter. The evening wasn't a complete disaster. Bumping against her with an exaggerated moan, I plucked the letter from its silk prison and tucked it inside my vest.

"Hey there, young fella," The farmer said. "What did you say about the Union and Confederate Armies?"

"Careful," Angelina warned in an urgent whisper. "Don't sour the waters of Lester for us."

The urgent need to share the ghostly soldier's warning abruptly faded when my vision cleared. Horrified stares filled the audience in a tableau of ugly suspicion.

Their unnerving glares took me back to boyhood. Frightened by my new ability to see the Dead, I'd told my father about the Ouroboros. The confession landed me into the walls of Grace Church Almshouse and Lunatic Asylum at age thirteen. Sharing such fantastical information in Lester might get me hanged.

I hurried into the wagon away from their questions. Lester's townsfolk could make their own choices. I'd delivered the ghostly soldier's dying wish. Whether or not the people of Lester believed the warning was their business. Damn that ghost and his bugle. The Dead never saw past their last duty. They didn't understand the burden they put upon my shoulders. Faced with eternity, I suspect they didn't care.

Garish petticoats and silk scarfs swept across my shoulder as I passed. Tin coins clinked in an angry chorus as the colorful fabrics swung slowly back into place. Angelina took pleasure in growing her gaudy collection of costumes. Her 'pretties,' as she was fond of calling them, had long ago spilled out of their allotted cabinet to spread across most of the wagon's living space.

I'd had a wagon with an exterior painted in beautiful hues of purple and green. Sighing at the memory, I had a little stitch of loss in my heart. A ragtag band of Johnny Rebs used my dearest possession as target practice. Lucky to escape unsinged, I had abandoned the wagon in a hurry. Angelina found it in her greedy little heart to charge me a low rental fee for a thin cot under the leaky section of her roof.

Tiptoeing over Angelina's abandoned sandals and decorative headdresses, I moved to the small pane window overlooking the dirt field hosting the medicine show. A line of calico dresses waited for a chance to seek guidance from mystical forces visiting Madame Angelina's tent. Shadows hid their faces from the low torchlight. Their gloved hands made a curious pantomime in the patterns. News of Lester's impending doom had little effect upon them.

Angelina's coins bounced upon the silks of her skirts as she stormed inside. She pulled the curtains closed with a harsh tug. Then turning on me, she folded her arms and tapped long fingernails against bare skin. Hard eyes gripped my face in their glare. A tempest was about to hit, and I was the focus of its fury.

"What is the matter with you, Dun? You just threw away good money." The angry twang of her native Tennessee thundered in the cramped space. All traces of the Madame's Romany accent were gone.

"Listen, Angelina. We need to leave right now. There's no time to pack up."

"What are you talking about?" Angelina tossed her tambourine upon her bed. "We have a chance to make some good money here. Think of the show. We could be rolling in silks and cigars for months."

I leaned against the chipped mirror. My reflection leered back at me. A trim mustache curled upward precisely two fingers' width beyond my nose. It was Angelina's idea. She wanted me to look like a sophisticated gentleman. Wayward strands of my heavily oiled hair broke free to wander liberally across the starched white collar of my silk shirt. Angelina came to stand behind me and slicked the dusty blond locks back in place. She'd changed tactics. The loving caretaker was her most dangerous persona.

"I thought you wanted to go to San Francisco. It's an expensive city. We need a stake, don't we?" Angelina gave the mirror her best pout. "Trip and Silent Dan are anxious to see the ocean. Don't let us down. We need the professor back on stage."

She gripped my shoulders and turned me around. Angelina began meticulously brushing the dust off my tailored suit jacket. It was a gift from a grateful widow in Saint Louis whose husband hid the family nest egg a little too well. I'd coaxed the strong box's location out of the old boy, much to the delight of his relieved wife.

Angelina's fingers fussed with the elegant blue ascot, held in place with a silver horse-head pin. I tugged absently at the honey-colored waistcoat hanging about my body. It didn't fit. None of these dowdy scholastic clothes were me. I pulled off the new frock coat and threw the ill-fitting garment at Angelina's overflowing wardrobe. It had outlived its usefulness.

"Stop. Listen to me." I grabbed her wrists. "A murdered Confederate soldier came to warn me. Lester is about to be a huge hole in the ground. We must leave."

"And what about little murdering Martha? She is ripe for the plucking! Stick with the plan and help me find granny's body." She pulled from my grasp and waved at the small window overlooking the dirt field. "And then there's all these corn-fed farmer's wives who want their fortunes told. I've had a few from a neighboring town tonight. We haven't begun to tap this county." Angelina shook the strands of dark hair from her bare shoulders. "Do you want me to read the letter again?"

"I contemplate Sal's offer at every opportunity," I said, producing the letter I'd lifted from her earlier.

"Give it back!"

"To Mister Dunham Raynor. Care of Bartlet Boarding House. Saint Louis," I read aloud. "Dear Mr.

Raynor. Word of your exceptional skill has impressed me. I wish to discuss a mutually beneficial opportunity in San Francisco...." I glared at Angelina. "This could make my future. Why would you keep it from me?"

"We're a family, Dun. You would've left Trip, Silent Dan, and me behind."

"That's not true, and you know it." I threw the letter in her face. "You should have been honest with me. Not that any of this matters right now. We need to leave Lester before the soldiers get here."

"You said it yourself. These spirits you talk to aren't always right. They get confused. You're starting to believe your own act, Dun. What is happening in that head of yours?" Angelina rolled her eyes with an uncharitable laugh. "You're becoming more and more erratic with each new town."

I pushed away with a growl. Damn her. My time as a resident in the asylum was a sensitive subject. Angelina was aware of my past. She'd coaxed the story out of me when I was a frightened and desperate boy. Her casual mentions of the asylum were rare but always devastating. I slammed a fist into the cracked mirror, shattering the glass.

"You think I'm unstable now, is that it?" I grabbed my old brown hat from its hook and pulled it on my head. "Fine. Stay here. I'm leaving."

Angelina put her fists on her hips with a laugh. "Don't you remember what you were when I found you? Just a common sneak thief." The smile, enchanting for the audience, turned cruel as it fell upon my face. "You're nothing without me."

I grabbed my share of the money we'd made from shows in the last few towns and tucked it into my wallet.

Boxes of show props crowded the floor. I kicked them aside and headed for the door at the wagon's rear. Professor Eden's clothes remained behind, folded neatly on the one shelf I was allotted. That identity was over. It was time to reinvent myself.

"Last chance, Angelina. Come with me," I said from the doorway.

"We're partners!" She flew toward me in a wave of fake silk and coins. "You can't just leave me here." Angelina dropped her hands as all pretense of affection fell from her face. "One day soon, I'll make you sorry you abandoned me in this Missouri hell hole."

I climbed down from the wagon without looking back. Stopping before one of our mules, I patted it on the rump and kept walking. The least I could do was leave the team if Angelina changed her mind. It was a safe bet I'd find a few nags living on the outskirts of town. I could liberate one and be on my way.

"We both know you'll be back," she called. "How long did you make it on your own the last time you tried to leave? Six months? You came crawling back, hat in hand." She spat upon the dirt. "Run to the next town. Gamble. Carouse. Do what you like. Know this. You'd better crawl back in a hurry, or I'll find someone else to share the wealth. Now, if you'll excuse me. I must calm some Missouri nerves."

The flimsy door slammed with a dull boom. Lantern light drew Angelina's outline against the thin curtains covering the door's single window. She was waiting for me to turn around and plead for her forgiveness, as I always had. Not this time. I wouldn't be back. Not to a town that didn't know it was already dead.

A sour taste crawled up my throat. Guilt. It was an emotion I repressed at every opportunity. Angelina had taken me in, fed me, and taught me the trade. Yes, she'd done all those things, but not out of the goodness of her heart. She knew what I could do and saw me as just another mark to be used to her advantage. Still, I couldn't hate her. She was the reason I'd escaped starvation and jail.

"I'll wait for you outside of town at the last farm west of here," I called to the closed door. "Twenty minutes. Be there, or I'm going my own way."

CHAPTER SIX

Laughter from a rough throat thundered under the Missouri night. Old Trip sat on a water barrel. His empty sleeve flapped in the wind whisking between the supply barrels and the wagon he shared with Silent Dan. The boy, never far from Trip's side, shrugged as I approached.

"What are you two fussing about now?" Trip chuckled and elbowed Silent Dan with a wink. "Does Mama Hen have her apron strings tied too tight again?"

"Why don't you speak a little louder, Trip? We all know how much Angelina enjoys it when we mention her age."

"She won't come after Silent Dan or me," Trip said with a grin. "We're all that's left of her crew. "Besides, Dan and I have more sense than to shout gibberish about Confederate and Union soldiers coming to town. Why did you do that, Dun? You could get us run off from here."

"It's not gibberish," I said. "Listen, Trip. Get Silent Dan and Angelina out of Lester tonight. Trouble's coming. Have I ever steered you wrong?"

"I seem to recall a certain town in Texas…." Trip began.

"How many times do I have to tell you? My Spanish is no good."

Trip grunted and hopped off the water barrel. He shook his head at me and spat on the ground. "The only place I'm going tonight is to my bed. Come on, Silent Dan. Let's check on the mules."

I grabbed the boy's arm as he passed. Sixteen was too young to die. Large brown cow eyes blinked down at my hand. Then he gave me a big smile and grabbed my arm as well. His grip, however, had the strength of a vise behind it. Not for the first time, I was glad the hulk before me had a gentle disposition.

"Listen, Silent Dan. It isn't safe for you to stay here. Understand?" I tugged on his arm to make him listen. "Come with me. We'll go to San Francisco. You'd like to see the ocean, wouldn't you? I can talk to Lucky Sal. He'll have a job at the gambling hall for both of us."

Silent Dan stared anxiously after Trip's departing back. Then, finally, the boy shrugged and gently pulled away from my grip. He wouldn't leave Trip, and Trip wouldn't leave Angelina.

"It's on you, Trip! I'll wait at the last farm at the west edge of town," I called after them. "Twenty minutes and not a second longer!"

I turned my back to our camp and started walking west. The troupe needed convincing, but I had no more patience for heated exchanges. They'd come running when the bullets started flying. For my part, I planned to be well out of town before Heaven and Hell descended upon Lester.

A waning moon hung over the Missouri countryside as I crept past the last building at the edge of town. Jogging clumsily along the road, I kept my eyes on the dark fields trying to catch any hint of movement. The dim light from the thin crescent celestial body wasn't offering much illumination. Midnight wasn't far away now. Soldiers from both sides could be creeping in the darkness all around me. Then again - if I couldn't see them, they couldn't see me either.

Tin music and the distant sounds of Lester's residents rang dully at my back. The chorus of Missouri's nightlife would fade soon. One man wandering about in the dark was bound to draw attention once all other two-legged creatures went to bed. I remained silent, careful to keep my nervous feet from bolting. It was slow going as I stumbled around in the dark. Finally, finding wagon ruts dug deep in the road, I let them guide my steps.

Then a tiny light burst through the darkness, bobbing and swaying to my left. I froze. My heart pounded a frantic beat. Was I too late? Had the soldiers arrived early for their butchery? Union or Confederate? Neither side was particularly fond of me. Being a neutral soul, I'd taken money off both.

"You'll find a horse and gear in a barn down the road to your right."

The small circle of light expanded, revealing the voice's owner standing at the side of the road. Covered shoulder to toe in a black robe, the man leaned against a lone post once part of a dilapidated fence. Thick curls of raven hair framed a square face. His stylish mustache and beard gave the stranger a sophistication I hadn't captured in my stage personae. He was the living embodiment of my phony Professor Eden character. Except, perhaps, for the sandals upon his feet.

"I think you'll find Lester inhospitable with your type, friend. You sound like a foreigner to boot. Those stiffed-neck farmers won't offer you a warm welcome." I gave him a bitter grin and passed by without stopping. "If you insist on risking your life, you'll find a dark-haired hell cat looking for a new partner."

"Madame Angelina," he said. "No. She's not the one I need. Better hurry, Dunham. The horse is still a fair distance. You must be quick."

"I'll just borrow the animal for a few days," I said defensively.

"Will you?" He asked with a chuckle. "Come now. We both know the farmer won't be needing his animal again."

"Wait. How did you know about Angelina and me?"

I spun around, but the foreigner and his theatrical cloak were gone. He'd taken the small light with him as well. What the hell was happening? Was he a spy watching Lester for one of the armies? He didn't behave as if he had allegiance to either side. And how had he known my real identity? The troupe was careful to use stage names exclusively when the marks were around. Perhaps he was another spirit come to hurry me along? No. That didn't make sense either. The Ouroboros hadn't warned me of a ghostly presence. Whoever the stranger may be – ghost or spy - his advice made sense.

The prairie wind faded with an eerie abruptness. Its sudden stillness sent the snake upon my chest into fits of frantic writhing. An unearthly sensation stronger than I'd ever experienced was speeding toward Lester. I took the side road at a run. My heart thundered against my breast as I sucked in panicked breaths. Was I making too much noise?

Tripping on a lump in my path, I fell hard. Another dead soldier, a Yankee this time, stretched spread-eagle across the road. He'd died with a knife in his back. I kicked free from the tangle of his bugle with a yelp. A steady 'shhh' hissed at my side. The young bugler's ghost put an ethereal finger to his dead lips. He swung the appendage slowly toward the dark fields unfolding upon the endless horizon before us.

Then I heard it. Something rustled in the grass ahead of me on the right side of the dirt road. I slowly rolled to my knees and listened breathlessly for more sounds of movement. An eerie light emitted from the bugler's ghostly form. It pulsed with varying degrees of brightness as he floated to the edge of the grass. I saw their faces and uniforms under the dim light of Death's glow. They'd come just as the Confederate soldier had warned.

From every liar and cheat's account of battles I'd heard thrown about in card games, it was supposedly rare for either side to fight at night. Yet, here was a crawling army of Union soldiers looking confused and scared. They had no idea or didn't care the war had ended a few months ago when Lee surrendered to Grant at Appomattox Court House. Rumors of fighting in Texas had prompted Angelina and me to travel north. These prowling predators were proof we hadn't gone far enough.

The rustling grew distant as the Union troops drew closer to Lester. Their bugler, abandoned on the road, turned sad eyes upon me with a shrug. He took a tentative step into the grass. His boots passed silently through the tall blades as he began to follow his comrades. Sometimes people become confused by their deaths. They see their lifeless shells, but still, they refuse to accept the end has come.

"Wait!" I beckoned him urgently from my knees. "It's time for you to go to the Light. There's nothing for you here anymore."

My words fell wasted upon the dirt. The ghost, no longer attentive to my pleas, drifted through the grass and disappeared into the emptiness. Poor fellow. He was doomed to live this night over again throughout eternity. I'd run across many of these poor souls trapped in the houses of New Orleans.

The bugler was beyond my help. I had some Living acquaintances to consider now. Where were Angelina and our two hands? I prayed she'd heeded my warning and hitched the wagon. Lester's nighttime invaders would be blocking the road out of town soon. I impotently slammed a fist against the ground. Going back was impossible. I'd never get through the army crawling between my current location and Lester.

I hurried to my feet again and crept toward the barnyard. The silhouettes of a farmhouse and barn appeared intact from my vantage point upon the road. My luck was holding. The soldiers had left the structures and the animals in peace.

A soft whinny guided me to a mangy old mare lazily munching on her hay. She'd seen better days, but a horse was a horse. The stranger on the road had been correct. A saddle and reins hung conveniently in the barn next to the stall. I fumbled with the reins, my shaking hands rattling them with enough noise to wake the Dead. Gulping deep breaths, I slipped on her saddle. I'd bless it as a miracle if the fastens held until we reached safer surroundings.

The barn door's hinges creaked as I led the mare outside. Great Lord above! Every move I made seemed a hundred times louder in the still Missouri night. Where was the howling prairie wind when I needed its cover? Mounting the horse, I kept her off-road just far away enough to quiet her hooves.

"We're almost clear, old girl. No gunshots. No boots chasing us." Nervous laughter tumbled awkwardly from my lips. "You and I are going to make it."

Then the world exploded behind me. Fire and debris burst into the sky, reaching fiery arms toward an unheeding Heaven. Screams and cries rolled toward me across the landscape. Death was descending upon Lester.

CHAPTER SEVEN

Explosions pummeled the ground in a storm of cannon fire. The old mare bucked lamely under me, her frantic squeals warning the storm was coming closer. Flashes of light sent stark plumes of fire into the night sky. I gripped the reins tighter. Should I go back? Angelina had to believe now. I shifted in the saddle, festering with indecision.

Our troupe was the only family I'd had since leaving Pennsylvania. I couldn't let them die. Damn their stubborn souls. I'd collect Trip, Silent Dan, and our horses. Angelina wouldn't want to leave the wagons. We'd have to tie her up and throw her over a saddle. She'd be furious but alive. We'd gather what was left of our show after the fighting stopped.

"Come on, old girl. We must rescue a stubborn mule." The old mare resisted as I yanked her reins. She wasn't too keen on the plan.

Then came the thunder of rumbling wheels. Red lightning struck in biting whips of fire as the haunting screams of the damned echoed from below. It was too late for Angelina and Lester. Hell's agent was taking the field. I leaped off the horse and pulled her behind a broken-down buckboard gathering rust along the side of the road. Tying the reins tightly to prevent the old mare from bolting, I crawled under the wagon. I'm not too proud to admit I was terrified. The Death Coach isn't something any sane man wants to see.

Earth and air ripped open, exposing a terrifying maw of absolute black. A deafening cacophony of horses and wheels struck my ears. I slapped shaking hands over my head to block the noise. He was coming. Nothing could stop the horror about to plague Lester.

Charging out of the bowels of Hell and onto the road, the Death Coach raced toward town. Always adorned for a funeral, the coach was ready to perform its gruesome duty. The Coachman sat atop his driver's perch upon the midnight carriage. His heavy black cloak swept back in an invisible forever wind as he drove. His skeletal hand was sure as he cracked the whip over his team of frenzied black steeds. Six in all, they were massive beasts whose hooves rained terror down upon the Living every time they touched the ground. My heart thundered against their furious pace. The Coachman had many souls to collect. I was immeasurably grateful my name wasn't on his list.

An eerie silence fell over the fields as the Coachman and his hellish team disappeared into the night. The nightmare, I knew from experience, wasn't over. The Universe was about balance. Coins had two sides. A front must have a back. Ying and Yang. Take your pick of platitudes. Any one of them remains true.

Then the tinkling of millions of tiny bells filled the air about me. Their ringing was my only warning. I spun away from Lester and put a hand against my head to block the rays of the Eternal Flame. Heaven had come to claim its children. It may seem odd to think of Good and Evil working side-by-side, but I considered it an eternal game of Jacks. Heaven and Hell collected souls like little pieces on a game board.

The Ouroboros, as if tiring of my contemplations, writhe urgently along the skin of my chest. Constricting. Biting. Twisting. I'd never felt the snake's painful alarm with such intensity. Its warning was clear. A disturbingly large number of the Dead were approaching.

Gritting my teeth against the pain, I crawled from beneath the wagon. The old mare remained hitched where I'd left her, but not for want of trying to escape. She'd chewed and yanked at the reins until her mouth bled. I stroked a comforting hand along her neck and carefully untied the reins.

"There now, old girl." I gingerly put my foot in the stirrup and mounted her saddle. "We're leaving."

Animals were more attuned to the mysteries of the Universe than we humans. The old mare twisted her face toward Lester. I reluctantly turned my eyes to see what had drawn her attention. The first of the Dead wandered upon the road in a daze. It was the woman in pink - Martha, the murderess. The top of her skull was missing. Round cheeks had faded into a transparent gray. Confusion. Fear. Anger. Raw emotions showed upon her face and the faces of the others who shuffled behind her. The confused mob of the newly Dead rambled in an uncertain path toward me. I was often the focus of a ghost's attention for a short while, but something about the intensity of this mob warned me to run.

"Betrayer!"

A ghostly form swept through the shuffling crowd of transparent traveling companions. It flew at me like a dreadful banshee. Angelina. I put a trembling hand over my mouth to ward off the gore rising from my gut. Gone was her mesmerizing beauty. Remnants of lethal heat smoldered from the horrible burns covering her face and body. The coins she wore about her silks had melted into bubbling puddles of metal embedded in her charred skin. One strand of dark hair, fading now to gray, fell across the burns. The contempt sweltering in her glare made me recoil in fear.

"You betrayed me. You betrayed all of us!"

Angelina gripped at the ruins of her throat. Though not of this world any longer, her voice was raw as if strained from her death screams.

"We were partners, Dun. You broke the grifter's code. Never cheat a partner!"

I dropped my eyes, avoiding her accusing glare. She was right. Angelina may have been tight-fisted, but she'd never cheated me out of my due. She'd been a partner, teacher, and hell, if I were honest, she'd also been a parent and friend. I'd let her down. I'd let them all down.

She thrust a charred finger into my face. "I will have my revenge even if I have to hunt you from the depths of perdition!"

Hellish hooves thundered on the road from the east. Hell's agent had the scent of its missing souls. Shaken out of their daze at the visage of their damnation, Martha and the other rogue souls tried to run. The Coachman could not be fooled or swayed from his duty. He pulled on his reins with a vicious yank. His midnight coach rocked to a stop beside Angelina and Murdering Martha.

Transparent fists beat against the door from inside the coach. The gruesome visage of Trip's half-melted face was among them. My horrified eyes found another familiar face. Silent Dan's terrified eyes pleaded with me from inside the coach. Why had Hell collected Dan? The boy hadn't said or done anything cruel since the day I'd met him.

Then again, we all had our secrets.

"No!" Angelina screamed as a massive skeletal hand grasped her by the head. "You failed me once, Dun. Help me now!"

"You're past help." I swallowed hard, stuffing down my impotent grief.

The lame apology faded, unuttered upon my lips. I covered my ears as the next cannon volley struck the ground in the dying town of Lester. This time, the old mare showed her strength. She bolted down the road toward open country, taking me with her.

Greedy laughter boomed behind me. Those lost souls wouldn't be following me from the ruins of Lester. The Coachman had come and was reaping the Devil's due. Angelina, Trip, and Silent Dan. They were all gone, pulled into the depths of Hell. I alone had survived this night of horror. Now I would have to live with my cowardice.

CHAPTER EIGHT

Wayne City Landing (Upper Independence), Missouri - 1865

"Cross over already," I grumbled at the wispy form of my recently deceased mount.

The old mare had given up her ghost a few miles back. She'd done her best for the past two days, and I was grateful, but not to the point of spending eternity with her. After having raced wildly out of Lester, we'd headed southwest toward what I'd hoped was Westport Landing along the Missouri River. There, I could catch a northbound steamboat.

My journey to San Francisco would be rough going. First, I'd have to escape endless prairies before facing towering snow-covered peaks. Progress had yet to carve a friendly route through the Rocky Mountains. My options were limited. Lacking a horse or wagon, I'd have to follow the river up north and eventually find my way south along the California coast.

Steam whistled across the water and over the green barrier blocking my view. I pricked my ears like a thirsty bloodhound. Steamboats! Any soul who'd floated the Mississippi River would recognize their siren's call. Thank the generous Lord. I sucked in a deep breath. The sweet scents of water and wet grass were bliss to a parched soul.

Aching with miserable thirst, I hurried toward the wall of green leaves rimming the Missouri River. I parted the foliage and stood transfixed at the wide body of wet before me. Cheery red paddlewheels thrashed and churned, pushing brilliant white steamboats through the river's current. Known as the Big Muddy, the Missouri's sediment accumulated on its southeasterly journey from the Montana Territory. The river's murky hue may not welcome travelers searching for a cool drink of clean water, but wet was wet as far as I was concerned. Sunlight danced across the gentle ripples rolling toward the shore. I dived in still wearing my hat, boots, and ruined suit. Cool water on hot skin. Was there a better feeling? I couldn't remember any just then.

Casting aside my memories of the last few days, I floated contentedly beneath the big blue sky. Spying the old mare standing upon the shoreline, I splashed a long squirt of wet toward her nose. The stream passed through her body with a splat.

The ghostly horse ignored my playful exuberance. Ears laid back flat and teeth bared, her screaming whinny sent nervous shivers down my spine. She bolted back toward the horizon as if Hell itself were after her. My tattoo, as if to underscore the mare's terror, writhed angrily under the wet shirt. Something had spooked her and set off the Ouroboros. I turned toward the river's center. Nothing. No ghosts or coachmen waited on the distant shore that I could see.

Agonizing pain registered in my stunned body as steel teeth clamped down tightly upon the flesh of my thigh. Bright ribbons of red floated to the surface. Blood. My bewildered mind realized it was my own. Twisting my body in panicked jolts, I slapped my arms against the current in a desperate attempt to swim toward shore. The beast, unhindered, bit down harder.

Pulling my wits about me, I slammed anxious fists against what I perceived was the head of the creature. Each strike passed through my captor as if it were merely a shadow. The river began to spin in multiple cones of swirling current. Watery tentacles flew forward and wrapped around me, pinning my arms to my side. I kicked frantically at the iridescent bands as they squeezed the precious life's breath from my lungs. The unrelenting pressure constricted in firmer spasms.

This was it. The last curse from Angelina's dead lips had let loose. I was going to die in the Missouri River like a limp trout. At least Angelina would be pleased with the gruesome manner of her curse's manifestation.

A strange blue ball of light burned in the distance. Small at first, the radiant azure glow expanded at an alarming rate as it zipped through the muddy water toward me. A massive bulk floated at the center of the blue glow. Muscle, fins, and a tail took form. The bright blue body struck my invisible captor with the power of a runaway train. Its tentacles loosened enough for me to wiggle an arm free. Bubbles of panicked screams burst from my mouth as the blue light turned for another approach.

A mouth full of teeth, taller than my torso, stopped a few feet from me. Burning on the Great White Shark's head was a peculiar symbol blazing in blue fire. The strange letters and images weaved together in complex patterns. I may not recognize the markings, but I would never forget them.

The shark moved closer, its body swaying in the river's current. Cold black eyes stared into mine as blue light reflected against their glassy surface. Hatred burned in those orbs.

Questions popped into my thoughts like escaping bubbles. Two ponderings were foremost on my mind. First, what was a shark doing in the Missouri River? And did it intend to eat me?

Then a swirl of water raced downstream, striking the shark. My watery captor hadn't abandoned its prey quite yet. Blood formed a fleeting curtain trailing behind the reeling fish. The shark's fins and teeth whirled like a hideous version of a child's spinning top.

The water monster gripped my torso in a crushing embrace and pulled me downward. My last breath whooshed through gritted teeth toward the surface. Lungs burning, I kicked at the creature's tentacles. Radiant blue sparked at the edge of my vision. It was true what the newly departed said about drowning. Bright pinpricks of light really did appear just before the end.

My body propelled forward. Or was it upward? I couldn't distinguish directions anymore. Air and the slapping sounds of thrashing water suddenly surrounded me. I could breathe again. Savoring each gulp of air, I stared in awe at the brilliant blue sky.

Jagged teeth ripped at the river around me in a fury of gnashing hunger. Finally, the limp tentacles fell away, and I was free from the water creature. Kicking toward the riverbank like a fiend, I willed my aching lungs to ease their panic gulps of air. My body sunk below the surface again. Grasping. Kicking. Wheezing. I fought my way back toward the blue skies. My head broke the surface at last. The rolling water rising from the river's body prompted me to forgo my appreciation of full lungs. Deciding it prudent to get out of the water, I swam double time for shore.

Then a chill of warning rattled my body. Lifting my gaze, I noticed a man standing in the scrub along the riverbank. The wide-brimmed hat he wore cast shadows over his eyes. What I could see of his features were sharp and exotic, as if he'd traveled from the other side of the world to watch me drown from the banks of the Big Muddy.

For a wild moment, I thought I saw his hands aglow with crimson fire. Impossible. Magic didn't live in this world. There was Life, and there was Death. That was it. What I'd seen had to be the reflection of the sun or some other easily explained illusion. My near-death experience – shark and all – could be attributed to dehydration.

The stranger looked at me then, and in his eyes, I recognized loathing. This man wanted me dead. I wasn't keen to wait around and discuss his reasons. The 'why' didn't matter. I was more concerned with the 'how.'

Mr. Black Hat slammed a fist into his hand. He gave me a final seething glare before disappearing into the green branches. Confused, I stared after him. Suddenly reality's unyielding fist smacked me hard on the back of the skull while I bobbed in place. My head plunged under the water again, and I took in a deep gulp of the river.

CHAPTER NINE

Something grabbed my hair in a claw-like grip and pulled me upward. Air scented with the sweet smells of fresh water and wet rope filled my aching lungs. I slapped at the fingers clinging to the tendrils of my hair. The owner of the rough grip stubbornly refused to let go.

"You fixin' to swim across the river, mister?" A gasping cackle rolled over the waters at me. "I wouldn't advise it. Those steamers don't care who they hit."

An old man dressed in a tattered hat and suspenders grinned at me from his flatboat. Then seeing my wits had returned, he let go. He reached a hand down and helped me up with a surprising amount of strength.

"Where am I, besides floating in the Missouri River, I mean."

"That's Wayne City Landing over yonder. What's left of it anyway," he said, pointing toward the other side of the river. "Walk up the bluff, and you'll find a whole heap of folks headed to Independence. It's a good four-mile walk, but you won't be short on company."

If river traffic indicated what awaited me on shore, I was certain not to be the lone traveler toward Independence. Steamboats churned in the center of the Big Muddy as it ambled westward. Small flatboats carrying goods and animals maneuvered skillfully around them as they headed toward shore. I hadn't gone far enough west. No matter. It was still civilization, and with no horse or supplies, I'd have to make do. I handed him a gold coin which he took with a delighted grin full of missing teeth.

"Have a seat and hold on. I'll get you across." He gripped at the oars and started forward across the river.

"Can I still find Steamboat passage here?"

I took off my jacket and squeezed the water back into the river. The bleeding from my right leg wasn't as bad as it appeared underwater. I swallowed a spirited curse. The teeth had ripped the hell out of my trousers, staining my right leg with dark blood.

"You're about twenty years too late, young fella. We had a nasty flood back in 1851. It ruined the landing and left behind that sandbar. Ships can't land here anymore. Nearest place to board a steamboat is Westport."

The slight change in color and current was visible as we moved further into the river's body. It must have been an incredibly destructive force to alter the river's path. The sandbar waited beneath the water, ready to ambush the unsuspecting pilot headed along the western shore. Any steamboat foolish enough to venture too close would find its paddle wheels ripped apart.

He shook his head and spat in the river. "Some worried Independence and Wayne City Landing were done for after that damn flood. Westport may get the bulk of river traffic, but we still hold our own with the wagon trains. They called Independence the "Queen City of the Trails" before the war. Yes, sir. You're about twenty years too late to see Independence in her hay day. Traders and travelers still stop here and get their outfits and rigs for the wagon trains headed on the California, Oregon, and Santa Fe Trails. 'Course more folks are headed to Fort Leavenworth now, but we still see a good trade."

"I thank you for the ride," I said. "And the information."

I disembarked onto the muddy shore and pushed his flatboat back into the current. Returning his departing wave, I set my sights on climbing the bluff. It appeared to be a slow ramble up a steep rise. Nothing strong legs couldn't manage. Other travelers much older than I had made the climb. I took a deep breath and started the slow ascent on my aching leg. The blood had stopped, but the pain persisted.

Remnants of the landing still resisted time's relentless hand. It wouldn't be long, however, before any sign of steamboats and their passengers disappeared into history. A sudden melancholy came over me. I would miss the romance of river travel. It didn't seem likely I would revisit Missouri or the Mississippi. Passing into the waiting arms of thick forest, I let my past go downstream with the waters of the Big Muddy.

Leaves danced about me in the streamers of wind rising off the river. The sudden unexpected shade sent a shiver under my wet clothes. Rumbles of conversation and laughter pierced the trees. People. Thank the sweet, gentle lord. Where there were people, there was food and dry clothes.

Independence was a good stretch of the legs away from the landing. Limping a bit on my right leg, I was moving much slower than my fellow travelers. Most were too absorbed in their conversations to notice me hobbling along the side of the road. French, German,

Dutch, and a dozen more unfamiliar languages flooded the stream of people headed toward Independence. I'd not expected such a wealth of international culture in the middle of the prairie.

No longer feeling the chill from wet clothes, my body began to warm in the Missouri summer afternoon. The damp shirt and trousers chafed as I walked. Trying inconspicuously to adjust certain tender male parts, I didn't notice the buckboard pull alongside me.

"Young man, you have the look of a soul in need of assistance." She stood like a queen in her widow's lace and black dress. Gray-streaked hair stayed tidily under a practical bonnet. At the same time, her hard eyes examined me with the precision of a surgeon.

"Yes, ma'am." I made to tip my hat but remembered it had floated toward Westport without me.

"Horace Abernathy, slow this wagon down. I have a wounded man that needs mending."

I hobbled around to the back of the wagon and pulled my body over the gate. Two sets of hands helped pull me over. I landed on my stomach before the widow and a charming young thing in yellow.

"I'm Mrs. Calloway, and this is my daughter, Eugenia May Calloway."

"Ma'am," I said, smiling politely at my two angels of mercy. "I'm uh…."

Who was I? Professor Edgar Eden had died in Lester. My internal conundrum was made mute. The widow Calloway, introduced to a fresh pair of ears, was deep into a one-sided conversation.

"Off with those trousers, Mr., what did you say your name was? Well, I was a nurse for twenty years. I've seen more Union and Confederate backsides than I can count." She pushed at her daughter's shoulder. "You sit with Mr. Abernathy, Eugenia May, and keep your eyes straight ahead." The widow's lace swirled as she turned to me. "You aren't Confederate, are you?"

"No, Ma'am."

"Good. We stayed loyal to the Union. I wouldn't have turned you away, mind. It's my duty as a nurse to heal all of God's creatures."

Another stern look motivated me to strip off my wet trousers. The widow Calloway frowned tightly at the ugly gash on my thigh. She slapped her palms to her thighs with a nod.

"I've seen worse."

I was sure she had, but the conviction did little to ease my discomfort when she pulled a needle and thread from her bag. Mrs. Calloway fished a bottle from inside a sack near the driver's seat. She took the cork in her mouth and pulled it out with a pop. The pained expression on Mr. Abernathy's face told me he was unaware she'd known about his whiskey. Then the widow Calloway did the unthinkable. She poured the bottle's golden contents upon my wound. I let out an unmanly yelp.

"Don't look so wounded, Horace. You have plenty of whiskey hidden under the seat." She poured more liquor upon the needle and measured out a reasonable length of thread, talking all the while. "Mr. Abernathy is traveling to Westport for his supplies and has generously offered to take us along. What kind of merchant did you say you were, Mr. Abernathy? Well, my sister and her family live there. I'd planned to take the train from Saint Louis."

"A train?" My moment of elation vanished as she put the needle into my tender flesh.

"Of course, a train. You don't think we'd take a buckboard all that way, do you? We planned to take the train, but that heathen Major General Sterling Price and his confederate ruffians damaged the railroad between Independence and Westport."

"Those Confederate sympathizers are still stirring up trouble. They won't have the railroad tracks fixed until September, they say." Mr. Abernathy shook his head.

September. I couldn't wait that long. Lucky Sal was bound to pick his crew by then.

"I have no intention of waiting until September," the widow Calloway echoed my thoughts. "My sister's misery can't wait. Eugenia May Calloway, you keep your eyes forward, or so help me, I'll get the switch." She tugged at the thread with an alarming amount of irritation. "Mr. Abernathy has arranged for us to travel with one of the wagon trains until we reach the road to Westport."

"You could come with us," Eugenia May said, winking at me.

She pointed to a sea of white canvas bonnets nestled in clumps outside of town. Prairie Schooners headed west. There were easier ways to reach San Francisco than enduring life on a wagon train. Weeks of hard travel and endless empty country. It sounded horrible.

"What a delightful thought," I said, giving her a strained smile.

Her impish gaze drifted up the bare skin of my leg. A knowing grin lingered upon her lips. I had an inkling Eugenia May wasn't the innocent lamb her mother thought her to be. My spirit was willing, but my body remained under the stern ministrations of an army nurse.

"Thank you for the tender healing," I said, pulling up my trousers when Mrs. Calloway had finished.

"We've arrived at last," she said, ignoring my words of thanks.

The cacophony of multiple languages grew more pronounced as we entered Independence. Shops catering to the wagon train clientele lined the streets. The pounding of iron against anvil thundered from every direction. It was deafening. We were struck silent under the clamor of bustling activity. Mr. Abernathy, a resident of the city, took the opportunity to break into the widow Calloway's steady stream of conversation.

"You think this is busy? Train loads of pioneers used to flood Independence to buy gear for the wagon trains when I was a boy. The blacksmiths who built the wagons and the gear outnumbered the hotels. They worked around the clock to fill the demand. Now, commerce has greatly reduced after the flood and because of the war."

"It's busy enough to suit me," the widow Calloway said. "Here's our hotel. Come along, Eugenia May. I have a headache to beat the band. We'll see you first thing in the morning, Mr. Abernathy. It was nice meeting you, Mister?"

"Thank you for your kindness, Ma'am."

Mr. Abernathy whistled as Eugenia May gave me a wink behind her mother's departing back. He chuckled and set the wagon to moving again. I sat on the seat beside him as he gave me a brief tour of Independence proper. It certainly was a Queen compared to the rat hole towns I'd frequented over the past few months.

"You should have seen Independence in the height of her glory."

"I'll owe you a drink for giving me a ride and showing me around town," I said.

An unhappy scowl crossed his face. "I'm grateful for the offer, young fella. I am, but we leave at first light, and I can't face being hungover while trapped in the wagon with that woman. If you change your mind about traveling with us to Westport, I live at the Nebraska House. It's a merchant's hostelry. We leave at first light." He pointed a finger toward a group of Union soldiers parading aimlessly down the street. "You watch your step around them, friend. They don't mind taking a heavy hand with men like you."

I suppose he meant drifters. Trouble with Union Soldiers was the last thing I needed. My appearance did suggest tramp after the run I'd made over the last few days. A bath and shave would work wonders. Then I'd find new clothes for a new identity.

Chapter Ten

I stayed on the sidewalks, avoiding the rush of wagons in Independence's well-traveled streets. Unfortunately, life as a pedestrian wasn't much better. Crowds of pioneers bustled around the windows of shops, inspecting the gear and supplies. Children dressed in their best town clothes pressed sticky fingers against the windows. Oblivious to their offspring, parents muttered in spectrums of awe to outrage. They were learning their first harsh lesson about the westward expansion. Adventure costs money.

Bonnets and wide-brimmed hats leaned together in roared whispers. Their obsessive interest made navigating around them difficult. Enthralled by the window displays, the pioneers sucked me into their clumps of wool and gingham. My cheek struck the glass with an ungraceful thwack.

"Proud of their merchandise, aren't they? Those prices are obscene." I shook my head with a tsk-tsk and extracted myself from the crowd. Several ladies ran cursory glances over my ripped trousers and ruined shirt. I heard the terms "drunkard" and "bump" tossed about in their conversation, but my shabby presence didn't deter them from resuming their gawking through the store windows.

Keeping to the outer rim of gawkers, I moved down the row of shops. My goal was clean clothes and another pair of boots to replace my ruined ones. The merchants of Independence could keep their gear and months of dusty roads. Give me a steamboat or train over wagons any day.

The Widow Calloway had an undeniable point. Methods of transportation were limited. I suppose I could rent a flatboat to take me upriver. My thoughts wistfully turned to the rails running between here and Westport. Time on a speeding locomotive could afford me the opportunity to heal my leg a bit. Unfortunately, sabotage by disgruntled Confederate troops had snatched away my chances to ride in a comfortable railcar. I kicked a stray clump of dirt back onto the road from which it had strayed. My last resort, of course, would be traveling to Westport with the wagon train.

One of Independence's respectable citizens gave me a perspicacious glare. The elderly gentleman seemed too richly dressed for a typical day. Wait. Was it Sunday? I had no idea. Offering him a friendly nod, I limped past with a new sense of hope. The town had a little wealth in it. Saloons and gambling houses seemed to be doing a steady business even during the middle of the day. I might be able to grow my stake here before moving on to San Francisco.

Thugs dressed in Union blues – stolen, I was sure - pushed roughly through the mass of people. Their hoots of drunken laughter echoed above the clamorous activity of an Independence Sunday afternoon. Unshaven with dirty bellies bulging over their belts, this mob of cutthroats was no more army material than I.

"Damn the luck." I nodded an apology to a group of ladies window-shopping nearby.

Griswold Wilks - Grizz to his few friends and oceans of enemies - stomped down the sidewalk. Thick hair flowed over the collar of the great beast's phony uniform. Dirty black strands jutted in unpleasant sprouts from his big nose and grimy ears. Drunker than the rest and uglier too, Grizz led the mob.

A scar joined his fat lips to the mangled ear on the right side of his head. I knew the mark well, having given it to him. Grizz and I had a short run as partners a year ago. We'd made good money appropriating cargo from dock warehouses along the Mississippi. The partnership lasted for a few months before our contract abruptly ended. It was I who'd irreparably broken our bond. Even now, I harbor no regrets.

Recognition flickered in Grizz's bloodshot eyes when he saw me. His thick lips dropped open as drool cascaded over his stubble. It was time for me to beat a hasty retreat. Turning abruptly, I began swimming upstream in the thick crowd. My passage was a bit more polite than the gang of cutthroats behind me. Cold sweat bubbled along my forehead as vivid memories of Grizz's promised revenge invaded my mind. I wouldn't be leaving Independence if he caught me.

An alley, roughly the width of a slender man, opened to my left. I darted into its mouth and immediately regretted the decision. One of the merchants had cleverly added six inches to the width of his storeroom. I'd have to turn sideways to get through the claustrophobic space.

"Dun! I don't believe it," Grizz said, standing at the mouth of the alley. "Didn't I say today was my lucky day, boys? Here's the man I want dead most in all the world right in front of me. And in bloody rags to boot!"

"You haven't changed much, Grizz. I see you're still as ugly as the night I burned your ear off."

"Yeah. I owe you, partner." Grizz ran a fat finger down the length of his scar. "Why'd you turn on me, Dun? We was having fun."

"I don't like your kind of fun. You have some dubious tastes in entertainment. Many I ignored, but there are some things a man – if he is a man – cannot overlook."

"Tarnation! Is this about that little nobody again?"

"Her name was Emily." I gritted my teeth as the rage flooded my heart. "She was a child. You had no right to do what you did."

"I take what I want. Don't ever forget it, Dun."

Grizz lifted his shoulders and tilted his head from side to side. The boxer's stretch he was dancing through now was a favorite ritual he did before killing. His boys started to titter like eager schoolgirls. They knew what was coming as well as I.

Scurrying sideways like a crab on a hot rock, I turned toward the light of freedom and scrambled along the walls. I'd gone several feet before my escape registered in Grizz's booze-addled mind.

"Where are you going, little rabbit? We need to discuss this scar of mine." Grizz chuckled at my back. "I can't fit through there. Get in after him, Phelps."

Efram Phelps was a lanky sprout of a man. Toothless and a bit wrong in the head, he was one of Grizz's favorite lackeys. Phelps had an unpleasant gift for dispensing pain in creative and unique ways. Every time we worked a job together, he'd brought along a new handmade weapon. Today he had a wooden contraption with several rail spikes sticking out through its surface.

"That's an interesting new toy you have, Phelps. Why don't you try it on yourself first?"

"Who says I haven't!" Phelps giggled as air hissed through the empty spaces between his gums. His shoulders shook violently with laughter. "This here's a toy I'd love to try on you, Dun."

"Don't maim him too bad. I want my due." Grizz gave me a hungry sneer. "I'll see you on the other side."

Grizz and the remaining gang headed toward the back of the building to meet us. Should I choose rail spikes or Grizz's stale breath? I didn't like my options. Then again, there may be another way. I pressed my palms against both walls and began to climb. Phelps rushed forward with his club raised, but a well-placed kick in the face stunned him. The blow gave me enough time to ascend out of his reach.

Scrapes from the rough brick pricked my skin. Ignoring the discomfort, I continued to think happy thoughts and aimed for the top of the buildings. My legs shook as I forced them to thrust my body upward.

Then shadows blocked the thin patch of blue. Grizz peered over the side of the roof. He and several of his goons looked down at me like gargoyles on an unconsecrated cathedral. Phelps below me. Grizz above. It was like being a spittoon cleaner in the seventh circle of Hell.

"Look out below!"

I let my body slide downward. It was a long drop. I might have injured myself if it weren't for Phelps cushioning my fall. The air burst from his lungs with a loud whoosh as my boots came down upon his chest. Then this little rabbit darted for the other end of the alley.

Shouts rang over my head. I grinned and waved. *Pride goeth before a fall,* or so the Psalms says. Hands grabbed me as I broke free of the alley. Grizz wasn't the fool I'd hoped. He'd been ready for any escape attempts, and this little rabbit had fallen right into his trap.

CHAPTER ELEVEN

The alley – as most alleys do – opened into the hidden world of the town's forgotten trash. Old crates and garbage made tall piles around a messy open space. The skeleton of an abandoned wagon stood at the center like a lazy guard dog. A malodorous breeze brushed at the heap. It groaned and teetered precariously in the Missouri afternoon.

Shorty Bill and his partner, Two Fingered Eddie, greeted me with wet chuckles. Dim and worn around the edges, the two ruffs appeared in perfect accord with the garbage around them. One was wearing muddy Union blue trousers. His friend had taken the sweat-stained jacket.

"I take it you haven't ambushed enough soldiers to earn a full uniform each."

"Shut your pie hole," Eddie said, shoving me against the store wall. "This one looks squirrelly."

"Don't he just!" Bill waved his gun at my chest. "Better keep a tight hold on him."

"And I thought we were friends," I said. "Who warned you to duck when that riverboat captain tried to shoot you in the back, Bill?"

"He thought I cheated him at cards!" Bill rushed forward and threw a fist into my gut. "It was you that done the cheating. I swear, Dun, you are as crooked as they come."

I bent over, gasping for air. My empty stomach gurgled, and I heaved the muddy water I'd inhaled from the Missouri. Grizz's gang played rough. I'd wind up with broken ribs if I weren't careful.

"Easy there, Bill. Don't go too hard. The boss wants a word with him."

"Damn right I do!" Grizz stormed toward us with the rest of his gang in tow.

Alcohol-infused sweat seeped through the brim of his hat. My eyes followed the sweat's continuous journey as it raced downward. His tainted moisture finally soaked into the collar of Grizz's filthy shirt. The lingering odor of his brief run from atop the building permeated the alley. What Grizz lacked in charm, he made up for in aroma.

Thick fingers grasped at his straining belt, producing a long slender weapon. It was a ring bayonet designed to fit at the end of a Union rifle. Grizz was surprisingly sentimental over the broken bayonet. He'd filed the wicked-looking blade himself, not satisfied until it was a staggering fifteen inches of deadly steel.

By his own account, Grizz had taken it off a Union officer. They'd fought over a poker hand, and the officer had struck a lucky hit. He'd stabbed Grizz in the rib cage, and the bayonet tip broke off. Grizz, in turn, had pulled the weapon out of his own body and stabbed the officer, killing him.

"I'm going to enjoy cutting you, Dun. Maybe I'll give you a scar, so we match like twins."

Grizz rested the edge of the blade against my cheek and slowly brought it down. Hot blood curled in a thin trickle toward my neck. His sudden boisterous laugh sent me staggering backward, but I didn't get far. Grizz's henchmen pulled me upright. Spittle and bits of what I hoped was lunch peppered my face as they laughed. The steel grips holding my arm began to loosen.

"I couldn't hope to reach your level of ugly, Grizz."

A fist hammered against my kidney, dropping me to my knees. Sparkles of light fluttered like glowing starlight around a harvest moon. Shaking my head to clear the fuzzy vision, I fell on my backside in the dirt, gasping for air. Grizz had a punch that could rival any steer. He did, however, have the unfortunate habit of underestimating me. My gut may ache, but at least my arms were free.

"What in the devil is going on here!" A storekeeper came out of his backdoor holding a rifle. "I don't want the likes of you loitering around my store. Get on out of here before I call the sheriff. He's right inside."

"Too bad, Grizz," I said. "You'll have a witness now if you murder me here. Independence seems like a town that enjoys a good hanging."

I threw a punch at the most vulnerable spot between Eddie's legs. Rolling away from his hunched frame, I got my feet under me. The narrow alley was close. I darted inside and shuffled toward the other end as fast as I could. Phelps still lay unconscious where I'd dropped him. I jumped over his sprawled body and gifted him with a backward kick to his head. Grinning, I hurried toward the sounds of commerce.

"Watch where you're going!" A well-dressed woman gave me the evil eye and stormed off with a string of children following behind her.

"Pardon me, Ma'am."

I had to find a place to lay low until morning. Staying in this crowd would get me killed or arrested. My back to the buildings, I ran unsteady fingers down the reassuring solidness of the wall. A sudden absence of rough surface made me stagger into the mouth of a recessed storefront. Crouching low, I kept my eye on the street for any sign of my pursuers. Then I spotted them. Damn. Grizz and his gang stormed through the crowd. Their determined searching reinforced my notion of finding a hidey-hole.

Keeping an eye on Grizz, I ducked into the store. A frantic chiming above my head announced my presence as I closed it behind me. Grizz turned. A triumphant sneer curved his fat lips. He could out hunt a bloodhound when it came to revenge. On this occasion, his keen nose had caught my scent. The thin glass panels vibrated as Grizz pounded his fists violently upon them. His yellow teeth were at my eye level. I could almost smell his putrid breath through the glass.

"What's that, Grizz?" I slammed the door lock home. "I can't hear you."

He rammed a shoulder to the door. I stumbled back a few steps as the glass vibrated. Making him angrier wasn't in my best interest, but it did brighten the day. I turned to look over my shoulder at my surroundings. It was an outfitters' store full of farming implements and other sharp things. Not good. I didn't want Grizz to have anything deadly on hand if he caught up with me.

Accustomed to the hustle-bustle of busy trade, the store's owner barely lifted his eyes at the ruckus we were causing. Grizz put his shoulder into the push, bumping the lock askew. I slammed it back in place. My injured leg wouldn't last for long against Grizz and his gang. I pulled the blind down to cover the window. Then diving behind a row of hanging harnesses, I pulled them around me.

Wood cracked, and the door slammed against the wall. Grizz burst inside with a growl. His broad back blocked the sun, casting me into darkness in my cramped space. Then suddenly, he moved, and glaring light struck my eyes, momentarily blinding me. I withdrew from the small hole between the leather strips to blink away the irritation.

A soft tinkling of bells caught my attention. Pressing my watering eyes to the small hole again, I spied a young soldier – a private from the looks of his bare sleeves – sneaking out the door. He was a Union soldier – a real one this time. Showing a generous portion of common sense, he was going to get his friends. The store would be crawling with soldiers soon. Those bluecoats would take anyone who knew Grizz in for questioning. They wouldn't believe that I was innocent dressed as I was. Well. Innocent on this particular occasion.

I turned in my crouch to the other side of the rack of leather goods and slowly spread the ribbons of rawhide. Farm implements, buckets, feedbags, and other goods stood in neat rows for any soul looking to conquer the West with a plow rather than a gun. Of course, there were plenty of firearms too. They were locked up tight behind the counter. I couldn't get to one without giving myself away.

The sweet rotting scent of cow dung struck my senses. It was faint, but my nose could still find the direction of the animals. Dark curtains swung lazily to my left, giving me a peek at the back way out. Luck was still on my side. I waited until Grizz was harassing some of the patrons standing in line at the counter. Then I plunged between the leather goods and bolted through the curtains.

A generous storage room opened before me. Barrels and crates, stacked from floor to ceiling, lined the walls and center aisle. I couldn't see anything of use for my purposes among the goods. Following along the center aisle, I found an untidy spot in the northwest corner of the room. Broken goods littered a nearby workbench. Still, no guns that I could see. I'd have to liberate a weapon somewhere else.

The odor of cow hit me again. Someone had cracked the back door open. I peered out into a dirt road nestled close to the stockyards. What a stench. Sweaty cows stomped on yards and yards of their own muck. God, how I missed the wonderful aromas of sophisticated city life.

I stepped out into the road, moving quickly through patterns of sunshine and shade. Cowhands lined the rail fences. Their attention rested upon the docile herd. Conversations rose and fell in waves of uninteresting comments about feed. None of them took an interest in me as I passed.

"Come back here, Dun, you miserable coward!" Grizz lifted his gun, pointing it in my general direction. "You have a date with my bullet."

He'd found the storage room exit. Hopping the fence and creeping through the herd might have been a better idea. Instead, I'd chosen to leave myself open like a big target. Regrets were a waste of brainpower. Instead, I directed my thoughts toward escape.

"Clear out!" I yelled at the cowhands.

Spurs flew over the paddock fence and into the cows. Startled mooing welcomed them. I, unwilling to flee toward the muck, wasn't as lucky. Grizz's bullet struck a yard away from my foot. He was a deadly aim even when taxed with unaccustomed physical exertion.

Managing a rapid limp, I bolted down the dirt road toward a series of outbuildings. Men and animals ambled lazily about the entrances. Some of the two-legged visitors carried rifles. Their presence gave me a tiny bit of hope. Grizz might be stubborn and mean, but he wasn't one to rush into unfriendly guns.

The outbuildings suddenly converged, closing off my escape route. Curse the luck! My eyes found an irritating lack of objects to climb on or crawl underneath. I was trapped.

"My rabbit has stopped running at last," Grizz said, swiping the bayonet wickedly through the air. "Hold him, boys. I'm going to take a piece of skin for every day I wasted tracking him."

The burning hatred in his eyes foreshadowed the kind of death I could expect. No one was within shouting distance except me, my murderers, and a bunch of cows. They'd find my body and label me as a worthless drifter.

Then a loud snort forced my attention to the stockyards, where an unbelievable nightmare met my gaze. A huge cinnamon-colored bull stared at us from inside the paddock. Horns and tail blazing with red fire, the beast shook its head wildly as if it had gone mad. On its forehead burned the same symbol the shark had borne under the river water.

The fiery bull stomped its hooves on the ground and charged. I'm man enough to admit I screamed when the rail fence ripped apart as if it were twine on a paper package. The ground rumbled, and dust rose as if from the thundering of a thousand hooves. I pressed my back to the wall with a cry as the great bull charged toward us.

This time, the symbol seemed to enrage the other cattle. They kicked and shoved, desperate to follow the horned beast to freedom. Suddenly, the horned flood broke loose. Endless hooves stormed across the dirt road and into my captors. Grizz's thick head disappeared under the stampeding herd.

Heat, intense and angry, struck me. The bull's blazing horn swept inches away from my chest. It gave me a last indignant snort before leading the cattle down the dirt road toward open country. I didn't wait to see if Grizz had survived. He'd finally met a murderous hulk of muscle who could best him.

Lingering to feed any itching curiosity at what I'd just witnessed wasn't in my best interest. I flew over the broken fence and into the empty stockyard.

CHAPTER TWELVE

After the gallant endeavor of saving my skin, my wounded leg finally exhausted its patience with me. Attempting to push my limits further was foolish. My body was demanding rest. If I didn't accommodate it soon, there would be a rebellion.

Stacks of freshly cut lumber blocked the sidewalk to my right. I peered around the hill of wood and marveled at the foundations of a new building. Its stone pieces and freshly cut wooden planks covered a few thousand square feet of the city block. Two stories of skeletal wooden ribs stood guard around a massive oak bar. Independence was birthing a new saloon. Regrettably, I wouldn't be present to sample the first whiskey.

I hobbled around the corner of the new building and immediately regretted my choice in hiding places. Visitors and locals were fond of using the space as a dumping ground and toilet. Ignoring the stench of human waste and garbage, I plopped down and leaned my head against the unfinished wall. Ending up in a toilet was the inevitable end to my day.

A high-pitched whistle from the other side of the thin wall made my last nerve twang. "Get a wiggle on, you men! Captain Tyson don't like to be kept waiting."

The tension in my body eased as the thunderous rumble of many boots passed by without stopping. I let a strained laugh escape through my lips with a nervous whoosh. Great galloping grannies. Was I losing what remained of my wits!

"Magical creatures aren't roaming through Missouri," I said, gently chiding myself. "My mind is playing tricks." Then shaking my head, I chuckled at the absurdity. "I haven't eaten in a good long while. Then I drank half the river, giving my leg a good gash to boot! Anyone would be off their head. Magic does not exist in the world. Such whimsical ideas are for children. Get ahold of yourself."

Turning my thoughts to practical matters, I began planning my next steps toward survival. Sitting in a field of shite certainly wasn't doing me any good. I'd need a place to hole up in for a few days. Pushing my body upright again, I left the muck behind. I ventured back out into the busy streets of Independence to search for sanctuary.

Salvation came in the form of a fancy sign with golden letters reading, "Nebraska House." Abernathy, owner of the wagon I'd ridden in from the landing to Independence, was staying at the hostelry. He'd generously seconded Miss Eugenia May's invitation aboard their wagon to Westport. Traveling with a pretty girl and a few bottles of whiskey would compensate for the constant stream of chatter from the widow Calloway.

Dashing my hopes of a comfortable bed and hot food, Eddie leaned against the hostelry's window. He threw the butt of his spent cigarette onto the sidewalk and moved to the entrance. Hooded eyes watched the street with keen interest. After the savage blow to his manhood, I doubted Eddie would greet me with a heart full of forgiveness. Curse my rotten luck! Grizz was more tenacious than I'd supposed. But, of course, it was a given he'd have his men watching all the hotels in town.

Wagon wheels surged past me, coming dangerously close to ruining what was already a horrible day. The vehicle's owner shouted a rather impolite expletive in my direction. I froze. The colorful language captured Eddie's attention. Turning his gaze upon the departing wagon, he stepped away from the hostelry's entrance. I moved one tentative boot toward the sidewalk, hoping he'd follow the wagon. Disappointment, however, was becoming an all too frequent visitor. Suddenly satisfied the departing wagon was of no interest, Eddie returned to his post.

"Get out of the damn road, tin horn!" The driver of an east-bound wagon uncharitably spat a wad of spent tobacco at me.

I ducked to dodge the disgusting black tar just in time to avoid the searching eyes of Grizz's sentry. Two wagons, one to my front and the other to my rear, rumbled down the road. I held my breath, saying a little prayer to benefit the drivers' steady hands. Standing in the middle of the street was going to get me killed by wagon or by bullets. It was time to pick a new destination.

Whirling back toward the alley, I was suddenly in the path of a wagon racing west toward the edge of town. I jumped backward as it passed. Then, using the last strength my wounded leg possessed, I threw my body aboard. Careful not to raise the driver's attention, I pressed my body against the empty canvas.

Grizz and his men would continue to search every hotel and means of comfort I might frequent. A drunk and criminal he may be, but Grizz was no fool. There was no help for it. I'd have to hide outside of town until I could reach Abernathy.

The wagon slowed to make a turn. I took the opportunity to swing over its side and back onto the road. Locating a perch in the deep opening of an empty storefront at the edge of town, I pressed my ear against the door. It was Sunday, so I wasn't surprised no one was working inside. Strips of old newspaper covered the side windows of the entrance, hiding my body from everyone except those walking directly past me on the sidewalk. Satisfied with my hiding place, I settled in to wait.

The orange rays of sundown crept over Independence, sending the thinning crowds of pioneers back to their campsites. They'd taken most of the hustle and bustle that hid my presence with them. Seeking out Mr. Abernathy was no longer an option. Nightfall had brought other predators to the streets of town. Bluecoats – the real thing this time – marched down the road in pairs. The soldiers, rifles held ready, anticipated a fight. It would be impossible to avoid their notice for much longer.

Grizz and his friends had formed the same conclusion and had finally fled back into the safety of the nearest saloon. Their reluctant departure didn't leave me much time to make my escape. I hobbled out of Independence proper and headed toward the long lines of prairie schooners. Mr. Abernathy had said his friends traveled on a wagon train following the Oregon Trail. Our route would take us through Westport, where I could catch a steamboat. The wagon master or one of his men would know Abernathy and the Calloway Ladies.

Maybe they'd spare a plate while I waited. The thought of food sent my stomach growling.

Juice from roasting meat sizzled as it struck open flames. I quickened my pace as pangs of hunger prodded me forward. The amber glow of firelight danced between a veil of leaves skirting the nearest campsite.

"Excuse me," I called to a group of men sitting beside their campfire. "Are you with the Oregon Trail train?"

"*Ich verstehe dich nicht.*" One of the men pointed down the dirt road toward a camp full of schooners nestled close together. "*Sie sprechen Englisch.*"

"That's the correct wagon train?" I gave him a bewildered frown.

He tugged on his suspenders with a grunt. More German words raced around the fire as the men murmured to one another. Waving a hasty goodbye, I stayed on course toward the other camp. I didn't understand a lick of German. Either he pointed me in the right direction or told me he didn't understand me either. I was too tired to reason it out. It didn't matter. Honestly, how many wagon trains could be leaving Independence at any given time?

My thoughts turned back to Westport. I could always stay with the wagon train if I failed to find a passage by water. Our paths were sure to cross with another group traveling along the California Trail. I'd find a way from Sutter's Mill down to San Francisco after that. If my future became truly desperate, I could join one of the emigrant trails to the southern end of California. The thought made me cringe. I'd heard the nightmarish stories yarning about yearlong trips through ungodly deserts. Lucky Sal and his San Francisco venture wouldn't wait that long.

Clusters of white bonnets peppered the trees around Independence. Stopping abruptly in the middle of the road, I scanned the thousands of faces sharing their evening meal. Frustration rumbled in my throat. My old companion, disappointment, had joined me for an evening stroll. I counted at least four different crude campsite entrances. It was too dark to read any signs indicating wagon trains in the fading light. The German had sent me on a goose chase.

I faced an impossible challenge in a field of too many camps with too many wagons. Damn it. I'd neglected to ask where Abernathy was meeting his friends. What a tin horn move. Well, there was no help for it now. I'd have to find Mr. Abernathy and the Calloway ladies in the morning. It would mean an early start but catching them at the Nevada House seemed the only solution.

Weaving between the wagons, I came across a group of primly dressed men. Their white collars buttoned up tight against their necks were in sharp contrast to the black suits they wore. One of them, a thin-faced man with a severe expression, waved his bible at the others. He leaned against one of the wagons, taking a cup of water from a mousy-looking woman hovering inside. The jackass didn't thank her or acknowledge her presence in any way. Everything about him screamed arrogant and self-righteous. I'd grown up with insufferable men like him. Resentment, firmly rooted in my childhood, spurred my admittedly childish temper.

Black and white fabric swayed in the wind beside the wagon. Well, well. The reverend's wash day. He and I were about the same size. I walked quickly between the wagons with the confidence to suggest I belonged there. Then tugging at the clothes and collar, I disappeared between the rigs like a sticky-fingered wind.

The long line of wagons belonged mostly to families headed westward toward the promise of abundance. President Lincoln's Homestead Act of 1862 gave hopeful pioneers 160 acres of public land. If they could tame the wilderness, then they could keep their share. California or Oregon, their destination didn't matter. They were headed in the right direction to suit me.

Hiding among families, however, would draw suspicion to a blissfully single man. I kept walking until I heard the unmistakable sounds of my kindred. Bawdy laughter. Cursing over an impromptu poker game. Yes. These were my people. Single men, most likely merchants, gathered around several campfires to play cards, drink spirits, and share their thoughts about the upcoming road ahead. Several times a Captain Tyson was mentioned among the men. The name sounded familiar. Had Mr. Abernathy or one of the Calloway ladies spoken of him? Or was it someone else? My fuzzy head couldn't manage to remember.

A heavy ox cart filled with neatly positioned barrels stood just outside their firelight. Stretched canvas covered the barrels, holding them in place. The cart's side and front boards glistened with a bright cherry red. The back had no gate, while the front didn't accommodate a driver. Some unlucky soul would have to walk all the way to wherever they were going. I sent a little wish to the heavens on behalf of their feet.

Spotting a space large enough for a man to crawl through, I climbed inside. The cart swayed as I fought my way toward the front. Someone had thoughtfully stacked blankets against the boards. I had the makings of a reasonably comfortable bed for the night.

Pulling off my old clothes, I stuffed them through a small opening under the canvas cover. The constant prairie wind lifted my ruined shirt and pants, sending them back toward the river. Goodbye, Professor Eden. Hello Reverend Dun. I pulled on the clothes. They were abrasive, much like their previous owner. The collar I set aside for another time. No sense in being strangled by this new identity until absolutely necessary.

I left my boots on, regretting not finding a replacement pair. They were comfortable and had enough wear left in them to get me to San Francisco. I'd buy nothing but the best once I reached the city.

Curling up on the blankets, I quickly drifted off to sleep. Dreams crept across my mind as I slumbered. My body swayed gently as distant hooves and the abrasive laughter of a woman echoed in the misty dreamscape.

Chapter Thirteen

Jarred out of a deep sleep, I woke to the sensation of flying. Sailing through the air was pleasant enough, but my landing was an abrupt and unpleasant surprise. My face slammed against hardwood. Spewing a stream of expletives, I grabbed at my throbbing nose with a disgruntled curse. It wasn't bleeding or broken. Thank the Heavens for small blessings.

Filtered daylight streamed in through the canvas. My brain caught up with my eyes as I remembered crawling inside to hide. I didn't, however, remember the wagon and its contents being tilted dramatically to one side. So when had we moved, and why had we stopped now? More to the point, why had the fool of a driver parked sideways on a hill?

"You are a master of deduction, aren't you?"

My fellow stowaway sat behind the barrels across from me. The theatrical black cloak – folded neatly atop his leather sandals - made a thick pile between us. Daylight exposed a fit and muscular body. His thick black beard, neatly trimmed, connected to a head of full wavy hair. Bushy eyebrows lifted slightly over deep brown eyes. His broad nose wiggled as he sucked in a laugh.

We'd met in passing on the road out of Lester the night it became a battlefield. He'd pointed me toward the farm where my recently deceased mare had waited. I honestly hadn't thought about this stranger since.

"Are you following me, friend?" I asked, gingerly patting my nose. "What's so funny?"

"This costume you're wearing." He wiggled a thick finger at my stolen clothes. "I should think you'd choose another disguise after the hell your father put you through. Or are you working through childhood issues?"

I lunged at him, but vicious wings and sharp talons thwarted the attack. The blazing symbol burning with purple fire upon the large crow's forehead looked suspiciously like the blue markings on the shark I'd imagined I'd seen in the Big Muddy. I yanked my hand back with a yowl as its angry beak snapped at my outstretched fingers. Intense bird eyes glared at me as it ruffled its feathers with disdain in my general direction.

"Easy, Doran," the man said, flicking a finger at the crow. "Our young friend has had a trying few days. I'm sure he doesn't mean to be rude."

The crow gave me a decidedly contemptuous squawk as it ruffled its feathers. Then flipping a sleek black tail at us, Doran hopped across the blanket toward the barrels. Thrusting its beak inside, the crow returned, carrying a shapeless mess dripping with water. Doran jumped over my bent legs and unceremoniously dumped a waterlogged hat on my lap.

"Is this a puncture?"

I wiggled my finger through the hole in the felt, eyeing the crow for any signs of malicious intent. Doran hissed as if insulted and hopped back on its perch atop the man's cloak.

"Wear it, Dunham. You will fry out here without a hat."

"What's your game?" I glared at him, reaching for my absent emergency pistol.

"I'm not much for games. Now listen. Our time grows short. My name is Hesperos," he said, bowing his head in greeting. "You and I have met before. Let us say we were reacquainted in Lester when I helped you escape the soldiers and Death's coachman. Yes. I've seen Hell's coach too."

Hesperos leaned forward. His body seemed to grow until it took up all the remaining space inside the wagon. Shivers of warning rippled along my spine. Given the opportunity, I would have bolted - anything to escape the menacing power exuding from his eyes.

"I know everything about you, Dunham Raynor. I was there when you told your father about the things you saw. He was a cruel-hearted beast. Claiming you to be marked by a demon and then locking you in an asylum. Ha! The hypocrite."

I'd never told anyone, even Angelina, what I saw when souls crossed over. Not since Pennsylvania anyway. Being thrown into another insane asylum was something I'd avoid at any cost. Escape for a thirteen-year-old boy was more straightforward than it would be for a man full grown. Now here was this stranger nonchalantly describing my whole life to me.

"How do you know about my mark and the rest? Who the hell are you?"

"I know about the Ouroboros because I'm the one who marked you." Then he opened his shirt to the shoulder, revealing an Ouroboros with the same colors and patterns as mine. "We're connected, you and I. Stop running from me, Dunham. Our destinies are linked.

You will see." Then Hesperos turned his head sharply toward the back of the wagon. "Interfering jackanape!"

Two hands gripped the hem of the canvas cover and threw it open. I shielded my eyes from the sudden burst of sunlight. My imagination formed the faint halo of white encircling the outline of a man's head and shoulders. He leaned inside the wagon, lowering the canvas enough for me to see shapes again. Blinking, I made out the black cassock first. A Jesuit? Of all the creatures on God's earth to run into on my journey to California. I'd thought they kept their travels to the southwest, creating missions and schools.

"Stay quiet," I whispered. "It's just a priest."

Silence met my warning. Turning away from the priest, I found Hesperos and his pet crow had gone. How? I struck the sides of the wagon with frantic fists. There had to be a hidden door or latch he'd found. How else could he appear and disappear so quickly without me hearing him?

"Come out," the priest called. "I will do you no harm. Come along before I summon the wagon master."

Introduce myself to the priest or make a run for it and hope to find Hesperos? Neither option was appealing. Deciding to take my chances on Christian charity, I grabbed the white collar and fastened it to my shirt. The priest wasn't armed, but I didn't want to startle him. I needed a little of his goodwill to stay on the wagon train, so I took a leisurely pace as I climbed out the back.

Good God, the sun hadn't reached mid-day yet, and neither Independence Landing nor the Big Muddy was in sight. Open prairies surrounded me. In the emptiness of the windy landscape, I saw no signs of civilization.

Bringing forth my great mental agility despite the ungodly hour, I formulated our wagon was stuck in a rut. It wasn't going anywhere without human hands to help. My time spent traveling in comfort had officially come to an end.

Oxen teams snorted passively before the white bonnet wagons they pulled. Their dull cow eyes blinked at me as they slowly passed. Women and girls in gingham dresses stared out the back of the swaying schooners with sympathetic waves. The men and boys weren't as keen to show us compassion. They snorted and shook their heads as they walked by.

"Good day, father." I gave him a cordial tip of my soggy hat. "Did I climb aboard the wrong wagon?"

The priest was a good foot shorter than I. He took a step back as my boots dropped down into the dirt. My stiff leg reminded me it wasn't pleased to be on solid ground again. Wincing, I put on a friendly smile and looked him in the eye. His square face, framed by the shadows cast under his wide-brimmed hat, remained unnervingly serene.

"It would appear so, Reverend."

His accent marked him as a Spaniard. Many folks from his country still traveled from their home across the Atlantic to serve in Colorado and New Mexican Territory missions. I'd seen them in Texas and sometimes along the Mississippi but never had the opportunity to make friendly conversation.

"My friends call me Dun." I held out a hand, and he took it warmly. "I'm looking for my companions, Mr. Abernathy and the widow Calloway. They're traveling briefly with the wagon train until we reach the road headed toward Westport."

Whispers and troubled looks circulated amongst the cassocks. One of them, a thin prune-faced man, gave me tut-tuts and crossed himself. The priest beside him let loose a booming laugh. He rested plump hands over his belly. The cassock, wide enough to fit two priests, swayed in the prairie wind. It seemed about to take flight.

A quiet young man with hay-colored hair and startling blue eyes stood behind the big priest. He gave me a fleeting smile. Then he cast his eyes to the ground as if horrified he'd made eye contact with a protestant.

"I am Father Emilio of the Jesuit Order," the priest who'd found me out said. "And these are my brothers, Brother Ambrose of the Franciscan order, Brother Cuthbert, and our novice, Peter. You must excuse our youngest. He is newly arrived from Prussia and doesn't speak much English."

Brother Cuthbert, the lanky sour gentleman, gave me a curt nod. He softened a bit when I returned his greeting with a bow exuding Southern graciousness.

Large, plump hands suddenly engulfed my own. Brother Ambrose shook my arm until my whole skeleton rattled. His round belly shook all the while as he laughed.

"We are most glad to know you." Father Emilio gave me a warm smile. "My brothers and I are traveling to Santa Fe to visit the Missions."

"Santa Fe?" I spun around, weaving my head to catch a look at the landscape between the wagons as they rolled past. "This isn't the Oregon Trail?"

"You have made a dreadful mistake, Reverend Dun. The Oregon Trail does not journey this way. We split from the other wagon trains at Gardener this morning. Westport and the Missouri River are behind us by almost three days."

Had I slept for three days? Granted, this had been a traumatic week, but the long sleep could cost me my life. The Santa Fe Trail was nine hundred miles of rugged terrain, Indian attacks, and rattlesnake bites. I was making all sorts of poor decisions lately. Now here I was, headed south toward the New Mexico Territory. It had been dangerous before the war. Deadly battles had all but shut down travel on the trail. I couldn't imagine it would be any safer now the fighting was over – more or less.

Our path rambled across Western Kansas, through the Colorado Territory, and onto New Mexico. All of which, to my limited knowledge, were inhabited by Indian tribes none too happy with invaders in their lands. If we did make it to Santa Fe, how would I get to San Francisco? Nothing about the southwest interested me, so I'd not paid heed to any point on the map between Texas and California.

Should I hike back to Gardner? I could join a wagon train headed to California or Oregon and then travel toward Sutter's Mill from Fort Hall. San Francisco would have been a horse ride south from there. Then again, there was no guarantee I would catch anyone headed to the northwest.

A big man with dinner plate hands and a red face stomped toward us. Curls swirled with dusty brown and silver escaped from under the man's hat. A big bushy white mustache undulated between a frown and temper when he saw first the tilting wagon and then me.

"Oh, dear. It's the wagon Master, Captain Tyson," Father Emilio told me. He took a step closer to me as the massive man approached like a charging bull.

"What in the Devil's own bedpan is going on here? Who's this?"

"The wagon has found some deep ruts, Captain," Father Emilio explained in a cheerful tone. "But God has blessed us with a new traveling companion. May I present the good Reverend Dun? This poor soul crawled aboard the wrong wagon on the wrong train."

"That was a tinhorn move," Tyson grumbled. "No free rides on this train, friend, whether you're a man of the cloth or not. Why don't you beg a stake from your kind?"

Captain Tyson waved a hand at a familiar group of men dressed in severe black suits like the one I wore now. It was the same reverend I'd stolen the clothes from in Independence. What an unpleasant coincidence. Protestants on their way to claim a patch of land, no doubt. The Homestead Act had brought all sorts out West to start a new life on their 160 acres of government land.

The protestant clergy cast their noses down upon Father Emilio and his brothers. Typical. According to those whitewashed bible beaters, the priests wore the wrong color of skin and held a different version of the bible. I'm not saying every protestant in the good lord's kingdom lacked Christian charity. Many have been kind and generous to me in my hour of need. These cackling crows, however, represented the bitter side of their harsh faith. Of course, the Catholic Church wasn't free of severe behavior either. One simply had to remember the Spanish Inquisition.

"I prefer the fellowship of friendlier folk if the good father will endure my company in return," I said with a smile. "How much will this pleasant journey cost me, Captain? I appreciate charity, but I won't be a burden when I have the funds."

"No rig and no supplies? I have half a mind to kick your backside in the direction of Gardner." Tyson grunted. "Let me see your hands."

I held them out. The manicure Angelina had given me had long ago lost its shine. Tyson turned my hands over with a disgusted grunt.

"Soft hands. I might have known it from a professional kneeler."

"I'm a fair hand driving a rig," I said. "Come now, Captain. You'll only have to put up with me for a short time until I can find my way to California."

"You don't know nothing about nothing. These prairie schooners average about two miles per hour. That's twenty miles per day. We'll be in Santa Fe in a little over two months."

"Two months!" The world swayed beneath my feet. "I have to get to California."

"Do you think the world ends in Santa Fe? You can join a wagon train there traveling the Southern Emigrant Trail bound for Los Angeles." Captain Tyson let out a long sigh. "A tinhorn like you would die from sheer ignorance if I sent you back alone to Gardner. Since I'm no murderer, I'll have to find you a job on our train."

"We will share our meals with him, Captain Tyson." Father Emilio patted me on the shoulder. "There is always room for one more."

"No, sir! I can't abide a fit man lounging at his leisure while the rest of us toil. So, you walk along with the father today, Dun. I'll find you when we camp for the night. In the meantime, you can repay Father Emilio's generosity by helping push this wagon out of the ruts. Lend a hand, you men!" Tyson shouted at a few unlucky travelers.

"A careful hand, if you please," Brother Ambrose's massive bulk bumped me out of the way. "I'll not have my hops spilled all over the prairie. Beer is God's gift to the grateful man, gentlemen."

And like the Hymn, we put our shoulder to the wheel and pushed the wagon clear of the ruts. Tyson was right. I wasn't used to doing a hard day's work. I don't think I'd had to since I was a boy. Didn't care for it then, and it wasn't any more glamourous now. My good mood faded as the weeks of hard work, hot sun, and dismal company were laid out before me like one of Angelina's foreboding tarot readings.

Chapter Fourteen

"God has blessed us with a beautiful sunset, has he not?" Father Emilio gestured expansively at the skies.

Burning orange erupted along the horizon as waves of purple splashed across the sun's fading rays. The priests and I stood together, marveling as nature's glory blanketed the prairie. Many grand sunsets awaited me, I was sure, before my journey's end. I nodded my agreement to the priest, not possessing the words or energy to speak.

"Hold our team, Brother Cuthbert. The mules smell water." Brother Ambrose pointed at the white bonnets of prairie schooners before us. "They form the circles for our camp tonight beside the stream. You see. Captain Tyson is directing them."

Our large train, five hundred wagons in all, ambled in a slow curve along the stream. Hard men, ex-soldiers from the look of them, directed prairie schooners to their camp for the night. Most of the guards were unshaven and surly from the day's long ride. A few had lost a piece of themselves in the war. Empty sleeves and crude eye patches spoke of the horrors brother delivered against brother. I couldn't fault them for their ill mood. Herding creatures as stubborn and dull-witted as human beings would strain anyone's patience.

A shrill whistle brought me sharply around to witness an unexpected parade of Union soldiers cantering in step with their leader. His rank was indistinguishable across the distance. I'd guess lieutenant from the officious manner he exercised against his men. The Union officer didn't seem keen on mixing with our civilian lot. Barking orders, he directed his men to veer their wagons and the cluster of young horses further along the stream. The hired guards let them pass as if years of service dictated their actions. One of them smoothed a hand across the lump where his leg abruptly ended. Then he cast his eyes downward and turned away.

"Why are they forming two circles?" I asked.

"One circle is reserved for the government train. Ten soldiers from Fort Leavenworth are delivering supplies and horses to the new fort. The other circle is for we civilians," Brother Cuthbert said. "The Santa Fe Trail is a critical commerce route from Missouri to New Mexico. Unfortunately, it also takes us through dangerous Indian Tribal lands. We won't be dealing with warring armies on this trip. I suppose that is a blessing."

"Warring armies? The Union and Confederates?"

"Yes. The Cimarron Route became so deadly during the war that civilian travel on the Santa Fe Trail halted until recently. Our wagon train is one of the first to journey upon the trail again. Of course, we are taking the Mountain Route through the Colorado Territory this trip. Even so, I wish our army escort would see us all the way to Santa Fe. It will take soldiers and their guns to see us safely there."

"We must trust in God's protection, Brother Cuthbert. Look there." Father Emilio smiled as if he hadn't been walking all day. "The little children play between the two circles. They call it 'No Man's Land.' It is good to hear their laughter at the end of a long day."

I couldn't argue the point. There wasn't much to laugh about on this dull journey. Any sound of merriment was a gift. Keeping close to the priests, I followed directions obediently and tried to stay out of the way. Captain Tyson was dealing me a fair hand. I had no intention of souring his attitude toward me.

Brother Ambrose waved his arms in practiced signals, guiding the mules and Brother Cuthbert to their assigned campsite for the evening. We joined the other weary souls in a blessedly stationary circle under the massive skies of Kansas.

Our mules joined oxen from other wagons to graze upon the lush grass within the circle. Glad to be free of their burdens, the sweaty mules rolled in cool prairie grass and dirt. The animals were kept from roaming by ropes tied between the wagons. Those confines, however, didn't keep the children from escaping their rolling cages. I followed their laughter as they snuck between the two circles of wagons. Father Emilio had called the space 'No Man's Land.' Indeed, it seemed to belong exclusively to the children.

A spirited game of catch ensued between some of the boys. They lofted a ball made from bits of twine and old canvas. It wasn't easy to ascertain the rules, but I guessed the players made them up as the game went along.

My attention shifted to a small gang of entrepreneurs gathering what I was aghast to find were buffalo chips. Spiders, centipedes, and scorpions lived under the chips. They crawled – angry and confused – along the ground, looking for an escape or perhaps, revenge. Who could be certain with crawling things? Unfazed, the children made a game out of squashing them.

Tired parents appeared under the ropes to wrangle children with unlimited energy. The scene was the same around dozens of campfires. I nodded politely to each exhausted mother to reassure her I didn't think less of her parenting.

Offering a pleasant good evening to their departing backs, I remained the outsider looking in. Melancholy loneliness crept across my heart as I spied upon them sharing their meals. Angelina loved this time of day. She'd believed magic existed in the hours between sunset and midnight. So we indulged her superstitious nature by remaining within the firelight. Our little troupe spent many a pleasant evening by the campfire, listening to Trip's tall tales about his past. Sometimes Angelina would give us a song while Silent Dan was content to listen.

Perfumed memories haunted the prairie wind, immersing me in fond recollections of the moments we'd shared. Grief's sorrowful touch dug into my chest and squeezed. Angelina, Trip, and Silent Dan. I'd never see them again.

Curious sounds drifted from the dark fields of prairie grass to whisper in my ear. Music? Yes, but not just any collection of pipes and strings. Tinny melody. Sour notes. I immediately recognized the unmistakable bad playing of a medicine show. My boots took me toward the sound. They knew which way to go even though darkness began to engulf me.

The tune quickened to a fevered rhythm, its tempo increasing the further I moved away from our camp. I wandered forward, following the music as if irresistibly drawn by its sound. Then the ground tilted unexpectedly beneath my feet, and I tumbled down into the dark belly of a gulch. The tinny music stopped abruptly. I shook my head, clearing the last of the noise from my foggy mind. What was I doing here alone in the silence of a prairie night? Disoriented, I crawled to my feet and slapped the dirt off my trousers.

"Fool!" A low growl erupted next to my ear.

One forceful swat from its gigantic paw hurled me head over boots across the gulch. I landed on my backside in the dirt. Dinner plate eyes, glowing in wild rage, glared down at me. A symbol I well recognized blazed in orange between the beast's eyes. Doran. What manner of creature had Hesperos chosen as his pet? I wasn't a ready believer in magic, but the beast was beginning to change my mind for me.

"Human meat sack." Doran's breath came in hot bursts against my face. "He won't get the chance to wear you."

"You can speak? What manner of creature are you?"

"I am the only being of my nature in the world. Perhaps I am even rarer than you." A massive snout sniffed my head with ravenous interest. "I wonder if you taste the same as other men?"

Greedy eyes ran along the flesh of my torso, looking for bits of flesh to steal. Doran was hungry, and I was the only bit of living meat within range. Using my boots in the slippery prairie grass, I pushed away from the drooling jowls.

"Doran."

Hesperos appeared next to the creature, adding his light to the gulch. Green jade shone about his body, illuminating the landscape in a strange hue. A cluster of dead wolves circled us. Jaws dripping with rabid foam, the animals had met their end before they could menace the wagon train. Doran, I realized, had ripped them apart to protect me. The thought wasn't as comforting as one would hope. I had the sneaking suspicion my magical rescuer would try to eat me at every opportunity.

I looked a bit closer at the wolf nearest me. Chunks of rotting flesh clung stubbornly onto the sun-bleached bone. Large patches of fur had deserted its body days before. These wolves were not a fresh kill.

"Finally, you've noticed. These animals were brought back from the dead to hunt you," Hesperos said. "Use some common sense, Dunham. You're no good to me dead."

His body faded into the darkness. Doran, with one last murderous look at me, backed away to follow its master. Hesperos' words echoed in my befuddled brain as I stared into the emptiness.

You're no good to me dead.

I hadn't a clue what he wanted from me. Answers certainly wouldn't be found in the middle of rotting wolf carcasses. Better to join the safety of the Living. My body, though still shaking, managed to crawl back up the side of the gulch. I rested sweaty palms upon my thighs. The comforting glow of campfires greeted me as I caught my breath.

"What were you doing?"

A black coat stepped out of the wagons to confront me. The firelight cast shadows upon the man's harsh features. It was the preacher I'd stolen clothes from when I'd snuck aboard the wagon train. The good reverend looked none too pleased to see me.

"I didn't catch your name, friend."

"I'm Reverend Edgewater, leader of our small group of pioneers." His eyes swept contemptuously over my body until I felt the weight of his judgment upon my skin. "I'll ask again. What are you doing out here in the dark so close to the back of our wagons?"

"The good Lord gifted me with a normal man's bladder," I said. "Tell me. Do you piss or pray yours away?"

"You have quite the mouth, Reverend Dun, or so you call yourself." He sniffed with distaste. "If you prefer to lay with heathens, then perhaps that's the best place for you."

"I'm glad you didn't offer to share your camp, my Christian brother. It spares me delivering an awkward rejection to you." I slapped at the dirt on my suit jacket. "Would you look at that? Dust from the trail on the new suit I picked up in Independence. Pity."

"You're no man of God. I'll prove it." Reverend Edgewater shook a fist at me.

I, in turn, shook something else in his direction. It may have been impolite, but his sputtering attempts to return my insult brightened my mood. Then, sensing the daggers at my back, I turned away and headed toward a friendlier group of men.

Chapter Fifteen

"I see you're making friends," Captain Tyson said. "If that stiff-necked Edgewater dislikes you, Dun, I suppose you might not be too bad."

Father Emilio followed in the wagon master's purposeful wake. Placing his fingers together, the priest formed a steeple below his heart. He shook his head woefully at Captain Tyson.

"Reverend Edgewater has a great many under his care. We must make allowances."

"He tries my compassion, Father," I said. "You don't like the good Reverend either, Captain Tyson?"

"Edgewater is a self-righteous arse. Sorry Father," Tyson said with a shrug. "He and his band are headed to someplace outside Pueblo. I'll be glad when they split off from the train in the Colorado Territory."

"Pueblo? I thought that was further north." I wished I'd paid more attention to destinations when Trip decided our routes.

"We're taking the Mountain Route," Tyson said. "Lieutenant Saunders has a fortune in horses meant for Fort Union. The Cimarron Route has seen too many Indian attacks since the war made its way out here. We reckon the Colorado Territory is a bit safer. Besides, we'll need all the water we can get. I hope you haven't exaggerated your qualifications as a driver, Dun. We'll be headed over the Raton Pass."

"I think we may be getting ahead of ourselves, Captain." Father Emilio gave him a tolerant smile. "One of the wagons has agreed to take you on as a relief driver. Mrs. Maxwell journeys to Santa Fe to visit her daughter. She has a large wagon full of goods for their trading post."

"We'll take you to her now," Tyson said, leading us across the herd of tired animals. "She wants to take the measure of you herself before we agree. Then, if she likes you, she'll feed you and let you sleep under the wagon with Domingo. He's her regular driver." Tyson bit at his mustache. "Experienced drivers get twenty-five dollars a month plus rations. I told her you'd work for the rations and her cooking. You'll get the safety of the wagon train, too. That's nothing to sneeze at in these parts."

"I'm obliged to you, Captain."

Suspicious eyes observed each step as we followed Captain Tyson around the inner circled of wagons. Reverend Edgewater's band of obedient sheep hugged their bibles against their hollow chests. Murmuring silent prayers, mothers tugged gawking children behind their skirts. Were their superstitious fears inspired more by the priest or me? I couldn't guess. The wagon master, sensing the tension, gave them a wide berth. He shared my impatience for hellfire and damnation enthusiasts. Father Emilio, however, either hadn't had much exposure to the hatred of others. Or he was a soft-headed fool who believed patient understanding could change the human heart. I knew better.

"A blessed evening to you," he said with a cordial tip of his head to them.

Affronted silence met his salutations. Oh yes. A real-life priest amongst their flock was more a threat than an irreverent stranger. I did my best two-step, putting my body between the priest and the growing crowd of hate.

"I don't think they're the neighborly sort, Father."

"Perhaps," Father Emilio said. "They fear what they do not understand."

"Yeah, I know the type very well."

Indeed, I did. My father could give them a run for their money. Reverend Raynor of Grace Church Pennsylvania was a hellfire and damnation preacher who made a habit of scaring the bejesus out of his congregation. He'd called it his sacred duty.

"It's no good wasting energy on people like those bible beaters," I said.

Bringing two religious communities together was not on my itinerary for this trip. I had my own problems. Someone or something was trying to kill me. I had no idea why. Anyone with any claim on me for revenge was a two-week wagon ride away or already in the grave. There was Grizz, of course. He didn't have the mental capacity or charm to partner with someone like the man in the black hat. No. My enemy was someone with power and money. Tucking away that uncomfortable thought, I prepared my most genteel manners as we approached a large wagon stuffed with goods.

A distinctive aroma grabbed my full attention as I stepped into the camp. Hot biscuits and bacon. Thank the gracious Lord or rather the camp's cook. A woman in her late forties stood over the fire, large spoon in hand, expertly folding the bacon in a pot of beans. Flaky golden-brown biscuits warmed in a cast-iron skillet beside the pot. My mouth watered like a hungry wolf in a sheep herd. Head spinning, my empty belly roared. I hadn't had a hot meal for days. The piece of dried meat I'd eaten during the lunch stop had done little to sate my abused body.

"Evening, Mrs. Maxwell." Captain Tyson removed his hat, revealing thinning dust-brown hair.

"This is him, is it?" Mrs. Maxwell asked. "What happened to your cheek?"

I touched the tender line Grizz had drawn across my left cheek. "I cut myself shaving."

"Sure, you did. Found some trouble more like it."

She stood tall in her gingham dress. A crown of graying braids circled her head with the nobility of a prairie Cesar. Sharp blue eyes took me in with calculating intensity. Those keen orbs gazed probingly into my eyes. I had the suspicion she could read minds or at least intentions. Standing my ground for an uncomfortable eternity, I finally had the sense to remove my hat.

"Mrs. Maxwell," I said with a polite bow. "I'm Reverend Dun. May God bless you for your generosity."

She gave me a crooked smile and chuckled. "I've been led to believe you were a simpleton. No. I'd say you were a little too smart for your own good." Mrs. Maxwell turned to Tyson. "You've explained the job and the pay?"

"Yes, Ma'am." Captain Tyson nodded.

"You start now. I don't often pay upfront, but I can hear your gut growling from here. We eat as soon as Domingo is back from seeing to the team." Mrs. Maxwell pointed to a blanket on the ground, and I sat like an obedient mutt. "Can I tempt you with some beans and biscuits, Captain? Father Emilio?"

"No. Thank You, Ma'am. My cook will have grub on the fire by now." Captain Tyson turned a threatening look toward me. "Work hard, Dun. I'll be watching you."

"That is comforting, Captain."

"I must leave you as well," Father Emilio said. "My brothers are expecting me to lead prayers tonight. Sleep well."

Mrs. Maxwell handed me a hot biscuit. I passed it from hand to hand until it was cool enough to eat. Fluffy and dripping with butter, her bread was the best I'd ever eaten. But, of course, that could have been the hunger talking.

"What's your real story?" Mrs. Maxwell sat on a small stool she'd unloaded from the side of the wagon. "Don't lie to me either. Daddy was a gambler and a conman until someone shot him in the back for cheating. I grew up in the trade."

I thought about lying, but something in her manner exuded commonsense wisdom I couldn't fool. We stared each other down, she and I. In the distance, small talk around the campfire erupted in bouts of good humor. Oxen shook the flies away as they chewed the prairie grass. A guitar struck the first chord in a lonely tune. Here was the end of all pretenses. Real-life with genuine people was my new role.

I shook my head with a grin and loosened the uncomfortable collar. "How did you know?"

"Life with Daddy has given me a horse feather detector. I've spent too many years with your kind to be fooled. Let me see if I remember. Appraise the situation and look for an advantage or profit before you choose the con. I recognized the shrewd look you gave my goods the minute you stepped into camp. And you're right." She poked her thumb toward the wagon. "There's wealth under that bonnet. I'm taking it to Fort Union. The government won't pay me unless I deliver a full load, so don't get any ideas. I sleep inside with a loaded gun. Domingo sleeps under the wagon also with a gun."

"It seems like a long way to travel just to sell goods," I said, taking the tin plate of beans and bacon she offered.

"My daughter is expecting their first child. A woman needs her mother during such times, even though they won't admit it." Mrs. Maxwell sat down and started eating her dinner. "I hope we make the fort before she gives birth."

"Captain Tyson seems competent. I'm sure we'll make it."

"This is my third trip on the Santa Fe Trail," she said. "Enduring the journey takes courage, determination, and acceptance." Mrs. Maxwell ran her biscuit over the beans in a slow wave. "It won't be easy. You stick close to our camp and watch with both eyes for danger."

"So, you'll keep me on even though I'm a conman?" I asked with a grin.

"I have a feeling about you, Dun. I think you may be good to have along on this trip." Her eyes lifted to stare over my shoulder. "It's about time, Domingo. We started supper without you."

Mrs. Maxwell spooned another plate of beans and deposited three biscuits on top. She held it out to the massive man who'd dropped beside me on the blanket. I noticed his great bushy mustache first. Then I saw the rattlesnake hanging limply from his fist. Squealing with alarm, I fell backward on the blanket and scooted as far away from the snake as I could get.

Domingo slapped a vaquero's wide-brimmed, low-crowned hat against his lap with a thunderous chuckle. The plain long-sleeved shirt he wore strained across his muscular shoulders. Life on the trail had chiseled Domingo into a two-legged bull.

"Easy, my friend. These rattles don't have a head!" He shook the dead snake's tail at me. "Rattlesnakes are good meat for the pot."

"Did you bury the head?" Mrs. Maxwell asked, taking the snake after Domingo lopped off the rattles with a well-used machete. "I don't want any of the children poisoned."

"I buried it deep outside the wagon circle." Domingo swallowed a biscuit whole. "Do you want me to skin it?"

"No, I'll do it. We'll have him for breakfast." Mrs. Maxwell filled my plate again and handed it to me. "You show good sense, being afraid of those things. I've lost track of how many good folks have died after being bitten."

Domingo shook the rattles. "Learn to listen for their song. You may get a visit in the middle of the night as we sleep under the wagons. If you feel something trying to cuddle you, know it isn't me!"

"He's being funny, but he makes a good point. The Santa Fe Trail is a dangerous journey. We'll do our best to keep you alive."

"I'm obliged to you," I told her.

"Don't thank me just yet. We'll work you hard because that's what it takes to reach the end of the trail. Get some sleep. You'll need it. Captain Tyson plans to push us hard tomorrow. He wants to reach Council Grove before sunset." She took my empty plate with a faint smile. "Call me, Winnie."

"I won't let you down, Winnie," I said. "That's a promise."

This time I meant what I said. Winnie would get the best I had to offer until I found a way off the wagon train and back to civilization. I had no idea how deep in Grand Prairie country the town of Council Grove rested, but if it had buildings and a telegraph office, I was back in business.

Chapter Sixteen

Morning found me stretched out under the Maxwell wagon. Stiff and missing a proper feather bed, I ignored Domingo's nudge on my arm. He'd kept me awake with his hurricane-force snores until the twinkling stars peeking through the wheel spokes began to fade. Sleep finally found me for a few blessed moments until I heard rustling in the prairie grass outside our camp. Visions of snakes or vicious predators brought me to full consciousness again.

I stared forlornly at the underbelly of the wagon. Every conman and gambler knew our luck would run out one day, but I wasn't ready to tap on death's door yet. An opportunity to escape this prison train would present itself. I just needed to be patient.

"Every door has a handle."

"That so?" Winnie poked her head under the wagon. "You won't find it under there. Coffee's on. Better get up and start another beautiful Kansas day."

Biting back my current opinion of her cheery morning salutations, I crawled out from under the wagon with a grown. Brilliant bands of orange greeted me from on high. Rays of sunlight crept across the land, casting their gentle light upon the waving ocean of prairie grass. I rubbed my tired eyes until nature's beauty was a blurry mess.

"I love this time of day," Winnie said with a sigh.

"It's alright for some," I murmured, stretching the kinks out of my back. "Give me room service at noon in a fancy hotel."

Ignoring my grumbles, Winnie was quick to hand me a mug of coffee. A bitter mix of nuts and smoke assaulted my nostrils. Something floated listlessly on the surface. Satisfied it wasn't an insect, I hazard a sip of the black tar. Liquid soot burned my tongue and invaded the delicate lining of my throat. Gasping, I swallowed hard.

"I make my coffee strong," she said, shoving a plate of breakfast into my hand. "You need your wits about you out here."

"And a strong stomach," Domingo said with a snort.

"Is that a criticism of my cooking?"

Domingo shook his head and waved away her anger. He was already shoveling food in his mouth with remarkable gusto beside the campfire. I didn't share his enthusiasm for snake flesh, but the aroma of cooking meat was enough to make my stomach growl. I joined him by the fire and sat down with a groan. A good meal might ease my stiff muscles. Shoveling a load of white flesh nestled on the plate next to my cornmeal pancakes, I closed my eyes and took a bite.

"It's delicious," I said between bites. "If you put where the meat comes from out of your mind."

"What did I tell you?" Domingo held up the rattle he'd kept as a trophy and shook it. "Let me know when you see another one. Señor snake can join us for stew. Isn't that right?"

A tiny giggle chimed at my back. Our guest - a towheaded girl of six or seven - lifted her cupped hands to produce a patty of buffalo dung. Spiders and centipedes crawled all over it. My stomach took a tumble as she thrust her hands toward Winnie.

"The other children have already collected the buffalo chips we need for our fire this morning, Henrietta." Winnie prodded the child gently to the water barrel. "Come along. Let's wash your hands. I can't send you back to your mother covered in chips."

Henrietta's proud smile faded, and she dropped the chip to the ground. Tears welled up in those innocent blue eyes as Winnie washed her little hands. I defy anyone with an ounce of decency to keep their heart stone after witnessing the heartbreaking tears of a tiny girl in pigtails.

"How much do you want for the buffalo chip?" I asked her.

"I pay the children a penny to collect them for us," Winnie warned. "Her mother might not like you giving Henrietta a penny for nothing."

"It's not for nothing," I said, winking at the little girl. "I think this chip has a unique shape. It is, perhaps, the most unusual buffalo chip I've ever seen. I'll give you a penny for it."

She took the shiny coin I'd held out with a sincere gasp of delight. Then she hugged my neck and favored me with a peck on the cheek. We watched her pigtails bounce as Henrietta skipped off toward her kin.

Winnie laughed, shaking her head at me. "A conman who's a soft touch. I never thought I'd see the day."

"Henrietta isn't the first woman to take my money."

"I can imagine." She gave my shoulder a playful shove. "Go help Domingo bridle the team. We leave soon. Captain Tyson doesn't like dawdlers."

Driving prairie schooners along the Santa Fe Trail was every bit as dull as I'd supposed. We hadn't broken camp yet, and I was already bored. Domingo, my teacher, pointed out each part of the wagon from back to front. I listened with strained politeness. The schooner may have been larger than our medicine show wagon, but the remaining differences were minor.

Domingo, pleased by his own voice of wise experience, finally escorted me to our oxen team. They stood in a cluster, munching on the dew-wet prairie grass. Eight in all, the oxen gazed up at us with what I'd describe as sullen acceptance.

Two oxen we tied to the back as a reserve in the event of an ox rebellion. We herded the remaining six animals to the front of the wagon. Domingo insisted I brush each ox while politely introducing myself.

"You cannot charge over to an ox and expect it to move for you. Our team deserves a respectful greeting," Domingo explained, patting one of the beasts. "Isn't that right, Stanley."

"The ox's name is Stanley?"

"Winnie named them." Domingo shrugged. "She figures they deserve respectable names if we put the responsibility of taking us across the prairie on their shoulders. I agree with her, seeing what they've already gone through." He made snipping motions with his fingers. "Stanley and his friends are castrated bulls."

"You have my sympathy," I said, patting the ox.

Stanley made no reply. Instead, he placidly waited as Domingo lifted a sizeable wooden yoke upon his shoulders. The yoke rested sideways with its functioning bits avoiding the animal's body. Then Domingo told me to hold it in place while gently prodding another ox into position.

Arthur – a brown ox speckled with white – plodded over by his partner without hesitation. I slid the left side of the yoke onto its shoulders. Domingo showed me how to bolt both in place. Following the same steps, we moved on to the remaining oxen. Other wagons had already begun to pull out of the camp's circle as we worked. Domingo would not be hurried as he patiently explained how to hook the team to the wagon's tongue.

"You must remember, Dun. Terrible accidents happen when you don't position the tongue stop and metal rings in the correct position."

He stood away from the team and took the long whip I'd held for him. Not that he needed the whip. The oxen did what he asked without resistance. Domingo had shown himself as boss of the bovines this morning. I was duly impressed. The great lumbering beasts did not take my instruction with the same regard.

"Winnie is onboard," he told me. "Now we go."

I peered over the tall backs of the oxen team toward the wagon. Winnie sat on the buckboard, struggling with the ribbon on her bonnet. She looked comfortable. It was good to be queen, I thought uncharitably.

Domingo moved to the front of the team and began walking, dashing any hopes of saving my feet. The oxen followed, pulling the wagon behind them. I stared after him as the last of my stubborn denial abandoned me. Life as a pioneer was my lot until I found another method of transportation to San Francisco. I needed to ingratiate myself with my fellow travelers in the meantime. Wandering alone through the prairie with no provisions or protection was a death sentence. If I needed to spend the day walking with a team of oxen, then so be it.

Domingo walked alongside the herd during the morning, saving a hot walk in the afternoon for me. He curled up in the wagon after the lunch hour for a nap. I didn't begrudge him the rest. After all, he showed me trust after my few hours of training. Kansas was relatively flat. Our schooner didn't require any significant turns. I rested the whip on my shoulder and followed the schooner in front of me.

The steady clomps of the oxen lulled my mind into a contemplative reverie. My thoughts turned to fanciful daydreams of rich living in San Francisco. The first thing I'd do is find the best tailor in the city. Yes, sir. Only the best clothes, the best food, and the best drink for me from now on.

A large blackbird circled overhead. It made a slow circle over our wagon, cawed at me once, and flew west. Its black body remained directly over the wagons until it disappeared from my sight. A sudden hollowness spread inside my torso. My odd stalker and his bird were still with the wagon train. Were they watching me?

Winnie's light touch stirred me from my musings. I tore my thoughts away from the bird to regard her. The ribbon holding her bonnet in place whipped in the prairie wind. Skirts billowing over the dirt, Winnie matched my steady pace. She lifted her chin to view the wagon in front of our team. Giving me a pleased nod, she patted Stanley's flank.

"What brings you among us bulls?" I asked her with a grin.

"You looked bored stiff," she said. "Not much to keep the mind occupied out here. I love it, though. Being on the trail brings me peace." Winnie gave me a sad smile and sighed. "I've had my share of sorrow too."

"How so?"

The curtain of hard determination, a constant presence in her eyes, opened enough for me to glimpse the tenderness inside. An unaccustomed vulnerability seeped into the softened features of her face.

"I brought one daughter and four sons into this world," she said. "We lost our firstborn at three years old to Cholera on the Cimarron Route. Two of my sons died in the war between North and South." She pressed a hand lightly to her chest as if reliving the heartbreak. "They fought on different sides. Such a waste. It broke my husband's heart. He's buried next to them in Saint Louis."

Words of comfort escaped me. Winnie Maxwell didn't seem the sort of woman who'd accept pity graciously. Her eyes stared stoically at the horizon before us as the silence lingered. Rather than fumbling a response, I tapped Stanley on the shoulder and straightened his path upon the trail.

"Saint Louis doesn't seem your sort of town," I told her at last.

"You have me right! No, it's much too large and civilized." The hard determination was back in her voice. "Now, I own a mercantile in Fort Leavenworth. Evan, my remaining son, stayed behind to manage things while I'm gone. He claims he can't be away from the store for long, but I don't think he has the stomach for life on the trail."

"You have the pioneer spirit, Winnie. I think you're tougher than most men I know, including me."

"All the same, I'll be glad to reach Council Grove tonight. Captain Tyson says we'll spend the sabbath there. Maybe you can give a sermon," She said, giving me a wicked grin.

"I'd be stoned by the flock of God's purest." I waved the tip of the whip toward Reverend Edgewater's group.

"If he's what churches have to offer, I'm glad I don't step inside. You see, I belong to the Church of the West. Be kind, work hard, and keep your head down. That's my motto." Winnie laughed and waved a hand at my white collar. "If you were anything like Reverend Edgewater's flock of saints, I wouldn't have let you in my camp."

"He's all wind," I said.

"Don't be so sure. The reverend has taken an extreme dislike to you, Dun. It's best if you stay away from him and his flock," Winnie said. "They don't like outsiders."

Winnie's impressions of Reverend Edgewater and his group were comically accurate. They camped away from the rest of the wagon train on the outskirts of Council Grove as soon as we crossed the Neosho River. The reverend, taking an imperious air, marched to the local church and commandeered the complete attention of the town's pastor.

I gave them a cordial wave as I passed the church. The pastor, a timid-looking creature with gold spectacles, was brutally admonished when he returned my greeting. I suspect the poor man said a silent prayer to the almighty for a quick end to the sabbath day.

Council Grove, I was delighted to find, had a few gems of civilization within its borders. Several members of our wagon train walked through the inviting doors of the town's two trading posts. Bits and bobs of cloth hung in bright splashes of color along the walls of the first post. Leather goods formed a smooth wall to the back. The selection didn't compare with the choices presented to shoppers in Independence, but it was still impressive. I had my eye on a pair of boots. Running my finger across the stitching, I frowned at the haphazard craftsmanship. My old boots would do until I reached San Francisco.

A friendly commotion broke out at the counter. Little fingers pressed against the wood, once free of smudges. The children of our wagon train had found the candy jars. I smiled. Their laughter was like a seltzer for my mood.

Then I noticed the sign behind the counter above them and drew closer. "Stagecoach Schedule," it read.

"Can I help you, sir?" The proprietor called above the happy noise.

I lifted a finger and dug into my pocket for a silver dollar. "Alright, children! Candy's on me. You each get licorice." I took the jar from the proprietor and handed out the sweet stuff. "Take it outside. Give me ten minutes alone with this gentleman, and there's a piece of peppermint in it for you."

I tapped Henrietta on the shoulder and handed her a second piece of licorice on the sly. The wave of happy faces disappeared with a final squeal. I handed over the coin and another again for the remainder of my bribed of peppermints.

"The stagecoach passes through here."

"That's a fact, Reverend." He reached under the counter and pulled out a chalkboard. "I was about to update the schedule when you folks arrived."

My stomach sank as his hand wiped away the departing coach from this morning. I'd missed it by an hour. Scanning the chicken scratches on the board, I found a series of question marks beside the next coach.

"Are you expecting another coach soon?" I asked.

"We don't get the coach travelers like we used to before the drought. Then the war broke out too. Folks have all but stopped coming." He shrugged dismally. "The coach company plans to move the stage line station to Junction City next year. I suppose they figure it doesn't pay to push people through Council Grove as regular as they normally would." Shrewd eyes took me in for a moment. "Are you thinking of leaving the wagon train, Reverend?"

"I was trying to get a letter to a relative in San Francisco." Uncle Lucky Sal.

"We can send it with the government troops to Junction City. They can get the letter to Denver from there."

"An inspired suggestion," I said. "Tell me, Friend. Do they ever take passengers on that route?"

"Not typically," he said. "But you might convince them if your circumstances were dire."

I thanked him again and took the stationery supplies to a quiet spot at the back of his office. Writing what I'd hoped was a persuasive letter, I handed the sealed envelope to the proprietor. He took it with a nod.

The town's afternoon air seemed all the sweeter as I stepped back into the sunshine. Things were looking up! The government troops would arrive on Wednesday. I suppose I could kill some time in Council Grove while waiting for them. A sudden unwelcome thought soured my pleasant mood. How should I break the news of my departure to Winnie? I'd grown fond of her and Domingo. They'd given me friendship when I needed it most.

I found my traveling companions at the other trading post. Domingo sat on the steps watching bemusedly as Winnie adeptly bartered with an elderly Kaw man. Old he may be, but Winnie's opponent held the upper hand. I was certainly dazzled by his appearance. A graying braid, adorned with feathers, trailed down his back and ended with a dyed strip of leather. The Kaw man's neck and chest were covered in an impressive display of animal claws. A beautiful hand-painted bead accompanied each piece of bone.

Captivated by the artistry of the Kaw merchandise, I bought some beads intending to make a hatband for my old felt. Winnie clucked her tongue at me when I refused to hold firm on my offered price.

"Beads! Ha!" Domingo laughed and patted a jug he held tightly to his chest. "I have something better – Cactus Wine. I make it myself." He handed the drink to me. "To friendship!"

"Why not?" I popped the cork and sniffed. "You could strip off axle grease with this concoction, Domingo."

The expression on his expectant face goaded me into taking a swallow - one quick drink before I broke the news of our parting. I had hoped to wait until sundown when I could say a short farewell and then retire in comfort to the hotel. It was a coward's retreat, but I hated long goodbyes.

"You'd better take it easy," Winnie said. "That potion is the Devil's own liquor. I don't want both of my drivers passed out in the back of the wagon while I try to drive the team."

"Fear not, dear lady," I said with a wink. "A sip from the jug won't harm Domingo or me. We're made of stronger stuff."

"Wait! I have something better," Domingo cried. "Look what I won off a conjurer. He tried to fool me with his pea under the walnut shell game. Ha! I have a sharper eye than he."

He pulled out two silver cups from his pouch and placed them on the sidewalk beside him. Each cup had the image of a bird – one an eagle and the other a crow - etched into its shiny surface. Domingo filled both cups with cactus wine. Then he carefully lifted the crow cup and handed it to me.

We saluted each other and then tipped our cups back. I swallowed the wine in one gulp. My gaze ran across the cup's shimmering surface. Funny. For a moment, I imagined the silver crow had turned its head to look at me. Dropping my eyes from its silvery beak, I noticed my tongue was numb. Laughter bubbled from my chest in good-humored giggles. Gone was my concern about reaching San Francisco. Forgotten were the government troops expected in Council Grove. My only thoughts were those of levity. Everything the big man did was suddenly hilarious. I could not recollect a time I'd laughed so much.

All the while, a large blackbird with a burning symbol on its forehead circled the town. Its shrill caw joined our drunken laughter.

Chapter Seventeen

Sunday drifted away in a blur of laughter and rotgut. Made from tequila, peyote tea, and something Domingo called "Mule Skinner," the drink could undoubtedly bring down the hardest of men. I can't place the blame on Domingo, for he "ate the worm" more than I. Nor can I fault poor Winnie, who shoved us both under her wagon to sleep off the demon milk. It was I who took the first drink, and it was I who, once again, ruined my chances for a safer trip to San Francisco.

My memories of departing Council Grove consisted of swinging oxtails and bouts of nausea. Driving and walking with the king of all hangovers had been a particularly horrible form of torture. Hornets buzzed in my poor head for hours. Every unsteady step tormented the vicious swarm.

Our camp at Diamond Springs offered little opportunity for recovery as Domingo, and I took extra care guarding our oxen team. Once a popular stop on the Santa Fe Trail, the war had drawn Missouri bushwhackers to the station. They killed the postmaster and set fire to anything flammable adjacent to the stone buildings. Two years had passed since the renegades struck. Since then, the unlucky station had fallen into ruin. I was strangely saddened as I walked past the abandoned buildings no one had bothered to rebuild.

We'd passed the night without incident. Our good fortune, however, didn't ease my aching head. Now here I was, a day and a half's journey from Council Grove, still feeling rough from cactus wine. The buzzing in my ears had vanished, at least. Thank the good Lord for small mercies.

"You should have shot me," I told Winnie as we kept pace beside the plodding oxen.

"And now you know never to drink with Domingo." Winnie shook her head.

"Well, I'm off the drink for the rest of this trip. I plan to keep my eyes open and on the horizon. Stanley here has the right idea." I patted the Ox. "Keep your eyes forward and your feet moving."

Domingo, none the worse for our drinking binge, came to join us at a jog. The ends of his mustache drooped unhappily. Captain Tyson had called a few of the men he could trust to the front of the wagon train an hour before. I was happy not to be included. Though the buzzing in my head had stopped, I couldn't endure a barrage of conversation.

"Trouble?" I asked.

"Mac found someone," Domingo said, casting sorrowful eyes on Winnie. "She's dead."

The Ouroboros - suddenly awake - slithered under my shirt. A newly departed soul was drawing near. I'd learned to stifle any surprise at the snake tattoo's abrupt movement. Even so, the shock of finding a ghost in the middle of the grand prairie unsettled me.

I heard her first. The rich alto carried in the prairie wind, melodious and strong. In her voice, I found the desperate and utter anguish experienced by a soul who has lost everything dear.

"Cara! Gino!" Her mournful cry echoed among the wagons. *"Dove siete, bambini?"*

Then I saw her passing unhindered through the clumps of sunflowers. Blood covered her dark blouse as bits of hair and scalp clung to the garment's puffed sleeves. Wild, desperate eyes found mine. Bambini. I didn't speak Italian, but that word I knew. She was looking for her children.

A barrage of Italian rolled over me as the woman held grasping hands toward my body. Unnerving tingles raced up my arms as her fingers passed unimpeded through my living flesh. She'd been beautiful in life, this sad ghost. Strands of hair still attached to her skull fell in thick waves to her waist. The remains of her smooth and pleasant features twisted in despair as she stood before me. Bitter tears showered down the translucent cheeks.

"Where?" I asked her, hoping she could understand English. "Show me."

Hope. It was painful to see in her dead eyes. What harm would it do for me to look for clues? If she could show me where she'd been attacked, maybe I'd find the children alive? I could spare a little hope for the unlikely.

"Never mind, Domingo," I told him to cover my conversation with the ghostly woman. "I'll find Tyson."

Handing the whip to him, I followed the ghost as she passed through the wagons toward the front of the train. Her movements were steady as she maneuvered between the oxen teams. Looking back over her shoulder, she made sure I was close behind. The ghostly mother was taking an easy path for my benefit. Good. That meant she was still attached to this Earthly plane.

I followed her grimly. Souls bound to the world of the Living could still reason and communicate with me. Perhaps I could use the ghostly mother's will to help me find her children? We didn't have much time before the ghost's despair became her undoing. If I couldn't convince her to cross over soon, she'd stay eternally bound to the place of her death. I didn't want that fate for this woman's soul. She'd been through enough hell.

"You should stay here, Dun!" Domingo called after me. "It is not a pretty sight."

Empty prairie stretched to the endless horizons without a distinguishing landmark in any direction. No matter. The ghostly mother knew our destination. She'd be drawn to her corpse no matter how far her spirit tried to roam. I jogged after her, perplexed as to how she came to be in our path. A fresh wave of pity came over me. It was a lonely spot to die.

We outpaced the lead wagon. Its driver, shaken out of his thoughts, stared after me. Ignoring his calls and hastily shouted questions, I kept running.

"Please slow down."

Challenged by her rapid pace, I gulped in dry air. The afternoon heat beat down on the black fabric of my jacket, converting the garment into a sweatbox. I caught the sickly-sweet stench of stale tequila and gagged on the odor emanating from my body. Oh yes. I was off the drink for a long while.

For the first time in days, I was out of the protective body of the wagon train. Running into the middle of a hostile country with no weapons or protection. When had I become such a fool!

The ghost - sensing my dismay - turned and beckoned me onward. Transparent hands clasped together in a heart-wrenching plea. Cursing, I nodded breathlessly and pushed my legs to keep pace. I never could withstand the weight of a woman's tears.

Suddenly the ghostly mother stopped. She pointed down the deep ruts made by decades of travelers. I stopped beside her, pressing my hands to my thighs. Breathing hard, I lifted my gaze to follow her pale finger. The group of men stood on the trail just ahead. Soldiers, merchants, and hired guards clustered together, staring down at the path. Chugging like a steam locomotive, I sprinted forward to join them.

"I came to see if I could help," I said, holding up my hands as one of the soldiers raised his rifle toward me.

"Sorry, Reverend," he said, lowering the weapon. "What can be done has been done."

Captain Tyson stood in the ruts of decades-old wagon wheels with his back to the wind. He didn't turn. Rather, he remained still with his head bowed. Father Emilio was beside him. His cassock billowed in bursts of prairie gusts. The words of last rites drifted from his lips and were carried away with the wind.

Two soldiers hurriedly shoveled loose dirt into a hole they'd dug inside the ruts. The grave was just large enough to fit a slender body. It didn't take a great mental leap to determine who was buried directly in the path of the oncoming wagon train.

"What are they doing? You can't bury her there." I offered the ghost an apologetic look, but she didn't seem to notice. My ghostly companion kept her eyes to the horizon back in the direction of the wagon train.

"We're burying her body in the ruts to hide her grave from desecrators," Tyson told me. "I'd say this poor soul has gone through enough. Hurry, you men. The wagons are almost on top of us."

"This is a lonely stretch of trail. It's unlikely she traveled alone. Can you tell where she came from?" I asked.

"God only knows." He shook his head. "Maybe she wandered away from Six Mile Crossing and thought she was heading east toward Diamond Springs?"

We were a few hours west of Six Mile Crossing now. The landscape looked much the same. If Tyson's guess was correct, the poor soul and her family might have thought they traveled to Diamond Springs. If pressed, I wouldn't know the direction either if left on my own.

"Aren't we going to look for her family? What if they're in trouble?"

"Listen, Reverend. There's a reason they call this stretch of trail 'Journey of the Dead.'" One of the soldiers, a sergeant, sunk his shovel into the ground beside the trail. "We're in Western Kansas. The Indians in these parts are mighty angry with trespassers on their lands. That means wagon trains, soldiers, and other Indians not in their tribe. This here woman was scalped. Whatever attacked her could still be out there watching us." He took off his hat and slapped the bald spot. "I've served in this territory for near ten years and have managed to keep my scalp. I don't want to lose it now looking for folks who are dead already."

"Whatever? You don't think Indians did this?" Captain Tyson asked.

"No, sir. An Indian would use a knife. The scalp was ripped off that poor woman's skull by something powerful. A wild animal, maybe."

I turned toward the desperate mother, but she was already gone. Her ghost drifted back the length of the wagon train, flickered, and then returned to stand over her grave. Was she drifting aimlessly, or was she trying to follow those that had taken her children from her?

"Cara! Gino! Dove siete, bambini?"

"People die out here. I'm sorry, but that's the hard truth." Captain Tyson patted my shoulder. "I know you want to help, Dun, but she's past caring."

He was dead wrong. Here was a woman whose love for her children would never allow her to pass on. She was fated to spend eternity alone in this spot, calling for a family that wouldn't come.

CHAPTER EIGHTEEN

Winnie and Domingo didn't speak as I fell into place beside them. A grim mood hung over me like a shroud. I extended my hand for the whip. Domingo's eyes were full of sympathetic understanding as he gave it to me with a solemn nod. We walked silently beside the team, Winnie, Domingo, and I. Each of us remained lost in our troubled thoughts. Bathing in the normal state of boredom, it was easy to forget the dangers lying in wait for pioneers on the Santa Fe Trail. The unfortunate dead woman was a harsh reminder for our wagon train. Death could come for any of us at any moment.

The woman's ghost watched me solemnly as our team passed over her grave. In her features, I read accusations. Failure. Coward. Perhaps I deserved her ire. My argument to search for the woman's family was weak at best. In the end, I hadn't convinced Captain Tyson or the soldiers. Indeed, I hadn't convinced myself to search either.

I turned away, unable to bear those heartsick eyes. What good was this Ouroboros or my ability to see the newly Dead if I couldn't help poor souls like her? I tapped the whip irritably against my leg. Maybe my problem didn't lie with the Ouroboros? Perhaps it was a flaw deep in the core of my soul?

"Captain Tyson's coming," Winnie said, her lips descending in an anxious frown. "What's happened now?"

Tyson nodded a curt greeting. Sweat beaded beneath his hatband, trickling down to the bandana around his neck. He had the look of a man whose patience has been tried past the breaking point. Considering our recent gruesome experience, I understood completely.

"The little towheaded girl, Henrietta. She's missing."

Tyson's hard eyes met mine. His thoughts weren't difficult to guess. I'm certain he recalled the lingering memory of a shallow grave trampled by five hundred wagons. Would we be digging another soon? Not if I could help it. I may have failed the ghostly mother, but nothing would stop me from saving Henrietta.

"Could she be with one of her friends?" Winnie asked. "I hope she hasn't met with an accident or was left behind somehow."

"We have to go back and look for her."

"That would be foolish, Dun, and you know it." Tyson shook a finger at me. "We've gone more than six miles from last night's camp. It's too dangerous to ride outside the safety of the wagon train. You know it's true! I've got over a thousand souls to look after. I can't put the rest of these people at risk for the sake of one child."

"What you need is more folks to search." Winnie gripped my arm to stop the angry words from forming on my lips. "Let me gather volunteers. We'll turn over every wagon if need be. Dun, you can help while Domingo drives."

Her words drifted among the humming whispers in my ears. A sudden chill raised the hackles on my arms as I shivered in the hot Kansas afternoon. Raw survival instinct told me inhuman eyes were watching. Turning my head, I saw my stalker standing in the prairie grass away from the wagon train. Hesperos waited for me. A smug and expectant smile stretched across his thick lips. At that horrible moment, I knew we wouldn't find Henrietta among the wagons.

Shoving the whip into Domingo's hands, I took off my jacket and handed it to Winnie. "I'll be back in a moment. I need some time for quiet reflection."

"Wait!" Tyson called after me. "What the hell is that supposed to mean?"

Rolling up my sleeves and ready for a fight, I went to meet Hesperos. I took a purposeful gate, avoiding the men and boys herding their teams to the west. No one else seemed to see Hesperos standing on the northern side of the trail. I questioned again if he were a ghost or a figment of my imagination.

His thick eyebrows raised in amusement as he watched my shifting path through the clumps of prairie grass and oxen dung. I took the opportunity in kind to examine him thoroughly by the light of day. Despite his affinity for theatrical clothing, I found nothing extra-ordinary about the man's appearance. Hesperos had an oval face with a handsome Mediterranean complexion. Dark curls fell in thick waves about his cheeks, giving him a youthful look. Some might even consider him moderately attractive. I suppose I might have found his features pleasant except for the glint of suppressed cruelty in his eyes.

"What do you know about the missing little girl?"

I stopped a few feet away from him – close enough not to be overheard by passersby, but not too close. Hesperos was still an unknown. I'd have to keep my temper in check until I knew more about him. His fascination with me was unnerving. He wanted something and was determined to stay close until he got it.

"You'd better pretend to be praying, Reverend. Some might think you've gone mad talking to yourself as you are."

"Funny," I spat and slammed my fist into my palm. "Where's the little girl? I know she's not dead."

"Would you? I should think all that poison in your body has flooded your senses." He snorted, pleased with the clever jibe. "As it happens, she's been taken."

"You know who took her? Start talking."

"Mortality is a tricky thing, Dunham. Life is fragile." Hesperos sighed with a shrug. "So many dangers in this part of the world. I wonder how anyone survives. Take the poor mother you found earlier. Her death was rather cruel, don't you think?"

"What does she have to do with Henrietta?"

I didn't like the filament of suspicion wiggling in my mind. Here was a man – or whatever he was – willing to follow me across the Grand Prairie to get what he wanted. Was he ambitious enough to take a child to extort a yet undisclosed favor? Of course, I could think of others who were equally persistent. The man in the wide-brimmed hat, for instance. He'd zealously tried to kill me in the river. Then there was Grizz. That butcher wouldn't think twice about murdering an innocent child. He'd killed before and worse.

"Doran says the child is a few miles east behind the wagon train. Danger races quickly toward her." Hesperos gestured dismissively toward the last cluster of wagons bringing up the train's rear. "You'd better hurry, Dunham. A child's neck is easily broken."

"They're waiting for you." Doran stretched his wings with a hop. "Good luck hiding in the prairie grass, meat sack."

"Your pet talks now? I could've happily gone the rest of my life without experiencing its charm."

I held up a hand to block the sunlight and followed Doran's path as it took flight. The bird creature sailed east, gliding directly over the wagon ruts. Henrietta's kidnappers hadn't put too much effort into hiding her. She'd be easy for me to track. I suppose that was the idea.

Hesperos was gone when my gaze dropped back to the horizon. Perfect. I was on my own with no weapon and no horse. I turned to the east, watching the last of the wagons roll past me. Henrietta was out there in the middle of a vast sea of prairie. Others could look for her, it was true, but the villains controlling this sick game wouldn't reveal her. Someone wanted me out from among the safety of the wagon train. Why? I suppose I'd find out in short order. Keeping Henrietta's little face in my mind, I began walking east.

"Don't be a fool!" Winnie grabbed my arm. "Captain Tyson is right. You're no match for what lies out there."

"I know." I gently lifted her hand off my arm. "Keep an eye on my jacket, will you? Someone might steal it."

I kept to the worn ruts made by countless wagon wheels over the years, carefully stepping over the eight-inch-wide tracks running north and south. Domingo called them Buffalo Trails. The beasts had worn the narrow paths deep into the Earth for centuries as they ran to follow the streams of life-giving water.

My eyes swept the horizon to the sides and front of me. Memories of the murdered woman stayed near to my thoughts. She wasn't hovering beside her trampled grave anymore. I hoped that meant she'd moved on, but I didn't think so. She'd stay Earth-bound as long as her children were missing.

An ugly thought poked at my suspicious heart again. Had Hesperos used his pet to kill the woman? I'd seen Doran in action. The creature could have easily torn the woman apart. Then again, Doran had refrained from killing on past occasions until it knew I was in danger. It didn't seem the blood-thirsty type.

Suddenly aware of the absolute stillness about me, I brought my attention back to where it should be. I was alone and exposed in a hostile wilderness. Each step took me farther away from my fellow travelers and the comfort of their weapons. I tugged on the sleeves of my white shirt. Why had I left my black jacket behind? Dressed as I was, my torso stood out like a beacon to anyone with a rifle or arrow.

After I'd gone another nerve-racking mile, the Ouroboros began to wriggle on my chest. I was getting close. Of course, I didn't need its warning this time. The sky before me was painted with a sickly green tint as if the angry heavens were birthing a vengeful tornado. Yet, there was no moisture in the air. Then a violent gust of wind grabbed my face with insistent fingers, forcing me to look up. I stopped to stare, thunderstruck, at the impossible.

Henrietta's body swayed thirty feet above the ground as if suspended by invisible strings. Beneath her was a dried Buffalo Wallow. It was larger and deeper than any I'd seen along the Santa Fe Trail. No more than ten feet away from the northernmost rut, it had escaped my notice when our wagon had passed by earlier in the day.

The dusty circles were formed by two or more bull Buffalo as they fought. Heads together, the behemoths shuffled round and round until a winner emerged. Nature, never wasteful, fills the wallow with rainwater to make a lagoon for its creations. Unfortunately for Henrietta, the wallow was dry and hard. It could be deadly for her fragile body if she landed on it from a thirty-foot drop.

"Oh dear," Hesperos said beside me. "What will you do?"

He stood unfazed under the sickly green sky. The constant wind whisked around us, leaving his hair and clothes untouched. Doran, still in bird form, hopped and pecked the ground beside him. It didn't look happy.

"Can't Doran fly up and grab Henrietta? I could stand underneath to catch her."

"It's a test, moron. I can't help you this time."

Hesperos flicked his hand with a growl. Doran screamed as its feathery body collapsed to the ground. The poor creature flapped and shook as if in incredible pain. Bits of feathers collided with clumps of tan fur. It seemed Doran was no more a willing participant in Hesperos' sick plan than I.

Cruel glee washed over Hesperos' face as he held an outstretched hand toward Doran. Laughing hysterically, the mad man jutted his fingers at the poor creature again and again. He'd kill Doran if I didn't do something. Scanning his features, I looked for any weakness I could use against him. Odd. I hadn't taken Hesperos for a killer. But, seeing him now in such a violent rage, I wouldn't be surprised if blood was on his hands.

Then the harsh slap of realization struck me. Hesperos had taken Henrietta, not the man in the black hat. Curse him. He wanted me out here on my own. The sick bastard liked his victims helpless. Unfortunately for Hesperos, I still held the better hand in this card game. He couldn't kill me as long as I had what he wanted. I could use that to my advantage.

"Stop it, or I'm leaving right now," I spat. "That would end your little game."

"Have you become attached to this monster? How sweet." Hesperos released Doran with a derisive snort. "Do you expect me to believe you'd leave the human child in peril, Dunham? I don't think you will, not when you're trying so hard to play the hero."

"Tell me what you want from me, Hesperos. What will it take for you to let Henrietta go?"

"An unfortunate choice of words."

Thrusting his hand toward the little girl, Hesperos flicked his fingers in a clawing gesture. Henrietta fell. I ran to catch her, but Hesperos put an arm out to block my advance. Henrietta's body bounced to a stop twenty-five feet above the ground. Terrified screams proved she was alive. I was grateful for the sign, but I wished she were unconscious during Hesperos' cruel game.

"Stop it!" I tried to grab his arm, but my fingers passed through the air rather than flesh. "You want something from me, not Henrietta."

"Yes, I do. I want you to use the magic I gave you to save her."

"Come again?"

I stared at Hesperos' face, looking for any trace of sanity. No. I wouldn't find any. The man was mad. He'd kidnapped a little girl and dragged us all out into Cheyenne territory simply to make me do magic tricks.

Was Hesperos real, though? I recalled no one else on our wagon train had mentioned seeing him.

"Magic, Dunham. I gave it to you when I put the Ouroboros on your skin. Use the power I gave you or watch your little friend die."

"You're insane. Magic isn't real!"

"How can you still doubt? A living tattoo slithers upon your chest. You see and speak with the Dead. By Zeus! Death's coachman knows you by sight. How can you not believe in magic?" Hesperos flicked his hand again with a shake of his head. "You'd better become a believer quickly, Dunham. The little mortal's life depends on it."

Then the ground began to rumble. Dust rose from the north, blocking out the sun. Thunder from a thousand hooves crashed against my ears. The sound was unmistakable. Buffalo! Taller than a man and over a thousand pounds each, they were a charging mass of hide, horns, and hooves. Part growl. Part grunt. Their unique voice rose as one to fill the prairie.

"Stampede!" I screamed.

Doran took to the sky, but his master stood placidly in the prairie grass watching me. He made no comment even as the herd charged toward us. I took a step back as the first horned behemoth raced forward. It came within six feet and suddenly veered to the east, setting its path right underneath Henrietta.

"You have to stop this!"

"Do I?" Hesperos waved his hand, and Henrietta began to fall in short, jerking drops. Twenty-two feet. Twenty feet. Eighteen precarious feet from death. Henrietta's screams were drowned out by the thunderous hooves beneath her.

I paced back and forth, trying to find anything I could think of to save her. I had no blankets to catch her or rope to pull her out of the way of the stampeding herd. Some hero! I had no idea what to do. I could merely watch as her little body grew closer and closer to the horns.

"Magic will save her." Hesperos glared at me impatiently. "Use what I gave you."

"How? Tell me what to do, and I'll do it."

"If I told you, then it wouldn't be a test, now would it." Hesperos threw up his hands. "I am very disappointed in you. You seem to care for these mortals. I actually believed you'd have the courage to save one." He regarded me for a moment and tugged at his thick beard. "Unless you plan on using her ghost after she's dead. Interesting. I didn't think you were the type."

"I'm not, and oh, by the way. Go to hell."

My searching gaze found Henrietta's frightened eyes. She reached her arms out to me, begging to be snatched away from danger by her friend. This time, I wouldn't turn away. This time I would be the hero she needed. But how? I'd have to find a way and fast.

CHAPTER NINETEEN

Running among the buffalo with a day-old hangover was madness. Regretting the decision to wake up this morning, I eased closer to the charging herd of raging hooves. Thunder boomed across the prairie as they stormed over the dry Earth. Clouds of dust blurred my vision until all I could see was a solid wall of brown fury streaming directly underneath Henrietta. Each rumbling jolt threatened to shatter my resolve.

"This is the stupidest thing I've ever done," I grumbled.

"I seriously doubt it."

Stabbing Hesperos with a withering glare, I took a ready position a few feet from the furry brown wall of brawn. The thousand-pound bodies began to thin a bit, leaving holes between the clumps of horns. I rolled up my sleeves. Keeping my eyes fixed on the approaching buffalo, I waited for a wider gap between the beasts.

"No cheating," Hesperos said.

The sadistic ass wouldn't let me wait for safer opportunities to avoid horns and hooves. Hesperos stood with his arms folded. A triumphant smirk settled upon his face as he watched me. Flicking his fingers, he nodded toward his helpless victim. Henrietta screamed as her little body fell another five feet. Dangling inches above the fur and horns, the little girl's terror came through in the frantic flaying of her arms. Her wide eyes held me in a pleading embrace.

Adrenaline pumped through my veins, sending my heart racing in a frantic rhythm. Its pounding beat struck in time with the thundering hooves anxious to trample my fragile body. In all my days as a conman, I'd never known a bigger fool than the mark I'd become. Hesperos had his pigeon right where he wanted me. Damn it. Taking a deep breath, I leaped forward between two clumps of buffalo. Thick clouds of dust and grass rose to engulf me in their suffocating bodies. I kept my eyes on Henrietta and tried to stay focused.

Buffalos are surprisingly agile despite their massive bulk. The first horn caught my arm, its tip leaving a long red gash along my shirt sleeve. Wincing, I didn't have time to register the stinging of ripped flesh. Moments later, the next horn grazed my chest. Force and momentum were behind this buffalo's strike. The hit knocked me backward, planting me on my backside with a grunt.

"Do better, Dunham!" Hesperos called.

I turned and made a rude gesture to show him what I thought of his support. Regrettably, Hesperos missed my salute as an enormous brown head scarcely yards away filled my line of sight. I had mere moments to roll away from the beast's path. This was suicide. If I stayed in the herd any longer, one of the behemoths would stomp me to the ground.

Bounding to my feet, I headed toward the wallow again. Dust rose in spouts of brown all around me.

Chancing a quick look upward, I saw Henrietta's waving arms. She was close. I took a step and stumbled as my boot found a hole. The wallow! I'd finally made it.

Then Henrietta dropped as if the invisible strings holding her had been cut. I flew forward, catching her just as she was about to slam upon the hard floor of the wallow. Henrietta hugged my neck, her sobs stabbing angry thorns into my heart. One day there would be a reckoning for Hesperos. I'd make certain he got his due.

"Are you hurt?" I asked, pacing the wallow to curb my raging adrenaline.

"Dun," She cried, hugging me tighter. "They're coming back!"

I stopped in mid-stride and faced south. The giant wall of brown was collapsing in on itself. A massive bull – leader of the angry herd - shook its massive head as if chasing away a swarm of gnats. Those wild eyes locked on us. The bull, shaking its horns with a grunt, charged.

"I've passed your test!" I stormed toward Hesperos. "No magic needed. Now get us out of here."

"The test isn't over yet, Dunham." Hesperos pointed toward the buffalo.

Brown bodies colliding, the herd shoved and bit at each other in a wild attempt to follow their leader. The strange behavior couldn't be normal. I turned to Hesperos. A slow grin stretched across his thick lips, confirming my misgivings. Impossible! The bastard was controlling the herd somehow. Jutting two fingers toward the frenzied beasts, he murmured an unintelligible command. The great murderous mass charged as one toward us with horns lowered at a deadly angle.

Desperate to find cover, I spun around in the wallow. Nothing but flat prairie in every direction. How would I get Henrietta out of the way without getting us both killed? I stared down at my boots as if they held some cosmic truth that could save us. Loose dirt in the wallow bounced in time to the rhythm of the raging herd. The wave of horns widened. They were coming faster. My legs wouldn't be able to carry us out of their path in time even if I had someplace to run.

Then a strange pressure pressed at the skin beneath my Ouroboros. Its sudden intensity knocked me to my knees. Henrietta let go of my neck with a cry. Racing around my body, she fell to a trembling crouch behind me. The little girl and her fear, however, had inexplicably become a distant noise brushing against my consciousness. I was still aware of Henrietta's presence. Her lifeforce shimmered in the air like the sun's rays upon a calm pond, but she no longer held my complete attention. Something else had awakened into being. Upon its arrival, I was able to touch the power of creation itself.

Instinctively, I thrust my hand toward the bottom of the wallow. Faint green light, its hue the color of meadow grass, radiated about my fingers. I wiggled them, fascinated as the strange aura pulsed about my skin. Did I smell lilacs? I sniffed again. Perfume filled my nose, reminding me of fresh flowers in springtime. Dear God in Heaven! Either I was having some sort of fit, or the impossible was really happening.

Then the green flew from my hand and struck the ground with a boom. I leaped to my feet, pushing against the sheer force it exuded. Power exploded into the wallow, sending shockwaves between the approaching herd and me. I held my ground as the dirt before my body began to bubble. Something was becoming. I sensed it deep in my soul. Closing my eyes, I could see it. This new matter I'd created started as a tiny pea-sized object. Feeding upon my energy, it grew and expanded beneath the ground like the roots of a tree. I held my breath, feeling its excitement to break free of the Earth.

Sheets of solid rock exploded from the dirt at the center of the wallow, sending fresh clouds of dust and rock into the sky. Their stony surfaces crashed together with a teeth-grating clamor. I held my arms wider as the granite sheets stretched to form a barrier six feet high and six feet wide. Then, letting my arms drop, I stood awestruck at the wall I'd just created. Sparks of green flickered across its surface and then faded into the granite depths with a final flash of light.

I had little time to marvel at my handiwork. The charging herd was coming fast. I pulled Henrietta into my arms and hurled our bodies to the lee of the barrier wall. Pressing her body protectively against the hard surface, I leaned over her and kept my back to the open prairie. The herd – suddenly oblivious to us - raced around the barrier. Their numbers joined into a single mass of brown six feet behind me at the edge of the deep wallow.

Silence descended upon the prairie as the buffalo stampede rumbled toward the north. I kept my eyes on their departing tails until the billows of dust thinned along the horizon. Many extraordinary events had happened to me today, the least of which was surviving a buffalo stampede – twice. It was the solid wall of rock I found most curious. Smoothing a hand along its surface, I no longer felt the sensation of creation. Had I actually done magic? The rock wall wasn't there before. I was sure of it.

"I knew you had it in you," Hesperos said, suddenly inches away from me.

"You bastard!"

I threw a clump of buffalo dung at him. It sailed right through his body and landed with a disappointing thump. Ignoring the chip, he stepped closer to examine the rock with a fascinated intensity. Grunts of appreciation erupted from deep within his chest. They reverberated against the rock in boisterous waves.

Hesperos looked down at me with a triumphant grin. He took a step back, spreading his arms wide in a grand gesture of amazement. I fully expected him to cry, 'Ta-Da!'

"And thus, endeth the lesson," Hesperos said. "Come along, Doran. We must leave Dunham to contemplate his new knowledge."

My tormenter draped his cloak theatrically about his shoulders with a nod. The next instant, he was gone. Good riddance to him! I had an unpleasant inkling the devil wouldn't be gone long. This devious test had proven to both of us I could do magic. Hesperos wanted something from me, and it involved my new gift. Whatever the ghost or figment of my imagination had in mind, it wouldn't be in my best interests.

"Stay vigilant, meat sack." Doran pecked at my shaking finger. "Someone ripped the mortal woman's scalp from her head. Hesperos may have used her as a distraction, but she was merely an opportunity to exploit."

"If it wasn't Hesperos or Indians, then who killed her?"

"You'll have plenty of time to reason it out on your stroll back to the wagon train." Doran gave me a last long look before flying after its master.

"Funny," I called with an expressive gesture. "Another bastard."

Henrietta lifted her tear-stained face from my chest, her wide eyes gaping in awe. "You said a bad word to that buffalo."

I found the strength to chuckle. Of all the things the child's mind grasped ahold of during her harrowing adventure, my cursing was what she'd remembered. I suppose Henrietta's memory lapse was a blessing. It would save me some awkward explanations to her mother.

"I'll give you a penny for the swear jar."

I swiveled to lean my back against the stone with an exhausted sigh. Magic was real. I made a rock from dirt and panic. What else could I create with magic? I'd have to discover the extent of my gifts quickly before Hesperos could use someone else I cared about against me. Next time the test might turn deadly.

My tired thoughts drifted to the many faces of my traveling companions. The pioneers were God-fearing folk. Using magic wasn't an approved activity in the Puritan handbook. They'd tar and feather me as a witch if they saw the Ouroboros hiding under my shirt. Throw in my new magical powers, and things would get even more awkward. Reverend Edgewater, I was sure, would be giddy to hold a torch to my feet at the bonfire. No. I'd have to practice at night while everyone was asleep. Of course, Henrietta and I would have to find our wagon train first.

Hooves raced toward us. Their pounding rhythm beat a chaotic tempo against my rapidly forming headache. Hesperos said the lesson was over, so why had the buffalo returned? Henrietta squealed with a panicked cry and nestled against my shoulder. We couldn't stay here, hoping the beasts would leave us alone. I'd have to risk doing magic and provide a cover story for Henrietta later. Flicking my hands toward the ground, I tried to will the magic back into being. Nothing happened.

Then the pounding stopped. Metal rattled as a horse nickered and shook its reins. Horses meant humans. But were they friendly? I hoped so. I'd left the wagon without a gun or knife.

"Well, praise the Lord and pass the whiskey! You're alive!"

It was Captain Tyson. I scooted on my backside to the edge of the barrier and poked my head around. Tyson and three soldiers had ridden out to find us. Henrietta and I both gave a whoop to welcome them.

"We saw the tail end of that stampede. You were damn lucky to find cover," Tyson said, wiping the sweat from his face with a dirty bandana. "Angels must be guiding your steps. Especially you, Miss Henrietta! Clever girl, climbing on top of the rock as you did."

Tyson and the soldiers hadn't seen Henrietta suspended in midair? Hesperos must have used his magic to disguise the situation. Then again, your average person would naturally seek a rational explanation when faced with the impossible. They'd seen Henrietta in the middle of the stampede. Their minds put her on top of the rock despite what their eyes had seen.

"No time to pick flowers, Dun. Get up on this spare mount." Captain Tyson thrust his thumb to a horse tied behind one of the soldiers.

"I'm going to need a moment," I said as relief swept the last bit of energy from my body.

"You don't have a moment." Tyson pointed at the horizon, where several tribal warriors watched our group. "The Cheyenne have been shooting at our wagon train off and on for an hour. We need to get back before all of us are missing a scalp!"

I hadn't noticed armed men lining the ridge of a low bluff to our north in my anxious state. The Cheyenne remained still as their mounts shifted restlessly under them. Though I couldn't make out any faces in great detail, their weapons were conspicuous enough. I wasn't willing to bet my life on their continued patience.

"It's time to go back to your mother."

Sufficiently encouraged, my legs found the strength to rise with Henrietta clutched close in my arms. I sprinted past Tyson and the soldiers toward the horse like a hare chased by a hound. Lifting Henrietta on the saddle, I scrambled on behind her.

"Stay close and ride hard," Captain Tyson told us.

I regarded the Cheyenne as we followed the wagon tracks west. They stayed on the bluff, watching not us but the rock I'd created. Had they seen what happened? If they had, then what would that mean for our wagon train?

Captain Tyson slowed our pace when he was confident the Cheyenne weren't following. He brought his horse beside ours and fell into step. "I bet money you'd hop on a stagecoach in Council Grove, Dun. Never been so glad to lose twenty dollars in my life." He gave me a rare grin. "Mrs. Maxwell was right. You've turned out to be a good man."

"Thank you, Captain."

I turned my eyes away before he could see the guilt hiding within them. It was no use my denying the pestilence I'd dragged along on our journey. Hesperos wouldn't stop his cruel games until he got what he wanted from me. The bastard didn't care who he had to hurt along the way. Then there was the ghostly mother I'd failed to help. Doran had insinuated the same brutal killer who'd murdered her may be following us.

"Captain, I…" My words faded in a sudden gust of hot prairie wind.

A good man would leave the wagon train, sparing innocent lives. Instead, I spurred my horse onward, staying in the wagon ruts headed west. White bonnets dotted the prairie in the distance. Hating my cowardice, I galloped to join them.

CHAPTER TWENTY

Nature showed her beauty in the August heat. Black-eyed Susan daisies spread across the plains in vibrant yellow, mixing petals with prairie coneflowers, goldenrods, and pale pink milkweed blossoms. None were more beautiful than the native sunflower. Taller than a man, their bodies stretched out against the wind. Clusters of their bright yellow flowers greeted us as we passed. The children enjoyed trying to eat the tiny seeds that made spirals within the florets. More times than not, however, the birds reaped the rewards.

A few heavy thunderstorms found us on our march west, but they didn't stay long. Rainwater dropped during August storms was quickly swallowed by the thirsty ground, so mud didn't trouble us as it might have during other months. I didn't mind getting wet. Any escape from the heat was a blessing. Domingo and I, like-minded in our search to beat the heat, gratefully spent the Noon hour under our wagon. Winnie sometimes joined us for a cold lunch when the temperature grew suffocating inside her schooner.

Like most of my fellow travelers, I longed for the coolness of night. It was during these pleasant evening hours I exercised my more social proclivities. Having a gregarious nature, it wasn't long before I visited other camps. Many an evening found me walking with a pretty girl on my arm after dinner. It is a fact – in my experience - for every daughter, there is a father with a gun. Stern glares from their patriarch over the dancing flames of the fire warned me to limit my visits. It didn't take long to conclude my evenings were better spent with others of my kind.

Merchants, traders, and soldiers on the train held a nightly card game in the government wagon camp. Tentatively welcomed at first, the other players gave me a warmer reception after I purposely lost a few hands.

This evening I gave no quarter to my opponents as we played cards in the government camp. Sergeant Culvers, the soldier who'd helped dig the ghostly mother's grave, sat across the fire from me. His sharp features made a perfect triangle as he concentrated on his hand. Neither of us had mentioned what we'd seen in the poor woman's grave. I longed to cast out the memory and suspected Culvers felt the same.

"Hellfire! What a lousy draw." Culvers slapped his cards down on his thigh. "Who dealt this hand?"

Shaw, one of the traders, spat tobacco on the fire as he glared at me. "I see you've found your luck tonight, Reverend."

He was a careful man, meticulous with his cards and his cash. He had an annoying habit of turning his back to us before raising every bet. Shaw frequently peeked over his shoulder to ensure we couldn't see him counting his money. Penny pinchers brought out the mean in me. I took a little too much pleasure at times, separating them from their treasure. Caution and poker don't mix. Any gambler will tell you so.

"What can I say? I'm a blessed man," I said, taking the pot with a grin. "The money I win tonight is meant for charity." The Dunham Raynor wardrobe fund was my favorite cause. "Intent is everything in life."

Shaw grunted and gathered our spent cards. Suspicious eyes lifted to my face. He absently stroked a hand against his money belt as if it were a lover. I decided to ease up on the winning and lose a few hands. The misfortune of others where money was concerned often put a man in a better mood.

"You'd do better to spend your money on a gun," Bert Wiggs, one of the guards and our fourth hand, told me. "Fort Union is where all the trails bearing southwest converge. Not everybody headed this way is God-fearing. It can be a rough place." Bert snatched the deck from Shaw and began to shuffle the cards atop his thigh. "There's a saying about the New Mexico Territory. It's called the 'land without law.' Some say New Mexico is where only the brave or the criminal go."

"You just get me to Pawnee Rock tomorrow, and I'll be happy," Sergeant Culvers said. "Captain Tyson says no, but I believe we're being followed."

"The boys and I backtracked for three miles yesterday. We didn't see a damn thing." Bert thrust the cards unceremoniously into our hands. "You're imagining things, Sergeant."

Culvers had it right. Someone was following us. I had done my best to stay sharp, but my nerves couldn't withstand the effects of tedium. Of course, my current good luck was doing wonders to ease the malaise. I was up a few hands. Puffing on the expensive cigar I'd won off Shaw, I examined the hand I'd been dealt. Two cards short of a full house. Maybe I'd lose the next hand instead.

A sudden thud stilled our talk around the game. I turned a perplexed glance to Culvers, but his hard stare remained upon the gap between wagons just behind Bert, our dealer. The cigar dropped from my lips as I noticed Bert's eyes opened wide. Then his body slowly fell forward into the campfire. I stared, transfixed, at the arrow sprouting from Bert's back. The deck of cards spilled from his hands, the edges curling as their cardboard bodies burned within the flames.

"To arms! To arms!" Sergeant Culvers yelled, bolting away from our group.

Shouts answered him as the soldiers made ready to defend our camp. I was conscious of gunfire echoing among the wagons as chaos broke out around me. Still, my feet remained rooted to the ground. Fascinated, I watched as the flames licked at cloth and flesh.

"You can't let me burn," Bert's ghost cried, grasping impotently at his abandoned body. "I thought we were friends."

"Help me get him away from the flames!" I shouted over the chaos.

Shaw, as shaken as I, grabbed Bert's belt. We tugged and grunted as one until the corpse of our dealer rolled onto the dirt. Bert's ghost was gone as I stood away from his corpse. Stomach lurching, I turned from his smoldering body when a gust of prairie wind took up the nauseating odor.

"I may never eat again," I grumbled.

A bullet struck the ground a few inches from my boot. Jumping like a toad on a hot rock, I hurled my body under the nearest wagon. Someone had the foresight to park the schooner beside a large clump of milkweeds. Their broad leaves gave me a little extra cover as I lay flat beneath the wagon.

"Can you see them?" Shaw asked, skidding to a stop beside me.

"Not yet." I scanned the impenetrable darkness of a moonless night. "Doesn't mean they aren't there, though."

A uniform slid under the wagon to join us. The soldier thrust a small kerosene lantern into my hand. Then, turning the flame up just enough to see the workings of his Springfield rifle, he loaded a bullet into the chamber. Flickering light fell upon his uniform, giving me a first look at our would-be protector. A suspicious lack of stripes upon the sleeve and his hairless babyface marked him as an inexperienced private. Wonderful. I'd bet money the kid wasn't any older than seventeen.

He gave me a wink and made a turning motion with his fingers. I dimmed the flame again, nodding my understanding. He needed light to see, but so did our enemy. The private fell to his belly and positioned his weapon toward the endless prairies surrounding our circle. Regarding the eager concentration on his face, I silently hoped Private babyface was a good shot.

"Keep your eyes open. Let me know if you see a target," the private said. "I don't want to waste bullets."

"I can't see a damn thing!" Shaw cried. "Do you think it's Indians after the horses? Might be Cheyenne or Arapahoe. Neither of them like intruders on their lands."

Our attackers might not be from any tribe. The arrow stuck in Bert's back was the only one I'd seen so far. Advanced weapons bombarded us now. Their bullets found human targets within our camp with expert precision, suggesting the weapon's owner was someone specially trained to shoot at a great distance. My money was on a soldier or a professional killer. Grizz, I remembered, had a few men handy with a long-range rifle amongst his gang. It wouldn't surprise me if he'd orchestrated the attack.

"Well, I'll be a son of a goat," Shaw said, leaning his head through the screen of milkweed. "That ain't no Indian!"

"Get back under the…."

A blast of hot liquid splashed across my cheek. Shaw fell to his side, dead eyes staring at the bullet hole in his forehead. Kneeling beside the body was Shaw's ghost. Dead eyes found mine, but there was no time for comfort or an explanation. His ghost sent a painful shriek into the cold universe. Then Shaw's ethereal being flew into the darkened prairie as if pulled by a rope. I stared after it. Death's coachman and the Eternal Flame were suspiciously absent. If Heaven or Hell hadn't come for Shaw's soul, then who had?

"I can't see them!"

Private babyface, now firing his rifle like it was a holiday popper, seemed to have forgotten his concern about wasting ammunition. I covered my ears until the disheartening 'clicks' of an empty chamber filled our temporary haven. Private babyface grabbed the lantern from my grip and sent the flame to its full glow. His panicked fingers fumbled as he tried to reload. The bullets fell into the dirt. My hero's frantic grasping pushed most of his ammunition beyond the wagon's cover into the grass. Cursing, I snatched the lantern back and snuffed the flame. We sat in the shadows, waiting for the next bullet to strike.

Then I saw an unnatural red light moving slowly across the horizon. Its crimson glow clung to the silhouette of a man. I recognized his wide-brimmed hat and the distinct presence of magic. It was the assassin who tried to kill me in the Missouri River.

Mr. Black Hat's elaborate gestures made red symbols against the night sky. Bodies moved among the grass and flowers as his fingers danced. God in Heaven! He was using magic to direct our attackers. How in Heaven or Hell could I stop him?

"Those bushwhackers are going for the civilians!" Private babyface clutched his rifle as screams echoed across No Man's Land between the wagon camps.

Mr. Black Hat knew I was in the area, but not my exact location. Then a horrible realization struck me. If he'd followed me all this time, the mad man knew about Winnie and Domingo.

I rolled out from under the wagon and crouched beside the wheel. "This is a stupid plan."

"I wouldn't advise running out into the dark unarmed, Preacher." The private regarded me over his shoulder. "Wait for Sergeant Culvers to bring back a few more men. You'll make one hell of a target if you go alone."

"There's no time." I took three deep breaths before creeping to the front of the wagon bed.

"What do you think you're going to do?"

"What I can," I said and then ran into the Kansas night like a fool.

Chapter Twenty-One

Zips and pings chased my boots as I ran across No man's land. Our attackers had been waiting for an opportunity to flush me out, and I'd obliged them by leaping right into the line of fire. What was the saying about fools rushing in? Jumping like a jittery jackrabbit, I raced in through the gap between camps in wild patterns.

Straining my ear to the north, I heard gleeful laughter ringing above the chaos of battle. Wonderful. My assassin was thoroughly entertained. I suppose being the brunt of a malicious killer's joke was what I deserved. What if Winnie or Domingo were hurt? My selfish need for companionship had put my friends at risk. Why hadn't I learned how to properly use the Ouroboros rather than spending most of my evenings playing cards? Better still. I should have stayed in Council Grove and let them go on their way without me.

Stretching out my arms before me, I reached into my soul, searching for the magic hiding within. Tendrils of power greeted my touch with welcoming sparks of warm light. I called the magic forth, directing it toward my waiting fingers. Sparks of green light flickered and then died with an unimpressive pop.

"Come on," I grumbled at the magic. "This is sad and embarrassing."

My shin slammed against an inert mound several yards from the nearest wagon. Breath bursting from my lungs, I sprawled across dirt and grass with a groan. I raised my head a few inches and regarded the still body. The man's name escaped me, but I recognized him as one of the fathers with guns I'd dined with a few evenings ago. His weapon hadn't done him much good tonight.

Rolling onto my knees, I crawled up beside him. Shallow rhythmic breaths met my touch as I examined the arrow sprouting from the back of his shoulder. Grabbing its shaft, I snapped off the feathered tail and turned him over. The sharp head had gone clean through. I gripped the slippery wood at the base of the arrowhead and pulled hard. It came out with a wet whoosh. Screaming, the man grabbed my arm and spewed a few impolite words before passing out again.

"Henry?" A worried feminine voice called.

"Stay where you are," I hissed. "We'll come to you."

I thrust bloodied hands under Henry's armpits and pulled his unconscious form toward the sounds of anxious weeping. Explosions of dirt followed us, narrowly missing our boots. The gunman was playing with us as if Henry and I were two mice tormented by a rabid cat. Then two sets of hands grabbed Henry's arms, ending the game. His wife and daughter helped me drag him to safety beneath their wagon.

Henry's wife tore her petty coat with a merciless yank and pressed the material to her husband's wound. Their daughter – her name escaped me – leaned back and tugged at her petticoats. Two little boys huddled together, watching them. Eyes wide with fear, they stayed still, trying to remain as small as possible.

"Stay behind the damn wagons!" Tyson's voice boomed over the chaos. "Don't shoot until you can make out your target. We can't waste ammunition."

I grabbed the wounded pioneer's gun and headed toward Tyson's howling. Finding the wagon master wasn't hard. He stood outside the safety of the wagon circle, drawing fire away from the families under his protection. Blatant hypocrisy and excessive heroics aside, I had to admit the wagon master had guts.

"Better stay back with the women, Reverend." Tyson waved me off irritably. "This is for men who know how to defend themselves."

A shape crept along the dancing shadows peeking through the wagon wheels. It was a man, or at least it used to be. My trader friend had been correct. Our attackers weren't exclusively Indians. This assassin sported a dirty nightshirt stained down the front with dried patches of God only knew. A sizeable bullet hole from a previous encounter had burned through the cap upon his head. Impossible! Dead men can't fight, and neither can their ghosts. Yet proof to the contrary shuffled toward Captain Tyson with a hand poised to kill.

"Behind you, Captain!"

I raised my gun and put another hole in the killer's sleeping cap before he could get close enough to stab Tyson. A massive butcher's knife fell from the dead man's hand with a thump. The wagon master spun away from the falling body. He gave me a quick but appraising look before returning fire from another killer hiding in the prairie grass.

The Ouroboros, sensing immediate danger, wiggled urgently under my shirt. I took a step back seconds before a thick iron spike flew by inches from my face. The deadly projectile lodged deep into the wagon bed behind me. I stared at the six inches of raw metal embedded in wood. Impressive. Tremendous force was behind the throw. It would take strength and skill to send heavy iron across twenty feet of space.

Wūshī. The single word drifted upon an uneasy wind, its fingers sending shivers of apprehension down my spine.

Then a Chinese railroad worker stepped out of the darkness. He hoisted another spike and aimed it for my head. I leaped to the side just as iron whizzed past my ear. Railroad workers were common enough in the West, but to my knowledge, there wasn't a set of metal tracks for hundreds of miles. So why was he here in the prairie trying to kill me? Like his friend in the nightshirt, this man was already suffering from a case of corpse rot. He'd died of an ugly stab wound in the stomach. It was time I helped him along to the other side. I aimed again and heard the sickening click of an unloaded gun.

"Dun," Tyson yelled and tossed me a rifle.

My shot struck the spike thrower in his dead heart. His body, however, didn't fall. Instead, it lingered for a moment before disappearing into a dust cloud of disintegrated body parts. I stood gaping at the empty hole the railroad worker had vacated. What in all God's creation had just happened?

"Wake up, Reverend! You've got more headed this way."

Snapping out of my shocked stupor, I pivoted toward the next wave of attackers. We took down two more assassins, but four more rushed forward to replace them. All the while, Mr. Black Hat remained on the horizon, hands aglow in red fire. Taking out the Undead forces under his command was an impossible task. The sorcerer had an endless supply of corpses at his disposal, while our ammunition reserve was finite. So I had to eliminate the source.

Aiming my rifle at the glowing red target, I focused all my will on the next shot. "Join your friends in the grave, you scarlet bastard."

I let my bullet fly across the long distance. The red glow on the horizon suddenly winked out, plummeting the prairie into an eerie silence. Mr. Black Hat was down, but I tell if he were dead or merely stunned. Taking a shot in the dark at such a long-range had a fifty-fifty chance of hitting the target.

"Look, Captain! They're leaving," Peters, one of the guards, cried.

Keeping his rifle aimed at the departing ambushers, Peters moved out of cover to join the wagon master. I noticed the bloody line running along Tyson's right arm as I drew closer. He slapped me on the back with a snort.

"You are a surprise," Tyson said, shaking his head when I tried to hand back the rifle. "Keep it. We'll need you again, I'm sure."

"I ain't never seen no reverend shoot like that," Peters said. "Where the hell did you learn to fire a gun?"

During my early years with Angelina, she'd taken up with Clive, a sharpshooter and trick rider. His stage name was Colonel Glory, Hero of the Cavalry. He never said which regiment, but the crowd rarely asked once they saw him shoot. In our off hours between shows, Clive taught me how to use a gun and hit the target a fair amount of the time. His sudden departure with a golden-headed saloon singer remains a bitter memory for me.

"No one is born a reverend," I said. "I'm glad I wasn't too rusty tonight."

"Rusty, hell. I'm glad you're on our side." Tyson turned to his men. "Set up a guard. The rest of you check on the train. I think we've lost a few folks."

Brujo. Their voices drifted over the empty plains.

Leaving Tyson to direct the managed chaos, I stepped away from the wagons and into the darkness. A torch was unnecessary as I walked out to meet them. The newly Dead put off a unique glow. Shaw, Bert, and a few other men from our wagon train were the iridescent ghosts. Strangers - Cheyenne, Arapahoe, Caucasian, Asian, and Mexican - stood among them. Skin color and nationality didn't matter anymore. Every human body died eventually – Unless they didn't.

The strangers among my fellow travelers had died before. Their Undead bodies didn't give off a glow. They were simply there, rotting before my eyes. In all my years of seeing beyond the veil, the rare times the Undead had visited me always meant trouble. Both times had been in New Orleans. Their corpses had been up to no good then too.

They come for you, riding dead horses. The collective voices of the newly Dead told me.

"Hell comes for you," Bert said, the arrow still sticking out of his ethereal back. "They won't stop until you're dead."

"Who are they?" Vacant expressions met my question. I tried again. "Where is the man in the black hat? He was the one controlling the Undead."

A man dressed in suspenders shuffled toward me. Half his face was missing, and I could detect the rotting remnants of chest muscle through his tattered shirt. He'd probably been a clerk in a mercantile during his boring life. A few years into death, he looked hungry for human flesh.

"Gone. Ran." He thrust a rotting finger at me. "New master."

"Absolutely not," I said, holding my hands up in a vain attempt to stop the corpse from getting closer. "I don't keep pets, especially Undead ones."

"Go to your rest," A voice said beside me.

It was Hesperos. He'd decided to come out of hiding at last. Doran – appearing this time as a gigantic wolf - snapped at their heels as they left.

Hesperos and I turned away as the Eternal Flame burst upon the plains to collect those bound for Heaven. I heard the grunting growl of a buffalo. The tip of its white tail flicked inches from my leg as it passed. That was new. I suppose you saw what gave you comfort when passing over. The Cheyenne and Arapahoe responded, heading to join the great beast.

Raised in the bosom of a Christian parish, I learned my scriptures. Did I believe every word of the Bible? Let me put it this way. I've seen many a fortunate soul welcomed in Heaven's embrace. I've also seen Hell gather its share of the damned. There is an afterlife. Make no mistake. But who judges a soul's worth? And by what measure?

I once witnessed a lowly thief summoned toward the Eternal Flame, accepted into a Kingdom whose riches none can imagine. I've also heard the anguished cries of shock from the bishop of a large cathedral. He'd refused to cast his eye upon the poor in life. In Hell, he would see rags and flame until time stopped. No. I couldn't say for sure what or who judges a soul upon death, but I can say it bears a wiser eye than any two-legged creature with a pulpit or a station.

Then it struck me. The Dead and Undead had immediately obeyed Hesperos' word. I turned back to the prairie skies as small poofs of dust floated away upon the eternal breeze. Somehow, Hesperos had freed the Undead from their rotting corpses.

"How did you do that?" I asked. "Who are you? You said you'd marked me with this Ouroboros. Why?"

"So many questions." He gave me a tut. "I'll answer them all as I train you, Dunham. Our destinies are joined. Soon you will be able to do what I can do."

"Who says I want to do what you can," I snapped. "Listen, if you gave me this mark, you could take it away too."

"Is that what you really want?" Hesperos laughed. "I don't think it is. How would you make a living then? A cheap conman with no way to expose the secrets of the Dead. You would starve quickly." He sighed with irritation. "Find new friends, Dunham. The ones you have are vexing me."

Then he was gone. I hadn't seen him move, but Hesperos had vanished without a trace. The footprints left behind were mine and those of the gigantic wolf. Doran, at least, was real.

"Dun," Father Emilio said from behind me. "Are you well?"

"Father, yes, I was just…it's not important. Is everyone alright?"

"A bullet grazed Domingo's arm. Mrs. Maxwell is seeing to his injury now. She sent me to find you." He let his arms fall as if unable to hold the burden any longer. "Heaven has spared my brothers and me injury tonight. We are offering comfort to the rest of our traveling companions. Nine dead this night."

I nodded uncomfortably. Father Emilio regarded me with puzzlement and perhaps a bit of suspicion. Hesperos was right about one thing. The good father wasn't buying my story anymore. I don't know what he saw in me now, but it wasn't anything completely trustworthy.

"I once met a Buddhist pilgrim on my travels," Father Emilio said. "He told me we are all who we think we are. I believe we are who God made us, but the pilgrim's words have the ring of truth, do they not?" Then he put a gentle hand on my shoulder. "Your friends wait for you by the campfire, Dun. Come. No more fighting tonight. We must comfort our fellow travelers."

Every ounce of raw anger I had told me to search out Mr. Black Hat while the villain was hurt. I let the tip of the rifle barrel fall toward the ground with a sigh. If I took him out, would the killings stop? Bert and the other newly Dead souls warned me riders were coming for me on dead horses. If Mr. Black Hat controlled these mysterious riders, why weren't they part of the attack tonight? I needed to think things through. Running after killers in the dark would undoubtedly get me killed.

"You're right, father." I sighed and leaned the rifle against my shoulder. "Nothing more I can do tonight. Let's go see to the others."

Chapter Twenty-Two

Captain Tyson drove us hard until we reached Pawnee Rock late the following afternoon. He intended us to stay put for a few days to restock the water barrels from the Arkansas River. Tyson had hopes of finding some wild game as well. Refusing friendly invitations for hunting and fishing with the other men, I stayed among the wagons. There were better ways to occupy an afternoon.

"You sure you don't need a hand, either of you?" I asked, helping Domingo down on his blanket by the fire.

"I have my medicine." Having had several sips, Domingo patted the jug of cactus wine fondly.

"Sit down and relax, Dun. You've been driving all day." Winnie gave me a frown. "Stop fussing. We're both fine. Now, enjoy the quiet. It's not every day you camp under the shadow of something so impressive."

A hundred feet of towering sandstone, Pawnee Rock was the halfway point between Independence, Missouri, and Santa Fe. First popular as a meeting place for the Pawnee and Cheyenne, Pawnee Rock became a favorite stop for travelers headed west.

"Tyson took me to the top of the bluff earlier this afternoon," I told them. "He showed me the initials he carved as a boy on his first time traveling the Santa Fe

Trail. I tried to find an open spot, but names covered every inch of rock. I finally found a place at the base to carve a sloppy 'D R 1865'."

Winnie gave me a chuckle. "Are you planning to be a doctor next?"

"I might. You never know. Maybe I could become someone respectable."

"You are someone respectable to the people of this train. Keep your feet on the right path, and never forget the courage you've shown. Oh Lord, look what the wind blew in! The stray cats have come calling," Winnie said, jutting a disapproving chin at a group of young ladies walking together. They were eyeing our campfire and giggling. "If my daughter behaved that way, I'd have given her the switch until her backside glowed red."

"It's a lovely night," I said, giving Winnie a wink. "I think I'll take in the beauty of Pawnee Rock."

"Be careful, Dun," Domingo called with a laugh. "You may stumble into a wife!"

"I'm too sure-footed."

Strolling at a casual pace, I caught up to the flowers of the prairie. I tipped my hat to the cluster of girls gathered around Jason MacKinney's Mercantile wagon. Many thought him insane to waste space with fabric and fancy perfumes. I had to admit. The man knew what young ladies fancied.

One of the girls, Beth to her friends, waved at me with a giggle. When I returned the wave, the bright pink splotches spread like vibrant petals from her neck to her ears. Whispers and more giggles broke out amongst the young ladies. Most pretended to examine MacKinney's assortments of handkerchiefs, buttons, and bows. Beth stood in their midst, watching me with a level of interest no confirmed bachelor wants to see.

We'd walked together on the edge of camp the night before. It was all very chaste. Her father had seen to it. I'd spotted him following us, brandishing his gun. Young Beth, however, had been oblivious. I'd kept the talks to spiritual matters, privately cursing the girl's tendency to burst into giggles every few minutes. Beth was pretty, but her propensity for silliness inspired me to continue my stroll.

Ten small frames rush to circle about me. I lifted my hands in mock surrender. The boys of the wagon train ranged from ages six to twelve. Any older and their parents or Captain Tyson put the unlucky souls to work. Poor devils. Ready or not, adulthood came early for pioneers.

"You ain't gonna marry Bubbling Beth Brewster like they say, are you?" Paul, their leader, asked as he wiped his runny nose on a dusty sleeve.

"Who's saying that?"

"My Ma and all the other women." He sniffed again. "Well, you ain't, are ya?"

"No, I ain't." I flicked his hat from the head of straw-like hair. "I'm more of a wandering preacher. We nomads don't stay in one place long enough to get married."

Having a wife meant settling down on a small clump of land somewhere, breaking my back just to keep us out of the weather. It sounded like Hell on Earth to me. I preferred reveling in all the luxuries city life offered. Admittedly, weeks on the wagon train made me long for a roof and four walls. I shivered as the thought struck me. Respectability was one thing, but marriage? I actively avoided it.

The little boys continued to circle, their eager faces watching my every move. I knew what they were waiting for and suppressed a grin. Sleight of hand was a must for any confidence man. I was passable enough to entertain children, but I would never fill my belly with the craft. However, my magic tricks were as thrilling as miracles to my enthusiastic young audience.

I slipped quick fingers into the cuff of my jacket and pulled out a shiny Indian head penny. Eager faces watched the copper. It twisted and flipped through my fingers as the boys laughed. Then I tossed the penny up toward the sunset sky. Well, not really. The coin had returned to my cuff where I'd 'magically' produce it out of Paul's ear. What happened instead left me as stunned as my young audience.

Indian head pennies fell from the sky in a shower of copper. They plopped in the dirt and smashed the prairie grass around our feet. The boys gave cries of awe and delight. Falling to their knees, Paul and his friends gathered the pennies as fast as they could in the fading light.

"How'd you do that?" Paul asked, stuffing handfuls of pennies into his trouser pockets.

"I don't know."

The last little coins bounced off my boot and into the grass. Lifting my hands, I regarded the fading glow of magic. Not the pathetic sleight of hand I'd picked up from Angelina, but real magic.

Stuffing my hands under my arms, I sprinted away from the boys and into the comforting crowd of wagons. What had just happened? Days of attempting to use magic, and I'd gotten nothing for all my efforts. I'd tried countless times to prod the Ouroboros into action, but it remained still upon my skin. So why had it relented now?

"I saw that shameful display."

Reverend Edgewater stood before me like a black and white pillar of annoying self-righteousness. Sweat from the day's travel beaded on his forehead, escaping from under the brim of his hat. Fists upon his hips, he glared at me.

"You, Reverend Dun, are a wanderer." Edgewater lifted his weak chin with a grimace of disdain. "I disapprove of your antics with dawdling children whose parents should know better. As the proverb says, 'Give a man a fish, and he'll eat for a day. Teach a man to fish, and he'll eat for a lifetime.' What exactly did you expect to teach those boys today? Imagine! Handing out money for no reason. What are those boys to make of it?"

"Giving is good. Hoarding money is bad?"

"You love to twist my words, don't you?"

"Everybody needs a hobby."

"You are needed at our camp this evening," Edgewater said, choking on the words. "We have important concerns to discuss."

"And you thought of me? I'm touched."

"Don't be. We took a vote, and I lost. Regrettably, the group wants you there."

"Who am I to refuse such a cordial invitation? I'd be happy to attend your little soirée even if it simply serves to irritate you."

I followed him into the depths of puritan propriety. My neck was chafing already. Reverend Edgewater, true to his nature, hadn't been exaggerating. Every puritan male soul in the wagon train was in attendance. I recognized some of the guards, ex-soldiers, who road alongside the wagons during the day. Many I'd see at the cards later in the evening. What could bring my fellow sinners here among God's perfect children?

A few staunch Edgewater devotees quieted the other men as their leader took center stage beside the campfire. Edgewater assumed his best pulpit stance, refusing to speak until every voice stilled. His face turned an angry scarlet when he caught me rolling my eyes.

"Our children are falling ill. Ned, Donald's boy, is near death with fever." Edgewater basked in the murmurs of the collective voices of dismay. "Our doctor claims illnesses of this sort run rampant on many wagon trains. He won't listen to reason. What else can you expect from a foreigner."

"I will remind you, Reverend, that you are the foreigner in this land," Doc, the only real healer in our traveling party, told him.

Doctor Gonzales was born and raised in the New Mexico Territory. A keen mind and wealthy parents afforded him the opportunity to study medicine in England. Doc claimed he'd returned home to the territory to help his people, but I suspect he was homesick for the ruggedness of the West.

"That prattling ass Edgewater is more of a foreign threat than the Doc and a damn site less useful if you asked me," Reese murmured.

"Do you mind?" One of Edgewater's faithful gave him a sour look.

"If it isn't fever, then what is it?" Reese asked. "Get to the point. I'm on guard duty in twenty minutes."

"Listen to me, you men! Satan has come among us." Reverend Edgewater paused for full effect. "He wants our children for some dark purposes."

The camp was silent as even Edgewater's supporters shifted uncomfortably in the dirt. Reverend Edgewater, as if expecting this, lifted his chin higher. I could make out the fiery conviction of a religious zealot in his eyes. Childhood memories and their unpleasant emotions curdled in my stomach. Edgewater had found my rawest nerve.

"Let me see if I have this right," I said. "You believe a horned beast with a pitchfork is sneezing on these children. That's how they're getting sick?" I shook my head. "I think we should listen to the only person qualified to express an opinion. Doc, what do you make of it?"

"Always so quick to deny your own kind, aren't you?" Edgewater swept a finger around the crowd. "I warned you he would reject anything I had to say."

"First of all. I am not your kind." I lifted my voice over the multitude of conversations. "Second, I'm not going to needlessly frighten the families on this wagon train by joining you on a witch hunt."

"A curious choice of words considering the evidence I've found under Ned's mattress."

Edgewater tossed a little brown bundle over the fire. I caught it and stared down at the leather bag. The aroma of herbs touched my nose. Hard bits of something crumpled the dried leaves when I squeezed the bag with my fingers.

It took every ounce of skill I possessed not to react. I'd recognized the symbol – an elaborately designed 'A' - burned in the leather when Edgewater had held it up to the firelight. The extravagant loops and sharp lines perfectly modeled Angelina's mark. Many a night, I'd watch her make the fake hex bags by our campfire. Angelina used to call them 'hate bags' because they were popular with her more vindictive clients. Whoever had placed the hex bag under the little boy's cot must have gotten it from our medicine show.

"It's called a hex bag." Edgewater lifted his voice above the low thunder of shock. "A witch has cast the sickness upon that boy."

"Give it to me," Doc Gonzales said, carefully lifting the bag by its leather tie.

He sniffed at the leather with a frown. Then, moving with an urgency that made me uneasy, he took an abandoned corn husk from someone's empty plate. Doc rested the bundle atop the open husk on a rock beside the campfire. He took a smoldering stick from the fire and held down the corner of the bag. Digging around in his medical implements, Doc pulled out a nasty-looking cutting tool. He sliced off the leather tie and carefully tipped the contents of the bag onto the corn husk. Bits of small animal bones mixed in with a dried herb. Pale white flowers still shaped a cloud above a broken stem with odd purple dots.

"Dear God! Poison hemlock," Doc said. "You men who handled this bag, wash your hands right now. And don't touch your mouth or eyes. I hope the leather has given you some protection."

"What are you saying?" I asked, following Edgewater to a pan of water. "That can't be a real hex bag. Someone is probably having a joke."

"This is no joke, Dun." Doc Gonzales tossed the husk along with the little bag in the fire. "Whoever put that under Ned's bed wanted the boy dead. The poor child must have opened the bag for a look. He'd simply have to touch it once to be poisoned. Damn me for a fool! I should have recognized the signs. I thought the boy was frightened because he'd been sneaking apples out of the barrel when his father wasn't looking."

Poison Hemlock? Angelina filled her hex bags with dried prairie sage and old bones we found on the road. There was nothing sinister in them - ever. She charged a pretty price for the bags, and no one complained. In truth, many came back for more.

"Mrs. Maxwell helped the doctor tend to our wounded after the last raid. She seems to know a great deal about herbs," One of the other black suits said.

"As do half the women on this train," I growled. "So does Father Emilio and his brothers. Would you like to cast doubts on the priests too?"

"Heathens! The Maxwell woman is too friendly with them to suit me. What about you, Reverend Dun?" Edgewater asked, thrusting a finger in my face. "Is there something you'd like to tell us?"

I slammed my fist in his soft gut and followed up with a strike in the pearly whites to finish the job. Edgewater dropped like a sack of sheep dip. The other black suits scattered back away from me, cawing like a murder of crows.

"Yes, there is something I'd like to say. You can tell your leader when he wakes up. I think you're all a bunch of superstitious idiots. Dance around the fire, waving your hands and beating your bibles on your heads if it pleases you. Just leave me out of whatever else you've got planned. That goes for Mrs. Maxwell, Domingo, and the priests too. You've all seen me shoot. Don't think I won't put a hole in your nice white collars."

"Heretic." The word circled about the crowd, slowly growing louder until it reached a crescendo.

"Easy, gents. Let's keep things cordial." Reese raised his rifle toward the black suits. "It might be a good idea to head back to your camp, Dun."

I gave him a nod of thanks. Pushing through the crowd, I walked past the still wagons. Whoever did this was human. Why would someone poison the boy? Ned was one of the clusters of children born into a farm family. He wasn't a threat to anyone.

"Damn," I grumbled and leaned against a nearby wagon with a frustrated sigh.

"Hello, meat sack," Doran whispered in my ear. "Rubbing elbows with the religious elite?"

I whirled around to find shining eyes regarding me from the driver's bench of the wagon. Hesperos' pet was in the form of a black house cat this evening. The orange symbol burned on his forehead, casting an eerie glow.

"I'm not in the mood for a visit this evening, Doran."

"Really? I should think a hex bag under a little boy's bed would jog a few memories for you." Doran stretched languidly upon the wagon's bench. "Little Ned is much younger than you were, of course. But Reverend Edgewater could easily be mistaken for your father. Am I right?"

A hissing fit of laughter wheezed out of the cat's mouth. Lunging forward, I pinned the cat against the bench. I lifted Doran by the scruff of his neck. Hissing, he slapped a paw at me, scratching the back of my hand.

"I know a couple of bored dogs who'd probably love to get their teeth on a stray cat. Start talking."

"Do you think the hex bag fell out of the sky? You've seen the sorcerer following you, meat sack. I know you have. I think he's trying to tell you something about your past." Doran hissed another derisive laugh. "The sorcerer probably assumed you were clever though we both know that isn't true." Cat eyes rolled at me with impatience upon noticing I didn't understand. "Poison hemlock killed Socrates, the Ancient Greek philosopher. Hesperos is also from Greece."

"Are you saying Hesperos used a hex bag on me when I was a boy?"

"He had to mark you somehow. Humans are so much more pliable when they're near death."

Doran took my distracted silence as an opportunity to sink his teeth into my finger. I howled with the pain and dropped him. Landing on his feet like a true cat, Doran flipped his tale in my general direction before darting under the wagon. His furry body disappeared in a blur. Hissing laughter echoed against my ears as I stared into the nothingness of night. I was beginning to despise my supernatural stalkers.

CHAPTER TWENTY-THREE

I kept to the exterior border of the wagon train's circle as I headed toward our camp. Cheery bands of firelight cast vibrant shapes through the wheel spokes as I walked. Absorbed in their evening chores and conversations, the pioneers didn't notice my silent passage through their temporary stretch of prairie.

Doran's revelation this evening brought back troubling memories of my boyhood illness with a sickening jolt. My first terrifying encounters with the Dead. The angry words and resulting beatings from my father. I was finally exiled to an insane asylum at thirteen. Hesperos had been behind all of it. I wasn't a vulnerable boy anymore, and as a man-full grown, I could be an obstinate ass when the mood struck me.

Hesperos and Mr. Black Hat had trapped me on this wagon train containing five hundred prairie schooners filled with potential victims. My options were severely limited. I may be unable to escape my tormenters, but perhaps I could outthink them.

Doran was certain Hesperos had given me the Ouroboros and its powers. Recollections of my chats with Hesperos seemed to confirm the creature's claims. Damn the man, or whatever he was. Then there was Mr. Black

Hat. He was extremely motivated to kill me by any means necessary. I think I could naturally assume they were enemies. Maybe I could use their rivalry for my benefit?

My hopes for quiet contemplation evaporated when I came upon the crowd at our campsite. Captain Tyson, Father Emilio, and a handful of armed men stood around our fire. Domingo had taken his medicine under the wagon, leaving Winnie to fend off an angry man with a gun.

I recognized his stubborn jaw, and the moss-green eyes continuously narrowed in a suspicious glare. His possessive attentions had followed Bubbling Beth and me upon our walk last evening. The patriarch of the Brewster clan ruled his womenfolk with a firm hand. I'd wondered if the same hand had struck flesh when I'd noticed his wife and daughter watching him as we'd shared a meal.

"Point your gun at me again, Ed Brewster, and I'll take it away from you," Winnie warned. "I have half a mind to march over and ask your wife what she thinks about her husband holding a loaded gun on an unarmed woman."

"Polly doesn't spend time with women like you. Traveling alone with two men. It's indecent." Mr. Brewster spat on the ground before him. "You ought to be home seeing to your own house."

A storm was about to break across Winnie's face. She grabbed her cast iron skillet from a pile of dishes she'd left to dry on the hot rocks. I rushed forward and caught her arm just as she was about to bring down the pan on Ed Brewster's head.

"What's going on here?" I asked.

"Where is she?" Mr. Brewster shifted his barrel to aim at my heart. "Where's my Beth?"

"Simmer down, Ed." Tyson pushed the gun, aiming it toward the ground. "Beth has gone missing, Dun. Do you know where she is?"

"Me? Why would I know?" I scanned the stern faces as my gut curdled.

Bubbling Beth was beginning to be a huge pain in my ass. Mr. Brewster's hands tightened around his gun as he searched my face for an answer. A lack of concern on my part would do me no favors among the group of fathers. I decided to be honest and go for a confused expression.

"I last saw Beth with the other young ladies at MacKinney's Mercantile wagon earlier this evening. Have you asked them?"

"Liar! You was out walking with her last night."

Brewster tried to lift his gun barrel again, but Captain Tyson wrestled it from his grip. Two of Brewster's friends hurried forward before he could do something stupid, like throw a punch at Tyson.

"Listen, friend. My interest in your daughter is merely spiritual, I assure you."

Of course, my intentions had been less than pure when I first saw Beth. Long auburn hair with curves where they should be, Beth was pretty. Her possessive father's skill with a gun, however, gave me pause. I'd seen him shoot rattlers among the clumps of grass. Not wanting to be Ed Brewster's next target, I'd decided to allow my common sense and self-preservation to win over my more animal instincts.

"Ask Reverend Edgewater. He and I were having an ecumenical disagreement this evening."

"Don't think we won't check your story."

"Rather than arguing, shouldn't we look for young Beth?" Father Emilio asked. "We could form groups and start searching in several directions about the camp."

"A sensible idea, Father. You men spread the word," Captain Tyson barked. "We meet at the base of Pawnee Rock in ten minutes."

Father Emilio moved closer, offering me another enigmatic smile. "We will search together."

I'd detected a slight change in the priest's demeanor toward me after we'd found the dead woman outside of Diamond Springs. Father Emilio remained pleasant enough. He treated me with the same politeness he'd shown when I'd first joined the pioneers. Nothing in his manner suggested the priest thought me a threat. However, the peculiar looks Father Emilio gave me when he thought I wasn't paying attention said otherwise. I wasn't sure why he found me suddenly worrying. A confrontation, I suspected, was inevitable.

"After you, Father," I said.

We walked together, the priest and I, through the prairie. Pawnee Rock was a dark tower before us. Keeping my eyes on its distinct outline, I stumbled over the clumps of dirt and rock in our path. Father Emilio maintained his steady pace, seemingly unaffected by the dim light.

"Five hundred wagons make a small group with little to do but gossip," Father Emilio said. "Word of any excitement spreads quickly."

"And what excitement are we talking about?"

"This unfortunate business about the hex bag is of great concern to my brothers and me."

"You don't believe it's a witch too?"

"I believe someone is playing a dangerous game. We must remain vigilant and stay together as a group. Fighting amongst ourselves only puts the wagon train in peril."

"Word does spread fast," I said with a snort.

"You knocked out a tooth." Father Emilio shook his head. "Reverend Edgewater and his followers are, how do you say, disgruntled."

"Fire and brimstone sermons only get you so far. Some people need a more hands-on approach to loving thy neighbor."

"You mustn't make light of the situation, Dun. Arguments with Reverend Edgewater make trouble for Captain Tyson. He has treated you with kindness."

"Yes, he has. Tyson's a good man," I said. "I don't want to cause him trouble, but I won't have those religious zealots threatening my friends. Don't worry. I'll keep my head down and stay out of trouble for a few days. Edgewater's anger will cool soon."

We found Captain Tyson standing among a torch-carrying crowd of men. His face was grave as he scanned the blackness settled over open prairie. I suspect he didn't hold much chance for Beth's safety at this point. Pawnee Rock was a meeting place for Indian tribes as well as pioneers headed west. Mac, our scout, had found traces of recent campfires around the base of the rock when we'd first arrived. It was possible someone might have watched our wagon train approach and waited until nightfall to return. Tyson had increased the patrols around our wagon circles after the ambush. Still, it was impossible to hide a large train like ours. The goods we carried – not to mention the government horses – would be a temptation for any thieves or rustlers.

Then there were the rattlesnakes that loved to hunt at night. Father Emilio and I had already cast one out of our path on the short trip from camp to the rock base. Beth wouldn't be the first of our number to suffer a rattler's bite.

"You all know Beth Brewster, Ed's daughter. She's gone off someplace and could be in trouble." Captain Tyson took Ed's arm. "Break into groups of three with at least one torch among you. Ed and I'll head to the top of the rock. Watch out for the damn rattlers."

Lieutenant Saunders joined Father Emilio and me. Lifting his torch higher, he gave us a silent nod. A youthful, clean-shaven face glowed under the light. Tonight's search party was the first occasion I'd had to examine the man closely. Smooth skin and neatly trimmed eyebrows disguised his actual age. I couldn't guess if he were older or younger than I. Saunders kept to himself, never joining in the card games or talks around the fire. I suppose he had to keep the boundaries between him and his men. Luckily for Father Emilio and me, his manner seemed pleasant enough toward us civilians.

"I think you can use an armed man." The lieutenant handed me his torch. "I hope this girl is up to mischief with some young man from the wagon train. She seems the silly sort."

"Silly or no, she is still an innocent," Father Emilio gently chided. "We must not judge unkindly."

He started toward the east. I shrugged at the lieutenant and followed. My money was on the priest seeing us safely along our path as we walked among the unknown. Stars twinkled in a vast sky above us. Though men and torches dotted the landscape, an eerie stillness fell upon the prairie. I hoped Lieutenant Saunders was right about Beth canoodling with some young man.

"If I wanted to take my sweetheart someplace romantic, I'd choose the top of Pawnee Rock or over this way among the wild sunflowers." Lieutenant Saunders gestured toward a point just around the base of the rock, away from the visible wagons. "Let's hope we find the love birds first for the young man's sake. Beth's father is overly keen with his gun."

"You don't have to tell me," I said.

The Ouroboros wriggled upon my torso at the exact moment I saw Beth's ghostly form standing among the sunflowers. Someone's brutal hand had pulled her long auburn hair out in bloody clumps. Beth, dress torn and dark with blood, stared out at the horizon with a confused cry. Her gaze, I noted uncomfortably, shared the same direction as the ghostly mother who'd been calling desperately for her children.

"What's that? It almost looks like a piece of gingham." Lieutenant Saunders hurried forward. "Oh, dear merciful God. It's Beth."

He lurched away and retched in a cluster of sunflowers. Father Emilio and I came to stand at the edge of the gruesome scene. I held the torch higher for the priest, having no need of its light myself. Beth's ghost was enough. She kept her eyes on the horizon as if she didn't notice our presence. I recognized the signs. Grief. Attachment to the circumstances of her death. Beth Brewster was in danger of becoming a lingering specter, stuck at Pawnee Rock for all time.

"Lieutenant," Father Emilio put a hand on the soldier's shoulder. "Perhaps you should go for help. Dun and I can remain here with Beth."

"Take the torch," I said, holding it to the side.

I couldn't look away from Beth's ghost, even as Saunder's trembling fingers pulled the torch from my hand. Wailing her heartbreak into the Kansas night, Beth clutched at the pieces of scalp and auburn strands hanging about her shoulders. Her torment brought back the memory of Angelina, Trip, and Silent Dan with crushing intensity. I'd seen plenty of souls like hers, but they had been strangers. She – like my old troupe - was someone I'd known. I'd let her down. I'd let them all down.

"Beth," I said low. "It's me."

She suddenly became alert, as if my voice woke her from a dream. "You were supposed to meet me. That's why I came, but it was a trick."

"Who tricked you, Beth?"

"The riders," she said. "They're hunting you, Dun."

Then Beth turned her eyes back to the horizon. She was lost once more in the confusing space between the Earthly plane and the afterlife. I couldn't leave her this way. Beth's death was my fault. I'd carelessly showed her some attention. Whoever was following me had noticed and used Beth to hurt me.

"I can't leave you like this," I said.

"What do you propose?" Father Emilio said behind me.

In my distracted shock and horror, I'd forgotten he was there. Trying to persuade Beth's ghost toward the afterlife would be problematic with an audience, especially a priest. My first problem, however, was finding a way to convince Beth to move on. Then a memory touched my mind and lingered for a moment. Hesperos had somehow managed to command the newly Dead toward the afterlife after our camp was attacked. If I shared a piece of the power, as he claimed, perhaps I could send Beth onward?

"I should cover her," I said, moving to take off my coat.

"I think it best Captain Tyson sees Beth first. He may be able to find a clue as to her killer."

Father Emilio lifted sorrowful eyes toward Beth's ghost. He shook his head and moaned with the anguish of a man weary of the world. For a fleeting moment, I wondered if the priest saw her. Impossible. The average human couldn't see the Dead. Some claimed to feel their presence, but not many could prove the otherworldly visitors existed.

"Poor soul," he said.

Then Father Emilio crossed himself and began to pray. Latin flowed across the bloody grass to swirl around Beth's ghost. Nothing happened at first. The priest's voice grew louder, more insistent. Finally, as if shaken from a dream, Beth turned slowly away from the horizon and drifted toward the priest. I stepped back to let her pass. Then I noticed Father Emilio. The good father was glowing in brilliant white light. I had seconds to turn as the Eternal Flame came upon him. Its power filled the bluff and was gone as suddenly as it had descended. I opened my eyes to find Beth's ghost was gone.

"God has given her soul peace."

Father Emilio was watching me. Disappointment reflected upon the priest's face. Cowering under his gaze, I turned away in inexplicable shame. Something important had just happened. Its meaning, however, escaped me. Why did I feel like my mortal soul was toying with damnation?

Torch lights formed a tight cluster back at the base of Pawnee Rock. Their circles of fire suddenly burst apart and reassembled into a fragmented line moments later. Rather than taking comfort in the fast-approaching searchers, my heart filled with dread as I watched the streaming line of fire race toward us.

Captain Tyson was the first to arrive. His eyes were stone as he met my gaze. What could I say to the man? Instead, I gestured toward poor Beth's body, having no words to give him. The wagon master didn't hesitate as he lifted his torch over the corpse. Each silent movement he made while examining the body spoke of his years dealing with death upon the trail.

Rage was on his face as he looked at me again. "Did either of you see anything?"

"No, Captain. Sadly, we were too late to save poor Beth." Father Emilio shook his head. "Evil found this innocent tonight."

Indeed. Evil and perhaps some madness had visited Pawnee Rock, alright. Who else would die because of me? Cold eyes pierced my back. I turned to find Reverend Edgewater and his friends gathered in a group. Ed Brewster was with them. Edgewater, his hand upon Mr. Brewster's shoulder, met my gaze with a triumphant arrogance.

"You take me to my daughter. I want to see her."

"Keep him out of here!" Captain Tyson barked.

Reverend Edgewater stopped the anxious father. "No, Mr. Brewster. There's been an unfortunate accident. Beth has been killed."

"You did this!" Mr. Brewster screamed at me, lifting his gun.

"He couldn't have," Reverend Edgewater squeezed the grieving father's shoulder. "As much as it pains me to be Reverend Dun's alibi, he was with me this evening. Come along. Your wife needs you."

Edgewater threw another gratified look in my direction as he and his blackbirds helped Mr. Brewster to his camp. As much as the heinous accusation offended me, I wasn't going to address it right then. There were too many guns out to suit me.

"What could have done something like that? A rabid pack of wolves? Coyotes, maybe?" Tyson asked. "That poor girl was ripped apart by something. Whatever killed Beth tossed her arms and legs into the grass like trash."

Mr. Black Hat had used subtle means to attack us thus far. This murder had been gruesome and violent. Vicious brutality was more in line with Grizz's style. It wouldn't be the first time he'd tortured a helpless young girl. I'd punished him then. This time, I'd make sure to stop Grizz permanently.

"Whatever it was, nobody goes off on their own from now on." Tyson gave me a frown. "You may want to watch your back for a few days, Dun. Ed is a grieving father. He may not want to listen to reason."

Perfect. I was stranded in the middle of nowhere with a vengeful father. Whoever was behind the hex bag and Beth's murder was making life uncomfortable for me. I needed to find the killers before they could cause more mayhem.

CHAPTER TWENTY-FOUR

Lightning split the world about me with its electric fingers. I stood alone, shivering under nature's violence. Dread engulfed me as my gaze locked upon Fate's minions. The riders stood on the horizon, making black shadows against the sky. Dusters bellowing behind them, they charge forward on their ghostly gray mounts. Hell had come for me. There was no escape this time. I gripped the rifle, knowing it wouldn't do any good against the killers who hunted me.

Tasting the salty blood in my mouth, I prepared to make my last stand.

Something slapped hard against my boot. I came awake with a start. Gray fingers – rotting and lifeless - reached for me from the haze of my dream. Falling short, they curled into angry fists. A woman's frustrated growl rang in my ears before fading away with the last traces of my nightmare.

Cold sweat seeped from my body, soaking my shirt and hair. Then lifting my hat off my face, I saw the wagon master standing over me. Tyson shook his head and pointed at the sun's pink and purple fingers touching the sky.

"We're burnin' daylight, Dun."

I kicked off my blanket with a relieved sigh. The chill of morning sent shivers racing along my body. Thank the generous Lord! Trapped in the tangles of my dream, I worried I might never see another sunrise.

Tyson tossed me a piece of jerky and a corn dodger. "Best not to stay up late praying or whatever you tinhorns do at night. I want to make Fort Wise by nightfall."

The wagon master moved on, passing through the bustle of breakfast and bedrolls. Tyson had recruited every spare man and boy who could hold a gun for guard duty. I had joined the other recruits sleeping in the camp we shared at the center of No Man's Land between the wagon circles.

Tyson and Lieutenant Saunders hadn't precisely agreed on how best to protect the train at night. Joining camps – my idea – had been fiercely rejected by both. Still, I did notice the civilian and government camps were considerably closer together. Beth's grisly death had rattled all of us. Mothers kept their children close in the evenings. No one was allowed to walk alone, not even inside the protective circle. I saw sense in Tyson's order, even though it meant an end to our nightly card game.

Beth's burial had been as disturbing as her death. Holding to the practice of burying their dead under the actual trail, we'd dug Beth's grave and placed her gruesome pieces in the hole. Captain Tyson had directed the Brewster wagon ahead before they'd carried down the body, so Mrs. Brewster wouldn't be forced to roll over her only daughter's bones. I honestly don't think she would have noticed. Mrs. Brewster hadn't said a word since she'd learned of Beth's murder. The poor woman's mind had drifted away. Doc said she was in shock. He didn't seem to hold much hope she'd recover her senses.

"You missed breakfast again," Sergeant Culvers said. "I don't think you'll ever be regular army, Dun."

As the most experienced soldier among us, Culvers had been assigned to babysit we civilian guards. In his mid-thirties, the sergeant had already seen more adventure than most. Life had blessed Culvers with a wicked sense of humor. Of course, I appreciated his skill with a long rifle most. The weapon was a comfort as we guarded the north section of the camp from midnight to two in the morning.

"I'd feel better with four walls about me," Tim Pritchett grumbled, rolling up his blanket. "We should have headed south along the Cimarron Cutoff with the others. It's madness to go the Mountain Route after what happened."

Tim was a young man in his thirties with the soul of a nervous old maid. He'd brought his wife and three children out west in a wagon filled with sharp tools and barrels of perfumed water. Trained as a big city barber, Pritchett had grand plans of taming the West one head at a time. I didn't hold much confidence in Tim's ability to tame anything. He seemed the type to be more comfortable in the safety of a township. Nevertheless, the man gave a good shave. I had to give him that.

"You aren't going to start that again, are you?" Culvers rolled his eyes. "Why don't you go back to Lakin then? It's about five days that way. Or stay in Lamar. I'm sure a slick fellow like yourself can find business. Plenty of beards here."

We'd parted ways with fifty wagons at Lakin, Kansas. They'd taken a route of the Santa Fe Trail cutting through Oklahoma. Granted, it was a hundred miles shorter than the Mountain Route, but Tyson had warned our departing friends the Cimarron Route lacked water this time of year. It had also become deadly during the war. Indian raids had increased with fewer soldiers to protect travelers. Our departing comrades had insisted things were bound to return to normal now the war was over. I wasn't willing to bet my life on it. Most people agreed after Lieutenant Sanders announced he would continue traveling on the Mountain Route to ensure the horses had plenty of water.

"I don't find your sense of humor endearing, Sergeant." Pritchett tugged his hat on with a huff. "We are in the Colorado Territory, don't forget. I dare say the Cheyenne and the Arapahoe are still seeking vengeance for what happened up at Sand Creek last year."

On November 29, 1864, Colonel John Chivington led 675 men to a village north of Lamar. The animals attacked and killed hundreds of Cheyenne and Arapahoe. I'd heard conversations about the massacre over a few card games. One of the players was an ex-military man. He reckoned over two-thirds of the victims had been women and children. I couldn't blame the Cheyenne or the Arapahoe for wanting vengeance, though I kept my opinions to myself in the present company.

"The Sioux may be involved as well, or so I've heard. It's an all-out war on the civilized, gentlemen, and I don't want to be the next victim," Pritchett said.

"Any coffee left, Culvers?" I asked, cutting Tim off before he could build up a full head of steam.

"Sorry, no." Culvers stood and slapped his hands together. "Get packing. We leave in ten minutes."

The strange dream still clung to my mind, making my brain foggy as I packed up my bedroll. None of us could afford to daydream or dawdle. The Colorado Territory was dangerous country. Word around our campfire suggested many of the soldiers and guards expected to fight our way to Fort Wise.

I mounted my army mule, Pepe, with a yawn and prodded him forward. "I'll give you an extra sugar cube tonight, Pepe, if you stay on the smooth part of the trail."

Weeks of prairie grass and dust were wearing on my patience. A sore backside was making my temper worse. Tyson had said we were close to Fort Wise. If this was the Colorado Territory, where were the mountains and evergreen trees? I slapped away a fly buzzing around my nose. According to my calendar, summer should be fading into early fall. Instead, the heat, much like the prairie land about me, spanned on forever. Maybe I had landed in Hell and didn't know it.

Sleepy faces waited for Captain Tyson to start the wagons moving. They barely acknowledged my passing, but I wasn't offended. No one was getting much sleep after the events of Pawnee Rock. Edgewater's blackbirds had found six more hex bags. Using the little bags to spread suspicion, he and his cronies continued to stir up trouble around the camp. The zealots insisted Beth's death proved their nonsensical witchcraft theory.

Steering Pepe toward the middle of the long line of civilian wagons, I made a sleepy effort to catch up to my friends. I didn't like leaving Winnie and Domingo to carry on without me. Edgewater's faithful had tried to intrude on them a few times. Between Winnie's temper and my gun, we prodded them back to their side of the camp circle.

"Hello, my friend."

Father Emilio's scrawny legs bounced wildly against the army mule he straddled. White knuckles awkwardly gripping the reins, the priest was at the mercy of his mount. He flapped his arms toward Heaven as if praying for salvation from the beast's ire. The mule, utterly unsympathetic to its rider's precarious balance, fell at last into a lazy walk beside Pepe.

Swallowing a grunt of unexpected laughter, I nodded my head in greeting. "Where are you headed in such a hurry?"

"Captain Tyson has summoned me to the front of the train." The priest's head swiveled to look over his shoulder. "It would appear others answer the summons as well."

His usual quick smile absent, Sergeant Culvers galloped around the oxen teams to join us. Grumbling a rushed greeting to me, he grabbed Father Emilio's reins. The startled mule gave the sergeant an angry heehaw. Culvers tugged the reins again and wrapped them around his saddle horn.

"I've got to get you to Tyson in double time, Father. We need a translator." Culvers turned his worried eyes to me. "You too, Dun. We have some unfriendly guests calling on our wagon train. Bring your rifle."

CHAPTER TWENTY-FIVE

Following Culvers toward the front of the wagon train, I stayed at the rear as Father Emilio rode between us. The Ouroboros suddenly came awake. Its body writhed frantically under my shirt. Something had brought the Dead out among the prairie grass. Considering the snake's wild undulations, I'd guessed their number to be more than a mere handful.

The Dead sprouted out of the prairie grass and rushed toward me. They brandished their fleshless fists and lifted their voices in a cacophony of unintelligible words. Some were Cheyenne or Arapahoe, but others among their numbers wore garments suggestive of many different tribes.

I scanned the plains for red lights, but Mr. Black Hat seemed to be sitting this attack out today. Unlike the Undead that attacked our camp, these souls were in spirit form. Angry, they may be, but they were powerless to attack. Still, I wasn't keen to have a few dozen angry ghosts surrounding me.

Ten Cheyenne – Living this time – rode their horses through the angry Dead. An explosion of feathers protruded in every direction from the headdresses they wore. Porcupine quills and beads decorated buffalo skin sashes resting against their bodies. The Cheyenne braves, armed for battle, were ready for any misstep on our part. These warriors, however, didn't need weapons to get their point across. Their venomous mask of pure hatred radiated under the startling monochromatic war paint they wore.

"Oh dear," Father Emilio said. "These are dog soldiers. It would seem our visitors aren't here for friendly conversation."

"Dog soldiers?"

"They are the Cheyenne's deadliest warriors. I have heard tales of their ferocity in battle." The priest crossed himself with a troubled frown. "They are opposed to colonizers in their lands. I don't believe they will exercise patience for much longer. We must hurry."

Tyson waited for us with a few of his men. Their bodies made a thin line between our new guests and the families they protected. The train was deathly still as Pioneer and Cheyenne sat on their mounts, regarding each other with tense suspicion.

"It's about damn time," Tyson said as Culvers brought us to a stop. "Father, can you translate for us? We want to be on our way in peace. It's less than a day to Fort Wise."

Father Emilio maneuvered his donkey a few paces before their horses. The priest's voice remained steady as he began to speak in the Cheyenne's tongue. Angry words met his calm ones. One of the dog soldiers lifted a rifle and gestured pointedly at the priest's heart. I took my rifle out of the holster and rested it pointedly across my lap as a show of support. Father Emilio turned and motioned for me to holster my rifle back on Pepe.

"Where did he learn to speak Cheyenne?" I asked.

"Who knows?" Tyson murmured. "I'm just damn glad he can."

A man steered his horse slowly around the line of dog soldiers. He seemed different from the rest. Rather than the elaborate headdress of the Cheyenne warriors, this man wore an animal skull atop his head, fastened with braids of dark hair. Black paint made horizontal stripes down his face. Intense eyes, glaring between the thick lines, locked upon me. He carried no weapons, but something about the man gave my already ragged nerves a fresh jolt of apprehension.

Father Emilio turned his mule to see both the Cheyenne and Captain Tyson. "Their leader will not give me his name. He believes we are unworthy of such pleasantries."

"Considering how well armed they are, I'm not about to argue over the social niceties," Culvers murmured.

"He says there have been killings on the plains," Father Emilio told us. "Men, women, and children from the southern villages were brutally slaughtered. They believe it was us. No one else has traveled upon their lands for many days."

"We've stayed on the trail. Tell him, Father. Nobody in this group has left the train." Tyson shifted in his saddle. "We're no murderers."

"Depends on who you ask, I suppose."

Hesperos stood inches away from Pepe. Why he'd chosen now to reappear was anyone's guess. The Dead certainly noticed his sudden appearance. They backed away from him, nervously whispering to one another. Hesperos, for his part, ignored them.

"Careful, Dunham." He waved a finger at me. "Best not to speak to me out loud. Some might mistake you for a lunatic again."

"You realize I don't miss you when you're away?"

"That's hurtful." Hesperos gestured toward the Cheyenne. "I believe you have an admirer."

The lone rider with the black stripes down his face thrust a finger at me. His words were sharp and urgent. Whatever he said made the dog soldiers pull their weapons. The lone rider lifted a short staff from the fasten on his horse and waved it in the space between us. Bones affixed to the wood by leather strands banged together as it moved.

"I think this is a holy man. He carries a spirit staff. If I understand him correctly, he believes you to be a demon. I cannot entirely understand what he says. My Sioux is not good." Father Emilio frowned at me. "One thing is clear. He has ordered your death."

"Oh dear," Hesperos cried in mock concern. "The Cheyenne have such inventive methods of killing their enemies. Add a touch of Sioux, and we are in for an interesting time. I suppose there's only one thing to do. Show them your Ouroboros."

I shook my head. There was no way I'd expose the snake tattoo. If the Sioux holy man suspected I was evil now, what would he think after seeing what the Ouroboros could do? And what would Tyson and the others think? I dare say any pagan shenanigans would get me kicked off the wagon train or worse. I could almost smell the tar and feathers.

"Very well," Hesperos said and turned to go. "Enjoy the torture. Call for me when you've had enough pain. I might come."

The holy man lifted his voice in a single command, gesticulating his spirit staff at me. His companions rode forward, weapons out. Echoing war cries in the prairie grass surrounded us. The wagon train was doomed if I didn't do something. Damn it. I had no other choice.

Fumbling with the fastens on my vest, I threw the garment to the ground and began unbuttoning my shirt. I was moving too slowly. The dog soldiers were almost upon me. I ripped the buttons away and opened the fabric, exposing the Ouroboros. The snake undulated in angry slithers upon my chest. It was ready to strike.

"Brujo!"

The holy man muttered several more words. Eyes wild with fear, he continued to stab the staff toward me. The leader of the dog soldiers moved his horse beside his chanting companion. I held my breath as they exchanged heated words. Their leader gave me a final contemptuous look before ordering his men to retreat behind the chanting holy man.

"What in God's name is going on?" Tyson managed to ask.

"The holy man says Reverend Dun is a brujo. It is a Spanish word. I'd prefer not to speak its meaning," Father Emilio said, crossing himself as he stared at the Ouroboros. "What have you brought among us?"

"You know what this is?" I prodded Pepe forward closer to the holy man. "Tell me!"

"Be still, Dun. Their leader asks the holy man if our deaths would remove the evil from among them. Oh, my young friend. What have you brought down upon us?"

"Ask him what this tattoo is," I growled. "I need to know if he can remove it."

"He repeats the word brujo. The rest is in Sioux. I don't understand him."

Tyson grabbed my arm with a warning squeeze. He'd have to make a move soon, but would he still be on my side? Damn it. I'd put Tyson in an impossible situation. The honorable thing for me to do was to go with the Cheyenne. Then again, I'd done the right thing when I was thirteen. Look where honestly had landed me back then. I'd survived by my wits for most of my life. My brains would have to see us through this now.

"Tell them I'll call to their dead if they don't let us go." I ignored the horrified look on Father Emilio's face. "Do it, Father."

The unhappy priest repeated the words, nearly retching on them. I kept my eyes on the nervous Cheyenne. They were watching. The dog soldiers hesitated as I opened my shirt wider. Writhing along my skin, the snake seemed to grow. Its teeth bit down savagely upon its own flesh. Power began to build along its long body. This con had better work soon. I had no way of controlling where the Ouroboros would strike.

Humans weren't always the most aware creatures the good lord put on the Earth. Animals, on the other hand, could see through the veil. Screaming, the horses began to buck and kick. Our mules, including the loyal Pepe, stomped and heehawed as they tried to back away.

Fear blanketed the holy man's eyes. It was as if he couldn't tear his gaze away from the snake's mesmerizing dance. Finally, he snapped his face toward Father Emilio. He shouted a stream of words at the priest and kicked his panicked mount into a run.

The dog soldiers swung their horses about and followed the holy man. Their leader remained behind long enough to deliver final threatening words to Father Emilio. Then thundering off toward the west, he disappeared with the others in the grass and wildflowers of the prairie. Their dead lingered, watching me with lifeless eyes. Then they slowly drifted away, following the Living Cheyenne. I'd have to worry about them later.

"Well?" Tyson asked. "Are we going to see tomorrow?"

"He warned they would follow us as long as they are able. I believe he means to track us until our train leaves the banks of the Arkansas River at the stage stop near La Junta. We are to leave their lands and make sure the Brujo doesn't remain behind," Father Emilio said. "If we try to…to kill Dun, then their weapons will rain down upon us. They do not want his death curse visited upon their lands. I suggest we do as they ask."

"Agreed," Tyson said.

Then the butt of his rifle struck hard against my skull. So much for friendship and mutual respect. Black covered my vision as my body tumbled backward over Pepe's tail and into oblivion.

CHAPTER TWENTY-SIX

Swaying and bouncing until my head pounded, I woke to the musky smell of hot canvas and kerosene. My wrists were bound tightly behind my back. Lifting my face off the fabric, I twisted awkwardly to position my nose away from the flammable liquid. Damn that, Tyson. My head was a fuzzy mess of pain from when he struck me.

Shifting my face toward the sky, I laid back again with a disheartened moan. Something hard poked at my backside under the cover. I smoothed at the lump with numb fingertips. Farm tools ready to trade at Boggsville or maybe Pueblo. I'd put those in the 'assets' column upon my mental tally board.

Summoning my wits, I began to take stock of my situation. Someone had ripped off my collar. My money was on Reverend Edgewater. He was most likely trying to prevent me from continuing the pretense. I wondered if the jackass had any idea he'd been ripping his garments. My shirt was intact, at least. Heaven's children didn't want the painted snake free to tempt the curious.

Two oxen at the front of a team nodded at the trail behind me. Pulling a loaded prairie schooner, they seemed resigned to their fate. The driver of the team, who'd been staring at me, quickly turned away. He smoothed a hand upon the nearest ox and fixed his eyes straight ahead. I didn't recognize him or the little blond girl waving at me from the wagon seat. Clad in a pretty blue dress and hat, she was ready for Sunday church.

"Hello," I said.

"Easy now, mister. We had a hell of a time finding anyone to carry you. Don't make these folks more uneasy than they are."

I twisted my head a little more to identify the rider. Ned Walters. I'd noticed him riding alongside the wagons while on guard duty, but we'd never met. The man had a reputation for being hard, and not the sort of person Tyson wanted amongst the sensitive ears of the ladies or children. If the stories around the camps were true, Walters wasn't the sort you wanted to make angry. Those who had ended up with a knife in their back, or so the rumors said.

"What happened to your fingers?" I asked, eyeing the red splotches dotting the bandages around his hand. "Cut yourself shaving?"

"Dios nos proteja!"

I tilted my head toward the front of the buckboard. Another new traveler stared back at me. Red-faced and sweating like a boiler, the driver of my wagon gave me an unhappy frown. Sweat dripped off his bushy mustache. Droplets dotted what I supposed was a new shirt. He and the family behind us weren't pioneers.

Walters spat a clump of tobacco in the space between us, earning him a glare from the wagon's driver. Ignoring the merchant, he waved his bandaged hand at my chest with a grunt.

"Thought I'd skin me a snake, but it bit back."

I laughed and shook my head. "Don't you think I've tried knives to be rid of it? You should have asked me first. I might have spared you a few fingers."

My probing hands found a small opening in the canvas. Suppressing a wince as my skin met steel, I allowed the small sliver of hope to creep into my mind. Lady Luck had decided to put her helping hand upon me. My friend, the merchant, hadn't secured his farm equipment as he should, leaving me a way to get clear of the wagon train. Perfect timing too. It wouldn't be long before other curious men with knives came to have a go at my tattoo. Carefully positioning the rope against the bare blade, I began to rub slowly. Still fascinated with the bites on his fingers, Walters didn't notice my wrists moving.

"Reverend Edgewater says your magic is what keeps the snake alive,"

he said, still staring at his blood-stained bandages.

Naturally, that stuffed-up old goat was behind the wagon train's fear of me. We'd gotten off to an ugly start the first moment we'd met. In retrospect, I supposed I could have done more to smooth things over.

"Nonsense," I said. "No one believes I'm an evil spirit."

Walters pointed north over the wagon bed. "They do."

Distant riders matched our pace over the grasslands. The Cheyenne dog soldiers were following us with the intensity of a bear watching fish swim upriver. Eyes glued to my wagon, the dog soldiers appeared ready to charge us at any moment.

"They won't give up. The commander at Fort Wise took one look at them and told us to keep moving."

"That wasn't very neighborly," I said.

"Can't say that I blame him. Fort Wise was hit hard by the Cheyenne a few days ago. They have troubles of their own."

"I and others travel with you for protection. Thank our merciful God, the journey to La Junta is quick!" The merchant issued a stream of Spanish to his bored mule team and crossed himself. "Many on the wagon train have grown angry because the commander turned you away. Reverend Edgewater has threatened to take action." He crossed himself again. "May God grant us mercy."

"I have a feeling God is busy with other things," I said. "Oh. And thank you for giving me a ride, friend."

"No. No, you would not be in this wagon if not for Father Emilio." The driver's frightened eyes nervously shifted away from the snake hidden beneath my shirt. "He blessed me with extra protection against whatever demon you have inside you."

"And where is the good father?" I asked.

"The holy men ride at the front of the wagon train now. They protect us from evil," he said. "I wish they had not left me alone with a demon and the unholy who plays with snakes."

"Which one are you?" I asked Walters.

"Let's ask our new visitors," Walters said with a grunt.

Men, angry and armed, marched up the long line of wagons toward us. Edgewater was at the head of the mob, beaming with righteous indignation. He waved the bible over his head like a banner. His flock had grown. I recognized a few heathens I'd played cards with among them.

"It looks like you are a curiosity now, Dun." Walters grinned.

Rubbing my restraints harder against the blade, I began weighing my options. If I ran into the plains, the Cheyenne and their allies would capture me. If I stayed where I was, the zealots would kill me. I looked at Walters. He gave me a lazy shrug.

"Stop!" Edgewater called. "You have the Devil's own in your wagon."

"Better do as he says, Amigo," Walters told the merchant. "Ain't no priest around to protect you from a mob."

The merchant pulled his mule team to a halt and climbed off his perch. He gave me one last troubled frown before joining the mules at the front of the wagon. I couldn't blame him. A mob, like a hungry animal, can turn vicious. The beast doesn't care about harming innocent bystanders when its rage is fully fueled. Regret comes afterward.

Winnie, dress pulled up past her ankles, ran toward us from the west. Domingo matched her pace. He carried a rifle resting on the sling, holding his injured arm in place. They beat the mob to my wagon. My friends stood stubbornly in the thin ribbon of dirt between the angry mob and me. I well recognized the determined look on Winnie's face. They'd get themselves killed protecting me. Edgewater already suspected Winnie of being a witch.

"You have no right to take justice into your own hands. The Wagon Master and the Army will decide what happens to Dun," she said.

"Foul creature! You dare speak to Heaven's children? It is my sacred duty to kill any witch I come across. It says so in the Old Testament." Edgewater thrust his finger at Winnie. "Take her."

The reverend's face twisted into a distorted mask of hateful glee. Leathery skin, bubbling with boils, covered Edgewater's head from chin to crown. In his eyes, I imagined I saw the fires of Hell dancing within the black orbs. Then the moment passed, and he was human again. What had I just witnessed? Perhaps his brief metamorphosis was the concoction of my panicked mind.

I pulled at the fraying ropes binding my wrists and gave one last tug. My restraints came free. I dove for the container of kerosene I'd smelled in the back of the wagon. Angelina had shown me a cheap conjuror's trick using fuel to 'magically' summon a ball of fire in my hand. Making flame out of seemingly thin air would hold off the mob until Winnie, Domingo, and I could find Tyson. If the zealots were convinced I was a demon, then it was high time I acted like one. I just needed a catalyst to light the flame.

"Look!" One of the men cried. "He's on fire!"

I held my hands before me. They were aglow alright, but not with real fire. Magic pulsed bright red about me, engulfing my body in angry power. Fire sparked in bursts along my arms. I twisted my wrist and gasped with the crowd as a ball of flame floated inches above my palm.

"Leave her alone," I warned. "If I can make fire, don't you think I could bewitch a woman? Maybe I bewitched the whole train?"

"Spawn of the Devil! I knew it!" Edgewater let the triumphant grin spread across his face. "You deserve to die after what you did to those children. Where are your hex bags and Devil's tricks now? I say we burn him right here."

"Try it!" I extended the fireball out toward the crowd. "Who do you suppose will burn who?"

Then a shot struck close to the toe of Edgewater's boot. Captain Tyson rode his horse into the mob and sent them scrambling. Several soldiers were with him, as was Father Emilio riding hard on his borrowed mule. Their sudden appearance chased the fiery hue from my body.

"I've had my fill of trouble from you, Edgewater. You and your flock are off the wagon train. Go back to Fort Wise and stay there until another train comes along. I expect one will turn up in about a month." Captain Tyson lowered his barrel toward Edgewater's nose. "The Cheyenne want Dun alive, and he's going to stay that way until I see we're safe. I have a responsibility to the people of this wagon train. If keeping Dun in one piece holds off an Indian attack, then that's the way it's going to be." Tyson lifted his eyes to the other men standing among the cluster of black coats. "You other men get back to your families, or you'll be joining Edgewater at Fort Wise."

Edgewater - thwarted and humiliated - slunk toward his wagon with the rest of the mob. The parting glare he gave me was anything but friendly. It wasn't over. Not for him.

"That light show of yours was pretty impressive," Winnie said, coming to stand beside the wagon. "You alright?"

I'd warned Winnie I wasn't a good person. She knew better than anyone what a con artist could do. I tried to be the man she thought I could become, but trouble always seemed to find me no matter what guise I put on. Seeing the disappointment on her face was more than I could stand. I shook my head and turned away. Friendship with me would cost Winnie more than she knew. So, I'd do the decent thing this time for her sake and end it.

"Now you're acting like a mark. I don't have any more use for you," I said, closing the door on the only friends I had in the world. "Take Domingo with you, and don't come back."

"Just you remember this, Dun," she said. "I know you're a good man at heart. Keep your feet on the right path, and you'll find your way."

Then Winnie was gone, taking all my faith with her. I was alone again with just the Ouroboros for company. The snake had guarded my money belt out of sheer spite rather than loyalty. But gold wasn't doing me much good here in the middle of nowhere. San Francisco and Lucky Sal's gambling house were a fantasy now, far out of my reach. Here in the harsh realities of life on the Santa Fe Trail, my fate rested once again upon Captain Tyson's strength and goodwill.

Chapter Twenty-Seven

Tyson kept us on the move, bypassing the expected stop at Boggsville to trade goods. Many of our group were disappointed, but no one openly complained. Our perilous situation remained at the forefront of everyone's mind. How could any of us forget? The dog soldiers were a constant presence. True to their word, they rode through the prairie grass parallel to our train. The Cheyenne would not allow us to ignore Captain Tyson promise.

Most of the pioneers kept their eyes straight ahead as we traveled along the banks of the Arkansas River. Making the most of my comfortable spot inside the merchant's wagon, I contemplated the horizons in all directions. Mountains and evergreen trees were still absent from the Colorado landscape. The river, at least, added a bit of interest.

Many of my former comrades were outspoken in resenting of my humane treatment. Indeed, if not for Father Emilio's reassurances, I'd have been shuffling behind the wagon train as a prisoner on a chain gang. My host, the merchant, continued to refuse me his name. Demons and their masters, he insisted, could use such knowledge to take his soul.

Morning had passed into afternoon before the driver spoke again. "I'll soon be rid of you, thank the Holy Lord."

Walters, equally startled, dropped a practiced hand to his gun. He shook his head and gave me a grunt when the merchant said an incoherent prayer of thanks to the heavens. Gesturing toward our escorts with his empty gun hand, Walters whistled a signal to another guard riding beside a group of wagons ahead of us.

Dust clouds swelled in explosions of dirt as the dog soldiers rode their mounts back toward the east. The Sioux holy man remained behind. He pressed his hand to his chest, mirroring the same position as the Ouroboros upon mine. Then he pointed at me with the tip of his knife. The warning was clear. An ugly death awaited me if I ever returned. I released an anxious breath as the holy man turned his horse and took an urgent pace after his companions.

"Why now?" I asked. "I'd assumed they'd follow us until our train turned south."

"There's your answer." Walters pointed at a large pile of crumbling ruins. "We've reached Bent's Old Fort. A great many folks died in this area from Cholera back in '49. The tribes have a long memory." He wiped the sweat from his face with a dusty sleeve. "As I recall from some old duffers back in Lakin, William Bent burned it down."

Located in the middle of nowhere, Bent's Old Fort once was a gathering place in the wilderness where people of many different cultures and languages had coexisted in the name of Capitalism. I ran an appraising eye over the decrepit buildings. The fort wasn't a merchant's paradise anymore. Abandoned by its owner and clientele, the blackened remains fell into ruin decades ago. Now it was simply another vanishing landmark to guide travelers to a popular junction on the Santa Fe Trail.

Sergeant Culvers had talked the other volunteer guards and me through our route one night at the campfire. He'd told us La Junta was a few hours west of Bent's Old Fort. If I headed south at the junction in La Junta, I'd continue to Santa Fe. Going north on the pioneer trail would eventually lead me to Denver.

An idea began to grow, bringing much-needed hope with it. Pueblo was roughly seventy-five miles up the pioneer road after splitting with the Santa Fe Trail. I'd make it if I stuck close to the Arkansas River. Its waters would feed me and quench my thirst. Then again, traveling on foot would certainly slow me down. It might take four or five days if I matched a wagon's pace. Stealing a mule would solve my problem, but Culvers might take it personally and come after me.

I wiped the sweat off my forehead with a ragged sleeve. Planning my journey was easy when the weather was good, but winter came quicker to the Rockies than it did for most places. I might not make San Francisco this year. Hell, I seriously doubted I'd make it out of Colorado before snow flies.

Spending the Winter months in Pueblo wasn't ideal, but the stopover would ensure I'd stay alive. Then I could travel the remaining one hundred miles to Denver when Spring arrived. Not that I'd stay in the troubled city for long. A fire had burned the city's business district to the ground two years ago. Then a devastating flood killed twenty residents the following year.

Denver's current misfortune, however, troubled me the most. News of an Indian war in the area had put the territory on alert. Violence had cut off all food supplies to the city. I wasn't counting on a quick end to the war. Best to give Denver a wide birth.

Yes. It was a good plan, provided I could escape first. My old traveling companions hadn't taken their eyes off me for a moment. I wasn't aware of Captain Tyson's plans, but I'd guessed they didn't involve a warm welcome back into the fold for poor Reverend Dun.

"Pull up here, driver," Walters called to the merchant.

Our wagon swayed as its wheels moved out of the worn trail ruts. Brittle prairie grass and tall sunflowers crumbled beneath our weight as we rolled to a stop. Walters, unmoved by the destruction, dismounted and tied his reins to the side of the buckboard. Keeping his eyes fixed upon me, the guard shoved a hand against the back of the wagon bed. The wooden gate dropped open with a noisy thump.

Walters shook his head as he slipped the knife out of his belt and sliced the ropes binding my legs. "I don't mind saying, I'd have like to see you hang. That snake of yours would lose its bite once you were dead." He shrugged his shoulders with a sigh. "Not up to me, though."

"I'm glad to hear it."

"Stop, I implore you! Harming Dun is not necessary." Father Emilio waved as he made a surprisingly quick run toward us. "The dog soldiers are gone. No harm has come to the wagon train."

"I agree with the father," I said.

"Ain't no call for the heroics, Priest." Walters spat again and gave the knife to Father Emilio while he held the gun on me. "Captain Tyson says to cut Dun loose. I mean to drive him off if he won't go."

Father Emilio cut the bonds around my wrists and handed the knife back. "I will see to Dun. You should report to Captain Tyson."

"On your head, be it." Walters shrugged and mounted his horse again.

We watched in uncomfortable silence as he rode off. Good riddance! I was glad to see the back of him. Walters was a wild card in the deck. If Captain Tyson or Father Emilio hadn't taken an interest in my wellbeing, I might have a nasty hole in my head about now.

Walters wasn't the only soul anxious to see me go. Many of my fellow travelers cast uneasy glances in our direction as their wagons rolled past. Father Emilio met their eyes with uncharacteristic scorn. For my part, I avoided unfriendly gazes when guns were present. Luck was a fickle thing. I didn't want to sour the odds.

"That was pretty brave, father." I eased off the wagon and stood on solid ground at last. "The trip to Santa Fe might be a little chilly for you from now on. You've helped Satan's spawn after all."

"I do not think you're wicked, my young friend. Perhaps, instead, you are a victim by evil's hand? The Sioux holy man called you a "Brujo" back on the plains. It is a Spanish term meaning Sorcerer. His word is not quite right." The priest turned troubled eyes upon me. "You can see the Dead. I believe a Necromancer may have cast a spell upon you."

"You may be right," I told him. "My father was a fire and brimstone preacher back East. Of course, he wasn't as free-spirited as the good Reverend Dun."

"Ah! Now I understand how you managed your disguise so well."

"Some things you never forget," I said. "I fell ill with a high fever when I was thirteen. The sickness brought me close to death. It brought me other things too." I patted the snake upon my torso. "My father saw the Ouroboros and began all sorts of rituals to banish it. He sent me to Grace Church Almshouse and Asylum when he found out I could see the Dead."

"That was unnecessarily cruel," Father Emilio said.

"He wasn't the sympathetic or nurturing type. I was on my own. After a particularly violent incident in the asylum, I escaped." I pushed the memory back into the dark recesses of my mind. "I've been running since, but you can't elude the Dead."

I scanned the ruins of Bent's Old Fort, suddenly apprehensive about drawing Hesperos or his pet to us. "A few weeks ago, a man showed up and told me he was the one who gave me the Ouroboros. He and his monster have been following me ever since."

"The Necromancer," Father Emilio said with distaste. "Did he say what he wants with you?"

"He said something about the two of us joining." Father Emilio waited with strained patience as I hesitated. "Here's the thing. I think he really can use magic. I know it sounds crazy, but I've seen him do things I can't explain. And so can the other man, who keeps trying to kill me."

"I worry for you, Dun. Please come to Santa Fe with us. My brothers and I can find a way to release you from this curse."

"I'm not sure Tyson would allow it."

"He only objects to your mark," Father Emilio said, reaching out to touch my chest.

Large wings slapped at the air directly above us as ripples of energy surrounded me. The priest yanked his hand back as a sizzling zap struck his fingers. Father

Emilio growled at the crow flying over our heads. It cackled with laughter and soared high out of the priest's reach. Doran. Hesperos' pet was watching, after all. It wasn't going to be easy getting the creature off my trail.

The good-intentioned Father Emilio was bound to get hurt if I didn't part company with him soon. Ordinarily, I wouldn't have cared about a pliable mark like the priest, but I'd changed on the Santa Fe Trail. People had respected and befriended me. We'd counted on each other to survive. The experience may not have turned me into a good man, but it made me want to be.

Father Emilio gripped my arm. "We will find a way to sneak you onto the wagon train."

I shook my head with a frown. "You've risked too much for me already, Father. It's best if I head away from the train."

"Very well. Come to me if ever you want help ridding yourself of that cursed tattoo. I'll do what I can."

"One day, I might just take you up on the offer." I rubbed my wrist where the rope had chafed my skin. "Do you think a man can change his destiny, Father?"

"I do not know, my young friend. But, for your sake, I hope so."

A small parade of wagons rolled around the main group and headed along the deep tracks of a side trail. Most were newcomers who'd joined us at Fort Wise. My nervous driver, free of his burdensome passenger, spurred his mule team after them. The little blond girl and her family followed to bring up the rear.

"Someone's in a hurry."

"They try to make up time on the pioneer road headed to Pueblo." Father Emilio shook his head and crossed himself. "God guide their journey. Perhaps you could run and catch them?"

"Somehow, I don't think they'd like me as a passenger."

It was time to part company. I nodded my thanks to Father Emilio and turned pointedly toward the northwest. My boots hurried forward, kicking dust as I went. Winnie and Domingo would be coming along soon. My courage would fail me if I saw their disappointed faces.

A horse approached from the west. It was Tyson. He stopped his mount, blocking my path. The wagon master tossed me a bedroll and a small sack of food. The rifle I'd used to protect the train was conspicuously absent.

"I don't know what devilment you're involved in, Dun, but I'm no murderer," he said. "It's not right leaving you out here alone. I'd rather take you as far as Fort Union to repay what you've done for our wagon train, but I was outvoted." Tyson rubbed at the stubble on his chin. "Stay close to the riverbank. You might run into a few trappers. Maybe they'll take you as far as Trinidad."

Then the wagon master nodded silently and spurred his mount back toward his place at the head of the train. I sat down out of sight under a thin cluster of trees, watching as the last wagon disappeared into the western horizon. Pueblo was a long walk. It was best to start after a good night's sleep.

Day slowly abandoned me to a Colorado night. I stretched across my bedroll and stared at the vast expanse of stars. It was lonely without the comfortable company of my friends. Leaving Winnie and Domingo resurrected the profound loss I'd experienced after the deaths of Angelina, Trip, and Silent Dan.

I rubbed at the thick beard forming along my jawline. It wasn't my favorite look, but I supposed it suited me for now. The reverend's disguise had played out. Time for a change, but what would fit? Dunham Raynor. Now that was a character I didn't know how to play. Maybe here in the Colorado wilderness, I'd found my opportunity to redefine him. Letting my eyes close, I relaxed to the distant sounds of the Arkansas running along its banks. Plans for future adventures could wait until morning.

A sudden touch of evil invaded my peaceful reverie. Then I saw them. Thundering hooves and billowing dusters. Ghostly hands clutched at ethereal reins as their steeds raced along the banks of a river. Screams and impotent shots rang out into the night.

"No time for dreaming, Dunham." My stalker knelt beside my bedroll. "You've got company. Put the Santa Fe Trail behind you."

I threw off the blanket in a daze. What had I just seen? Were the images some sort of vision? I didn't recognize the riders invading my dreams, but their anger with me was evident. Hesperos waited impatiently for the fog to leave my brain. His concern for my sake left me with the impression he knew about the nightmarish riders.

"What do you want from me?"

"How many times must I explain, Dunham? I suppose we could sit and chat until Reverend Edgewater's witch-burning party comes."

Hesperos stood away and moved like a wraith deeper into the shadows. Following his robed form, I stayed low and kept to the edge of the tree line. My campfire had died hours before. It must be well past midnight. Then my sleepy eyes spotted the danger. Reverend Edgewater and his fellow blackbirds were coming. Their torches swayed and bounced along the road. Murder was easier in the dark, I supposed.

Religious zealots never changed. They were the same from one end of the country to the other. I wondered, not for the first time, what Heaven thought about such madmen killing in its name. This particular set of witch-burners had enough firepower to make me consider abandoning my bedroll and supplies. No. I'd have to risk the extra seconds it would take to pack my things. Traveling through such a rugged territory without supplies was suicide.

"Show yourself, Dun!" Edgewater shouted. "I know Tyson threw you off the wagon train here."

"Join with me now and never fear men such as these again," Hesperos said.

"I'm not doing anything blindly for you, Hesperos. You need to explain yourself and your intentions."

"Reckless fool." Hesperos stepped into the shadows and was gone.

Tucking my bedroll and the food sack under my arm, I moved through the trees. An alarming number of torches set the ruts of the Santa Fe Trail alight. Losing them in the darkness would be tricky. I crept toward the west, hoping to head north once I'd left the mob behind.

"Going somewhere, Satan's Spawn?"

A wall of torches burst into flame, blocking my path. Reverend Edgewater was cleverer than I'd thought. Yes. Hunting down heathens required sharp thinking. Two of his followers stood beside him with guns pointed at my tattoo. They'd brought more firepower this time. It would appear by the hatred upon their faces that these men of God had left Christ's mercy back in Fort Wise.

Chapter Twenty-Eight

The thick odor of burning kerosene soured the air. Torches, their flames flickering wildly in the wind, bobbed atop the midnight prairie. Faces began to form in the narrow light beneath their burning bodies. Men from Edgewater's group mixed with a handful of unfamiliar faces. Soldiers, still dressed in uniform, were among them. I'd guess they had temporarily deserted Fort Wise for tonight's party. Armed to kill, they weren't roaming in hostile territory for tea and cookies in the middle of the night.

Rushing blood pounded in my ears, sending a wave of panic over me. Every con artist feared the day they'd be snared. Planning escape routes and glancing over our shoulders on the lookout for zealous enemies was a way of life. Most of us believed a shot in the back was preferable to judgment from an angry mob. Of course, I wasn't in the grave yet. If I was breathing, I still had a chance to talk my way to freedom.

"Oh, thank our merciful God," I cried. "A search party at last! I've been abandoned here in the wilderness."

"Foul creature of Satan's teat!" Edgewater lifted his bible before him though it was too dark to read the words. "God's justice has found you."

"Listen to me! My name is Reverend Dun. I've been wrongly accused of witchcraft and left here to die."

A few of the fresh faces exchanged unsure whispers as they looked from me to Reverend Edgewater. Good. All I needed was a few seeds of doubt. The blackbirds I recognized from our wagon train, however, were undeterred. They waved their torches like swords of devouring fire. Outraged cries of 'demon' and 'sorcerer' circled the mob. The choir reached a crescendo but abruptly fell silent when a single gunshot rang above our heads.

"You didn't say nothing about no preacher!"

My somewhat tattered savior stood at the edge of the torches. Dressed in pelts and a badger cap, the trapper chewed enthusiastically on his wad of tobacco. Shrewd eyes looked me over. Finally, he grunted and spat a dark stream onto the ground.

"I tracked him down for ye," he said. "Pay me my ten dollars. I've earned the money ye owe me. What you do after I leave is your business."

"How many others among you have been paid to harass me? Reverend Edgewater took an instant dislike to me the moment we met. He seems willing to commit murder in his hatred," I said, hoping to address the more reasonable souls in the mob. "As the good book says, 'refrain from anger and turn from wrath; do not fret – it leads only to evil. For those who are evil will be destroyed, but those who hope in the Lord will inherit the land.' Psalm 37:8-9"

"Demons know God's word when it suits them." Reverend Edgewater held his torch up higher. "You take pleasure in mocking me. That tongue of yours made me look foolish among our traveling companions."

"You didn't need my help."

"Ah! The famous wit. You beguiled Mrs. Maxwell and Captain Tyson. Even the priest succumbed to your lies." Edgewater leaned closer with the confidence of a man holding a royal flush. "Why don't you open your shirt? Let these men see the snake hiding under your skin."

Edgewater had me, and he knew it. The Ouroboros, even as it slept, was still a snake. It hissed and bit when provoked. I wasn't keen on seeing how it behaved when agitated by an angry mob.

"No retorts? No gests at my expense?" Edgewater sneered. "We'll listen to no more of your lies. In Salem, they hung witches. I prefer to cleanse and purify with fire. Take him. The others should have the wood ready by now."

I'd learned a universal truth when I was in the insane asylum. You couldn't argue with crazy. Nothing was more demented than a religious zealot convinced he's doing God's work. Convincing arguments or desperate pleading wouldn't change hearts in this crowd. I twisted around and charged blindly in the dark. More torches suddenly flared into life, resembling tacky dancing girls in a cheap saloon. I was trapped. No sign of sanity or reason glimmered in the eyes of my executioners. It was time to put my pride behind me and ask for help.

"Hesperos! Doran!"

I scanned the darkness, waiting anxiously for Doran to appear shaped like a great magic bear or a buffalo. Perhaps my reluctant protector planned a stealthy entrance? Straining my ears, I listened for any signs of wings or hooves. Nothing. Hesperos and his pet were standing down from this fight.

The circle was closing fast as the mob marched toward me. Some of the dried grass caught on fire from the weeping torches. Then, withered and brittle from the heat of summer, the ground burst into a rapidly spreading blaze. Reverend Edgewater was about to get more of a witch-burning than he'd first supposed.

"Stop! What you're doing is murder," I shouted, but the unceasing march of hatred smothered my words.

Then Edgewater stepped into the shrinking circle. He sauntered toward me, stopping when we were feet apart. His grin widened, drawing the lips and skin on his face into an unnatural cavern of jagged teeth. Eyes of hellfire blazed with triumphant satisfaction.

"What are you?"

"Oh Dun, you are such a fool." His voice rumbled low like metal striking against a rock. "Heaven showered its mercy on you for the sake of those pathetic humans. Did you not think Hell would send its scorn?" He leaned closer, teeth snapping inches from my nose. "The balance must be maintained."

"I don't understand what you mean." I leaned away from the stench of rotting flesh.

"You'll have an eternity in Hell to contemplate my words." The beast known as Edgewater threw its head back and laughed. "Why are you men hesitating? Show him what it means to burn!"

Then the Ouroboros began to swell upon my chest. Power – hot and wild – raced through my veins. It formed in a pulsing mass in my palms. As if by their own volition, my arms thrust out before me and pointed at the men blocking my path. Blinding white fire burst from my palms. Hot and full of power, the magic felt like a stream of the Eternal Flame. I turned my face away. Screams and shouts of fear circled about me as the horror spanned for what seemed a lifetime.

Silence fell with abrupt finality. I blinked and tentatively turned my face back toward the crowd. The supernatural fire had died, leaving pockets of earthly flames in the grass. I was alone. The demon, Reverend Edgewater, and his blackbirds had been reduced to glowing piles of cinder.

Holding my hands before me, I marveled at my unscathed skin. No burn marks or pain registered upon my skin that I could see. Unfortunately, Colorado wasn't as lucky. The Earth about me was scorched in a circular pattern spanning twenty feet to my north. It curved back toward the Santa Fe Trail, stopping at its edge.

Swallowing the gore rising in my throat, I ran as fast as I could away from the scene of destruction. Bits of charred trees and grass still glowed from the unimaginable heat of the Eternal Flame. I used their light to avoid breaking my neck as I raced west upon the pioneer road. The route, much like the Santa Fe Trail, had deep ruts from years of wagons rolling across its dirt surface.

San Francisco was a long way off, but there was no time like the present to get started. No horse. No wagon. No supplies. I was going to need all the luck I could get.

CHAPTER TWENTY-NINE

Terror chased me through the night, menacing my mind with images of the horrific carnage I'd left behind. I was afraid to stop or close my eyes, worried I'd see the faces of each life I'd taken. How could I ever control this new power with the destructive force to burn men to ash?

My wild run ended when I stumbled over loose gravel and took a painful tumble. I collapsed across the trail ruts and fell instantly into an uneasy sleep. My mind, unwilling to rest in peaceful slumber, haunted my dreams with one worrying thought. What if my father had been right all those years ago? Had I become the monster he predicted?

Aching thirst rousted me from my dirt bed. Lifting a hand to block the mid-morning sun, I turned my gaze eastward. Nothing. Not a wagon, man, or beast to be seen. The trail was empty. I must be the only living thing on two legs for fifty miles in every direction.

Sitting in the dirt and nursing a foggy brain wasn't doing me much good. I needed to keep moving toward Pueblo for any hope of survival. Crawling to the banks of the nearby Arkansas, I dunked my head in its healing body. The river's cool water chased away my exhaustion.

Mind and body somewhat restored, my thoughts turned to practical matters like breakfast. My supplies waited for me where I'd left them on the trail. I snatched up the pack and sorted through the contents. Tyson, bless him, had tucked away a few apples, jerky, and some corn dodgers for me. I gulped down the meal, taking in my surroundings as I chewed. The rugged mountains I'd expected to reside in Colorado were still absent from the landscape. I shrugged. The view was pretty enough with its kaleidoscope of Autumn leaves running along the riverbanks.

Food, water, and comforting daylight did wonders to brighten my outlook. Lady Luck was still with me. If I kept my wits and stayed close to the river, I'd make it to Pueblo.

"The name's Dunham Raynor," I shouted into the wilderness. "And I am not going to die out here!"

Slapping my drenched hat atop my head, I stepped back into the trail ruts and lifted my bedroll over my shoulder. I had no idea what waited for me on the road to Pueblo, but I'd face it with the new sense of confidence I'd earned on the Santa Fe Trail.

"How philosophical and self-aware you've become," Hesperos said, suddenly appearing beside me. "Aristotle's bones are rattling in his grave."

"What the hell do you want?" I kicked dirt through his ethereal robes. "I'd thought you'd left after you'd abandoned me to those religious nuts."

"Your recent ill fortune is due entirely to your foolish decisions." He put his clasped hands behind his back as if he were about to give me a lecture. "I chose you for a specific reason, Dunham, and quite frankly, you've been nothing but a disappointment."

"Oh really?" I growled. "Who asked you to choose me anyway? My life would have been better without this mark and your company."

"Indeed! I can picture it now." Hesperos sneered. "Reverend Raynor, Jr., meekly agreeing to join the clergy to please your abusive father. You'd wear his old clothes while preaching the sermons he's already delivered a hundred times. Perhaps some dreary woman would agree to marry you. I suppose she'd give you a litter of dullard children. Frankly, the notion sickens me to the core." Hesperos thrust a finger at me. "I have a higher purpose for you, Dunham."

"Does it involve dying out here in the middle of the Colorado Territory?"

Hesperos shook his head with a snort. "Allow me to explain. I was born in Athens during an era you'd refer to as Ancient Greece. In retrospect, my time seems a more modern and enlightened age than yours. I was a Priest of the God Hades at the Necromanteion in Epirus."

"He was supposed to be the God of the Underworld, right?"

"The very same. I was one of several priests who went to worship Hades in a special Necromancy Ceremony." He shifted uncomfortably as if the memory from thousands of years ago still caused him pain. "The spell went terribly wrong, killing everyone in the chamber." Hesperos gritted his teeth. "Naturally, I felt betrayed when neither Hades nor Charon, the ferryman for the River Stix, came for us. After all, I'd been a devoted priest, willingly sacrificing for my god for most of my life.

Hades and the ferryman didn't come, but others did. You know of whom I speak. The burning light of Heaven shined upon some while the jagged claws of Hell grabbed others. Twelve souls – I one of them – remained."

"Why? Did you resist?" I asked. "You don't seem like a poltergeist, though you are as annoying as one."

"No. Something else came to claim we twelve remaining souls."

Hesperos fell silent, lifting his gaze to the horizon. In the troubled arrangement of his facial features, I read the strain of a long life lived with heavy secrets. If the fantastical tale he told was true, then the structure of the Universe was more complex than anyone had supposed.

"A massive shroud, towering well over twenty feet, came among us. Faceless and showing no limbs, the being ignored the agents of Heaven and Hell. These representatives of the afterlife, for their part, stood aside. They waited in utter silence for the shroud to pass by them.

I cowered in the presence of the being, terrified as it floated before we remaining priests of Hades. Then the creature spoke, and Hades' temple trembled. It proclaimed its name as Il Separatio or The Separation, the personification of neutrality. It explained that neither Heaven nor Hell had a claim on the priests who remained. Our souls belonged to Il Separatio because we had done as much good as evil in life. If we maintained our neutrality, Il Separatio would allow us to live unnaturally long lives. Then it restored our bodies and left us to carry on as we wished."

I regarded Hesperos with reluctant curiosity. Every Sunday school lesson I'd ever suffered through spoke of Heaven and Hell exclusively. No mention or evidence of the existence of a third party ever presented itself. My experiences with the Eternal Flame of Good and Hell's coachman had never included this so-called Il Separatio either. Yet, I detected honesty as Hesperos spoke of the unknown being.

"You didn't stay one big happy bunch for long, I take it."

"Long Life wasn't the only gift Il Separatio bestowed upon us. What once was fake ritual and trickery transformed into real magic." Hesperos gave me an indecipherable smile. "We named our group 'The Apeiron.' It means the origin of all things. We were the first and only of our kind. In the beginning, we remained together and prospered for many years. Then the Romans came. Honestly, I don't harbor any ill feelings. I saw Rome burn as well.

By the fall of the empire, three of my fellow Necromancers had succumbed to the temptations of evil. Il Separatio, true to its word, took away their immortality, and the darkness came for them."

"Let me stop you right there," I said. "It's 1865, and we're walking along the Pioneer Trail in the Colorado Territory. That's a Hell of a long way from Ancient Rome. So how come you are still roaming the Earth bothering me?"

"Well, Dunham. I'm happy to know you aren't a complete fool." Hesperos laughed. "As you've guessed, there's more to my tale. The remaining members of the Apeiron resented Il Separatio's heavy hand. We'd grown arrogant in our magic, thinking we could hide from our master. The Apeiron created a spell which would allow us to jump to a new host body when our current one died."

"And what did this God of Neutrality think about that?"

"Il Separatio wasn't fooled but rather amused by our efforts. It would allow us twelve total jumps until eternity finally found us, but whether we would go to Hell or Heaven or remain with Il Separatio would depend upon the Host rather than the Necromancer." Hesperos lifted his fists into the air as if pleading with fate. "Should the host be a perfectly neutral soul, Il Separatio promised to grant the Necromancer true immortality." He looked at me with the flames of ambition in his eyes. "You, Dunham, are my last jump. Your life will determine where I end up."

"You sure can pick 'em." I shook my head. "I'm not exactly the poster boy for good honest values."

"But you aren't entirely evil either," he said. "I believed you to be a soul capable of neutrality, so I marked you. While you have larceny in your blood, your heart is good." Hesperos tightened his fists as craving glistened in his eyes. "You are equal parts good and evil. Soon, I will possess Il Separatio's gift of immortality. And with it, infinite power."

"Has anyone achieved this special state of balanced immortality?"

"Only once. We don't speak of HER." Hesperos jaw tightened, and he dropped his fists to his side.

Every movement of his translucent body, no matter how minuscule, communicated Hesperos' unwillingness to discuss the mysterious HER. Curiosity banished any lingering fear from my wild run during the night. His past was none of my business, so I'd leave it alone. But any plan Hesperos had for the future had to have my consent.

"And what's in it for the Host? You've been a little slim on the details."

Burning pain ignited along my chest as the Ouroboros pierced my skin with its painted teeth. Fixing my gaze on the trail ahead, I spotted what had provoked the tattoo's warning. She was standing beside the road, clutching at her small bonnet. The little girl from the wagon train was no longer part of the Earthly realm. I'd last seen her alive the day I'd been cordially invited to leave our wagon train. She'd been among the travelers headed north along the Pioneer Road. The little girl and her family wouldn't be making Pueblo.

"I wouldn't go any closer. She's a harbinger." Hesperos shrugged when I ignored him. "Such curiosity. We'll have fun together."

Her small transparent hand pointed at black wings circling against the blue heavens. Vultures. Hovering like a thunder cloud, the scavenger birds dove toward the ground and climbed again in a feeding frenzy. Those many buzzards in one place meant the prairie meadow had seen more death than a single child. I held a hand up to block the sun as I moved closer. Then the smell hit me. Blood. Unfortunately, I was used to its copper odor.

The first body lay ten feet away from the circle of wagons. It belonged to the little girl. Her corpse rested in the crimson-tipped prairie grass while what remained of her being skipped along behind me. The physical version of the blue dress, showing no signs of violence, was clean and well-kept. Her hair and boots were Sunday School tidy as if she'd just arrived at church. If not for the little girl's ghost, I'd have guessed she was peacefully napping in the grass.

Kneeling beside her, I turned the small body over. Handling dead bodies was nothing new for me. I'd gotten used to the cold skin and rigid remains. Children were the exception. I'd never get used to the loss of such innocence, and this occasion would give me nightmares for months to come. Wide lifeless eyes stared at me while her blue lips contorted in a silent scream. This poor child looked as if she'd died of fright.

"I don't want to stay here anymore." The little girl's ghost pointed at a pile of fabric a few feet away. "Mama went to the light."

Her mother's corpse lay curled in a tight ball as if she'd tried to escape into herself. The woman had yanked out large clumps of hair from her scalp in her terror. White fists, still clutching strands of yellow, remained pressed against her forehead as if she were preparing to tug again. I parted the veil of hair covering her face with a gentle finger and quickly let the strands fall back in place again. Though the little girl was past caring, I didn't want her to see her mother's face. The expression of absolute terror had contorted the woman's features into a hideous mask.

"I can't find any signs of violence on either of them," I said, looking to Hesperos. "What could cause a person to literarily be frightened to death?"

"Join with me, and you'll have the answers to all your questions." Hesperos grinned when I gave him a rude gesture in response.

"Do you know what happened to you and the others?" I asked the little ghost.

Her small hand reached out to touch mine, but it passed through my living flesh unhindered. "They made me stay behind so that you would find us. They said they'd be coming for you soon. Can I go now? Mama is calling for me."

"Soon. I promise." I rubbed where her phantom fingers had passed through my skin. "Who told you to stay?"

The little girl wasn't looking at me anymore. Something held her gaze on the other side of the road just past my shoulder. I didn't look. Instead, I stayed still with my eyes shut tightly. The Living weren't supposed to see through the veil.

Moving away from mother and daughter, I edged closer to the silent camp. The wagons were positioned in a circle as if their occupants were preparing for the evening meal. Pots and flour sacks sat upon the wagon gates, waiting for an absent cook to take them in hand. Yes, everything seemed as it should be, except the suspicious absence of noise or movement.

I entered the circle of wagons and stopped abruptly with a gag. The smell was enough to knock a man over. Now I knew the source of the blood odor. Someone had butchered a mule. I ripped a strip off my shirt and used it to cover my nose.

The eerie sight awaiting me within the camp was far worse than a bloodied animal. Men, women, and children - about fifty in all - had met the same fate as the little girl. Their corpses had dropped in random spots about the camp as if they'd dropped dead trying to escape an invisible predator. What could have caused something like this? Sickness? Disease? I didn't think so. I'd been visited by enough newly departed to see just about every way a body could die. This was new.

"The killers following you are relentless, Dunham. They come from an evil you're not prepared to meet. Join with me, and we can face them as one."

"What killers?" I stared hard at him. "Don't think you can con a conman. You aren't telling me the whole story."

"Very well," he gave me a cordial nod. "I'll leave you to discover for yourself. We'll talk soon, Dunham. I hope for both our sakes you are in one piece."

Then he was gone, leaving me with more questions. Damn him. I kicked at a buzzard snatching up a piece of flesh in the center of the circle of wagons. I'd love a chance to beat the tar out of Hesperos. Too bad for me, he was untouchable.

One of the bloated corpses still gripped a rifle in his hands. I recognized him and the wagon of farm implements. It was the reluctant driver who'd carried me to Bent's Old Fort. His wagon was the only one broken apart. It was as if the gang of murderous thieves had been searching for something. Or someone.

Another smell touched my nose. Its familiar odor stayed on the vague ridges of my memory. Perfume. It hung in the hot air about the camp, refusing to diminish despite the gore upon the ground. Wild and exotic, nature hadn't made this scent.

Dismissing the puzzle for more practical concerns, I searched the bodies for suitable clothes and a good pair of boots. Cash and coin, I pocketed. After dressing in fresh garments, my attention turned to weapons and food. The oxen and mules were missing, leaving me to continue traveling on foot. A mule would have made it easier to carry more supplies, but I'd take what I could carry. Much like my old boots, the supplies would last until I hit Pueblo.

Exiting the last wagon, I glanced at the center of the circle. Whoever did this hadn't just piled animal parts for fun. They'd formed gruesome letters in the camp. I climbed up on the driver's seat for a better view. Though crudely written, my instinct recognized the letters. Entrails and legs spelled out one word in gore.

Lester.

Whoever wrote this gruesome message had found out what I'd done. Now they were hunting me like a cat playing with a field mouse. I gripped at the rifle I'd found in one of the wagons. This mouse planned to bite back.

CHAPTER THIRTY

Standing on the bluff, I stopped to admire the plains stretching out to an unlimited horizon. Gold brushed against the fading green of a dying summer. Gigantic clouds towering to God's Heaven cast massive patches of shadow over the landscape. A forceful wind pushed their enormous bodies across the darkening sky. I put a hand atop my hat as the wind's fingers tried to snatch it off my head.

Distant rumbles signaled a fast-moving storm headed my way. Then a brilliant blast of raw energy whipped toward the ground a short mile from me. Thunder chased the lightning with a sudden Earth-shattering boom. The storm was getting closer. I spun around, looking for a haven away from the coming downpour. The Colorado mountains were notorious for birthing violent thunderstorms. Being on the high plains with no shelter during such times was dangerous. And here I was standing out in the open, doing my best impression of a lightning rod.

Hard pelts of hail pinged against my hat and torso in painful taps. Not willing to turn around and seek shelter among the gruesome wagon camp, I wrapped my arms about my body and kept moving. These storms formed quickly and faded fast. There was nothing to do but wait it out.

Shouldering the saddlebag containing my supplies, I continued north again. My mind wandered back to the unsettling deaths at the campsite. Something had terrorized those people until their hearts stopped. I'd guess the attack had taken mere minutes, based on the state of the camp.

A prickle of warning crept up my spine, bringing me back to the Pioneer Road. Years of looking over my shoulder and hiding from angry marks had taught me to pay careful attention to my surroundings. Instinct warned me I wasn't the only traveler enjoying the day. Someone was watching me.

Ears tuned to either side of the road, I waited for the inevitable tell of an attempted ambush. My efforts, however, proved unnecessary. The would-be highway-man following me was making enough noise to wake the Dead. Based on my new companion's bumbling movements, I doubted if he was the killer who possessed stealth enough to wipe out an entire wagon train before any of the men could get a shot off.

The storm, a quick-moving soaker, rolled to the northeast as swiftly as it had descended. Patches of warm sunshine struck the ground and began melting the tiny bits of ice pebbles left behind by the thunderstorm. I stopped for a moment on the trail, pretending to adjust my pack, and quickly scanned the landscape. A flash of light reflecting off some shiny doodad screamed my stalker's exact location. This was no bushwhacker.

The landscape was open, with a few rolling hills running along the Arkansas River. Not much to hide behind except some rock formations and tall clumps of brush. I kept an easy pace, forcing my eyes straight ahead.

If my pursuer wanted me dead, they'd have used one of the abandoned rifles from the wagons by now.

Dropping down into a gully carved by the river, I stomped on the loose rock bed. My clumsy companion slipped down into the gully a short distance away, just as I'd hoped they would. I climbed rapidly onto the Pioneer Road and darted into a cluster of rocks silhouetting the horizon. Crouching down low to hide my shadow, I waited.

A slight little man popped out of the gully like a skittish prairie dog. Covered in dust and bits of grass, his thin hands brushed at the front of his dirty shirt as he ran to catch up. He was a scrawny thing in his early thirties. Thinning blond hair, straw-straight and filthy, clung to his sunburned scalp. Sweat streamed down his face as he frantically looked for me. My nervous companion ran stained linen haphazardly across his gold-rimmed glasses. He looked as out of place in Colorado as a toddler in a fist fight. What the hell was this tinhorn doing so far from civilization?

I stepped out from behind the rocks as soon as he passed by. "Looking for me?"

Grabbing him in one fist, I frisked him with my free hand. He wasn't armed, but the mousy little man did have an intriguing mound wrapped around his waist. I recognized the shape as a money belt. Mine, though not as plump as his, never left my waist. Noting my interest in his hidden treasure, he pushed me away.

"Was manhandling me necessary? Honestly, I meant no harm." He moved a shaking fingertip to the bridge of his glasses and pushed the frames back in place. "I saw you passing by and wondered if you'd mind a traveling companion. You see, I've lost my way."

"Have you?" I grabbed my things from behind the rocks and shouldered the rifle. "Is that what happened to your friends in the wagon train back there?"

"Oh no. They weren't my friends. I mean, I wasn't with them. I found them same as you."

He was lying, of course. I hadn't seen any boot prints or traces of other travelers on the road. Running an evaluating glance over the man's face again, a moment of curiosity came upon me. Something in the overly eager way he held his body gave me pause. Nope. I had my own problems. The tinhorn's lies were none of my business.

"I prefer to travel alone."

A low moan gurgled out of the man's tightening throat as I pushed past him. "Wait! I need someone who knows their way through the territory and is good with a gun. I saw you shoot when we were with the wagon train!" The little man ran after me like a stray puppy. "Please! I'll pay you twenty dollars."

A good memory for faces was part of a con man's bag of tricks. Having spent several hard weeks with the caravan of pioneers, I could recollect each of them though their names would fade soon. I was sure I'd never laid eyes upon this man.

"Not interested." I kept walking. "And stop following me. I've got my own problems."

"A hundred! I can pay you one hundred dollars."

I stopped abruptly on the trail and turned around just as the little man bumped into me. Terrified eyes blinked up into my face through dusty lenses. My tag-along stumbled quickly away. He gripped at the hem of his shirt, twisting the garment around his fingers until their tips turned white.

"Let me see the color of your money."

Turning his back to me - he began digging inside his shirt. I rolled my eyes as he contorted his slight body, attempting to prevent me from seeing the treasure he tried to hide. Twisting back around, he clutched at a piece of paper and held it to his chest. A sudden sob shook his body as he edged the paper closer to me. It was a hundred-dollar banknote. The last time I'd seen one, Angelina was paying off a particularly greedy politician.

I grabbed the little man by the collar. "Where did you get this? Nobody walks around with hundred-dollar bank notes in their pocket."

"The name is James Meeks of Boston, Massachusetts. I should think a hundred dollars would get me to the next civilized place with no questions asked," he said, adjusting his glasses. "I've seen you shoot, Reverend Dun. Or are you pretending to be someone else now?"

I released my grip. Meeks' hundred-dollar banknote would get me through the Colorado Territory, but its friends would see me to San Francisco in style. I stepped back and regarded my tag along again. It was my bad luck to run into someone who had known me from the wagon train. Then again, he feared me, like I was a gunslinger. Well, why not let Meeks believe what he wanted? I may have decided to be myself from now on, but who was to say I had to be poor?

"The name's Dunham Raynor. A hundred dollars gets you to Pueblo. If you die on the way, then that's your business."

CHAPTER THIRTY-ONE

Shades of yellow and red-colored the leaves as they danced in the chill of an Autumn sunset. Time was shorter than I'd first supposed. Late September had descended upon the landscape. Snowfall couldn't be far now. I didn't want to be stranded in the wilderness when the first Winter storm hit.

Another chilly gust brushed against my naked skin. Yowling a shrill cry, I stumbled out of the icy river. Perhaps using the last rays of daylight to have a bath wasn't my brightest notion. Taking several quick breaths to prepare my body, I tiptoed on bare feet toward our campfire.

Meeks hadn't been idle while I was playing in the river. A large pile of tinder lay at his feet. God only knew where he'd found that much wood in this treeless expanse of land. Frowning at my antics, he meticulously placed each piece of tinder he'd gathered on top of a large pile of firewood.

Whistling at the stack of fuel he'd collected, I said, "We're only here for one night."

Snorting as Meeks averted his eyes from my nakedness, I pulled my trousers on and sat down close to the fire. Any sense of modesty had left me while traveling in tight quarters on the medicine show. Moving my frozen feet nearer to the heat, I sighed.

"I plan to keep this fire going all night, Mr. Raynor. You never know what's waiting in the darkness."

"Call me, Dun. Everyone does," I said. "Open skies above me, food in my belly, and money in my pocket. Life has taken a turn for the better. Why be sour?"

Meeks stood shivering in the dancing circle of firelight. Staring anxiously into the still night, he cleared his throat and tossed me another corn dodger. Something was rattling my jittery companion. Meeks was jumpy enough during the day. Here in the dark, he was acting like a frightened old woman. I held out the last of the whiskey I'd found in the wagons to Meeks. He took it with a nod and sat down on the other side of the campfire. Sipping the bottle, he stared sullenly into the flames as they popped and crackled.

"Say, how did you hide all that time from Captain Tyson?" I asked.

"What?"

"I'm curious. You claim to know me from the wagon train. I have a good memory for faces, but I don't remember seeing you."

"I don't want to talk about it." Meeks threw a piece of tinder into the fire.

"Come on. I'm curious."

His eyes shifted to my face and lingered before dropping to the flames. "You'll laugh."

"Probably." I shrugged. "I can appreciate a good con. You fooled a whole wagon train, after all."

"I suppose." He shrugged with a shaky smile. "Very well. I hid in a small open space in the Pritchett wagon. Old Tim will be furious when he discovers all his towels are missing. And Mrs. Pritchett's Sunday dress? She'll be in hysterics."

"Her dress? You don't mean to say you wore it." I threw my head back, howling with laughter.

"I knew you'd think my hardship was funny!" Meeks threw his arms in the air. "Yes. There, I said it. I disguised myself as a woman around the camps. Behave like an adult! We have more important things to think about right now. Darkness is not our friend. We must keep the fire burning," Meeks said. "I'm not going to shut my eyes for a moment."

"Good. You can take the first watch. Ma'am."

I laid back on my bed roll and gazed up at the diamond sky. Marveling at the night's sparkling beauty, I took a deep breath. Meeks muttered something about shadows and threw another log onto the fire. I ignored him, letting my thoughts drift away on the chilly breeze. It was peaceful out here with nothing to do but watch the full moon float across an indigo sunset. Eyelids growing heavy, I relaxed as sleep blanketed my eyes.

Then the dreams came for me.

I stood alone in a field of blood. Nauseated by the intense feeling of dread, I fought to stay put. Nothing would make me run this time. Lightning struck the ground about me with its electric fingers. The ferocity of its attack made me jump. I gripped my rifle tighter as laughter smacked my ears. Let them have their fun. I wouldn't play the mouse any longer. It was time to end our sick game.

My gaze locked upon the nine riders. Their still frames made black shadows against the crimson horizon. Why weren't they moving? Was this another jest at my expense? Then their leader gave the command to attack. Dusters bellowing behind them, they charge forward on their ghostly gray mounts. I lifted the rifle, knowing it wouldn't do any good against the killers who hunted me.

Crimson fire blazed within the eye sockets of the demon mounts. The beasts cut through my dreamscape, charging at unimaginable speed toward me. Terror attacked my resolve as each thundering hoof moved closer. I froze, unable to squeeze my trigger finger.

"We're coming, Dun. Perdition wants you."

Then a gigantic chasm opened before the demon mounts. Screaming in outraged frustration, they descended deep into the Earth. I caught the putrid odor of sulfur and rotten flesh. Gagging, I turned away from the Gates of Hell.

The dreamscape suddenly faded as fists pounded against my chest. The punches were desperate and weak as those of a frightened child. I caught Meek's fist as his next strike fell toward me.

"What the hell?"

"We have company!" Meeks fell onto his backside with a cry.

I threw off my blanket. Rolling into a crouch, I aimed my rifle toward the southeast. Riders – a dozen or more – made dark shadows under a bright moon. Terror sent my heart on a wild dance as I scanned the approaching forms. Were these the demon riders back from Hell to take me?

Then the cold tip of a rifle barrel came to rest against my temple. An ox of a man stepped into the dying light of our fire. Bright copper hair and a bushy mustache to match framed our visitor's weather-worn face. The star on his chest said, 'United States Marshal.'

Hard brown eyes glared into mine. I found no signs of mercy or tolerance in the marshal's manner. Judging by the lawman's rough appearance and stone demeanor, he had challenged the wilderness on more than one occasion and won.

Outmatched, I lowered my gun and carefully rested it on the ground. What were the odds a posse would find me out here in the middle of nowhere? I slowly lifted my hands. Damn my luck! I hadn't done anything to attract the wrath of the territory law - lately.

"Is there a problem?" I asked, hoping I sounded innocent.

"James Meeks?" His deep baritone growled. "Sergeant Milton, build up that fire. I can't see their faces."

Another man stepped out of the darkness carrying an armful of tinder Meeks had so helpfully gathered earlier. The gold stripes on his blue uniform marked him as a sergeant in the Union Army. Dashes of silver dotted the sergeant's coal hair and mustache. He was regular army. Wood crackled behind me as the sergeant threw his load into the flames. Light exploded outward, banishing the dark as the fire grew. Bright beams danced off the faces surrounding us. Sergeant Milton had brought friends with him into our camp. I groaned under my breath as a posse – consisting of union soldiers and a few lawmen – made themselves at home by our fire.

"Are you James Meeks?" The marshal asked again.

It took a few moments for the marshal's words to cut through the shock. He wasn't after Dunham Raynor, con man. Instead, the posse had come for Meeks, the weasel who'd conned his way into my company. I stuck a thumb toward the bawling little coward clutching at my blankets.

"James Meeks. You're under arrest for robbing the Wagon City bank and evading the law, resulting in the death of my deputy. The name's Marshal John Barlow. I'm the man who's going to take you back for trial. Behave yourself, and you'll make it there without any broken bones." Barlow lowered his rifle. "Take him, sergeant. If I look at this little bastard any longer, I'll kill him."

"Give us a reason, Meeks." Sergeant Milton fingered his sidearm. "We found the wagon train. God, what you did to those people."

"I didn't kill anyone! Swear to God!" Meeks cried. "It was them."

"Them? Don't give me any lies," the sergeant warned. "What Cheyenne do you know who can spell Lester, huh?"

"They weren't Indians. They were ghosts – nine in all."

Meeks had seen the riders too! How was that possible? I stabbed Meeks with an accusing glare, but my searching eyes didn't find anything unusual about him. Of course, being new to the world of magic, how would I know? Honestly, I'd like to believe those hell-sent terrors haunting my dreams were figments of my guilty imagination. The ambushes on our wagon train, however, proved what a necromancer could do with the Dead.

The marshal backhanded Meeks, sending him to the ground. "Don't try it on with me, you miserable coward. You killed one man. Now you've got a taste for it."

Marshal Barlow turned his attention to me and asked, "So, who are you?"

"Me? I'm nobody, just a good Samaritan helping this little tinhorn to the next town. He said he was lost."

"Did you see these so-called ghosts kill those people on the wagon train?"

"I didn't see a damn thing." I looked the marshal in the eye, unaccustomed honesty rushing from my mouth.

"I found them after they'd been dead for hours. Listen, I just helped myself to some fresh clothes and supplies. That's all. Those killings had nothing to do with me."

Barlow's mustache fell over a stern frown. "The tip of my nose starts to sting a mite when someone lies to me. And boy is it ever stinging," The Marshal said. "Search him."

Rough hands hoisted me to my feet. I kept my eyes on Barlow while two soldiers ran roughshod over me. It didn't take them long to find the hundred-dollar banknote and my belt with the money I'd damn well earned from the medicine show. The marshal held the banknote and lifted his bushy eyebrow at me. Damn it. I should have kept walking and left Meeks with the Dead. I swallowed my anger when the marshal held up a pair of irons.

"Meeks has himself an accomplice. You're coming along with us, Mr. Good Samaritan."

CHAPTER THIRTY-TWO

Fog rolled off the surface of the river, covering my new campmates and me in a chilly drizzle. Patches of sunlight tried to pierce the gray morning but merely managed to make a dull yellow glow. We would be socked in until the fog decided to release its grip on the Pioneer Road. Marshal Barlow, our new leader, hadn't stopped cussing the weather since he'd opened his eyes at dawn.

Sniffing at the strip of dried meat and ancient square of hardtack dangling between my shackled wrists, I wrinkled my nose at the distinct smell of leather and age. Disgusting. I wasn't about to complain, though. The marshal was in a sour mood. Provoking him would be foolhardy. Keeping my eyes on Barlow, I softened the granite piece of hardtack in a cup of lousy coffee.

"Are we headed to Pueblo then, Marshal?" Sergeant Milton asked, his stormy gray eyes lifted as he waited for Barlow to swallow the last dregs of coffee.

"Edwards and his men should have met us here last night after checking that false trail Meeks and his new partner made," Marshal Barlow said, handing his empty cup to a young soldier waiting impatiently for orders. "We were a day late. They would have waited for us if they'd gotten here first."

Damnable Meeks had been the one who'd insisted we stop in this spot. I'd wanted to keep going a bit further, but the little tinhorn was terrified of the dark and refused to travel after sundown. So now, we were surrounded by a posse, glumly eating their dried breakfast. I don't know who set the false trail Barlow was talking about, but it was a pity the ploy didn't work. Our current company had already worn out its welcome.

"We'll have to backtrack to the southwest and retrace their trail." Barlow glared steel daggers at Meeks. "I don't like it. No sir, I don't like it one bit."

"Marshal, I ask you to reconsider," Milton said, standing when Barlow got to his feet. "Wouldn't it be better to head back to Pueblo? My men and I are already a week overdue. We need to send word to Fort Leavenworth."

"I'm not having this conversation again." Barlow came at Milton, leaning threateningly over the sergeant's shorter frame. "Keep your opinions to yourself unless I ask for them."

"Edwards will know to ride for Pueblo. We all agreed that was the plan if something went wrong. Backtracking takes us twenty or thirty miles in the wrong direction!"

"These are civilian volunteers, not soldiers. I'm not leaving them out here in hostile territory! That's final." Barlow shoved a thick finger at the buttons on Milton's uniform. "Your colonel put you men under my command, sergeant. I know what I'm doing."

Splotchy patches of purple covered Milton's face. His brows, mustache, and lips fell in unified resentment. Clearly, he and the marshal had covered this ground before, and Milton wasn't willing to let it go. The expression corrected its descent within a millisecond.

Then a mask of cool indifference nestled upon his face. I hid my grin. Milton was a career soldier accustomed to taking orders from less experienced officers.

Marshal Barlow, however, didn't strike me as a novice or pushover. Stone features, rigid and immovable, reflected the nature of the man. Barlow was a creature made from the wild country he patrolled. Unruly copper hair defied the confines of his Stetson hat. Several white curls swirled amongst the red as his unruly tuft fell across his bushy eyebrows. The thick mustache prickled in anger as he waited for Milton to speak. Barlow reminded me of a charging buffalo I'd had the misfortune to face on the Santa Fe Trail.

"Yes, sir." The sergeant glared at Barlow and turned his eyes toward the yellow-gray gloom. "Looks like the fog is starting to thin."

"Have your men break camp. We're burning daylight," Barlow said, turning toward his horse.

I didn't catch the grumbled curse Sergeant Milton gave the marshal under his breath. The sergeant, well-trained though he may be, looked close to mutiny. Barking orders to break camp, Milton painstakingly packed his kit. I regarded his practiced movements. Order and routine seemed to calm the sergeant's temper. Discord among the troops could make a promising opportunity for me to slip away.

Then I saw the sergeant take a long blade from its place beside his bedroll. It was a bayonet fashioned into a knife about fifteen inches long. I recognized it, of course. How could I forget Grizz's favorite weapon? But how had Sergeant Milton come by it?

"Can I help you with something, prisoner?" he asked, giving me an ill-tempered look.

"No, Sergeant. I plan to mind my own business for the entirety of our time together."

"Good. You'll stay healthier." Milton pointed at two unlucky soldiers not quick enough to escape his notice. "Mason. Peterman. You two laze abouts will guard the prisoners until Corporal Nichols tells you otherwise."

"Yes, Sergeant."

I regarded my two nannies over the rim of my tin coffee cup. Mason was a lanky man with a ruddy complexion whose wrists peeked out constantly from under the sleeve of his uniform. I gathered from the private's periodic tugging upon his hem that the uniform's ill fit was a sore point for their sergeant.

Peterman was a foot shorter than his friend, but what the private lacked in height, he made up for in belly mass. Startled by Milton's sudden focus upon him, Peterman drizzled hot coffee down his tunic. Yes indeed. Milton had entrusted Meeks and me to a couple of crackerjack soldiers. My chances for escape had significantly improved.

Our posse left the Pioneer Road a mile north of the campsite. Determined to escape Barlow and his men, I made a note of the departure point as we headed south. Distinguishing landmarks, unfortunately for me, were rare in Colorado's plains and sage country. It'd be tricky to make my way back to the Arkansas River after giving them the slip.

All signs of the fog had passed a few hours later as a bright blue sky stretched above my head. I lifted my face to let the sun warm my cheeks. The journey might have been pleasant if circumstances were a bit different. Perhaps a change in traveling companions, for instance.

"Watch your head, Meeks," I grumbled at the back of his sweaty head. "Hit me in the nose, and it will be the last thing you do."

Our nannies had chained Meeks and me together on one of the pack ponies. Wrists bound before our bodies, we grabbed onto whatever we could find to stay upright. I leaned as far back as possible, not wanting anyone to accuse me of cuddling against Meeks.

"Marshal Barlow is calling for a stop," Meeks said over his shoulder. "I wonder why?"

"Grub stop," Mason said. "Off your horse. Hurry up. Barlow doesn't look to be in a good mood."

"Does he ever," I murmured.

Chewing gingerly on the strip of dried meat, I wordlessly promised that should I survive this ordeal, I'd never eat jerky again. Meeks sniffed his lunch and then gagged. I took the jerky from his outstretched hand with a shrug. The meat might taste like old socks, but it was filling, and I was hungry.

Our company remained standing as we ate. The marshal kept a silent vigil at the edge of the group and locked his gaze upon the south. I cast a glance in the direction he watched so intently. Outlines of a mountain range rose in the distance. Their faded blue peaks stretched across the world in an unsurmountable line impossible to traverse. I had to escape before we reached their foothills. Venturing into the Sangre De Cristos or any part of the Rockies in late September was a crapshoot weather-wise. And it was my bad luck we were headed straight for them.

"Are those the Sangre De Cristos up ahead?" I asked Mason.

"Naw. Those are the Wet Mountains. They're baby brothers to the Sangre De Cristos." He cast a careful glance over at the marshal. "Just hope we don't have to cross them after snow flies."

"What does he mean?" Meeks asked me in a whisper.

"Look at the riders. Do you see anyone here carrying winter gear?" I gave Meeks an acid frown. "Barlow won't stop until he finds his men, even if that means risking a mountain storm. Damn you, Meeks. You've landed me deep in it."

We mounted our horses again and followed the marshal south. Fall touched lightly at the tips of foliage, brushing against my boots. Usually, I found the burnt colors of Autumn enchanting. Today, however, the dying leaves were a sobering reminder of how little time I had left to escape.

"Are those buzzards?" Mason asked, pointing at a flock of dark shapes circling over the landscape.

The Ouroboros slithered anxiously upon my chest as if in answer to the vultures' ravenous cries. Barlow wasn't going to find his men alive. The marshal glared back at Meeks and me. Then he prodded his horse faster. As if anticipating what we'd find, the posse hurried to catch up.

"I dare say escape should be your main priority now, Dunham," Hesperos said as he sat behind Peterman on the mount next to ours. "Ready to join with me yet?"

Barlow pulled the reins with a curse, stopping abruptly at the edge of a shallow ravine. His horse snorted and tried to back away. The marshal smoothed a hand across the horse's neck.

My nose caught the coppery odor of dried blood permeating the air as the soldiers brought our horse to a stop beside Barlow. The group of men – farmers and ranchers, I'd guess – were lying in a small dry gulch. They'd tried to find cover to protect themselves against whatever band of cutthroats had ambushed them. The effort had been pointless. Whatever had butchered them had done a thorough job. Even the horses had been torn apart.

"Great God in Heaven. All three men are dead." Milton spat and wrinkled his nose as one of his men vomited. "They spelled out 'Lester' in body parts this time. What kind of a mad man does this?"

Marshal Barlow spurred his horse over toward us. Murder brewed in his eyes. The marshal's powerful hands were shaking as they gripped the reins. I spared a glance at the rest of the posse. They were watching Barlow, waiting to see what he would do.

"What do you know about this?" The marshal asked with barely contained rage.

"It doesn't look good for either of you," Hesperos said. "You and your new friend are at the top of the marshal's list of suspects. His men were killed well over a day ago, ample time for you and Meeks to kill them and then travel to the river."

"You don't understand!" Meeks cried. "They did this! Nine pale riders found us. They ambushed our wagons on the Pioneer Road and killed every last soul but me. Those murderers have done this to your men too, I'm sure of it."

"An interesting theory, isn't it?" Hesperos gave me a sideways smirk. "You know nothing of the other realm. What hunts you will never stop until it has what it wants."

Then he disappeared again, leaving me to face one pissed-off lawman and his trail-weary posse.

Chapter Thirty-Three

My weary arms lifted another shovel and hurled the contents atop the growing pile. I thrust the shovel into the ground with a satisfied sigh. Then, wiping the sweat from my face with a filthy sleeve, I surveyed my handiwork. The two holes I'd dug weren't quite four feet deep, but their depths were close enough for prairie land.

Determined boots crunched on unearthed gravel. It was Sergeant Milton coming to inspect our progress. I rested a hand on the shovel handle with a low curse. The man had an uncanny knack for sensing dawdlers. He'd caught me sneaking a break earlier and had taken my water ration away as punishment.

"Dig faster, Meeks," The sergeant said, hovering over the hole next to me. "Corporal Nichols is ready to bury these men. By all rights, you should carry what's left of the bodies by yourself." Then Milton glared over at me. "Raynor. Get in there and help him finish."

I kept my grumbles to myself and crawled out of the grave I'd been digging. Swinging the shovel over my shoulder, I regarded the pathetic pothole. Meek's thin body shook with the struggle of lifting dirt and rock. His face red with exertion, he was in danger of fainting at any moment.

"Thank you," Meeks muttered when I landed next to him.

"Thank you? Is that all you have to say to me?" I shoved him to the side and took over digging. "I wish I'd shot you on the road."

"You'd have done us both a favor," Marshal Barlow said, joining Milton to watch our work. "Three more good men are dead because of this pathetic excuse for a human being. I'll get Meeks back to Fort Leavenworth, but I can't guarantee he'll make it through the first night. Mark my words. There's a necktie party waiting for Meeks when we arrive."

"How can I prove to you I had nothing to do with Meeks or his crimes, Marshal," I said. "Nobody wants to see an innocent man ripped apart by an angry mob, especially me."

"That's for a judge and jury to decide. I just track them. I don't try them." Barlow gave me an impatient frown. "Hurry. We've got to get these men buried before sundown."

Blue caps moved silently over the tops of the dirt piles. The soldiers were wasting no time burying their dead. Throwing the last shovel full of dirt atop the mound, I scrambled out of the hole to watch the corporal and his soldiers lower what were essentially body parts into the individual graves. They weren't sure which pieces went with which torso. The horrified confusion made them uneasy and angry. I eased away from the grave site, unwilling to be a target for their vengeance.

Meeks, the idiot, didn't share my practicality and vomited into one of the graves. He was lucky to crawl away with just a black eye and bloodied lip. However, his disrespect for the honored dead earned us a seat on the hard ground away from the campfire. Bound by the wrists and ankles, I managed to rub a finger along the fresh blisters on my palm. There went the possibility of a gentleman's disguise when I reached San Francisco.

Though Marshal Barlow had ordered his men to make camp well away from the graves, the proximity to their Dead unsettled our company. I preferred to push on a mile or two but traveling across the plains in the dark was too dangerous. Not that anyone wanted a prisoner's opinion.

Exhausted from the day, I rested my head on the ground and closed my eyes. The hum of campfire conversation about Pueblo gossip and tactical discussions lulled me toward sleep. I was one war story away from blissful slumber when the tone of their talk took a more sinister turn.

"Who do you suppose this Lester is anyway?" Corporal Nichols asked.

"I don't think it's a person," young Davis said. "Our newspaper ran a story about a town in Missouri called Lester right before I joined up. The Union Army and the Confederates fought there. No one knows why, but some think they made a mistake and chose Lester because they thought the town was abandoned."

"It wasn't, I take it," Barlow said, his face darkening.

"No, sir. Over three hundred souls were lost that night when cannon fire hit the town. It was a massacre." He stopped to rub his fuzzy chin. "I wonder if the men who killed Edwards and those folks on the Pioneer Road are renegade soldiers looking to get revenge for what happened in Lester?"

"It's not a bad theory," Sergeant Milton said. "We've had reports of vigilante soldiers on the fringes of the western wilderness who aren't ready to concede defeat."

Vengeful renegades on a killing spree? The theory sounded a bit outlandish to me. Of course, the idea was better than Meeks and his ghosts. Sitting up to face the fire, I cast an uncomfortable glance at the crude graves of Barlow's men. Regrettably, I had a disturbing theory of my own to consider.

"You got something to say, Raynor?" Barlow asked.

"I think I might have an idea who is behind these killings," I said. "Sergeant Milton's knife gave me a clue. I recognize it."

"That so?" Milton pulled the weapon out and let the blade flash in the firelight. The other men leaned in closer for a look. It was an unusual weapon, and the chances of there being two like it in the world were slim.

"It belongs to a bear of a man named Griswold Wilks. Grizz claims to have been stabbed by a Union Officer. The way he tells the story, the tip of the bayonet broke off between his ribs as they fought. He loves showing off the scar." I lifted my gaze to Barlow. "Grizz is a nasty character. He cut the officer's head off and took that bayonet as a trophy." I frowned at the blade. "Grizz and the hellions that ride with him enjoy killing Union soldiers. I wouldn't be surprised to find they've included civilians in their games."

"Sounds like an unpleasant character. I'm glad you're wrong, Raynor." Milton tapped the hilt of the makeshift weapon with his fingertip. "I took this off a dead man a few miles outside Fort Leavenworth. Wish I could describe his features for you, but when I found him, he didn't have a face left."

I had mixed feelings about the news. Happy to have Grizz dead. Pleased that someone gave the bastard what he dished out to others. Uneasy that our unknown killers still couldn't be identified. Unfortunately, Meeks' theory about Undead riders was the only explanation left. But who possessed enough power to control such ruthless supernatural killers?

"The things you don't know about Necromancy are too numerous to mention," Hesperos said, squatting beside me. "Spare me any attempts at a clever retort. Your new friend seems anxious enough without suspecting his shackle mate is insane."

I glanced at my fellow prisoner, who was listening intently to the men at the campfire. Sweat bubbled from Meeks' skin, staining the collar of his filthy shirt with wet despite the coolness of the evening. His wild eyes darted from the soldiers to some invisible objects hidden in the darkness encircling the camp. Meeks was a terrified animal caught in a trap. I imagine he'd chew through his shackles if he could.

"He knows," Hesperos said. "They're coming, Dunham. It won't be long now before the riders try to take you. Join with me, and we can stop them with my power." A hungry glint flashed in his eyes. "I'll take control of the riders and then use them."

"Use them how?" I asked. "They're killers, not clerks."

"I have a few notions. For example, they can get us to this San Francisco you so desperately want to visit."

"Then what happens to me?"

"What?" Meeks asked.

"Careful, even this coward isn't a complete fool."

Hesperos brushed ghostly fingers across the spot where the Ouroboros lived upon my chest. "Your time on this earth is almost at an end, Dunham. Join with me now, and you'll play a part in our eternal life. A small one, but a part nonetheless."

"No." I spat. "I control who I am in this life."

"Look at these pillars of the law. Do you see the fear in their eyes?" He stood and took a step back toward the shadows. "Soon, they will understand what tracks them. You'll see. These men will do anything to escape alive. How long will you last once they discover it is you who these Hell-sent creatures are hunting?"

On the constant wind came the roar of thundering hooves. The deafening sound clamored from every direction. I twisted my head around, trying to pinpoint the coming riders. Instead, I found creeping fingers of thick fog crawling across the ground. Its thick body encircled our camp in a barrier of eerie gray. Then a scent wafted in the swirling mist to lightly touch my nose. Perfume. The same aroma I'd smelled at the killings on the Pioneer Road.

Upon my chest, the Ouroboros writhed anxiously, ready to fight. "What in the hell is coming?"

"Hell. Precisely. I hope you survive the night, Dunham. Call for me when you change your mind." Hesperos disappeared, giving me one last superior grin.

A sudden powerful gust of frigid wind reduced the campfire's flames to a sputtering flicker. Marshal Barlow and the soldiers jumped to their feet with weapons drawn. I, unable to protect myself or the camp, stayed put and stared helplessly into the wall of fog.

"Build up the fire, for God's sake!" Meeks cried. "They'll be on us at any moment!"

"Shut your mouth, Prisoner!" Barlow edged closer to the sergeant. "Milton, what do you make of this fog. Ever see anything in nature come up so fast?"

"No, sir," Milton said, using the end of his rifle barrel to trace the shrinking circle of light made by our campfire. "It must be a trick. A smoke bomb, maybe?"

Then something moved inside the wall of fog a few feet from my left. I thought I saw the brim of a hat, but the shape retreated again before I could be sure. Other objects – moving impossibly fast – swept along the barrier just out of sight. I couldn't see them, but the Ouroboros' magic helped me sense they were there. After months of hunting, the Undead had found me.

"What demon's magic is this?" Barlow aimed at the fog. "Fire your weapons, fools."

"What are we supposed to shoot at?" Milton asked. "There's nothing there."

Corporal Nichols flew across the camp and landed at the edge of the fog. Pulling against my restraints, I reached bound hands toward the corporal. His fingers grasped through the distance between us, trying to reach me. Our eyes locked. Gazing into his soul, I recognized mortal fear. Suddenly, the same invisible hand grabbed Nichols and dragged him through the sagebrush into the night.

"Get after him!" Barlow ordered.

His words struck weakly upon the members of the posse. Mouths open in horrified astonishment, we listened as Nichols' pleading cries penetrated the fog. I, not fairing much better against the terror visiting our group, tugged helplessly against my restraints. Then Nichols' screams abruptly stopped as a malicious laugh penetrated the fog. Pieces of the corporal's body flew back into camp. I pulled in my legs, narrowly avoiding his severed head.

Like a fleeing storm, the laughter died as the wall of fog slowly retreated. God in Heaven, what were those things? Then I saw a red light glowing around a wide-brimmed hat and knew the good Lord had nothing to do with this nightmare. My favorite assassin was back, and he was riding with Hell's own posse this time. The necromancer gave me a vicious grin and stepped back into the shadows.

CHAPTER THIRTY-FOUR

The corporal's burial was a quick hole and a hallelujah. Not trusting the task to Meeks or me, Sergeant Milton dug the grave for Nichols himself. His men looked on in uneasy silence, leaving their sergeant to brood.

"You men get over there and fill in the grave," Marshal Barlow said, thrusting a finger at two unlucky soldiers. "I'm sorry, Sergeant, but we don't have time for eulogies. You've seen what those killers can do. We can't stay out here in the open."

Milton threw down his shovel and flew at the marshal. His fist slammed against Barlow's jaw with an audible whack. Milton's strike barely nudged the man's buffalo-sized head. Spitting a dribble of blood, the marshal grabbed Milton's brass buttons and picked him up like a sack of flour. I made a mental note not to provoke Marshal Barlow as the big man carried Sergeant Milton to the side. Though they were out of earshot, I deduced the depths of their disagreement in the tense positions of their bodies and the barrage of threatening arm gestures.

"Oh, dear," Meeks said, frowning as he watched the two men argue. "This isn't good. They must work together if we are to have any hope of surviving."

"That's one theory, I suppose." I lifted my face to the gentle rays of a September sun. Discord was a good thing. The more time Milton and Barlow focused on their hatred of each other, the more opportunities I would have to slip away.

Stomping past us like a bull buffalo, Barlow was on his horse before the last shovel full of dirt landed atop the corporal's shallow grave. The animal stomped the ground, echoing its rider's mood.

"Well, don't stand around waiting for the angels to sing!" The marshal growled. "If these bastards are renegades, then we won't make Pueblo. I know a place with plenty of men and arms. Hell, at least there was when I was last there two months ago. Now, mount up! We head west to Greenhorn Mountain."

"Shit. Barlow's taking us to Fort Victory," Mason said, exchanging an uneasy look with Peterman.

I scanned their unhappy faces, not liking what I saw there. "What's Fort Victory?"

"You ask too many questions, prisoner." Mason eyed me. "Get on the horse."

Peterman rubbed at the stubble on his chin and shrugged. "Hell. I guess he has a right to know what's ahead, seeing as he and his partner there might not see a court of law after this journey.

The army built a temporary fort around an abandoned trading post in the foothills of Greenhorn Mountain. It stationed a single battalion of experienced soldiers there during the war. Their assignment was to patrol the territory and protect travelers along the Santa Fe Trail and the Pioneer Road. The fort was supposed to be shuttered, and the soldiers reassigned when the war ended a few months back." Peterman shook his head. "I hope the marshal is right about the men and arms."

"And if he's wrong?" I asked.

"Fort Vic is in the middle of nowhere. There isn't a sign of civilization for hundreds of miles," Mason said. "We'd be on our own."

"Then why does Marshal Barlow believe soldiers are still there?"

"Well, that's a good question, prisoner," he said. "Rebels aren't the only ones who don't want to admit the war is over. Let's just say Fort Vic's commander is an ambitious man."

"Mason. Peterman," Sergeant Milton barked. "Stop gossiping like a pair of old women and get those prisoners moving."

Greenhorn Mountain burst from the plains like a 12,000-foot herald of doom. Though Fall laced the plains with color, snow blanketed Greenhorn's peak. A strange foreboding snatched the last of my hope as we drew closer to the mountain's foothills. Had Peterman been correct? Would I see civilization again?

Barlow suddenly called a stop and dismounted. His large body leaned over to examine something on the ground. Mason drew our horse close to the marshal, giving me an excellent view of the gore Barlow was poking at with a stick. A cluster of dead birds had been torn to pieces, their severed wings forming an arrow pointing toward Greenhorn Mountain's forest-covered foothills.

"The bastards are playing with us." Barlow spat on the ground.

"Let's not play their game, marshal," I said. "We could go back to the Arkansas River."

"And give you a chance to escape?" Barlow grunted. "My daddy didn't raise no stupid children, Raynor."

"Just trying to be helpful."

"Nice try, prisoner," Mason murmured. "We're being herded to Fort Vic. The marshal is the only one who won't admit it."

Leaving the tattered wings behind, we headed ever closer to Greenhorn Mountain. Sullen silence hung over the group as we rode. I cast uneasy glances upon the faces of my fellow wanderers. Dread rather than hope filled their eyes. Somewhere Hesperos was getting great pleasure out of being right.

Great plumes of wet-ladened clouds crept over the mountain's peak. Their bodies grew darker as the miles fell away. Then, as if warning us to turn back, nature sent a thunderstorm down upon our posse. Rain soaked the ground until rivulets of water tumbled toward prairie land on the mountain trails. Thwarted by the weather, Barlow reluctantly gave the order to make camp at the base of the foothills.

I eased off our horse, narrowly avoiding a large mud puddle, anxious to swallow my boot. Meeks wasn't as lucky and landed on his knees in the belly of the dirty pool. Any hope of saving my footwear was dashed when Mason ordered me in to help Meeks to his feet. Nothing put a man in a sour mood quicker than cold, wet feet. Naturally, I took the opportunity to lash out at the man responsible for my predicament.

"Your fort seems to be missing, marshal," I said, glaring at Barlow through the sheets of cold rain. "Now what?"

"It's here, Raynor." Barlow shot me a murderous glare. "The storm may have sent us off course a mile or two, but Fort Victory is somewhere in these foothills."

Milton whistled from between two parted evergreen boughs. "I found a reasonably dry patch of ground inside these trees. Shall we?"

Anxious to get out of the storm, the posse led their horses through the thick evergreens. Though the air was still damp, I found the green canopy comforting. It was a relief to leave the freezing rain behind.

"Listen to me, Raynor," Sergeant Milton grabbed my arm as we passed. "I would appreciate it if you keep your observations to yourself. The men are nervous enough without provocation."

I shrugged. "I'll do my best."

"That's all I can ask. Make sure you secure those shackles to the tree," Milton told Peterman.

"Come on, Sergeant. Take these off." I shook my irons at him. "We aren't going to run. Where would we go? If the wilderness doesn't kill us, then those renegades will."

"You just won't cooperate, Raynor." The sergeant shook his head. "Not a chance. I trust you about as much as I trust Meeks."

Sergent Milton nodded as Peterman tugged at our chains. The sergeant, satisfied we were secured to his liking, turned his back, and walked away. Milton gave me a parting gesture I considered beneath him.

"Can't you build the fire up?" Meeks called after him. "They won't come inside the firelight."

"You think," I said. "It seems to me these killers don't fear much."

A sudden nip from the Ouroboros was all the warning I had before the first tendrils of fog crept between the tree boughs. Laughter, not of this world, filled the darkness around our camp. I froze as the back of my neck crawled under the wrongness of the sensation.

Barlow and his men were on their feet with weapons drawn in an instant. They made a tight circle around the camp, but our supernatural visitors hid behind a veil of thick fog.

Professor. Where is your audience now?

The voice sounded strangled as if strained from endless screaming. I kept my face blank, emotionless. I don't know who my stalkers were or how they learned about Lester, but I wasn't going to give anything away.

"There's no Professor here," Barlow shouted at the disembodied voice. "You've got the wrong men."

"Do we?" Cackles struck our ears from every direction, confirming they had us surrounded.

Then two men on both ends of Barlow's armed line fell to the ground. Invisible hands dragged them toward the body of fog. Screaming and clawing at the Earth, they were gone before anyone could move to help them.

"Come into the light, cowards!" Barlow shouted.

Those are hasty words you WON'T live to regret, lawman. Are you so eager for death?

"I'm the law, damn you! And by God, I will take you in for the atrocities you've committed."

How can we refuse such a cordial invitation?

The Ouroboros bucked wildly beneath my shirt as nine figures stepped out of the fog. Every instinct I possessed warned that evil was among us. Nine riders stood at the edge of the light, their storm-gray dusters billowing in a constant wind fueled by Hell itself. Masked in the shadows of their hats, I couldn't see any defined facial features.

You can't hide from Hell's punishment, Professor," they said as one. *"We're coming for you. Death will be slow in giving its sweet release.*

A massive wave of fog rolled forward to engulf the riders. Its thick body moved backward until it finally disappeared into the darkness, leaving us with a clear night sky overhead. I shivered under the cold stars. Hell was hunting me. I knew better than most you couldn't escape your fate.

"What do you know about this, Meeks? Are you the professor they're hunting for?" Barlow backhanded him hard. "By God, you better tell me. Our lives depend on it."

Meeks wiped at the blood trickling from his ears. "I swear I don't know who they are."

"According to your story, they tracked the wagon train and followed you on the road to Pueblo." Barlow put the barrel of his gun to Meek's head. "Why would they be so keen if they didn't have a beef with you?"

"I wasn't the only one in all those places." Meeks, the little weasel, turned anxious eyes upon me. "Raynor was on the wagon train too."

"And yet they didn't attack me."

It was true – for the most part. I don't know why the riders were playing with Meeks. I didn't care. It was time to look for an escape before Barlow forgot his hatred of Meeks and started believing the little weasel.

"Listen, does it matter?" I chimed in before Meeks could speak. "They don't seem shy about killing any of us. If we can make Fort Victory tomorrow, we can do something about them."

"How?" Sergeant Milton stuffed his gun irritably in its holster. "They've spooked the horses."

"We'll have to risk the dark to catch them," Barlow said. "Let's move before the horses run clear to Kansas!" Barlow turned his heavy glare on Milton. "We make for Fort Victory at first light, and I do mean the second the horses can see well enough to move on the trail."

The marshal shoved Meeks away and joined the other men in search of our horses. Meeks, in response, fell against me with a whoosh of air. His eyes rolled back, exposing the white. Fainted, probably. I shoved him off and scooted away.

A sudden prickling of apprehension raced along my arms and neck. My gaze was drawn instinctively toward a sparse clump of trees outside the camp. Orange-red fire glowed through the trunks. Damn. It was the man in the wide-brimmed hat. I scooted on my backside until the chains chafed my skin. Meeks was still unconscious from his fainting spell while the marshal and his men were chasing after the horses. Hands bound, I was alone and unable to defend myself.

Mr. Black Hat lifted his hands, swirling them in the air. Intricate patterns of red glowed for a moment before a jet of blazing magic streaked toward me. I rolled out of the way, barely escaping the heat of burning flames left behind from his attack. Mr. Black Hat's blazing streams scorched the ground about me until hot, blackened patches of Earth boxed me in.

"Who are you? Why are you trying to kill me?"

"Hapless fool! You don't know?"

His voice was a rich baritone laced with traces of an exotic accent. Sharp features and porcelain skin marked him as a visitor from the orient, while his perfect English suggested he was from an upper-class family. But, posh or not, Mr. Black Hat was motivated to kill me and had traveled a long way to do the deed.

"Hesperos! Doran!"

Damn those two to the Devil. Hesperos and his pet seemed to come when it was least convenient for me. Apparently, they couldn't be bothered when I was in real trouble. Then reluctantly, my mind flashed back to the banks of the Arkansas. I'd used my terrible power on the Reverend Edgewater's mob. The beam of white light had utterly scorched all those men in seconds. It might take care of Mr. Black Hat.

I closed my eyes and focused. Reaching down into the depths of my soul, I summoned every ambient memory I could muster. My mind conjured sensations from the burning heat of purity to the odor of charred flesh. Then I called to the power.

Nothing happened.

Panicked by my failure, I called until sweat rolled down my forehead. All the while, Mr. Black Hat watched with condescending amusement. What good was magic to me if it didn't work when I needed it?

"Stop it, Meat sack," Doran whispered in my ear. "You'll hurt yourself."

I twisted against my bonds but couldn't move enough to make eye contact with my reluctant rescuer. Not wanting to irritate the abrasions already rankling my skin from the chains, I gave up with a huff.

"Who is he? Scratch that. What is he, and why is he trying to kill me?"

"I should think that would be obvious," Doran said, the sneer heavy in his words. "That is a real-life necromancer. He is commanding the Undead killers hunting you." Doran gave me a derisive snort. "Do you imagine he cares about what happened in Lester? He's after you, dimwit, because you're Hesperos' new body bag. Nothing more."

"How do we stop him?"

"We? You are a presumptuous meat sack, aren't you?" Doran gave me a humorless laugh. "Better for me if he were to kill you." The creature winced as if struck with sudden and harsh pain. "Hesperos is near."

"He can hear you?" I asked. "I take it he doesn't want you to share any tidbits of information."

"Capture the fire necromancer, and you may have a chance to escape Hesperos' plans for you."

Then the ground rumbled as Doran – taking the form of a green elephant made of stone – charged at the necromancer. Green tusks knocked Mr. Black Hat off his feet and into the night. I heard cursing and stomping, but the battle was either abandoned or had moved too far away from the camp.

"What the hell was that sound?" Barlow approached the campfire with his recovered horse in tow.

"Storm's coming, I suppose," I said with a shrug.

Meeks sat up and rubbed at his face with a groan. "What happened?"

"That's twice you owe me, Meeks," I grumbled. "I'm a generous man, but you've screwed me too many times. I won't save your ass again."

"Well, that's not very Christian of you, Reverend," Meeks hissed in a harsh whisper. "Yes, I remember what you were on the Santa Fe Trail. Or would you prefer I call you, Professor?"

"You can't call me anything if I shove your teeth down your throat."

Meeks couldn't wait to rat me out to save his own skin. Doran wanted to kill me while Hesperos planned to wear me like a new suit. It was official. I needed new traveling companions.

CHAPTER THIRTY-FIVE

"It was here two months ago." Marshal Barlow twisted his body around in the saddle, searching the empty hilltop with impatient eyes. A sudden gust of wind bit at the brim of his hat. Its chilly teeth threatened to tear the garment from atop his head. He absently tugged on the bonnet string to secure his hat in place.

Two small twisters rose from the ground beside our horses. Dirt and dead leaves swirled at a mad pace as the dust devils danced around one another. My gaze followed their waltz as they raced each other down the steep hill.

"The hell it was," I told Barlow. "You're lost."

The marshal met my incredulous glare with gritted teeth. Face glowing red under his unkempt whiskers, Barlow pulled his pistol and aimed it at my head. Hard lines of stubborn will made deep crevices around his eyes. He cocked his gun, telling me I'd gone too far this time.

"Call me a liar again and see what happens."

Then a fist full of knuckles struck my chin, sending me rocking backward on the horse. Sergeant Milton eyed me with his other fist, ready to deliver another blow. I got the hint. My obvious insights weren't appreciated.

"I warned you about keeping your opinions to yourself, prisoner," Sergeant Milton said.

The sergeant prodded his horse forward, blocking me from Barlow's view. He kept his hands away from his weapons and patiently waited for Barlow's temper to subside. I held my breath as the moments slipped away.

"He's not worth the bullet," Barlow uttered a final curse and holstered his gun. "I take it you have some thoughts, Sergeant."

"The army would have sent word to close Fort Victory when the war ended, Marshal." Sergeant Milton said. "Maybe the fort's commander destroyed all the buildings so the wrong sort of men wouldn't use them?"

"Thieves and rustlers, you mean?" Barlow shrugged. "It's a good theory, but I don't think so. My gut tells me different. We'll keep searching."

"The weather is against us," Milton said, glancing at the approaching clouds. "I suggest a compromise. Can we agree to give your search one more day? Then, if we don't find anything, we'll head back to Pueblo in the morning."

"We keep searching as long as I say we keep searching," Barlow said.

Sergeant Milton gave his men a slight shake of his head as Barlow turned his horse north. Mason nodded his acknowledgment and uncovered the barrel of a gun he'd had hidden beneath a piece of cloth. He holstered the weapon with a wink at me. Interesting. The sergeant had plans to mutiny against the marshal. His soldiers were ready to follow suit. I suspected the remaining three civilian posse members wouldn't resist either. They didn't seem keen on Barlow's obsessive need to keep wandering among the frigid trees.

Greenhorn Mountain and its forest-covered foothills were neighbors to the Sangre De Cristo mountains at the southern end of the Rockies. I'd wanted to avoid these snowmakers and get out of the Colorado Territory before winter hit. This early snowfall better be some fluke rather than a sign of what lay ahead for me.

The clouds parted, exposing a round bald peak poking through the treetops. Standing at over 12,000 feet, the mountaintop was covered in shards of rock. It dipped into a saddle-like formation before rolling back toward the tree line.

We continued up the narrow trail ascending the foothills. White mixed in the wind as signs of a mountain Autumn fluttered upon the swirling air. Sharp, biting wind gusts gnawed at my fingers as I tugged my jacket tighter. Its touch made me nostalgic for the suffocating heat of the Grand Prairie.

"Shit weather. Folks don't call these the Wet Mountains for nothing," Peterman groused. "That's not good for us. We're dead men if we get trapped in deep snow with no shelter."

"Do you think Fort Victory is close by?" Meeks asked, teeth chattering in the bitter wind.

"It should have been back on the hilltop like Marshal Barlow said." Mason spat and gripped his reins tighter. "If the damn place existed at all."

"I don't like being closed in by all these trees," Meeks said, scanning the branches surrounding us.

"Were the plains any better?" I asked with a grunt. "The killers chasing us seem to be able to hide in any terrain."

Barlow held up his arm, signaling another stop. It was the third time the marshal had made us wait while he examined the ground for signs of his missing fort. Barlow seemed almost manic as he stared at the dirt. I, for my part, couldn't see a damn thing except for muddy animal prints and a whole lot of nothing.

"Enough. We need to turn back, Marshal," Sergeant Milton said. "My men and I have been patient while you've looked for signs, but we're about to run into some bad weather. You must face the facts, Sir. Fort Victory isn't here anymore. Its men and arms are long gone."

Apparently, Sergeant Milton was the only soul among us who could voice his concerns. Even so, Barlow's back stiffened. I waited for the inevitable outburst. Instead, he laughed and pointed to the ground.

"Are you so sure, Sergeant?" Barlow asked. "Then tell me why there are fresh horseshoe prints in the mud! Look. Iron made those marks, not wild horses."

"He's right," Milton said. "The tracks trample each other in a single file formation to conceal their numbers."

Careful to hide their passing, the riders had taken great care not to break branches or disturb their surroundings. If not for the keen eye of the marshal, I would have written off the tracks in the mud as belonging to deer or wild horses.

Then a sharp whistle sounded upon the wind. A dozen or more Union bluecoats with rifles trained on our posse poured out of the trees to surround us. Marshal Barlow had been right about Fort Victory, but unfortunately for us, he'd not considered if we'd be welcome.

"What the hell is going on? I'm a United States Marshal."

A Union officer with bright brass buttons and a clean-shaven face slowly rode toward Barlow. He gave the marshal a chilly nod and then took in the Union soldiers in our posse with a raised eyebrow.

"Silvers! What game are you playing?" Barlow growled. "Why point your weapons at us?"

"Lieutenant." Sergeant Milton saluted, cutting the marshal's angry cursing short. "We're stationed out of Fort Leavenworth. My men and I were assigned to assist Marshal Barlow in his search for a prisoner." He pointed to Meeks and me. "We're requesting aid."

"Perhaps you are who you say you are, Sergeant." Lieutenant Silvers let his disapproving gaze sweep across our company.

"As to whether you serve the true United States Government, that's for the captain to decide," he said. "You'll come with us to Fort Victory as our prisoners."

Barlow and Sergeant Milton exchanged flabbergasted looks as they handed over their weapons. The rest of the posse followed suit. They didn't have much choice. Fort Victory's defenders had us caught in their ambush.

CHAPTER THIRTY-SIX

Fort Victory wasn't the stronghold of military might I'd hoped. After a long, ass-blistering journey, our mounts shifted under the evening shadows of a disappointing eight-foot log fence. We approached from the northeast, giving me an underwhelming glimpse of the fort's size. Honestly, I'd seen bigger farmyards. Where were the battalions of men and arms Barlow had promised?

Two army bluecoats pulled open the gates, their suspicious eyes following as we passed. I couldn't fault their inquisitiveness. We were probably the first entertainment the soldiers had for months. Curiosities of any kind would be a treat. I'd felt the same on the Santa Fe Trail.

"They all look like they're ready for a damn parade," Mason said, glaring at the clean uniforms and shiny boots of the fort's men.

Ignoring the curious stares, I swept my gaze around our new temporary home. My visual tour didn't take long. Built around the ruins of an abandoned trading post, Fort Victory was no bigger than the cattle yard at a train station. Canvas tents lined the back wall giving the fort a temporary feel. These fabric shelters had room enough to hold about thirty men, but not comfortably. I didn't envy the men sleeping within canvas walls during a Colorado snowstorm.

The fragrance of horse flesh and hay struck me as we moved closer to the main building. Several roughly built lean-to shelters dotted the compound. These structures were tied together with rope, giving them a portable appearance. The shelters housed the fort's resident horses. Large dull eyes lazily followed us as they chewed their dried mountain grass.

In the very center of the yard was the only other permanent structure in the entire fort. A stockade rose from the wilderness like a frightening monument to justice. Freshly painted trim accentuated thick iron bars in the windows. The cells lay in a diagonal line from the entrance to the trading post and had a nice view of the gates.

A questionably hygienic doctor's surgery leaned against the back of the stockade while a clean tent anchored against its south side. Based on the United States flag flapping next to its opening and the stiff guard standing to one side, I guessed this was the fort's headquarters.

The tent's flap opened, and a man exited the tent. He was tall with a neat mustache and shiny brass buttons on his uniform. Puffing on his large pipe, he waited as we pulled to a stop before the stockade. The officer's raven hair was neatly slicked against his scalp, contrasting Barlow's ruddy and rough appearance. Trim eyebrows and a thin mustache were the only signs of hair on his face.

"You've come for another unexpected visit, Marshal Barlow. It would appear you've been hunting dangerous criminals again." His mouth curled, taking its sparse mustache upward. "The skinny one has all the markings of a hardened thug."

His distinctive lack of a recognizable accent marked him as one of the east coast elites. I'd guess he was either a courtier of Washington or aspired to be. In my travels from state to state, I'd met ambitious social climbers like the captain. They were dangerous animals best avoided, especially the ones who played their power games in the name of patriotism.

"It wasn't exactly our choice," Barlow said, glaring at Silvers.

"Can I assume you'll be leaving us soon then?"

The marshal dismounted with a grunt. "Just as soon as I can, Captain Farley. I've got two prisoners who'll need the use of your stockade for tonight. We ran into some trouble with a band of renegade soldiers. They've killed some of my men."

"And you'd like us to help track them down." Farley's smile was slow and indulgent. "You have our aid, naturally. Whatever we can do to help speed you on your way."

Strained politeness. These two didn't like each other. It was possible they'd been on different sides of the war. Things didn't get any friendlier when the posse dismounted, and the marshal prodded Meeks and me coldly past the captain toward the entrance of the stockade.

"This is a well-built stockade for a fort that's not supposed to be open, Captain. I thought you men had been reassigned," Barlow said.

"Is that what you thought, Marshal?" Captain Farley raised his arm, and Silvers pointed his rifle at Barlow. "Who sent you? Was it Johnston? Cooper, perhaps?"

"Sir," Sergeant Milton stepped beside Barlow and saluted the captain. "I'm Sergeant Milton. My men and I are out of Fort Leavenworth. Our orders are to assist

Marshal Barlow with hunting down the murderer Meeks. I can assure you. The marshal is loyal to the United States government."

"How would you know if he secretly wasn't, Sergent?" Farley asked with an odd sort of glimmer in his eyes. "I, too, once trusted a man who pretended to be honorable. He cut my throat as I slept."

Farley unbuttoned his collar and opened the tunic, exposing an ugly strip of red leather. Whoever wielded the knife did a lousy job at cutting a straight line. Either that or Farley had put up one hell of a fight. Clearly, the experience had left him unsettled.

"No, Sergeant, I don't give my trust freely anymore. Anyone could be a confederate spy. Fort Victory is still desperately needed to protect our interests in the Northwest."

"Spies?" Milton cast a quick warning glance to Barlow. "You moved the fort from its original location to keep it secret, Sir?"

"Well done, Sergeant." Farley gave him an appreciative nod. "Our stockade has held quite a few spies now. How many since we've moved up into the foothills, Silvers?"

"Twenty-eight, Sir." Silvers cocked the rifle he had aimed at Barlow. "Every last one of them claiming to be trappers or pioneers headed west."

Eyes widening in troubled confusion, Milton said, "Yes, Sir."

"Barlow, you've always been a crude man. I suppose I must overlook your rather rude and probing questions for the time being." Farley nodded for Silvers to lower his weapon. "Our stockade is at your disposal for the night."

CHAPTER THIRTY-SEVEN

The building's interior was no less austere than its facade. Six empty cells stood at attention against the exterior walls with no privacy between them. A single desk faced the door, offering its occupant an unobstructed view of future visitors. Behind the guard's perch was a well-built gun case with a firm iron lock.

Barlow pushed me into the farthest cell adjacent to the courtyard as Milton shoved Meeks into a cell across from me. Iron bars rattled as the doors shut hard. Moving to the window, I caught the tantalizing view of Fort Victory's open gates. Freedom was a mere two hundred feet away. Unfortunately, I wouldn't be breaking out of here any time soon. The bars were too sturdy and the security too tight for escape. I'd have to pick my moment when they moved me to a larger town for trial.

"I don't like being unarmed while I'm locked up with such unfriendly company," Barlow said, eyeing the soldiers as they delivered the posse's confiscated weapons to the stockade guard.

"Please don't make trouble, Marshal," Milton told him. "Captain Farley holds all the power here. If you press him too hard, he might lock you up with Raynor and Meeks."

Barlow, snatching our money belts from one of the soldier's arms, marched out of the stockade. I stared after him through the bars as he stormed across the courtyard toward the stables. Curse the hardheaded fool! If someone stole my money during the night, I'd take it out of Barlow's hide.

"That all of them?" The stockade guard asked as the last gun belts clattered atop his desk. "Well, go on about your duties then."

His friends shuffled back into the cold Colorado afternoon, leaving the stockade guard with a pile of iron. He made a great show of listing each of our belongings in a ledger book. I shook my head as I watched him scribble. The army may be meticulous in its records, but I'd bet some of our guns would go missing by the time we left. If we left. The guard unlocked the gun case and stuffed the weapons inside. His job done, he poured himself a cup of coffee from the simmering pot and sat down to ignore us.

Staring through the bars in my cell window again, I let Fort Victory's structured life play out before me. The soldiers, not on guard duty at the gates or watching the forests along the fences, formed two perfect lines. They began drills and marched across the courtyard like Fort Victory was a key military stronghold. All these exhausting activities were performed under the watchful eyes of Captain Farley and Lieutenant Silvers.

The marshal didn't share their interest in daily routines. He stood beside them, having a one-sided argument. I chuckled when he finally threw his arms in the air and stormed back to the stables. Farley didn't plan to search out the riders quite yet. Maybe he'd do so tomorrow? Or maybe he'd make Barlow wait a few more days. I'd have to trust Lady Luck to keep me off the captain's spy list until it was time for us to depart.

"I wonder how long it will take for Captain Farley to decide we're spies," I said, turning to Meeks. "Did you notice the stretch of the fence next to the fort's gates? It's full of bullet holes. Farley likes to shoot the poor souls he believes are Confederate spies."

Meeks lifted his head from his hands. He sighed and nodded. Taking his spectacles off, he pinched them between his fingers. His other hand lifted an edge of the clean blanket and began to wipe the glass gently.

"Justice has found me. I can't say I don't deserve to be shot." Meeks lifted his eyes, finding my gaze. "Have you ever been to Wagon City? No, I suppose not. It's not Boston, but it's my hometown."

"So why did you do it, then?" I asked.

"The town got a new train station. Folks started making more money shipping their crops to the next county." He looked down at his hands. "Harvest time came. Well, I'd never seen so much money in one place. I suppose I couldn't help myself." He lifted his head when I laughed. "You don't understand. Many of my neighbors lost everything they had because of me. I hate myself for what I've done."

"You're sorry you got caught. I guarantee you'd do the same thing if you saw that much money again."

"I'd like to think I wouldn't."

"Marshal Barlow may be a lawman, Meeks, but I'm almost sure he's human. You're responsible for his friend's death. I wouldn't take bets on you reaching civilization." I flicked a finger against the bars between us. "Hell, I don't like our chances escaping this fort alive."

Cool mountain air swept in as the outside door opened. An old soldier with a wooden leg gave us a cursory glance. Then, leaning his thin body on a wooden crutch, he moved to the guard desk. Two more soldiers carried a pot of stew and fresh coffee. My mouth watered as the scent of food touched my nose. Marshal Barlow hadn't been too free with his vittles.

"Go fetch yourself some chow, Donaldson. I can sit with the prisoners while they eat."

"Much obliged, Spoons."

The one-legged old soldier hobbled down the line of cells toward Meeks and me. His silent helpers shoved full bowls of stew through a small opening in our cell doors. Clumps of what I hoped were potatoes floated on the surface.

"What is it?" Meeks asked, poking at the bowl of stew with his spoon.

"That there is hellfire stew. Gotta do something with all that hardtack." Spoons slapped his knee as he laughed.

Goody. More hardtack. I had to admit the food was decent despite its main ingredient. Hot coffee served to boost my mood considerably. I downed my portion and took Meeks' untouched share. Nothing ruined my hunger for food. You ate when you could. A man who'd gone without knew the wisdom in that.

"It's good to see a man with an appetite for my cooking, Mr. Raynor. Not many other choices in old Fort Vic."

"Call me, Dun. You been with the fort long?"

Spoons passed his flask to me. "Captain Farley says the army will build a bigger fort in these foothills with fancy barracks and tall walls once they see how important Fort Vic is for the West. I suppose the territory needs it, but just the same, I'll miss the ruggedness of this place."

I decided not to risk testing Spoons' loyalty to his mad captain. The fort's soldiers had willingly followed Farley up the side of the mountain despite clear orders from Washington. Still, I needed to test the waters if I were going to escape.

"And what about your fancy captain? Is he going to stay in command?"

Spoons grinned, exposing more gum than teeth. "You mean old Fussy Farley? Oh no, sir, our good captain has a hankering for a post back east. He misses all those white-gloved dances and brushing elbows with the gentry."

"He and Marshal Barlow don't seem to like each other much."

"I've never seen two men hate each other quicker in my life. Captain don't like people coming into his backyard and barking orders, you see. That Marshal Barlow is a hard man. He wants your friend Meeks here in the worst way." He grinned and took the flask from my hand. "I like you, Dun. Don't care what you done. You seem like a decent enough fella. Just you keep your head down on the road. What's between Meeks and the marshal is their business. Remember that, and you'll stay alive longer."

"Best advice I've heard in a long time, Spoons."

The old cook's shuffling gait made lonely echoes in the nearly empty stockade. He waved to Donaldson, who'd just returned from his meal, and exited into our tiny safety bubble in the middle of the hostile wilderness.

Chapter Thirty-Eight

My appreciation for the stockade had slightly improved by the following day. I'd gotten a decent night's sleep on the plank, passing for a cot. It was better than being on the cold ground, but not by much.

Hours passed as I watched the courtyard through my window. Finally, I spotted Mason and Peterman as they passed within the small vantage point afforded me by the cell window. Shaved and sporting clean uniforms, my former traveling companions didn't seem thrilled with their new stations among the fort's men. Barlow and Sergeant Milton, however, were worryingly absent. I'll admit thoughts of my missing money belt rather than concern for their welfare rested heavily on my mind.

Spoons delivered our evening meal as the last sliver of sun dropped below the gates. He sunk onto a stool outside my cell door with a long sigh. A broad smile filled with missing teeth formed as he watched Meeks take a few bites of bread.

"Eat up. You'll need to keep your strength for the trip back to Fort Leavenworth. Marshal Barlow's keen to leave as soon as the way is clear," Spoons told us. "Captain Farley decided to send scouts back down to the fort's old location the night you arrived. They've been gone a good long while. 'Course, they're supposed to cover their tracks, so no one follows them back here."

"Sure," I said, glancing at Meeks' troubled face. "That's probably it."

I suspected the scouts wouldn't be seen again on this side of the veil. The thought soured my good humor. I'd allowed myself the brief illusion of safety only a heavily guarded fort could provide.

"Well, can't stay here gossiping all night," Spoons said, lifting his old body to a swaying stand. "Captain wants me to guard the supplies. Some varmint is stealing corn."

I shook my head as I regarded the cook's useless leg dragging along the floor. Captain Farley earned a little more of my ill will for ordering a crippled old man to perform night guard duty. I'd seen my share of the night watch. It was hard on younger men than Spoons.

"They've killed the scouts, haven't they?" Meeks asked in a quiet voice.

"You don't say!" I slammed a palm against one of the bars of my cell. "I've got to get out of here."

"What would you do?" Meeks asked. "If you could escape, I mean."

"Ride like hell for Denver," I said. "It doesn't matter now. All I can do is watch and wait."

I laid back in my cot with an exasperated sigh. My perch at the window gave me a good view of the guards and their routine. None of the soldiers, including our babysitter, seemed too concerned about their missing friends. Then again, Farley's scouts weren't any of my business either. I had my own problems. Once I found a way out of this cell, I'd snatched my money belt and the bank notes back from the marshal. I'd have a nice stake for life down in San Francisco then. Or Mexico. Hell, maybe I'd buy one of those haciendas by the ocean?

Tiny tickles of annoying conscience derailed my pleasant fantasy. I'd gone straight back to my old ways. Wasn't I trying to be a good man? Yes. But nobody was one hundred percent honest all the time. I could borrow the money – temporarily. Once I struck success, then I could return the bank notes. Shifting uncomfortably, I dismissed images of forlorn farmers. Maybe I'd pay them back with interest.

A distant howl broke through my thoughts. Odd. I hadn't noticed any dogs running around Fort Vic. Then more baying echoed against the fort's walls. Bloodhounds. The law had hunted me down in Louisiana when I was still a kid. I'd never forget the relentless baying of the dogs on my trail.

"Do you hear it?" Meeks sprang out of bed and threw his body against the bars.

The howls lifted into an unnerving crescendo. My gut did a flip. The pack of bloodhounds was getting closer. Good, God. Could the beast be right outside the stockade?

Then the Ouroboros wriggled on my chest. I bolted off my plank cot and moved to the window. The street looked clear. No sign of any hounds or other wild animals. Had I imagined the horrific howling?

An incorporeal mass rolled into the yard, blanketing everything in a thick cloud of foul-smelling mist. Two guards standing beside the closed gates caught my attention. Staring down at their boots, they danced a jig as they tried to extricate their feet from the fog.

Someone fired their rifle to my right. The soldier's scream was silenced with abrupt finality. Then, another scream pierced the mist to my left. It had come from the gates. I pressed my face against the window bars, straining to see. One of the guards slumped against the wood. The other was missing. How had our attackers gotten inside the fort and then attacked the soldiers by the gate afterward?

Shouts of alarm clamored about me as chaos broke out in Fort Victory. As if emboldened by their victim's terror, the hounds bayed louder. Gunfire amid screams of terror filled the night. I could merely watch out my window like a transfixed voyeur of death.

"Give me a damn gun!" Marshal Barlow growled as he ran inside the square landscape of my window.

"Can I trust you not to shoot me in the back?" Captain Farley asked.

"I've got other targets to worry about," the marshal said.

The two men raced toward the gates just as an invisible force snuffed all the torchlight from Fort Victory. Amid the baying of the hounds, I imagined I heard a woman's shrill laughter. The grating noise gave the woman a hysterical tenor as if she were standing on the edge of madness.

Behind me, Meeks shook the bars of his cell. Screams choked by incessant bawling, he looked as if he were having a mad fit. I pushed away from the window and reached for Meeks through the bars.

"It's them! They're here!"

"You saw them from inside the wagons, didn't you? Stop screaming and tell me who they are!"

Meeks faced me at last. He looked like hell itself was at the door. "I've told you! They came for us just like this the night the wagon train was attacked. Fog came in a wave, catching us off guard. Then the horrible baying of hounds circled about the wagons. We couldn't see them. Finally, when the killing started, I saw them, Dun. I saw them through the fog. Riders dressed in dusters and hats. I'm not making this up. You must believe me."

"Okay, Meeks. How did you escape then?"

"I crawled up inside of a wagon and closed my eyes. I didn't dare open them until the sun came back. Then I ran as fast as I could, but I didn't escape, did I? They've come back for me."

Riders dressed in hats and dusters. I dropped my hands away from the bars. No. The riders hadn't come for Meeks. They were here for me. I moved back to the window and gazed out into the street. The howling had stopped. The riders and their hounds were gone, but had they left anything behind them?

Then I saw the red glow of magic just outside the cell window. The necromancer who rode with the Dead was staring at me. Contempt radiated from his face in waves of disturbing hate. Something thudded behind me, but I was too transfixed by the man to turn around. Then the murderous sneer on the necromancer's face suddenly disappeared. He stepped back into the shadows and was gone.

"Hello, Meat Sack."

I spun away from the window and found Doran, sporting the body of a cattle dog, standing beside the unconscious Meeks. It chuckled with mischievous glee as if daring me to defend the thief.

"I'm tired of stumbling around in the dark. Who is the man in the wide-brimmed hat? Tell me!" I slammed the flat of my hand against the cold bars. "I want the whole truth this time, Doran. No more teasing."

"Why? Aren't you having fun? Very well. His name is Athan. He's a particularly nasty fire necromancer." Doran trotted over on padded paws and sat beside me with a huff. "Hesperos doesn't want you to know of Athan."

"And that's why you'll tell me, right?"

"We are beginning to understand each other, Meat Sack." Doran scratched behind his ear for a moment. "Athan was a priest of Hades like Hesperos. Unlike my captor, he was sold into the life by his parents. He, too, felt betrayed and bitter when Hades turned out to be a false god. Rather than focusing on living his many lives, he searched for a replacement for Hades. Athan soon found his new religion. Crime. He joined forces with Melampus for a time, but they had a falling out. Two massive egos don't tolerate each other for long."

"Melampus? Is he in Hesperos' necromancer club too?"

"They are called the Apeiron, Idiot. Melampus is known as the Alpha Mage. He's the most powerful among them. I believe your kind would call him a crime lord. Pray you never meet him." Doran stretched as he rose. "Athan wants to kill you so he may have Hesperos' power. He's strong and will not be easily defeated."

"Are you saying you want me to join with Hesperos too?"

"Don't be a fool! Hesperos keeps me his prisoner with this enchanted mark." Doran slapped a paw against the burning symbol on his forehead. "I was a sprite once. Sometimes I can still feel the wind calling me as it used to when I raced along the treetops." The cells grew still as I waited for Doran's mind to drift back into the confines of the bars. "Then Hesperos trapped me and others of my kind. He did experiments on us, trying to harness our power. I alone survived." Doran pierced me with a glare. "There isn't another creature on Earth like me. I will remain trapped as I am until Hesperos is dead. Never imagine I will allow you to join with him."

Doran's body shuttered with fast-moving colors until my eyes lost the edges of his body. Then the crow was back. It hopped onto the lip of the cell window and gave me a final caw before flying away.

Was there anyone that didn't want me dead? Of course, I couldn't blame Doran. Being a prisoner to someone else was a fate I also wanted to avoid. We had something in common, the creature and me. Neither one of us, however, could help the other or ourselves. Hesperos had us both trapped, but when the final test came, would Doran help me? Or would it kill me? Time would tell.

CHAPTER THIRTY-NINE

The putrid aroma of spent weapons and blood seeped into my cell in the brisk air of early dawn. Moans from the injured or dying had finally stopped. I'd listened to their eerie dirge for what seemed an eternity as I waited for the comfort of daylight.

Heavy boots stomped outside the stockade door stopping a few feet beyond my vantage point. Shouts followed by an occasional stray elbow poking into my line of sight indicated a scuffle. And was that a rope? It wasn't a great deductive leap to assume we were the subject of their argument.

Hell had visited its horrors upon Fort Victory last night. I was sure there'd been deaths. The soldiers needed someone to blame, and it was my bad luck to be one of their hapless targets. I doubted I could charm the terrified mob this time.

"We have company." I turned from the window and leaned against the cell's exterior wall.

The door banged open, and Captain Farley marched inside with an armed escort. Sergeant Milton trailed behind them. Eyes bright with fear and exhaustion examined us with eager care. Then Milton looked away, unable to meet my gaze. That couldn't be good.

Captain Farley stood with his chin up and hands clasped behind his back. His heavy glare scanned every inch of Meeks before his attention turned to me. I had the impression Farley was weighing me against an impossible standard.

"On your feet, Gentlemen. I've something to show you, and I certainly hope you can explain it."

Meeks shook his head with a whimper. "It wasn't my fault."

"You owe me answers, Mr. Meeks. If not for my insistence and Marshal Barlow's rifle, several men would have taken the law into their own hands last night."

Captain Farley nodded to Milton. The sergeant opened Meek's cell and stood aside as two soldiers carrying irons entered the cell. After a brief and pointless struggle, they slapped irons on the little thief and dragged him forward to the guard desk.

The captain turned to regard me. "You look the type to think before you make mistakes. Will you come quietly?"

I shrugged and held up my wrists to Milton. The sergeant kept his eyes on his work, not meeting my gaze as the irons clicked shut on my wrist. Then, walking with my chin up, I marched to the door. Meeks was watching me. He stopped fussing and let his shoulders drop with a moan.

Captain Farley headed the group as we marched into the yard and passed the entrance to Fort Victory. The gates had been ripped off their hinges and thrown several feet into the forest. Athan and his Undead friends were strong. They could easily break through the bars of the stockade and take me. So why didn't they?

The captain guided us toward two groups of soldiers tossing bodies into the back of a wagon. I didn't like the enraged looks they threw in my direction. Captain Farley hadn't been exaggerating. Meeks and I were lucky not to hang at the end of a rope this morning.

Terrified and unnatural sounds penetrated the stable walls as we passed. I'd experienced things decent men shouldn't know about, but those sounds were unlike anything hell had made. Then gunshots shattered the hushed morning.

"The horses all went mad." Captain Farley tugged at the tight collar of his uniform. "Many tried breaking through the stable walls with their rear legs. They kept kicking even as their bones broke. We've had to shoot every one of them."

I steadied myself under the weight of his glare. An unspoken accusation smoldered around the captain's being. He'd seen his animals terrified enough to break their own legs. It wouldn't take much to prompt Farley into a more brutal line of questioning when next confronting Meeks and me. I turned away, trying not to flinch at the next shot.

The trading post waited in the center of the chaos. A crowd of soldiers had gathered at the base of its short set of stairs. Marshal Barlow, rifle cradled in his arms, stood by the door. His glare followed us to the steps. Peterman was hunched over a few feet from him, his violent retching keeping time to the gunshots from the stables.

Lieutenant Silvers, left arm in a sling and the other holding a rifle, passed through the crowd. "Go about your duties, or I'll find other, more unpleasant things for you to do."

Low grumbles circled among the crowd as Captain Farley passed with his prisoners. The soldiers eyed Silvers' rifle as they dispersed. Military training would keep them obedient for the time being. Any more brutal attacks by Athan's monsters would surely break their discipline.

"I still say it's damn foolish to bring these two out in the open. You should've let me take them out of here before sunup."

"To what end, Marshal? How far do you think you'd get on foot before whoever did this caught up to you?"

Captain Farley stepped aside to let Meeks and me upon the porch of the trading post. A stench, so foul it made me gag, struck us as they moved around the corner of the building. Several bodies made a gruesome pile on the porch. Their throats and wrists had been cut to drain the blood to fill a large pail. Young Davis was among them. I wanted to turn away, but the gory centerpiece held my attention. Written above the bodies in blood-soaked letters was "Lester."

Meeks covered his mouth with a thin arm. He turned wide eyes to me but said nothing. A little tick at the side of his face began to flutter. Meeks was thinking, reasoning things out. Would he keep his mouth shut or betray me?

The captain gave me a suspicious look. "I don't think it's a coincidence this shows up the night you two arrived."

"Anybody who'd drain the blood out of five men can't be sane. Don't ask me to explain what a mad man thinks." I turned to Barlow. "Are we going to hold up here waiting to see who they'll butcher next, or are you going to do your duty, Marshal? Meeks and I have the right to a fair trial."

"Don't you tell me my business, Raynor."

Marshal Barlow chewed at his mustache as angry red splotches formed upon his cheeks. He was a hard man, tenacious and good at his job. It was dangerous to provoke him, but I needed to get out of my cell. Fort Vic's stockade was too solid. Even if I could escape from my cell, getting past all these bluecoats would be impossible.

"You seemed concerned, Mr. Raynor." Captain Farley gave me another appraising look. "Any special reason?"

"Meeks here won't last much longer in the middle of a fort full of soldiers who want him and me dead. If he dies, then I'm the one looking at taking the blame for his crimes. I need him alive to prove my innocence. A judge may believe me when Marshal Barlow won't."

Captain Farley shook his head with a cold smile. "I wouldn't classify you as innocent, Mr. Raynor. Regardless, I've lost eleven men and all of our horses. Murmurs of possible desertion are running wild around the troops. I need all the good men I have on hand to protect the remaining souls in this fort."

"I'm flattered."

"Don't be, Mr. Raynor. I was speaking of Marshal Barlow. You and Mr. Meeks will remain safely locked behind bars for the duration."

"Wait just a minute, Captain!" The marshal's finger hovered over the trigger of his rifle. "It sounds like you're keeping me a prisoner here too."

"Not at all. I'm simply asking for your assistance as a loyal citizen of these United States." Captain Farley started down the stairs. "Please see your prisoners back to their cells, Marshal. We must prepare for more trouble."

"Damn, Jakey Yank. You heard the man. Back to the stockade. Looks like you'll be staying another night."

CHAPTER FORTY

We walked across the blood-soaked yard toward the stockade. Though the bodies were gone, it would take a steady rain to wash away the gore. Fear still lingered in the eyes of the soldiers who watched us. Their panic was my greatest threat. How long would their adherence to Fort Victory's waning discipline hold them in check?

Marshal Barlow stood aside when the guard opened the stockade door. He kept the rifle handy until his prisoners were locked up tight in their cells. Then he opened his shirt and unstrapped both money belts. Meeks came out of his stupor momentarily as we both watched Donaldson lock our treasures in the gun cabinet.

The marshal turned to stare at me, arms folded and a frown upon his face. "I've been doing this job for a long time, Raynor. I know when someone's lying to me. Why don't you tell me what's going on, so we can stop these killings?"

"I'm telling you I don't know."

"And if you did?"

I leaned against the bars. "Let me out. You'll need another man good with a gun."

"So, you can shoot me in the back and escape. Nope," Barlow said. "Last chance to tell me what you know."

I sat on the cot and leaned against the wall. "See you in the morning. Maybe."

"Go to hell." The marshal spat and headed toward the door.

"Please! Move me to another cell." Meeks rattled his door. "I want to be as far away from…from the door as I can get."

"Shut up, Meeks. Don't forget how much I'd enjoy finding you drained of blood in the morning." Then Barlow left with Donaldson following sullenly behind. Meeks and I stood abandoned in the eerie stillness of the stockade.

Banging. Slamming. Shouting. Fort Victory shuddered with the thundering sounds of men preparing for a siege. I stood at the window most of the day, watching bluecoats run back and forth past the window. They'd managed to find the gates and had dragged them inside the fort. Mending them would take more than a hammer and nails.

"I know what you are," Meeks said low.

I turned and caught him staring at me through the bars. The little weasel's mind was working fast behind those spectacles. Had he already figured out I'd been in Lester? And what did he plan to do with the information?

"And what do you think I am?"

"You all make fun of me for being small, but my size has its advantages. I can hide in cramped spaces." He gave me a triumphant smirk. "I saw you pretending to be a man of God. What a laugh! Playing cards with the other men around the campfire. Ogling the young ladies. Then there is the way you can shoot. So who are you really, Dun? I bet you're an outlaw."

"Shut it, Meeks." I snorted. "You're dead wrong."

"Am I?" He pushed away from his cot on unsteady legs. "I don't think so. Those things hunting us know who you are. They called you a professor. Is that one of your disguises? Did you steal from them? And what has Lester got to do with your crime?"

I turned back to stare out the window. Bluecoats walked across my limited view at an anxious pace. Peterman was with them. He didn't spare me a look as he hurried to help mend the gate.

"No quick-witted response?" Meeks asked. "No denials? I wonder if Captain Farley or Marshal Barlow would accept your silence as an explanation?"

I spun around and lunged an arm through the bars. Meeks fell back onto the cot with a cry. "If you think I'm a dangerous outlaw, then it's not a good idea to provoke me."

He laid down on the cot and turned away from me with a sullen sigh. I'd kept him silent for now, but I suspect Meeks was waiting for his chance to rat me out. The little fink. It wasn't enough to get himself hung, but he wanted me to join him at the end of a rope.

Whatever Meeks' plans, he didn't get the opportunity to betray me. Spoons was our only visitor the entire day. He'd finally brought our supper as the last rays of sunlight sunk below the edges of the stockade windows.

"What's happening?" Meeks asked Spoons.

The old cook didn't answer. Instead, he handed a portion of hardtack and salted meat to each of us through the bars. I examined Spoons' face as he went about his tasks. Any sign of his typical good humor was absent from his features. Fear had taken its place.

"Are you staying with us for a while?" I asked, accepting the cup of water through the bars. "Can't say I won't appreciate the company. Meeks isn't much fun."

"Nope. I can't stay long. Captain has me guarding the trading post with a few other men." Spoons sniffed and took my empty cup. "I suppose he's desperate enough to use a half-blind war horse like me."

"Let me out. You need more men," I said.

"Wish I could." Spoons hobbled toward the door and gave me a last look. "But I have orders."

"Do me a favor," I called to the old cook. "Keep your head down."

"That's good advice, Dun. Remember it."

Meeks turned accusing eyes on me as the door closed behind Spoons. "You're going to let him go without telling him the truth? And they call me a killer."

It was my turn to succumb to indecisive guilt. I moved back to the window and leaned against the wall to resume my watch. Darkness covered the yard like a shroud. Someone coughed. The abrupt sound sent a jolt through my strained nerves. I let out a soft laugh. Meeks and his antics were getting to me. Nothing unearthly was lurking in the dark tonight.

Then a creeping mist rolled across the ground a few feet away from my window. It hovered in place for a moment and shifted direction upward. Finally, its body rose five feet and began to take on form. I could make out a figure in the filtered light from the window. My visitor stood silently before me, dressed in a long duster and large brimmed hat. The shadows lifted slowly, finally revealing the bottom half of a woman's face. My gut twisted. Half a woman's face was more like it. The other half was charred bone.

"Dun." Her voice echoed in whispers across the distance between us. *"Hell's come knocking for you. Come out. Let me take you easy, or more of these pretty soldiers will die."*

"Who the hell are you?"

"They call us the Hounds of Perdition. We're bounty hunters, Dun, and we've got your scent."

Her skeletal smile drew back burned lips as an emaciated hand flicked colorless hair over her shoulders. She was no living creature. I was finally meeting face to face with the Undead killers who'd been hunting me.

"Don't you recognize me? We were such good friends once until you deserted me in Lester."

"Angelina?"

This charred piece of rotting flesh bore little resemblance to the beautiful enchantress I'd once known. Gone was her striking beauty and alluring charm. Hideous blemishes covered her once lovely face. The smokey richness of Angelina's voice, too, had been traded for the rasping gravel tones earned in the fires of Hell. Athan had summoned the one person who knew me best.

Guilt's fingers strangled me as I forced my eyes to look at her face. "God, I'm sorry about Lester. I should've locked you in the wagon and drove the team out of town that night."

"Do I hear Dunham Raynor expressing remorse?" She laughed. "I thought you believed guilt was for suckers." Then, a boney finger pointed at me. "You deserve what you'll get."

Then I remembered the pleading cries of the ghostly mother. Angelina and her posse had tortured and abandoned her on the Santa Fe Trail. My memory shifted to Beth's brutalized body strewn among the wild sunflowers. Both tormented souls had stared out into the horizon, robbed of their love, their life, and their futures. Someone had to stand for them.

"You've hurt innocent people, Angelina. They didn't deserve the torture you put them through," I said, casting what remained of my weakness aside. "I warned you to leave Lester with me, but you wouldn't listen. Blame your own greed for what happened. Not me."

"Poor, Dun. Never man enough to face responsibility. I looked after you in life, and now I've come to escort you to the gates of Hell. The Devil has a room ready for you. He wants his due, and so do all of us you burned alive. We're waiting to throw you a party like the one those cannons gave Lester."

Spurs clattered within the mist, echoing as if they didn't quite exist in the world. I stared into the darkness as the sound grew louder. Sweat bubbled along my neck and face. The rest of my body had gone cold with terror.

Then the spurs suddenly stilled. Two Undead men stood beside Angelina. I let loose an anguished cry. Once familiar and dear to me, their faces contorted with tortured hysteria. Trip's body burned with hellfire. Its glow filled the eerie mist with a sickly light. In his hand, he held taut a chain attached to the collar around Silent Dan's throat. The boy growled and pulled at his bonds to get to me.

"You remember Trip and Silent Dan, don't you?" Angelina asked. *"Trip was a thief from the day he was born, but Silent Dan is a surprise. We had a mass murderer in our camp and had no idea."*

Silent Dan's white face cracked in a ghastly grin. He lifted a sickle and twisted it anxiously before me. Muted laughter gurgled from his swollen lips as he strained against his iron collar.

"Easy, Dan." Trip's boney hand yanked harder on the chain. *"We're not quite ready to butcher him yet."*

"Silent Dan locked all his neighbors inside their town church and burned them alive. He doesn't like it when people make fun of his feeble mind. I was surprised to learn how many times he'd come close to killing me!" Angelina put a hand on her duster in mock shock. *"Then again. He didn't have to, now did he. Dunham Raynor, medium extraordinaire. Look at you now, standing there trying to master your fear. But it won't work. I can smell it on you."*

Hate swirled in her mad eyes. Angelina was never easy to sway after she'd made up her mind. Nothing I could say now would persuade her from exacting her revenge. I had to find a way to stop them, even if it meant casting Angelina and my friends back to Hell for eternity.

"Justice has found you, Dun. Admit that your cowardice is responsible for all their deaths, or soon, you'll be as terrified as the rest of these unfortunate souls in Fort Victory. The boys and I will kill every one of these soldiers to get to you. In the end, you'll be on your knees begging for mercy."

"That'll be a cold day in Hell." I spat. "I'll be damned twice before I let the likes of you take me."

"And these souls with you? Are you going to let them die too?" Thin wisps of hair fell about her boney shoulders as she shook her head. *"You were always a selfish bastard. So be it. I'll give you one more day to change your mind."* Then she turned her back on me and stepped into the thick fog. *"Come on, boys. Let's make this fort bleed."*

CHAPTER FORTY-ONE

A trumpet sounded through the night like Gabriel's horn heralding the second coming. Rushing to the window, I half expected to see angels and demons battling in the yard. Judgement Day, however, wasn't upon me yet. Rather the stomping boots of Fort Victory's soldiers sounded a harsh reminder of the night's unholy visitors.

Captain Farley, marching at their head, brought his men to a stop across from my window. The captain's harsh features darkened in the flickering light of the fort's braziers. His mouth foamed as he barked orders in rapid succession.

Then Captain Farley thrust his sword toward the fog and shouted, "I condemn you as Confederate spies! Drop your weapons or face the might of the United States Army!"

The ensuing laughter thundered around Fort Victory in terrible waves. I covered my ears against the horrible clamor. Angelina never was one to respect authority.

I lowered my hands again when the last of the grating titters faded. Though the soldiers in the yard had also recoiled from the ear-splitting laughter, Farley stood defiant upon the field. His face was a mask of ugly rage. Unphased by the tendrils of mist reaching for his terrified men, he held his sword before him like a gladiator.

"Charge!"

Then Farley rushed headlong into the fog bank and disappeared. His men, unsure of what else to do, followed. Their backs disappeared as they blindly ran into Hell after their mad captain.

"What's happening?" Meeks cried behind me.

I gripped the bars of my cell window, rattling them in a vain attempt to loosen the iron. The mad man was going to get all his men killed, and I was helpless to stop it.

Screams replaced gunfire in the fog's belly. I stayed glued to the window as I tried to penetrate the gray gloom with my gaze. It was no use. Nothing, not even a stray bullet, was getting out of the fog's body without Angelina's permission.

Eerie stillness suddenly descended upon Fort Victory. I waited breathlessly as the shroud of gloom rolled across the ground and through the broken gates. Swallowing down the gore edging upward in my throat, I surveyed the gruesome scene Angelina's hounds had left behind them. Body parts littered the ground like fleshy ticker tape. The soldiers spared from Hell's fury sat on their backsides in pools of blood. A few were screaming for salvation from the Heavens. I hit the wall of my cell with an angry fist. Damn it! Angelina was playing cat and mouse.

"Lieutenant Silvers?" Captain Farley stared down at the broken body of his second.

Then he suddenly lifted his head as if sensing he was being watched. Insanity churned within the captain's orbs as his gaze locked upon mine. Stepping over Silvers' body, the captain stormed toward the stockade door brandishing his sword.

"Oh hell!" I backed away from the window. "We've just run out of time."

The door opened with a boom. Farley, covered in sweat and blood, stood in the doorway. His boots echoed dully on the floorboards as he came at me in a rush. I pressed my back against the stockade wall as his body slammed against the bars of my cell door.

"You did this," He cried, mouth foaming with white spittle. "I knew you were Confederate sympathizers. You left a trail for these animals to follow, didn't you?"

"No, Captain," I said. "You must listen to me. We are victims just like you."

Boots shuffled into the stockade. Farley's remaining men had come to join their mad captain. Fear. Rage. Confusion. The three emotions painted the faces of Fort Victory's remaining defenders.

"Lieutenant Silvers is the victim. So are half my men!" Captain Farley shook his head, his eyes twitching wildly. "By God, they will see justice this day. Take them to the wall. And fetch Barlow too. He's in this as well."

"Please don't do this, Captain. You'll be murdering innocent men." I lifted my fists as the soldiers came for me. "The killings won't stop if you shoot us!"

"Your Confederate friends are desperate to take the Northwest and capture all the logging resources for their own. But Fort Victory will stand in their way. We won't let you destroy the United States." Captain Farley gave me a murderous sneer. "Take them to the wall."

Struggle as we may, Meeks and I were no match for soldiers emboldened by terror. I winced as the cold air of a Colorado Autumn night struck me. My mind raced for ideas. I wouldn't die in the middle of the wilderness, not if I still had my wits about me. Then I noticed the bullet hole-ridden patch of wall, and my optimism faded. How many men before me had pleaded their innocence to mad ears?

"Stand up like men," one of the soldiers said, shoving me against the fence. "It'll be over quick."

"Get off me, damn you! I'm a United States Marshal." Barlow's voice boomed across the courtyard. "Where's Farley? I want to speak with your captain."

Barlow hadn't come easy from the looks of him. Dark clumps of blood covered the shaggy hair on the left side of his big head. Someone had torn his lip, but the punch hadn't broken his stubborn jaw. He wiped the trickle of red from his mouth with a torn shirt sleeve.

"Well, Barlow, lying until the end, I see." Captain Farley's eyes narrowed as his men thrust Barlow against the wall beside Meeks and me. "I can't say I'll be sorry to see you dead."

"You know damn well I'm a United States Marshal, loyal to our government." Barlow glowered at the captain. "We aren't Confederate spies. You're about to murder innocent men." Barlow cast a glance at Meeks. "Innocent of spying, that is. Meeks must be taken back to civilization for a fair trial."

Meeks let out a long sigh. "Marshal Barlow and Dun are innocent bystanders, Captain. If you must shoot someone, I suppose it must be me. It isn't fair they have to die because of what I've done."

"Are you telling me what happened to Lieutenant Silvers and the others was fair?" Captain Farley thrust a finger toward us. "You left a trail for your gang to follow. They killed good men trying to break you out of our custody."

"Listen to me, Captain," I said. "The creatures who killed your men aren't human. They don't care about politics or governments or even riches. The man who sent them is hell-bent on killing anything that moves. You must let us go. We can help defend the fort."

"Let you go?" Captain Farley laughed. "And I suppose you'd like me to hand you a weapon as well?"

"I'm good with a gun, sir."

"He is, Captain. I've seen him shoot," Meeks said.

"I knew you two were in cahoots," Barlow grumbled.

"The point we're trying to make, Captain, is that you'll need every gun you've got to keep those killers at bay." I lifted my voice, sending it out to the ears of the remaining defenders. "They'll be back! We must work together to build a better barricade if you want any hope of surviving another night."

Rumblings of agreement circled about the crowd. A little sliver of hope touched my soul as some of the guns began to lower. Perhaps Farley's men didn't share their captain's madness after all.

"Fantasy!" Farley waved the sword uncomfortably close to my neck. "Would you listen to Confederate lies? They want weapons, so they can kill you and save their friends the trouble."

"Let us go, you mad man!" Barlow pulled against his bonds.

"Subtle," I murmured. "And very unhelpful. Shut up before you get us shot."

Captain Farley shook his head, eyeing the soldiers. "You've all turned on me! One slick-talking spy comes among us, and you forget your allegiance."

The captain dropped his sword and pulled his revolver. Sweat glistened on his face in the light of the braziers. Farley took a hesitant step back and swept the barrel of his gun across the crowd before pointing it at Barlow.

"You've all lost your nerve! I know my duty to this country. Shooting Confederate spies is at the top of the list."

Then Captain Farley's eyes rolled back into his head, and he dropped like a rock. Sergeant Milton stood with the butt of his revolver hovering over Farley's unconscious form. He nodded at Barlow. I didn't like the sergeant, but I had to admit he was a welcome sight.

"Untie them," He ordered Peterman and Mason. "The rest of you men get to work on building a barricade. Dun may not be a soldier, but his idea is a good one."

I nodded my thanks to Peterman as he untied me. "I'm best with a rifle."

"Not so fast, Dun," Barlow said, retrieving his weapon from Mason. "You gave a pretty speech, but it didn't convince me to trust you."

"Unbelievable! Barlow, you are the stubbornest ass I've ever met." I threw my hands in the air with a curse. "I can help you."

"Would that be before or after your escape?" Barlow turned to Milton. "Farley's off his head. He better be locked up as well."

But Captain Farley had other ideas. He'd disappeared while Barlow and the soldiers were distracted. Much like the plague, crazy wouldn't stay gone for long. I suspected we'd see the captain again.

Chapter Forty-Two

I walked sullenly beside Meeks as our keepers herded us back to the stockade. Peterman and Mason marched behind with their rifles at the ready while Sergeant Milton brought up the rear. I glanced over my shoulder with a final plea. The sergeant, however, remained unmoved.

"Don't start. Barlow is still in charge," Milton said. "Be grateful you're not in irons again."

"That stubborn ass is going to get us all killed," I said, reaching for the stockade door.

"Shut it, Raynor. Listen," Mason said. "Do you hear that?"

I swallowed my pithy response and listened as a shrill screech rose over the treetops. Branches snapped, and rocks exploded outside the broken gates. Fort Victory rumbled as if in the path of a runaway locomotive. Mason yelled a curse. Suddenly a violent whirlwind swirled its body across the yard toward us. Tents and upended supplies disintegrated in its path. The Ouroboros wriggled wildly on my chest, warning me the cyclone headed toward us was not of this world.

Then Silent Dan appeared in the twisting air brandishing his scythe. He gave me a gleeful grin as Peterman and Mason sailed into the air. Their abandoned rifles clattered to the ground just out of my reach.

"Get inside!" I yelled, finally having the presence of mind to open the door.

Meeks ran past me and threw his skinny body over the threshold. I searched the whirlwind for Sergeant Milton. He stood frozen before the tempest, staring wide-eyed at the wall of nature's fury surrounding us.

"Milton!" I yelled. "We must get inside the building! Run!"

"What are you?" The sergeant, half-crazed with fear, lifted his rifle and fired into the spinning wall of debris.

"You can't kill them, Milton. They're already dead."

Sergeant Milton's eyes opened wide as his body lurched upward. Silent Dan grabbed Milton and twisted the sergeant's back with a sickening crunch. Lifeless eyes stared into the nothingness as the sergeant's body dropped into the mud.

"Murdering bastards!" Barlow's buffalo body charged at Silent Dan. Their battling forms disappeared in the gray mist settling in the yard.

I tumbled backward into the stockade and slammed the door behind me. Shoving the lock home, I staggered away from the door until my back hit the bars of the nearest cell. Then turning to the walls, I kicked against the wood, trying to find a loose board. It was no use. The building was solid. Not for the first time, I wondered at the permanent feel of a stockade constructed in a supposedly temporary fort.

"Are you mad? We're safer in here," Meeks said. "I think we should stay put until help arrives."

"What help? I don't think our attackers will be satisfied with letting us die a peaceful death. Do you?" I yanked hard at the window's bar above the guard desk.

"Damn it. They set these bars too well. Check the other windows and cells. See if you can find a weakness in the walls. Maybe we can break through and escape without the hounds seeing us. Hurry! Milton and the others won't keep them entertained for long."

"I think they're tired of waiting, Dun." Meeks pointed at the floor.

Tendrils of fog oozed through the cracks around the door jamb. The misty fingers reached upward and tugged at the handle. I held my breath as it turned and then suddenly stilled. The lock was holding.

"Break it down!"

A heavy mass slammed against the door, striking with a harsh rhythmic boom. I watched helplessly as the hinges started to groan. Meeks backed away and plopped down in the farthest corner from the door. He pulled his legs against his chest and rocked. His eyes were wild like a frightened animal trapped by a pack of wolves.

"Put your back into it, Silent Dan!" Angelina growled. *"Break that door down. We've been patient long enough. It's time for Dun to die."*

An unearthly cackle surrounded the stockade. Its echoes rang in my ears and sent tremors down my spine. The wood, unable to withstand such a beating, cracked. I braced my body against the cell bars. Angelina and her hounds would be inside within moments. My luck had finally run out.

A tiny green light pulsed within the door lock. It flared, suddenly bursting out of the handle and stretching across the door. Its bright body jumped from surface to surface until a green glow engulfed the entire building. Then the green flared in angry bursts. I flinched as the Earth magic threw a surge of power from the walls into the night.

"No!" Angelina howled from the other side of the magical barrier. *"You can't stay in there forever, Dun. I will have my revenge."*

"You can help those soldier friends of yours, Dunham."

Hesperos stood beside the cell across from me. His face remained placid, but the unspoken gloat was still there. He watched my face, searching into the depths of my squirming soul. Somehow, he knew about the guilt I refused to acknowledge.

"Join with me. Use my power to drive these hounds away. They have no real claim upon you. Not if we join." Hesperos closed the gap between us. "No more soldiers need to die here. We'll cast the hounds back to Hell, and then we can get on with our business."

"We?"

"Well, mostly me," he said with a grin. "Have you seen anything as powerful as these hounds, Dunham? Of course not. The Dead have no power unless someone gives it to them."

"I was wondering when you'd get around to telling me about Athan. He's a Necromancer, isn't he? Why is he giving Angelina power?"

"Doran has been talkative. I'll have to do something about him soon. Very well. Athan wants my new host body dead. It wouldn't be in our best interests if that were to happen now, would it? I just need your body to bring my powers to full strength."

"And what about me?"

"What about you?" Hesperos shook his head. "The fever should have killed you at thirteen years old. I kept you alive for my use. You've been living on borrowed time, Dunham. That body belongs to me."

"I'm not through using it." I tossed a small piece of wood through the bars and snorted when it passed unhindered through his torso. "Go find another puppet."

Hesperos sighed. "A stubborn fool to the last. Very well. I'll return when your situation grows desperate. You won't be able to refuse our joining." He leaned in with a glint of malicious amusement in his eyes. "Practice being contrite. I'll need you to beg for my help next time."

I threw another plank at his dissolving form. The wood smacked loudly against the iron and clattered on the ground. Hesperos was gone, and he'd taken his green light with him. Curse him. My situation looked grim, but I wasn't out of options yet. I yanked the drawers out of the guard's desk. The keys to the gun cabinet weren't there. Cursing, I picked up the discarded plank and slammed the end against the cabinet's lock.

"The plank isn't making a scratch on the metal lock," I told Meeks. "Look around for something harder I can use."

Meeks sat quietly on the desk. Solemn acceptance filled his eyes as he watched me. He sighed. Thin lips formed a straight line over his gritted teeth. The little thief had lost his fear.

"I supposed we both deserve to die a long, painful death."

"Go to hell, Meeks. I'm not ready to give up just yet. If I had one of those rifles…"

"What would you do? Shoot?" Meeks shook his head with a grunt. "For whatever reason, I heard that woman, Angelina, last night. She's coming for you. Guns won't help. The Devil wants the soul he's owed."

"Are you judging me now? I'm not the murderer in this stockade."

Meeks shook his head again, placing steady hands on his knees. "No. I have blood on my own hands. Barlow was right. I should pay for what I've done. Why can't you accept your fate too?"

Something banged against the door sending Meeks and me racing behind the guard desk. Silent Dan had returned now that Hesperos had lifted his magical barrier. I was defenseless, trapped in this escape-proof box. Then Keys banged against the stockade door. Spoons limped toward us. Dried blood stained his hair and face. His uniform had so many rips he was barely recognizable as a soldier in the United States Army.

Leaning heavily upon the bars, he made his way toward us. "Captain's gone. Sergeant Milton's dead. I'm the poor bastard who ranks highest here. Now, I don't know what you done, and I don't care much, but I reckon a man has the right to defend himself. To hell with what that Marshal said."

Spoons pushed the key into the gun cabinet lock and threw open the door. A dozen rifles lined the interior. Ammunition was stacked neatly beneath them. I whistled and stepped back when I saw the explosives.

"I've been eating and sleeping within spitting distance of dynamite?"

"Where else would we keep it?" Spoons shrugged. "Don't be so skittish. We only have four sticks left. 'Course they'd still make a hell of a bang."

The old soldier was a good man. He'd been the only one in the fort willing to treat Meeks and me as men. I owed him the truth.

"Listen to me, Spoons. I know who these killers are. They're led by a crazy woman named Angelina. She used to be my partner back in Lester." I took a deep breath, knowing how insane I was about to sound. "She blames me for her death and wants revenge."

Wrinkles on the weather-worn forehead grew deeper as Spoons regarded me sadly. "Fort Victory has fallen to these godless vermin. Me and four other souls are all that's left of our troop. Don't go loco on me now, Dun. We need your help getting out of this cursed place. Grab as many weapons as you can." Spoons grabbed one of the rifles. "I'll meet you at the trading post. The rest of us are hold up there."

I stepped to the cabinet and began grabbing ammunition. Meeks reached over my shoulder. His finger trailed along two pieces of leather hanging inside. The money belts. We exchanged glances. I grabbed my belt with a free hand and threw it over my shoulder. Meeks hesitated for a moment and then took up the belt with his stolen money.

"I'm not going to leave it here in the wilderness," he told me defensively. "I'm going to take it back to Wagon City."

"You do what you need to do, Meeks. I'm not leaving Spoons to die."

I grabbed as many weapons and ammo as I could fit in my arms. They wouldn't do much good against the ghostly posse, but it was worth a try. Hesitating, I finally grabbed the small supply of dynamite. It was bound to come in handy.

"None of this is going to help." Meeks leaned against the desk, watching me.

"Maybe not, but I'm not going to make it easy for Angelina. Have a little trust in me, Meeks. I make my own fate. Who knows? If you save a few lives tonight, maybe you really can buy your way to heaven?"

I was surprised to hear his footsteps behind me. Whether he stayed out of fear or a need for redemption, it didn't matter anymore. Meeks retched, pointing toward a dark red pile of shredded cloth a few feet away. I took tentative steps closer and stopped as the smell hit me. Sergeant Milton, barely recognizable except for the tattered stripes hanging from his torn sleeve, rested on the threshold of the gates. Peterman, Mason, and several of the men fell beside him, trampled under Angelina's wrath.

"Do you see Marshal Barlow?" Meeks asked, his head turning toward the exterior wall.

"It's hard to tell," I said.

The fort's entrance was unguarded. I could walk right through, but I wouldn't get very far when Angelina and her posse discovered I'd left. Then there was Spoons and the others. What about them? How many more would suffer because of my actions?

It was time I admitted the truth, even if it was just to myself. I could have stayed and warned the people of Lester, maybe helped them get out or stop the armies somehow. Then there was Fort Vic. If I'd been honest, perhaps I could have drawn Angelina away before the killings started. How many soldiers had lost their lives because of me?

I turned and shoved a rifle in Meek's arms. "We don't have much time. Let's go join the rest while we wait for Hell."

CHAPTER FORTY-THREE

Cheery beams of sunlight made an incongruous backdrop for swarming insects devouring their afternoon meal. I rubbed at the stubble on my chin to keep the gore from rising in my throat. Death wasn't pretty, and it got uglier the longer a corpse spent in the sun.

We'd found Marshal Barlow's body in the middle of the yard, stubbornly clutching his gun. The marshal's dead eyes, as if in a final insult against me, glared at us from where he'd met his end.

Meeks peeked out over our makeshift barrier of crates and sacks of flour. His wide eyes stared at the marshal's bloating form. The little thief turned away, gagging. I pushed him toward the back of the trading post.

"Don't spill your stomach here," I said.

"Can't we at least turn his head?" Meeks asked.

"Go ahead, mister." Spoons patted the barrel of his rifle. "I'm staying here."

The Ouroboros sank its teeth into my skin. Its bite drew my attention back to the yard where misty fingers caressed Marshal Barlow's body. The supernatural fog rolled over him, blanketing the dead man in its thick mass.

"Get ready," I said. "They're coming."

The Hounds of Perdition hadn't bothered to wait for the witching hour. Riders materialized out of the mist. Angelina was at their head with Trip and Silent Dan half a horse length behind her on either side. Their phantom steeds took a slow trot across the yard.

"You weren't off your head, were you?" Spoons looked at me with wide eyes. "These killers really are demons from Hell."

"They call themselves the Hounds of Perdition. They're the Devil's bounty hunters," I told Spoons. "Our bullets are useless. We need to find another way to send them back to Hell."

Crimson light flashed to my left. I spotted Athan on the porch of the stockade, his hands ablaze with red energy. He was coming out into the open at last and, in doing so, had created a hole in the fog. I returned the smirk he gave me. The man looked solid enough. If he was human, then he could be killed.

I took careful aim at his hat and squeezed the trigger. Splinters of wood from the stockade wall flew into the air. I lowered my rifle, hoping to see blood. But Athan was gone. I'd missed the shot. Damn, he was quick!

"Look!" Spoons pointed at the yard. "The fog is gone."

Angelina and her hounds remained in the open without their protective blanket of dread. Their Undead forms flickered as if they'd lost all sense of awareness. So, not only was Athan holding their leash, but his power was also holding them here in the human realm. If I could take Athan out, the hounds should return to Hell.

I spotted Athan's hat sticking out around the corner of the stockade. Firing again, I cheered as the hat flew out into the yard. My glee was short-lived. Athan stuck his head out from the other corner with a laugh. Tricky.

"Stop firing at the hounds," I said. "You're looking for the man holding their leash."

As if on cue, Athan took the opportunity to run into the makeshift surgery. I fired at the tent's opening, but my bullet found fabric rather than flesh. Athan was getting closer. Well, let him come. I'd never wanted to stomp somebody so much in my life.

"Who is he?" Spoons asked.

"His name is Athan, and he's the necromancer controlling the Dead." I lifted my eyes to the unbelieving stares around me. "And the Undead. We kill him, and the hounds go back to Hell."

"Right," Spoons said, spitting out his tobacco. "Kill the magician, boys."

A swarm of bullets struck the surgery tent. Fabric, liquid, and powder exploded into a sickly-smelling cloud. Finally, the tent collapsed over lumps of furniture. I fired as a bump in the canvas moved toward the back of the flattened tent. Athan burst out of the ruins with unimaginable speed. White powder and different shades of liquid cures covered his suit. Giving me a rude gesture, his hands flamed crimson again.

"Ruined his suit!" Spoons cackled, taking another pot shot at Athan's departing back. "He's fast. Maybe too fast to kill."

"It's time, Dun. Give the Devil his due."

The Hounds of Perdition, made whole again by Athan, waited in the center of the yard. Mounted on their phantom steeds, they were towering specters of death. Guns hadn't helped against the hounds. One chance remained. I had to distract Angelina until the others could take out Athan.

"You set your sights on the necromancer and don't stop shooting until he's dead," I told Spoons. "I'll distract Angelina."

"I don't like this, Dun."

"Yeah, neither do I."

I handed Spoons the sticks of dynamite. "Take these. See if you can find something constructive to do with them."

Reloading my rifle, I slowly got to my feet. One of the soldiers pulled the top crate off a section of our makeshift barrier. I put a leg over it and crossed the distance to face the Undead. Standing silently before them, I clutched at my rifle.

"You've decided to accept your punishment at last." Angelina's skeletal grin held a malicious glee. *"Hell will be pleased."*

"Why pretend you still have your own will, Angelina? We both know someone is using you like a flesh puppet. You're no more commanding these Undead animals than I am."

"The necromancer and I are partners! Not that you'd know the meaning of the word." She thrust a finger at me. *"It's time to make you pay! Boys, take care of Dun's friends."*

"Stop, Angelina," I cried. "Let's keep this between you and me. I'm the one you want."

"I'll let you in on a little secret, Dun," Angelina said, her boney jaw grinding as she spoke. "I enjoy the killing. Get going, boys!"

Angelina's hounds charged toward the barrier, their horses snorting red fire. I stared as they passed. All nine faces were exposed to their victims this time. My fear had conjured terrifying images of the riders hiding inside their protective fog. Their true forms, however, were more frightening than any nightmare I could imagine. To my horror, Grizz and Phelps rode with my old troupe and the damned of Lester. Athan had summoned my past when he'd conjured the Hounds of Perdition.

Chaos filled the trading post as the defenders met Hell's posse. I fired as the phantom horses circled about the building, killing as they went.

Then Spoons stood atop the barrier with a stick of dynamite in his hand. He winked and lifted the lantern to ignite the fuse. Hope surged within me. Athan's power couldn't save him from the destructive energy of dynamite.

A flash of steel swept through Spoons. Silent Dan stood on the barrier, his scythe dripping with blood. He giggled as the old soldier's body split into two gruesome pieces. Spoons' dead hand clutched the inert dynamite as he tumbled into the mud.

"Make them all bleed! I want Dun broken."

Angelina kept her horse steady throughout the carnage. Her laughter circled about me, stabbing like iron pokers taken from Hellfire. The malicious hatred she and her hounds held for their innocent victims was unnerving. Was Athan aware of their barely contained blood lust? Did he care?

Spoons and the others stood within the barrier. Their ghostly forms were confused at first. Then the brilliant light of the Eternal Flame called them home. Turning away, I listened for Hell's coach. It didn't come. Strange. Perhaps Heaven had made room for Meeks after all.

Lifting my eyes back to the vengeful Dead before me, I spat in the narrow space between us. I'd made a mistake provoking Angelina. Her hate only made her stronger. Now I was alone in Fort Victory with only the Undead for company.

CHAPTER FORTY-FOUR

Angelina pointed her finger toward the ground. The Earth shook and rumbled as if a great quake would pull the fort asunder. I balanced in the trembling yard, holding my rifle like a pole. I'd be damned twice before falling on my backside in front of Angelina.

Then the Earth opened next to the hounds. A team of midnight horses exploded from the cracked ground pulling a funeral coach behind them. Fire and brimstone spewed under its wheels. My courage was in jeopardy of waning as I lifted my gaze toward the front of the coach. A hulking form wrapped in shadows sat upon the driver's seat. His gigantic hand pulled the rabid horses to a stop.

"*The coachman's come to take you to Perdition.*" Angelina laughed with malicious glee.

"Why so eager? I thought you wanted to see me suffer."

"*Are you trying to buy time? Give it up. I warned you, Dun. Nobody cheats me.*" Angelina waved a rotting hand at the coachman. "*Take him. Let's banish this coward. I think it's high time we ride against the Living who butchered us! We'll have our fill of blood before we've done. Right, boys!*"

Screeching laughter from the Undead hounds sent icy shivers down my spine. The monsters were hungry for violence. I feared there wasn't enough flesh in all the world to satisfy their blood lust.

Red light burned through the broken remnants of a wagon bed behind the hounds. Athan. So, the hounds weren't quite out of control. Their puppet master was still instigating the violence. His head bobbed over the broken wood as he watched us. I'd have to be quick with my aim to kill this ferret before he went to ground.

"You've slaughtered innocent people, Angelina! I won't let you hurt anyone else."

"And what makes you think you can stop me? Coachman! Do your duty."

Wheels rolled over the Dead, crushing bones under the weight of the hellish coach. Then like a shot, a clawed hand reached out of the depths of the coachman's black cloak and flew at me. My body froze as terror held me in its tight grip. I kept my eyes on the clawed hand, determined not to shrink away. I wouldn't give Angelina the satisfaction of seeing me cower.

Athan stood, anxious to watch my exit to Hell. I lifted my rifle and shot through the coachman's eternal body. Athan flew backward as he cried out with shock and pain. Blood blossomed from his shoulder where my bullet struck flesh. Damn! I'd missed the necromancer's heart.

The Hounds of Perdition screamed as if they, too, had been struck. Body's flickering between Earth and the Spirit Realm, they grasped at the air about them as if trying to find a handhold anchoring them to reality. Athan's hold on his puppets was failing.

Solid hands pushed me. I went sprawling in the dust of the yard. Meeks squirmed in the coachman's massive grip. He gave one last yowl as the hand shoved him into the depths of the coach. The door slammed shut with terrible finality. Meeks' pale face pushed against the window.

"Meeks!" I screamed. "Why?"

"You must stop them! There's no one else!"

The little tinhorn thief had saved me from Hell. Meeks, in the act of ultimate selflessness, had finally shown his true worth. By God, his sacrifice wouldn't go to waste. I tore my gaze away from the coach and ran for the gates. Knowing myself for a fool, I turned and stood my ground. I had no powers or weapons to stop the hounds, but I had to try.

The Hounds of Perdition roared as the death coach descended back to Hell. Long howls of impotent anger filled the yard. I tried not to think of Meeks trapped inside or where his abandoned body rested after taking a blow from Hell's emissary.

"Someone has taken your place tonight, Dun." Angelina glared at me. *"Don't stop looking over your shoulder just yet. We'll be back soon. Come on, boys. Let's ride."*

"Stop! I command you to kill Dun!"

Athan stumbled into the yard, his left arm hanging uselessly beside his body. He held a glowing hand toward the hounds, but his pets weren't listening. Not good. The necromancer seemed as surprised as I was by his lack of hold over the Undead. He sent a fiery red beam of magic at Angelina, but the strike bounced off her body like a child's ball.

"I guess I don't need you as a partner anymore, Magician." Angelina spat a stream of brimstone toward him. *"The hounds follow only me now."*

"Hey! Remember me?" I took a pot shot at her boot. "I won't let you leave, Angelina."

Athan took the opportunity to run for cover, leaving me to stand alone in a field of blood. I fired at his departing back as red lightning struck the Earth around me. Athan was sending his attacks at me rather than trying to capture his wayward pets. The ass was as vicious as Hesperos. Neither cared what happened to the innocent people caught in their magical struggle.

A memory came at me in a rush. I'd lived this scene the night Marshal Barlow found Meeks and me. Had I seen a vision of my end? I was going to pay closer attention to my dreams if I somehow survived this mess.

"Having delusions of heroism?" Back in its dog form, Doran sat behind one of the broken gates. Its tail wagged as it laughed.

"What are you doing here, Doran? Come to see me get a bullet through my heart."

"Whether you make a last stand with Athan or run away, it makes no difference. Hesperos is growing weaker. Soon he will lose all his magic." Doran stood and pranced over to me with an impatient sigh. "If he doesn't have his magic, he can't take your body. I'll help you escape. We simply walk through the gates, down the trail, and right through the trees. No one is guarding the way."

"And why would you do me any favors?"

"I owe Hesperos a few anxious hours to suffer. And nothing is more painful than desperation. Except maybe dashed hope. Come on, Dun. I'm not wrong. You certainly didn't like being locked in an abandoned jail with no way out."

"No. I can't leave."

"Why? To save humans who don't give a damn about you?" Doran shook its head. "This is foolishness. Those killers will cut you down."

"I can't let Angelina and her hounds kill more innocent people. You've seen what they can do."

"Don't be stupid, meat sack," Doran said, rolling its eyes in exasperation. "Why do you care about the Living? You've never cared before. I've seen you take their money without a second thought."

"Maybe I have enough blood on my hands," I said. "Father Emilio was right. A man must stand up to his past before he can move forward. I need to do the right thing."

Then a rope dropped over my head to settle around my neck. Angelina pulled it taut before I had time to react. My fingers tugged at the rope's coarse fiber, but it wouldn't budge. She had me.

"*You should have listened to Hesperos' abomination, Dun. It more than anyone knows what evil tyrants the necromancers can be.*" Angelina laughed, yanking me closer.

I fired, but the bullets went through her ghostly body. The rope grew tighter. Yanked off my feet, I dropped to the ground like a gunnysack. Angelina cackled as she dragged my body toward her.

"*Goodbye, Dun. Say hello to the Devil for me.*"

Then Angelina fired. Her bullet burned through me as its path cut a flaming hole into my heart.

Chapter Forty-Five

Memories scrolled in quick jerks across my mind's eye. Joy. Love. Tears. They pressed upon my bleeding heart in waves of regret. My turn on the planet contained pain, but I'd had sweet moments too. It was these little flashes of happiness I would hold onto when the coachman came.

"Not yet, Dunham." Hesperos knelt beside me, his words forcing me back to the present. "There's still time. Join with me."

Doran, muzzled and bloodied, sat beside its master. Hesperos hadn't spared the whip on his slave. It stared into my dying eyes and then quickly turned away. The look spoke of utter defeat. My loathing of Hesperos grew with each drop of the creature's blood. The bastard enjoyed being in control. I forced my mind to move past hate and resentment. One chance remained to save innocent lives. Athan and I couldn't stop the hounds, but Hesperos might be strong enough.

"I'll join with you if you promise to stop the Hounds of Perdition and Athan. Don't let them kill any more innocent people." I looked to Doran again. "One last condition. You set Doran free. Those are my terms."

"I'll agree to stop Athan. Adding his power to mine will be very satisfying."

"What about the hounds? You can't let them loose to kill again."

"You are a stubborn soul." Hesperos shrugged. "Very well. I will dispatch Athan and the hounds. Doran, however, is none of your concern. I made the creature, and I intend to keep it." His fingers drifted down my cheek. "We are short on time. Pity. I looked forward to making you beg."

Then Hesperos rested his hand upon my Ouroboros, and the world exploded in a swirl of colors and lights. My mind searched for any signs of physical sensations, but I couldn't feel my body anymore. Then my awareness peered down. It was as if I was looking at the ground from a great distance. My consciousness drifted over Fort Victory, hovering as I watched my body rise to its feet.

Hesperos turned my body to face the Hounds of Perdition. Dried blood clung to the shirt where the bullet had penetrated my heart. The bits of spent iron and gunpowder sprang from my flesh to land on the dirt with a thud.

Angelina leaped from her mount and marched toward my body. Eyes flaming wildly within her rotting skull, she pointed her gun at my forehead.

"How is this possible? I shot you!"

"Silence your tongue, demon whore. Dunham Raynor is out of your reach," My mouth said, sending waves of power toward her.

Angelina flew backward, tumbling head over spurs. She slammed into the hounds with a crack of bones. Her band of cutthroats backed away from Angelina. Surprise and fear circled about them. I took resentful glee. It was good to see these murderers afraid for once.

"Necromancer! You may not take what Hell has claimed."

The new voice rumbled across the yard like boulders crushing gravel. Hesperos turned my body toward the terrible noise. It was the coachman. I'd never heard him speak and hoped never to have the experience again. He'd likely come back to collect my soul after Angelina shot me.

"I marked him first," Hesperos said.

"He's mine!" Angelina flew at Hesperos.

He lifted my hand, sending a beam of green light bursting from my palm. Green flame surrounded Angelina's body. The magic fed upon her remaining flesh with a ravenous appetite. I tried to turn my awareness away as my former friend screamed, but it was pointless. Whatever power was holding my consciousness wanted me to witness Angelina's fate.

Hesperos extended a finger toward the hounds. Green flamed pounced upon Angelina's minions, greedily devouring their Undead bodies with its heat. Fort Victory glowed brightly until their ashes smoldered upon the muddy yard.

"I command Death!" Hesperos thrust both hands outward.

Bands of power circled about the Death Coach, binding the horses' legs and throwing them to the ground. Hell's emissary struggled against his bonds as he balanced on the driver's seat. Great God in Heaven! Hesperos could bind and control death? Clearly, there was a great deal about the supernatural world I didn't understand. I was, however, an expert in reading a person's face. The coachman looked as if he would crush Hesperos with his bare hands.

A blast of red power struck Hesperos, sending him staggering backward. Athan had joined the battle covered in colorful remnants of our earlier exchange in the surgery. His left arm was miraculously functional despite me having shot him in his shoulder.

"We face each other at last, Hesperos," Athan said. "I've been looking forward to this for centuries."

"Always so ambitious." Hesperos lifted glowing hands. "You are overextending again, Athan."

"Ha! It wasn't I who tried to overthrow the Alpha Mage's rule. You, too, have expensive ambitions, Hesperos. Why don't we join forces? Together, we can defeat Melampus and divide his criminal empire between us."

Hesperos shot a green burst of power at Athan, sending his opponent reeling. "I don't share."

"Melampus is Alpha Mage of the Apeiron. You've tried to take his power before and failed miserably," Athan said, slapping away Hesperos' attack. "If you won't join with me against him, then it is best for me to put you down."

Athan's red fire struck the ground. Nothing happened at first. Then I saw the Earth rip and heard the thunder of hooves. The Hounds of Perdition were rising from Hell again.

Hesperos sent a bolt of green lightning at the Undead as they rode through the opening in the Earth. Angelina and her Hounds shook off his magic with boney grins. How? I'd seen Hesperos easily defeat Angelina and her minions. Had Athan somehow made them stronger?

Silent Dan swung his scythe at Hesperos' head, but Doran knocked the weapon from his hand with a mighty strike of its claws. Compelled to protect its master, Doran snapped and tore at the Undead killer's face. Trip, ever Silent Dan's protector, came at the creature. Doran was outmatched and bleeding hard.

"I'll have your soul, Necromancer!" The coachman burst out of the magical bonds.

Athan whirled toward Hell's coachman with a laugh. "Take him to Hell. His death is long overdue."

"Never imagine I don't crave your soul with as much ravenous desire as I do Hesperos." The coachman hesitated as if unsure which necromancer to attack. Finally, coming to a decision, he and his hellish horses charged toward Hesperos. The whip flashed upon the ground about my body. Though I no longer was a resident, I mentally flinched.

"Traitors! Get out of my fort!" Captain Farley ran toward us, his eyes glowing with the wild flame of madness.

Hesperos and Athan sent bolts of power at the man, wrapping him in deadly hues. As they watched the captain struggle, the malicious glee upon Hesperos' face made my heart sink. He sent a sudden bolt at Athan's foot to distract him. Then Hesperos twisted my wrist and flicked a finger at Farley. The captain gave one last scream and then collapsed in the red mud with his men.

"Is there anything more intoxicating than the taste of madness?" Hesperos sucked in what I'd guessed was Farley's remaining lifeforce.

Great God in Heaven! What had I done by joining with the necromancer? Hesperos was a ruthless cannibal who devoured the souls of those he killed. What would stop him from killing more people? I understood why necromancers were hated by Heaven and Hell.

"Dear God, what have I done?" Captain Farley's ghost stared around the yard as it hovered above his body. "All those men I ordered killed. What have I done?"

Then the Eternal Flame cascaded from Heaven to touch down in Fort Victory. Its light danced in the space between Hesperos and the coachman. Good and Evil, equally matched, faced each other. It was a standoff. Now a bodiless observer, I watched their exchange without fear of madness or oblivion. Captain Farley, I'd guessed, was once an honorable man until he'd lost his mind. Then he'd become a crazed murderer. I was glad I wasn't responsible for deciding Farley's eternal destination.

"That's my kill!" Hesperos growled and jutted a hand toward Farley's ghost.

The captain screamed as he was dragged into Hesperos' sucking mouth. Sickened, I watched my body grow brighter as the necromancer devoured the captain's soul.

"Stop it!" My voiceless mind screamed. "Let him go! You're breaking our deal! No more killings. You gave your word!"

I'd told myself I was choosing the lesser of two evils when I agreed to join with Hesperos. Experiencing his savage delight as he savored Farley's soul proved I'd been dead wrong. Hesperos was worse than any Undead killer or monstrous fiend. He was an insatiable glutton for power, willing to kill innocents to feed his obsession. And I had just handed him the world.

CHAPTER FORTY-SIX

Despair descended upon my consciousness like a shroud, blocking any hope I had left. My vision dimmed as the black of doom filled the fort. Was this my true Hell? After a lifetime of self-centered aspiration, I finally found the humanity to care for others. But my change of heart had come too late to save anyone, especially my soul.

Then Hesperos and Athan paused as well, turning toward the growing black. Heaven and Hell vanished as an ancient presence took the field of battle. I was aware of a strange emptiness that materialized in the middle of Fort Victory. Yet, I could detect subtle lines and dips of black cloth. Shivering in terror, I realized true power had come to Fort Victory.

"Il Separatio!" Hesperos fell to our knees and bowed his head.

Il Separatio, or the Great Separation, was the embodiment of the perfect balance between Good and Evil. Hesperos had told me how he and the other Apeiron were judged to be in perfect balance by Il Separatio. They'd been priests of Hades in Ancient Greece then. So why had the Great Separation chosen this moment in time to appear again?

A massive set of scales materialized between Hesperos and Il Separatio. The contraption was made of ancient metal as if the balance between Good and Evil were all about iron will. Then Il Separatio lifted its hood and found my shapeless mind. It held me in a mental embrace, and as I peered into the depths of the black hole where its face should have been, I knew eternity.

It released me and pointed to the waiting scales. One side filled with all the black-hearted deeds I'd done in my miserable life. The other filled with white shapes of gentle hope, flickering in gold. The scales teetered briefly and stopped to hang even. A higher power had measured my life and found it to be balanced.

The Great Separation waved a covered arm. I flew back into my body and had control of it again. But I wasn't the only one living inside my flesh. Hesperos was there too, though his being remained whispered memories. Dunham Raynor and Hesperos were no longer individual entities. We were truly one. And we were alive.

Then Il Separatio was gone, leaving me to wonder at its justice. It hadn't appeared for thousands of years. Why now? Why for me? Perhaps I would never know.

I patted my arms and torso with trembling hands. Something was different about my body. The aches and pain of mortality were gone. I felt – for lack of a better word – perfect. Then I looked inward. The necromancer's mind and mine had meshed. I retained memories of traveling about America with Angelina. Mixed with those were the thousands of years Hesperos had spent upon the world.

Time resumed its pace, and we – no, I – slowly turned to Athan. The necromancer's fiery fists hurled a red beam at Doran's neck. I summoned the magic inside me and thrust my palm toward the necromancer. Projectiles made of stone flew at him with the speed and force of a Gatling gun barrage. Athan threw up a wall of fierce flames between us and retreated.

So, Hesperos' memories and knowledge were still with me. No more struggling to make sparks. The magic was coming naturally now, fortunately for me. Athan would be hard to kill. Despite the new magic living inside of me, I'd still need help to take the necromancer out.

Hesperos' pet lay in the mud, panting to catch its breath. Unbidden memories of potions and cutting flesh made my stomach lurch as I looked at the creature. Doran hadn't exaggerated when he'd told me there wasn't another being like him in the world. According to Hesperos' memories, he mixed wind sprite with several other supernatural beings. The mad man had also mixed his genetic concoction inside a human. Doran had been a man once. But, no matter what he'd once been, Doran was nobody's slave now. I'd see to it.

I moved to Doran and helped him up. "Are you okay?"

"You saved my life. Why?" he asked.

"You've saved mine more than once."

"Yes, because Hesperos willed it so." Doran frowned at the blood along his paws and chest. "I was his prisoner."

"That's not something I want to remember," I said, pointing up at the mark on his forehead. "How do I take that off of you?"

Doran regarded me for an incredulous moment. "You really are a fool. I probably will kill you when I'm free."

"Probably is better than definitely." I shrugged. "Hurry, he's coming back."

"Athan is powerful. We'll both need to be at full strength to defeat him." Doran spat. "You'll release me after this is over? Your word?"

"Cross my heart." I turned back toward the wall of fire. "Get ready."

Athan slowly lowered the wall of fire until its flames danced a few feet tall. Fiery red magic burned along the blade of the sword he held. The weapon was a bit ostentatious for my tastes. I summoned my magic, letting it flow about my hands. We stood facing each other like a pair of glowing locomotive headlamps headed down the same track. Neither was willing to budge.

"Il Separatio transitioned you to a Whole Immortal when Hesperos was the larger part evil," Athan said, scanning my features. "What makes you special, I wonder?"

"I don't know what you mean," I said. "Then again, it doesn't matter. You and your hounds aren't leaving Fort Victory."

"Such bravado," Athan said with a grin. "You aren't the first, you know. Il Separatio has transitioned one other. I'm not sure how she'll feel about you." Athan shook his head when I shrugged. "You dare be flippant about HER? Don't be foolish. Even Melampus fears her."

"If this immortal woman and I meet, I'll tell her you said hello and goodbye."

I fired projectiles of stone and wood toward the hounds trying to sneak behind me. Athan, in turn, sent a burst of flame toward my head at the exact moment. I lifted a rock shield to stop its touch from reaching me.

My opponent was a tricky bastard. He had centuries of combat experience while I was green out of the gate.

"We need cover, meat sack." Doran roared at my back.

Athan's blade came toward me in a fiery blaze of red. I ducked, but not fast enough. Hot blood dripped down the side of my head. Damn it. The necromancer had come close to giving me a permanent haircut.

I followed Doran behind the barrier surrounding the trading post. It was a gory mess, but we didn't have much choice. Athan and the hounds were taking up positions at the center of the fort. We had moments before they made a full assault against us.

"I don't like our chances," Doran said.

Suddenly tendrils of light sparkled in the space between Athan and us. The Eternal Flame was back, but not in its full glory. It was powerful enough. Angelina held her boney arms before her face and screamed as the light of Heaven shone in Fort Victory.

A growl of defiance thundered as the ground ripped open beside Heaven's light. The coachman crawled out of the ruined Earth, his anxious fingers grasping the handle of his whip. Hell had also retaken the field. What was happening?

"Well, well," A familiar voice said from within the column of Holy light. "You have made a mess of things, my young friend."

CHAPTER FORTY-SEVEN

"Father Emilio?"

Gone was the dull cassock and old boots he'd worn as we'd traveled together on the Santa Fe Trail. Radiant white garments shimmering with the muted light of Heaven replaced them. We'd been fellow pioneers and friends. Now the priest resembled the statue his brothers might pray to at a shrine.

I regarded the man I thought I'd known. "Let me guess. You aren't a priest."

"It was a necessary deception to maintain the balance," he said with a shrug. "The demon Edgewater had found you out." He examined me more closely and shook his head with a shrug. "Il Separatio has left only Hesperos' memories and power. There is little of the man I knew. Perhaps that is good, or perhaps that is bad."

"Do you understand what happened to me?"

"I will explain. Absolute balance. That is the realm of Il Separatio." Emilio spread his arms with that knowing smile to which I'd become accustomed. "You may have run away, not helping the people of Lester. But you saved the Wagon Train, then gave your life to save countless innocent people. You are equally balanced. Neither Heaven nor Hell has a claim on your soul."

I crawled over the barricade with Doran following at my heels. "How do you know about Lester?"

"Haven't you guessed yet, my young friend?" Emilio gave me another tolerant smile. "I am one of God's angels."

The demon Edgewater's words back on the banks of the Arkansas River made sense now. Hell had sent its demon to travel the Santa Fe Trail, while Heaven provided angelic guidance. Demon and Angel had kept an eye on me. But why simply observe? Why hadn't they acted?

"If both sides knew of Hesperos' plans for me, why hadn't either of you tried to stop the necromancer before he could take my body? People died, Emilio."

"Always asking the wrong questions, Dun!" Angelina tapped the rope against her leg with an agitated beat. "What are you doing here now, light walker?"

"Heaven has sent me to maintain the balance."

"I thought lying was a sin," she said. "Tell the truth. Aren't you trying to make another deal with Hesperos' new host?"

Emilio snapped his fingers at Angelina. A thin stream of the Eternal Flame raced toward her body, gripping it within the light. Angelina screamed as her Undead body disintegrated. I cast a glance at the angel's face. Emilio showed no more emotion than if he'd killed a troublesome cockroach.

"She was quite vexing."

"I've always thought so," I said. "Was she right?"

"I've come to offer my help by leveling the playing field," Emilio said. "I think we can come to an arrangement. A favor for a favor."

"Don't trust him, Dun," Doran warned. "Hesperos was sorry when he made a deal with this light walker."

"Abomination." Emilio struck a finger toward Doran, but I stepped between them.

"Let's keep it friendly," I said. "What favor?"

"One to be named at a later time," Emilio said. "Come now. I'm a host of the light – an angel. You don't think I would try to trick you?"

Warning bells clanged inside my head as every instinct I had told me to decline the offer. But Father Emilio had saved my life. He'd been a good friend when I needed one most. Then again, I didn't know Angel Emilio.

"One favor from me in return for what?" I asked.

"Oh, something very productive and advantageous to you now."

Standing in the middle of a gruesome battlefield, I wasn't in a position to negotiate. Muttering a silent curse, I shook hands with the angel. Doran rolled his eyes in disgust. He was right. I was acting like a mark – easy prey for an experienced immortal. But we were in dire straits, and I couldn't see a way out.

Emilio pointed a finger toward the remaining hounds. Silent Dan dropped his scythe with an anguished cry and fell to his knees, clutching at the rotten flesh dissolving from his body. The remaining gang of Hell's bounty hunters collapsed in writhing piles. Their cries of misery were unbearable. I fought the urge to slap my hands over my ears.

The coachman gave a lusty laugh as he gathered their confused souls. Then, stomping the ground with a black boot, he threw them into the gaping maw leading to Hell. Silent Dan's fractured soul stared at me as he fell. The madness had left his eyes. Regret and sorrow haunted his soul now.

"And I'm done here," Emilio said cheerily. "We'll talk soon, Dun."

"Wait," I called. "Back at Bent's Old Fort. That burst of eternal flame wasn't me, was it?"

"I may have helped a bit," Emilio said with a smile. "Hesperos made quite the trade for that little bit of eternal flame. He still exists, so my deal with him stands. Be wary of the weapon, Dun. It extracts a heavy price."

Then he left as quickly as he appeared, leaving me with more questions than answers.

CHAPTER FORTY-EIGHT

Doran shoved me aside just as a blast of magic whizzed by my head. Athan strode to the center of the yard, sweeping the tip of his fiery blade in the air between us. Even after witnessing Emilio's appearance, the necromancer was calling me out. He wasn't a quitter. I'd give him points for that.

"Fool!" Athan shook his head with a laugh. "You owe an angel a favor. I'd rather die than carry such a burden."

"I'm happy to grant your wish."

I let loose a surge of green energy. It rocked the yard with the force of an Earthquake. Athan, taken off guard, lost his grip on the sword and teetered backward. The blade twirled as the flickering fire made trails in its wake. Finally, the sword came back to Earth and plunged tip first into the ground.

"Clever strike," Athan said, getting to his feet. "Few opponents can disarm me. I've underestimated you. Perhaps we can help each other?" He gave me the same disarming smile I'd used on dozens of marks. "Melampus knows Hesperos came to the Americas. He will be coming for you soon. I can help you to train in the art of necromancy. We can be partners."

"I've seen how you treat your partners," I said.

Then I nodded to Doran, who'd transformed into his feathery form. The bird dove for Athan's sword and yanked it from the ground in its talons. I held out my hand and caught the hilt as Doran threw it toward me.

Summoning my Earth magic, I infused it into the fiery blade. Earth and Fire magic meshed into one terrible bolt of vengeance. It struck Athan and sent the necromancer's body flying across the yard. He hit the wall of Fort Victory with a sickening crunch. Athan slipped down the wooden poles to land in a smoldering heap of ripped flesh.

"Nice shot, meat sack!" Doran landed on my shoulder with a cackle.

"It's not over yet," I warned.

The Earth rumbled as Hell's gate opened. Demon horses charged from the ground pulling the Death Coach behind them. The animals kept a cheerful pace as they trotted past us toward the bloodied wall. Athan's ghost squirmed along the fence line, his innards spilling onto his trousers as he moved. The coachman grabbed Athan's wriggling soul with a gleeful laugh.

"Your tasty soul may have slipped through my fingers, Dunham Raynor, but I hold no malice against you for it. For you have given me a better prize."

Death's hand yanked the necromancer from Fort Victory and threw him inside the coach. Athan's soul screamed as his ethereal fists beat against the coach door. Hell would celebrate tonight.

"Hear me, Dunham Raynor! Remember the sound of this necromancer's screams. Let the memory serve as a reminder for you to stay out of my way," The coachman warned me. "In fact, I've left you a little present to keep you company." Grating laughter filled the ruined fort. "John 15:13."

"What is that supposed to mean?" Doran asked.

"I'll figure it out later."

A wave of relief washed over me as the ground closed behind the coach. Having Death's coachman pissed at you wasn't good. I'd given him a soul he'd coveted for centuries, but that didn't make us best friends or allies.

"Should I be worried about the Alpha Mage?" I asked Doran.

"Melampus is someone you aren't ready to meet yet. You must train before he sniffs you out, or you'll end up another slave in his sphere."

"I'm not sure I want to know what that means."

"Consider yourself lucky." Doran shrugged and flew to the only gore-free surface in Fort Victory – the top of the stockade.

The bird had a good idea there. Whoever I was now, I wasn't going to stick around Fort Victory to find myself. Winter was on its way. Deep snow and frigid temperatures may or may not kill me. My battle wounds were already healing, but did that mean frostbitten fingers and toes would grow back? I wasn't willing to test my immortality in the Colorado wilderness.

Entering the ruins of the trading post, I started collecting supplies for the hike back to civilization. I found Meeks as well. The little thief's body lay crumpled in a pile next to the door. I leaned over to close his eyelids. It was the best I could do for him. He was another soul I had lost. Standing up again, I looked out across the fort. It was a graveyard now. Doran and I were the only things living within its cursed walls.

"Don't forget the money," someone said behind me.

It was Meeks. Or rather Meek's ghostly form. Of course! The coachman's gift to me.

John 15:13 stated, "Greater love has no one than this than to lay down one's life for his friends."

Meeks had given his life for mine.

"Aren't you going to say anything? I am back from Purgatory." Meeks folded his arms with a huff. "I'm supposed to help you stay on the straight and narrow. Don't look at me like that. I must work off my sins somehow. The coachman told me so. I don't want to end up in Hell again. Trust me. It isn't nice down there."

"And here I thought I escaped punishment," I said with a grin. "Come on, Let's get out of here. We need to reach Denver before the snow gets too deep."

"Seriously, don't forget the money. We need to make sure it gets back to Wagon City." Meeks pushed a finger on the bridge of his ghostly glasses. "We are going to return it, aren't we?"

"Yes, we are," I said with a nod. "I'll make sure of it. Because that's what a good man would do."

CHAPTER FORTY-NINE

I let my kit drop to the ground on the trail outside the entrance of Fort Victory. Extending my hand, I pulled the fort gates closed with my new magic. It was natural now, instinctive. Flicking my fingers, I pounded in the nails with the Earth's energy to seal the gate shut. Good men had died behind these walls because of my, or rather the old Dunham Raynor's selfishness. I wasn't going to let it happen again.

"We have company," Meeks said, floating beside me.

Several ghosts of the newly Dead wandered around the walls aimlessly. The sudden violence had confused them, and they didn't know what to do now. I could use them to do my bidding for power or money, but I wasn't Hesperos anymore either.

"You've seen enough war. It's time for you to rest in peace." I released them but didn't watch as the light and darkness took their souls.

"I didn't mean them," Meeks pointed to a rock at the tree line.

An old man sat upon the rock beside the path leading away from Fort Victory. He gave me a grin and spat out a long stream of tobacco. It was Spoons. I did a double take. Spoons had crossed over yesterday. This was something else.

"Didn't your mother ever tell you that if you make funny faces, you might get stuck looking like that?" I asked. "What are you still doing here, Doran? I released you hours ago. Shouldn't you be halfway home by now?"

Doran jumped off the rock and shook his body. A young man with dandy good looks and a nice suit strolled beside me. I eyed the fancy suit and shiny shoes with a snort.

"You may want to rethink the outfit. We're not parading around Chicago."

Swirls of color erupted around Doran's body. Then a sensible pair of boots, dark trousers, and a coat, looking suspiciously like mine, appeared on his body. I hadn't realized the creature could adopt human form. In a way, it was oddly comforting.

"Better? I saw this actor perform on the London stage once," Doran told me. "It's as good a form as any, I suppose. Besides, taking this human form will help me guide you through the world of magic."

"You're going to help me? Why?"

Doran shrugged. "This world takes money. Hesperos was rich."

Images of gold and jewels flickered across my memories. Hesperos may have been in favor of staying neutral, but that didn't stop him from using his power to amass a large fortune. Much of it had been stolen, but the victims were long dead.

"And by rich, you mean?" Meeks asked, his ghostly form nearly drooling.

"Disgustingly wealthy," Doran told him. "He left everything to a certain Dunham Raynor."

Ill-gotten gain or not, Doran was right. Living in this world took money. If I was going to find a way to keep this new world of magic from intruding on innocent people, I couldn't spare the time to hold down gainful employment.

"So why not take my form and steal the money?" I asked with a snort of laughter.

"I owe you my life." Doran brushed at his sleeves irritably. "I suppose that makes us friends."

"Yes, I suppose it does." I gave my new traveling companions a grin. "I'm not keen to spend the winter trapped in these mountains. We'd better get started back toward Wagon City."

"Where do we go after returning the money?" Meeks asked.

"Anywhere we want," I said. "We literally have forever."

Picking up my kit again, I headed toward the trail leading down Greenhorn Mountain. Doran walked gingerly beside me while Meeks floated happily overhead. If it were true that a man could be judged by the company he keeps, then I suppose that made me interesting as hell.

The End

ABOUT THE AUTHOR

C. R. Richards is the award-winning author of *The Mutant Casebook Series.* Her literary career began as a part-time columnist for a small entertainment newspaper. She wore several hats: food critic, entertainment reviewer, and cranky editor. A lover of horror and dark fantasy stories, she enjoys telling tales of intrigue and adventure. Her most recent literary projects include the epic dark fantasy series, *Heart of The Warrior,* and the novel-length dark fantasy thriller, *Pariah.* She is an affiliate member of the Horror Writers Association.

For more information on the author's books and upcoming events, please visit her website: www.crrichards.com

OTHER BOOKS BY C.R. RICHARDS

The Lords of Valdeon
(Heart of the Warrior Series - Book One)

The Obsidian Gates
(Heart of the Warrior Series – Book Two)

Creed of the Guardian
(Heart of the Warrior Series – Book Three)

Pariah

Lost Man's Parish (Short Fiction)

Phantom Harvest (The Mutant Casebook Series)

Did you enjoy the book? Please leave a review
and let me know. I'd love to hear from you!